Praise for *Runaway*

"A great crime novel [featuring] engaging characters." ALISTAIR I

"Dynamite … The author loves t types" SHARON BAIRDEN, CHAP

C000079818

Praise for *Burnout*

LONGLISTED FOR THE HEARST BIG BOOK AWARDS CRIME NOVEL OF THE YEAR 2018

"Gripping." GOOD HOUSEKEEPING

"A terrific writer." KIRSTY GUNN, SCOTSMAN

"Absorbing. This is a thoroughly entertaining series that could run and run." SHIRLEY WHITESIDE, SUNDAY HERALD

"An utterly riveting and often unexpected read, absolutely brilliantly done." LIZ LOVES BOOKS BLOG

"You should make time to get to know Maggie and Wilma." LOUISE FAIRBAIRN, SCOTSMAN

"Strong advocacy of and for women … that's what makes this such an engrossing read." LIVE AND DEADLY

"Incredibly gritty and compelling … absolutely superb writing." THE QUIET KNITTER

Praise for *Cross Purpose*

LONGLISTED FOR THE MCILVANNEY PRIZE FOR SCOTTISH CRIME BOOK OF THE YEAR 2017

"A brilliant new talent for the lover of crime…a vibrant crime partnership and sound forensic expertise." SUE BLACK, DBE, FORENSIC ANTHROPOLOGIST

"A refreshingly different approach to the private investigator genre… a fast-paced tale." – SHIRLEY WHITESIDE, *HERALD*

"MacLeary's prose is assured and engaging, bursting with the liveliness of the Aberdonian vernacular… an impressive debut." RAVEN CRIME READS

ALSO BY CLAIRE MACLEARY

Cross Purpose
Burnout
Runaway

PAYBACK

Claire MacLeary

CONTRABAND

Contraband is an imprint of Saraband

Published by Saraband,
Suite 202, 98 Woodlands Road
Glasgow, G3 6HB

and

Digital World Centre, 1 Lowry Plaza
The Quays, Salford, M50 3UB

www.saraband.net

Copyright © Claire MacLeary 2020

All rights reserved. No part of this publication may be reproduced, stored in a retrieval system, or transmitted, in any form or by any means, electronic, mechanical, photocopying, recording, or otherwise, without first obtaining the written permission of the copyright owner.

ISBN: 9781912235827
ebook: 9781912235834

10 9 8 7 6 5 4 3 2 1

Printed and bound in Great Britain by Clays Ltd, Elcograf S.p.A.

FSC www.fsc.org MIX Paper from responsible sources FSC® C018072

For Eleanor

I

Wilma

'Wilma Harcus?'

'You're looking at her,' Wilma replied, covering her nipples with spread fingers. Clamping a leopard print hand towel to her crotch, she demanded, 'What do you want?'

Averting his eyes, the taller of the two policemen, a lantern-jawed loon with cauliflower ears, answered, 'We're trying to establish the whereabouts of your neighbour, Mrs Laird.'

'Why do you want to know?' Wilma asked, water running off her hair and dripping down her back.

'I'm not at liberty to say.'

'Well, you've got me out the shower,' she complained. 'So, whatever it is, you'll have to come back.' Taking a step into the hallway, she made to kick the door shut.

'Hang on!' The second copper, a well-built lad with a broken nose, shot out a restraining hand. 'It's important we speak to Mrs Laird, if only to satisfy ourselves that she's safe and well.'

'Why wouldn't she be?'

'Do you know where she is?' he pressed.

'Out,' Wilma snapped, shaking with cold by now.

'Is it work-related? I believe you are business partners.'

'Work?' Wilma echoed. 'On a Friday night?' Leaping at the opportunity to put the woolly suits in their place, she fibbed, 'Us private investigators are not so hard up we have to work around the clock.' Then, following the two constables' eyes, she realised the towel had slipped, and hastily put it back.

'She's on a social visit, then, is she?' the taller policeman fished.

'My colleague has a dinner appointment,' Wilma pronounced in her poshest voice.

'Who with?'

'Even if I knew, it's not something I would be willing to share.'

'What about the venue?'

'That neither.'

'Look, Mrs Harcus,' the second copper said. 'This isn't the time to go coy on us. We have reason to believe Mrs Laird's life may be in danger.'

Wilma's mind whirled. Where was Maggie? And who was she with? Then the penny dropped. If it was who Wilma thought it was, Maggie was indeed in danger. And if anything happened to her, it would be all Wilma's fault.

Forgetting her nakedness, she threw up her hands. 'Why didn't you fucking say that in the first place?'

Four Weeks Earlier

'What's up?' Wilma demanded, breezing through the back door. 'You've a face on you like a slapped arse.'

Maggie carried on loading Colin's sweaty rugby kit into the washing machine. 'Money worries.'

Wilma groaned. 'Join the club. What is it this time?'

'I've direct debits coming up,' she replied, raising a tousled head of titian curls. 'And Harlaw Insurance invoice isn't due for settlement until the twentieth.'

'But the Milne fee note. Surely that will–'

Maggie cut her short. 'Scott Milne hasn't paid our bill.'

'Bastard! I'll go up there, and...'

'What?' Maggie challenged. 'Give him one of your boxing gym moves?'

'No. But didn't we get a result?' Scott's wife, Debbie, had disappeared a few months previously and he'd hired the two women's detective agency, Harcus & Laird, to investigate.

We? Maggie's green eyes flashed. Acting on a hunch, she had found Scott Milne's missing wife single-handed. 'Might have slipped his mind,' she replied. 'Things will be strained at home. They'll still be having counselling. And–'

'Counselling my arse. No reason for him not to cough up.'

'He's maybe a bit late,' Maggie reasoned, 'but he's not that late.'

'Regardless. Fella was all over us when we found the wife. High time he paid his dues.'

We, again. Maggie thought indignantly. But tempted as she was to take her business partner up on the subject, it was early in the day. And, besides, there was no arguing with Wilma. 'I suppose you'll be wanting tea?'

Wilma cocked her blonde head. 'If you've nothing stronger.'

Maggie filled the kettle, pulled a couple of mugs from a cupboard and stooped into the fridge for milk.

'What's the upshot?' Wilma pressed.

'If I can't raise some cash in the next couple of days, there's not enough in the bank to meet the direct debits.' Dropping a teabag into each mug, she splashed in milk and topped up with boiling water. 'And if the situation persists, I'll default on the mortgage.' A shiver ran down her spine. Keeping her kids safe and a roof over their heads was her number one priority.

'What are you going to do?'

Sticking the milk back in the fridge, Maggie fished out the teabags and dropped them in the bin. 'No idea.' She carried the tea through to the dining-room and set the mugs on the table.

Wilma followed. 'How much are we talking about?' she asked, lowering her ample rear onto a spindly Ercol chair.

'Couple of grand,' Maggie replied, taking the seat opposite.

Wilma reached for a mug and took a slurp. She did a quick mental calculation. 'I've a bittie put by.'

Maggie sighed. 'Thanks, but no thanks.'

'Mum?' Her son Colin stuck his head round the door.

Brightening, she turned. 'You're up early.'

'Wanted to catch you before you went out. I need forty pounds for new rugby boots.' He eyeballed her companion. 'Hi, Wilma.'

'Morning, pal.'

'But...' Maggie protested.

With a perplexed look, Colin added, 'I told you last week, remember?'

Maggie didn't remember. But, then, she always had such a lot on her mind.

'The ones I'm wearing are falling apart.'

She felt a rush of love. Poor kid. Still, 'Forty pounds?' she queried.

'They're the cheapest I could find in my size.'

Followed by an overwhelming sense of guilt. Why did her kids always have to wear cut-price stuff when other people's children flashed big-name products? If she hadn't been left a widow... She banished the thought. 'Does it have to be today?'

'If I'm to get them at that price. Sale ends tonight.'

Sighing, she fetched her handbag from the sideboard and dipped into her purse. 'I'm short,' she said, colour rising in her neck. 'Take this for now,' thrusting three ten pound notes into his hand. 'When I'm done with Wilma, I'll put the rest in your account.'

'Here,' Wilma stuck a podgy hand down her cleavage and rummaged in her bra. 'Be my guest,' she grinned, palming Colin a warm note. 'You crack on. Your mum and I will sort it out.'

Maggie didn't say a word. She should have felt grateful, but deep down she resented Wilma's constant interference.

'Thanks.' Pocketing the cash, Colin backed out the door.

Ian

Between the polyester satin sheets of their super-king bed, Wilma cosied up to her man. 'You know that money in the savings account?'

'For the new kitchen?' Ian spoke over his shoulder. 'Aye, what about it?'

'I was wondering...' She fished, flattening her boobs against his back. '...if I could use some of it?'

He turned. 'What for?'

'This and that.' Her divorce from ex-husband Darren had left Wilma with nothing. Less than nothing, when you counted the debts the bastard had left in his wake. From her part-time jobs in the Torry bar and at Aberdeen Royal Infirmary, she'd managed to build up a small nest-egg. But that had been raided to fund her arsenal of dodgy investigative tools.

Rubbing sleep from his eyes, Ian mumbled, 'You're needing more money for groceries, is that what you're saying?'

'That, and other things.'

'Well, I'll tell you now I'm not fussed about eating meat every night of the week, I'll be happy enough with fish.'

'Fish is dear these days.' Wilma asserted, conjuring a mental image of the fish processing factory she'd worked in when she left school, the stuff they'd let drop on the floor.

'Haddock, I grant you,' Ian allowed, wide awake now. 'But give me an Arbroath smokie or a tasty wee herring.'

'Even herring. But it's not so much the grocery shop, it's...'

His eyes narrowed. 'You've not been hitting the Bacardi again?'

Wilma snorted. 'In my dreams.'

He stuck his face in hers. 'It's that Maggie Laird, isn't it? She's at it again: trying to take advantage.'

Wilma tensed. 'She is not.' When she'd first moved into Ian's semi-detached bungalow in suburban Mannofield, she'd thought the neighbours - Maggie Laird included - a snooty bunch. Now she knew different. 'You know your problem, Ian Harcus, you don't like me doing my own thing. Trying to get on in the world. Better myself. You're jealous, that's what it boils down to. And if I can lend that poor woman some support, well...' She paused for breath. 'If you'd any sense in your head, instead of coming all macho on me...'

'"Macho" is it, now?' Ian blustered, cutting in. 'You're not complaining when we're...'

'...having it off.' Wilma supplied, as she inveigled a knee between his legs.

'Stop that.'

'Not in the mood?' she teased, running a hand up his inner thigh.

'Pack it in.' He batted her away. 'You think sex is the answer to everything.'

'No,' she contradicted, bringing the conversation back to the topic in hand. 'It's money.' Not that Ian was tight. But with one failed marriage already behind him, he'd been resistant to opening a joint account.

Wearily, he ran a hand across his brow. 'How much are you talking?'

Wilma braced herself. 'Couple of grand?' She could see her fancy new kitchen - marble worktop, pan drawers, tap that runs boiling water - going up in thin air.

'What!' Ian exclaimed.

'It would just be for a wee while, you understand.' Assuming an expression of supreme innocence, she moved to reassure him. 'We're only talking a month or two.'

'With what sort of guarantee it'll be repaid at the end of it?'

'Well...' In her mind Wilma ran through a series of facile excuses. Dismissed them one by one. Ian was no fool. He'd put her on the spot, and she knew it.

'It has taken us long enough to put that money together,' he went on. 'There's no way I'm letting you blow it on one of your mad schemes.'

'It's not a mad scheme,' she remonstrated. 'It's–'

'You've a good heart, Wilma,' he said, voice softening. 'But the answer is no.'

'But...' she protested.

'End of story.'

Wilma buttoned her lip. Ever since she'd talked Maggie Laird into picking up the reins of her late husband's ailing private investigation business, she'd been pushing her luck. Her second husband might be a pussycat most of the time, but maybe Ian had more balls than she gave him credit for. When he dug his heels in over something... She cast her mind back to the ultimatum he'd served up after yet another run of late nights and ready-meals, their ensuing separation. He'd given her a fright, no question. And Wilma didn't scare easily, not with the upbringing she'd had.

He dropped a light kiss on the end of her nose. 'Now go back to sleep.'

Wilma's mouth stretched in a huge yawn.

Good try!

She closed her eyes.

Pity the bugger had her sussed.

A Bombshell

Thirteen grand? The figures swam before Maggie's eyes. And that was before you took into account the books and the uniform and the extra-curricular activities: sports, music, educational trips. Things that were part and parcel of private education. Things the deprived kids at Seaton School, where she worked part-time as a classroom assistant, would never see.

It hadn't been unexpected – the fee-note from Robert Gordon's College – but time had flown since Maggie's meeting with the guidance master earlier that summer, when she'd been faced with the choice between withdrawing her son from school to pursue a vocational career or sending him back to do a sixth year.

She read the invoice again: forty percent due by the end of August. Over five grand! Maggie's heart missed a beat. And that was just weeks away. Her mind churned. The Harlaw Insurance cheque should be in by then, but there was the mortgage to pay. She'd come to an arrangement after her husband, George, died and couldn't renege on that. Plus, there were other small bills outstanding, and they all added up. She scanned the small print. In her panic over the headline figure, she'd forgotten she'd paid Colin's fifth year fees by monthly direct debit. Still, she'd need to find over a thousand pounds by the first of September. And the first of each month after that.

'Braw day.' Wilma announced, barging through the back door. Scotland was enjoying a mini heatwave, and she'd stripped down to sawn-off denim shorts and a bright orange vest top.

'Is it?' Maggie asked. She hadn't heard her neighbour approach. She cast a glance through the kitchen window. Sure enough, the sun was out, bathing the back garden in a golden halo. 'Hadn't noticed.'

'What's that?' Wilma was on the piece of paper in a flash.

'None of your business,' Maggie retorted, whipping her hand behind her back.

Wilma's eyes narrowed. 'Wouldn't be another bill, would it? Might explain why you're in such a foul mood.'

'I am not in a foul mood.'

Shrugging, Wilma said, 'Could have fooled me.'

'Is there a reason for this visit?' Maggie asked, pointedly. In her experience, Wilma rarely made a move without an ulterior motive.

'Social call. Brought you this,' she grinned brandishing a glossy magazine. 'Thought it might be of interest. Though I did wonder...' Setting the magazine down, she leaned back against the sink, causing a roll of perma-tanned flesh to settle on the work surface. '...if your mannie had paid up?'

'Not yet,' Maggie responded, trying to keep her voice light.

Wilma gave her a pointed look. 'Now, will you let me chase him up?'

'Not on your life! The Milnes have enough on their plate, without us...'

Wilma cut her short. 'What's the plan, then?'

'I don't know.' Maggie replied, chin quivering.

Spreading her arms wide, Wilma said, 'Come for a bosie,'

For a few moments, Maggie let herself be smothered in Wilma's embrace, then she broke free. 'I have to get on.' She took a backward step, letting the invoice fall to the floor.

Wilma pounced. 'Christ, no wonder you're in bad humour,' she said, scanning the content. 'Couldn't you pay it up?'

'I already do. And before you suggest it, they only grant bursaries in S1.'

'Can't you ask your folks for a loan?'

Maggie groaned. 'No way.'

'Why not? They've savings, haven't they? And for all the interest they'll be earning...' She frowned in concentration. '...you could always offer them a better rate.'

'I'm not involving my folks,' Maggie insisted. 'They have enough on their minds after my dad's health scare.' What she didn't say was she'd never seen eye to eye with her mother. The most recent example of this was when her mum had gone off in a huff after the trial run of helping Maggie out in the house had gone disastrously wrong. Besides, Maggie was too proud to go cap in hand asking for money.

'Well, there's no point getting in a stushie.'

'It's all right for you,' Maggie retorted. 'You don't have a growing boy to feed.'

Hands on hips, Wilma challenged, 'That right?' Despite the fact her two loons, Wayne and Kevin, had long since flown the nest, she regularly had to bail them out.

'Plus, I've Kirsty to think about. Her rent's paid until the end of August, but I'll have to find it after that.'

'Hmm!' Wilma had a soft spot for Colin, but in her opinion Maggie's daughter, Kirsty - studying for a law degree in Dundee - was a little minx. 'Does he have to do his sixth year at Gordon's?'

'Yes.' Maggie had already weighed her options, but transferring her son to a state school at this late stage didn't bear thinking about. They'd made the decision, she and George, to educate their children privately. Or rather Maggie had made the decision, and George had gone along with it. 'All his friends are there.'

'There's colleges and that,' Wilma chuntered on. 'Thon place in the Gallowgate...'

Another option Maggie had flirted with. 'And the quality of the teaching to consider.' She'd told herself it wasn't Colin's fault his father's resignation under a cloud from the police service had diverted him from his school work. In truth, Maggie hadn't wanted to lose face. *False Pride!* The words rang in her ears. If she hadn't been such a snob, Kirsty and Colin could as easily have gone to one of several excellent state secondary schools in the city. 'Your magazine?' she queried, in an attempt to divert Wilma's attention.

'It has a big spread on Annabel Imray.'

'The PR woman?' Annabel Imray was a fixture on Aberdeen's social circuit, and featured regularly in the weekend magazine of the *Press and Journal,* chock full as it invariably was of local events, at which underdressed women in over-the-top outfits were photographed standing side-on to camera.

'The very same,' Wilma answered. 'Talk about rags to riches,' she exclaimed, eyes filled with admiration.

'You're a fan, then?' Maggie asked.

Wilma nodded. 'Knew her way back when. Started out as a hairdresser. Used to do my regrowth when Darren and me were first married and Annabel was still a junior. She's done well for herself. Must be worth a packet, now.'

'That right?' Maggie said, non-committal. Whilst she applauded Wilma's drive for self-improvement, Annabel Imray - all show and no substance - wasn't her cup of tea.

'Plus, she's well-connected. Might be worth our while making contact.'

'Yes, well, thanks, I'll enjoy the read,' Maggie lied. 'Now, if there's nothing else...'

'I get the message,' Wilma said, heading for the door. 'But dinna fret about money,' chucking Maggie under the chin. 'It'll sort.'

Val

'Without Wilma?' Maggie questioned, her voice rising a full octave.

'Think about it,' said her friend Val. The two were on one of what had become their regular FaceTime calls. 'You'd halve your overheads.'

'Not halve.'

'Near enough. Plus, cut down on the stress factor. Didn't you say the woman has been giving you grief?'

'Not grief, so much as...' Maggie hesitated. '...she's full-on, Wilma. But not in a bad way,' she hastened to add. She recalled the day her new neighbour had first appeared on her doorstep, all fake tan and sprayed-on leggings. How sniffy she, Maggie, had been. And look at them, now, like an old married couple. 'Wilma means well,' she argued, somewhat lamely.

'That's as may be. But wasn't it Wilma who talked you into taking on that missing person case?'

'It was, yes. But with the best of intentions.'

Val ignored this. 'And isn't that the root of your current financial crisis: that the client hasn't paid your bill?'

'That,' Maggie conceded, 'and other things.' She hadn't yet reached a final decision on Colin's sixth year studies.

'All I'm saying is, now you're a lone parent, you have to look after number one.'

'But...'

'Let me ask you a question: what's most important to you?'

Maggie deliberated for a moment, then, 'Two things. My kids, obviously: keeping a roof over their heads.'

'My point, exactly,' Val said. 'And in order to achieve that, you need to maintain a steady income stream. If you off-loaded

Wilma, it would be a major cost saving. You'd be able to run the agency without outside influence, and...'

'That's all very well in theory,' Maggie countered, 'but I couldn't do it on my own. Wilma gets through a ton of work. She does most of the computer research, runs virtually all the credit checks, and...'

'You could employ an intern: some bright young thing who would not only be computer-savvy but full of energy. Cost you nothing, or next to nothing.'

'Mmm.' Maggie pondered, furrowing her brow. The idea had never crossed her mind. 'Notwithstanding. Wilma's way more savvy than me. Knows...'

'...all sorts of dodgy stuff,' Val finished the sentence for her. 'From what you've told me, that neighbour of yours may well have been a Godsend when you were starting out. But now the agency is established, ask yourself this: does Wilma Harcus reflect the image I want to present?'

'No, but...' Pictures flashed in front of Maggie's eyes: the countless times she'd been embarrassed by Wilma's appearance, like when she'd turned up to an important presentation in skin-tight Lycra and white stilettos. Not to mention the questionable investigative tactics Maggie had learned to turn a blind eye to: picking locks, sticking trackers on vehicles. And those were just the ones Wilma had admitted to.

'You could sell it to her as a temporary lay-off, just until you get back on your feet financially.'

'I'd find that hard,' Maggie protested. 'Wilma worked for no wages when we first started out. She's put in countless hours since that she hasn't billed for. She has a lot invested in the business.'

'She's got other jobs, hasn't she?'

'Yes, but...'

'Two things, you said?'

'Keeping my kids safe and clearing the Laird name. But I've hit a brick wall with that one. Inspector Chisolm has tried to persuade his superiors to re-open George's case, but they don't want to know. And as time goes on...' She broke off, voice wavering.

'I'd forget about it,' Val counselled, her face filled with concern. 'Consign it to the past. No point worrying over something you can't change.'

'But I've come so far,' Maggie wailed. 'Getting George's partner, Jimmy Craigmyle, to give a statement was a big step forward.'

'That I grant you. Who'd have believed something as minor as turning off a tape recorder could have had such far-reaching consequences?'

'Tell me about it,' Maggie concurred. 'Turned my whole life upside down.'

'Yes, but what you have to remember is it wasn't your decision that caused this situation, so stop beating yourself about the head over it.'

'Easier said than done.'

'The other chap - the drug dealer - didn't you tell me he'd gone missing.'

'Bobby Brannigan? That's right.'

'Any news on him?'

'Not at the last count.'

'The police,' Val prompted. 'Are they active?'

'No.'

'Well, then. My advice to you is to drop the whole thing. I've watched it eating away at you, and that can't be good. Life has moved on, Maggie. Time you did, too.'

'I suppose,' Maggie conceded, unconvinced.

'Talking of moving on, isn't it high time you packed in your Seaton job?'

'It's only a few hours out my week, and...'

'...by your own admission earns peanuts. Seems a lot of effort for not a lot.'

'That's as may be. But those kids, Val, they need me. If you could see them: undersized, underweight. They come into school hungry, some of them. Steal food - sachets of sugar, sauce, you name it -just to stay alive. It's Dickensian.'

'Sometimes, you have to make hard decisions in order to...'

'Well, I don't know,' Maggie debated, her head spinning. It was all very well for Val, sitting in Dubai with a wealthy husband and a houseful of servants. And, besides, Val didn't have children.

'Couldn't you take out a short-term loan? I'd offer, but I'd have to ask...'

'No way.'

'Then, it seems to me cutting Wilma's salary is the quickest route to solving your problems. Don't you agree?'

'Yes, but...' It's not just about salary, Maggie thought. Wilma looked up to her, looked out for her. They'd become friends. More than friends. Wilma *loved* her, of that Maggie was sure. And - the realisation hit home - she loved Wilma.

'Promise me you'll think about it,' Val urged.

'I promise,' Maggie replied. Though in her heart she knew it wasn't much of a promise at all.

Some Other Way

Maggie lay in the dark, mind churning: the house, the kids, the bills. How in hell was she going to square the circle? A tear formed in the corner of one eye. She made a knuckle of her forefinger and wiped it away. When she'd walked down the aisle with George all those years ago, she couldn't have imagined she'd be left like this.

She'd gone to a dark place after he'd been found dead in his office: too maddened by grief to retain perspective, seeing conspiracies at every turn. Too proud to ask for help in her quest to clear his name. Time hadn't healed. There was still a yawning void in her life, her bed at the end of a long day a cold tundra.

She hadn't had sex since George died. Way before that. For all through that bad business, when he'd been on medication and she trying to hold things together, their sex life had gone out the window. Since then, she'd had neither the opportunity nor the inclination. That wasn't true. There was Brian. They'd come close, but nice as he was, she couldn't picture them in bed together. Same for DI Chisolm. Or was it? Even now, Maggie felt a tingle in her spine as she recalled their fleeting embrace. She was strongly attracted to the man, of that she had no doubt. So what was stopping her? The agency, for a start. She'd sailed close to the wind cutting across police business, been warned off more than once. After all she'd been through, she couldn't risk endangering her main source of income.

She was too picky, that was another thing. Too obsessed with appearances. She'd have to lower her standards. Wasn't Wilma always on at her to loosen up? And she was right. Maggie had been strung out for as long as she could remember. Had she always been like that? She thought not. Before things fell apart, her life with George had been quietly harmonious, sex like a warm blanket tucked around her at the end of the day. Since he died, she'd been so busy trying to keep a home together her own needs had slipped way down the list. Maybe what she needed was a casual relationship. Straight sex. No strings. Just enough to ease the tension accumulated by juggling two jobs and a household.

Her thoughts turned to Wilma, sleeping through the party wall, spooned with Ian. Safe. Whereas she... Lightning images flashed through her brain: drug dealer Fatboy lunging at her with a branding iron, imprisoned in the dark under the railway arches, picking her way through discarded hypodermic needles in the hunt for Debbie Milne. Maggie batted them away. She was overtired, that was all. Tired and stressed and... Her right hand slipped under the bedcovers, slid between her thighs, felt the wetness there. Maggie's spirits sank even lower. Her period was all she needed. With her free hand, she groped for the bedside light and switched it on. But, no. Her mouth curved into a rueful smile. One less thing.

Wide awake, now, she threw back the covers and swung her legs onto the floor. She padded, barefoot, across the bedroom. Noiselessly, she turned the door-handle and tiptoed up the stairs. Colin's door lay ajar, a hump in the duvet testifying to the bed's occupant, one large bare foot protruding from the end. The half-drawn curtains hung untidily, revealing a cluttered desk, a floor strewn with discarded clothing. The room was stuffy: an amalgam of cheap aftershave, soiled laundry and sweat. Maggie experienced a rush of love. *Bless!* For all his teenage angst Colin was a gentle soul, the polar opposite of Kirsty, who'd pick a fight with a post-box. She crept to his side. Her son lay on his back, hair tousled, soft snores emanating from his open mouth. She balled her fists, resisting the urge to reach out, tuck the duvet tight, smooth his hair, drop a kiss on the top of his head. Turning, she crossed the landing, drawing the door to behind her.

Kirsty's room was in total darkness. Maggie switched on the light. The curtains were fully drawn, the bed neatly made, the desk devoid of clutter. Above it, shelves held colour-coded books and files. A rainbow garland of necklaces hung from one end. Maggie's eye was drawn to the bed, where a handful of battered soft toys formed an untidy chorus line against the pillow. She recognised Mandy, a dog-eared Dalmatian that dated from Kirsty's primary school days, Toast the brown rabbit, Minnie the field mouse. Her throat constricted. For all her daughter's airs and graces, Kirsty was still a wee girl.

Maggie sank onto the edge of the bed and reached for the toy dog, burying her face in its soft fur, hoping to invoke some sense of her absent daughter. But all she could smell was a combination of detergent and dust. She wondered what Kirsty was doing that very moment? Said a silent prayer she, like Colin, was safely asleep.

In that moment she realised Val was right: the time had come to make hard decisions. If she were to keep the agency afloat and her family secure she would have to let Wilma go. Either that or Maggie would have to find some other way.

Brian

Brian Burnett flopped down onto the black leather sofa of his new home in Spring Garden. Running between George Street and the Gallowgate, it was handy for Queen Street divisional police headquarters and a short walk from Union Street, Aberdeen's main thoroughfare. When he first moved in, Brian thought he'd died and gone to heaven: good-sized lounge furnished with a widescreen television and modern suite, two proper bedrooms with double beds and fitted wardrobes. In place of the cramped cupboard he'd been used to, there was a dining kitchen with blond wood units and faux marble worktops. This came complete with brand new washing machine, fridge/freezer and microwave. The bathroom was fitted with a full-size bath. It was double-glazed throughout. There was even a designated parking space.

It was only after he settled in, Brian began to tot up the downside: his rent - £600 per calendar month - was fifty percent more than he'd been paying previously. Plus, he hadn't recouped his deposit - largely due to damage occasioned by the high jinks upstairs at Urquhart Road - and had to stump up another £600 from his savings to secure the new flat. The council tax was higher, too. Then there was the electric heating, not the most cost-effective. Nor was Spring Garden devoid of student tenants, testified to by the numerous bicycles chained outside, since Aberdeen College lay just across the road, Aberdeen University up and over the High Street and Robert Gordon's city centre campus within easy walking distance. Granted, there was dedicated student accommodation nearby, but it came at a price: en-suite rooms costing over a hundred pounds a week in term time. Much more practical to rent a two-bedroom flat and squeeze a few extra bodies in.

He put his feet up, luxuriating in the softness of the cushions.

Changed days from the lumpy bed-settee he'd suffered too long in Urquhart Road. He'd have to cut back on the takeaway meals, that and his visits to the pub, which had become more regular since Maggie Laird gave him the bum's rush. Still, the move was a positive step, and long overdue. Why he'd stuck with that shit-hole he couldn't imagine. Apathy, he supposed. Well, it was all going to be different from now on. Brian's confidence had hit the skids after his ex-wife, Bev, cheated on him. He resolved to make the most of himself: eat healthily, exercise more, smarten up his appearance. He might even push for that promotion. His DI, Allan Chisolm, a stickler for protocol, had relaxed somewhat of late, and the atmosphere at work had improved. Brian's fellow sergeant Bob Duffy was solid. Wee constable Susan Strachan had the makings of a first-class detective. Even graduate entrant Douglas Dunn was less of an arse. Maybe, going forward, they'd pull as a team. Yes, Brian decided, he'd have another try at making inspector.

One thing was for sure: he wouldn't be going anywhere near Maggie Laird. Not that his feelings for her had waned. Brian had carried a torch for Maggie ever since they first met. But he'd been a callow youth: slender, fair-skinned, looking younger than his years. Once George Laird - he of the dark good looks and athletic physique - looked in her direction, it was game over.

There was a wee girl in Comms Brian reckoned had given him the glad eye. But you couldn't be too careful nowadays. Best keep romantic overtures out of the workplace. Besides, it wasn't that long since he'd dated young civilian officer Megan, she of the blond hair and Welsh lilt, and that was over in short order. Mind you, catching him and Megan together had caused Maggie Laird to throw some sharp looks. Brian hadn't thought much of it at the time, but now, looking back, she'd acted proprietorial, if not downright jealous. No bad thing, he mused. Might even be the way to snare her. It would be a long game. He wouldn't make the mistake of instigating a hasty courtship twice running. No, softly, softly, Brian resolved, that was the way to go.

Going Forward

'Going forward,' Maggie began, hands twisting nervously in her lap. The two women were in Wilma's conservatory, ensconced in the colourful patterned cushions of her rattan armchairs. On the windowsill, a glass fragrance diffuser emanated a cloying scent. 'Seems to me there are two options: either we bring in new business. And fast. Or...'

Wilma wondered what was coming? On the one hand, she was pleased Maggie had found her mojo. On the other, a voice nagged inside her head. '*Where does this leave me?*'

...I go it alone. For days Maggie had rehearsed the phrase. She opened her mouth to speak. Found it was dry. She'd mulled over the pros and cons of taking Val's counsel: the freedom to set her own timetable, make her own decisions, set against the lack of tactical support. Plus, the agency's image was let down by Wilma's wayward appearance and manner. And she was a loose cannon. But when it came to the crunch Maggie didn't have the heart or - despite her recent displays of initiative - the nerve to cut Wilma loose. She drew a deep breath. 'We call it quits.'

'But,' Wilma turned a stricken face. 'Six months you said. And that was in May.'

'The end of May,' Maggie corrected.

'You wouldn't go back on your word,' Wilma maintained, picturing a long line of dead-end jobs, her hopes of bettering herself flying out the window.

'Not willingly. But the agency is in trouble. If I can't find a way out of this mess, I might have to sell the house.'

'You're kidding,' Wilma said. She took in the worry lines on Maggie's forehead, that lazy left eye drifting off to one side, as it often did when she was stressed.

'If I downsized to a flat, there would be significant cost savings,' Maggie justified. 'Plus, think of the convenience. If I didn't have this house to run, I'd really be able to focus on the business.'

'But your kids, wouldn't they have something to say?'

'Kirsty's as good as left home already. As for Colin, I doubt he'd notice where he slept.'

'How about you, though? You wouldn't want to leave all those memories behind?'

'You're the one always telling me to move on.'

'I know, but there's other things,' Wilma argued.

'Such as?'

'The garden, for one.'

'That's nothing but a nuisance,' Maggie countered. 'If I didn't have my dad's help, it would be just one more thing to worry about.'

'You've good neighbours where you are,' Wilma teased, elbowing Maggie in the ribs.

She pursed her lips. 'You don't have to spell it out. One thing's for sure,' Maggie insisted, assuming a stern expression. 'No more headline cases. We've allowed ourselves to be diverted from our core business, and that's what keeps us afloat.'

Wilma's lower lip jutted. 'Not my fault you got in too deep with that bunch of toe-rags.'

'Fair comment. But then we landed ourselves in more trouble with Sheena Struthers.'

'Another one down to you, chum.'

'Accepted. And that proves my point. We put in countless man hours for no discernible result.'

'We got paid, didn't we?'

'Granted.'

'And she got shot of that wee nyaff she was married to.'

'She did, indeed. Though I doubt she's any happier.'

Wilma sniffed. 'Not our problem.'

'And let's not forget Debbie Milne.'

Wilma couldn't look Maggie in the eye. She'd lobbied hard for the agency to take on the case, and the fact they hadn't been paid weighed heavily.

'Admit it, we've got in over our heads. Not just by taking on clients we had no business with in the first place–'

'Told you before,' Wilma persisted, 'it was you–'

'...trying to take on the world single-handed. But, as I was saying, we've made the wrong call, both of us, on several major cases. Crossed the line with police investigations. We could have done real harm. It's only down to Brian's help and DI Chisolm's forbearance we haven't ended up in front of the sheriff.'

'Okay,' Wilma turned a sulky face. 'I get you.'

'We've put a sound framework in place,' Maggie continued. 'Served our apprenticeship. We need to go back to first base: running credit checks, taking witness statements, tracing miscreants in debt and divorce cases, chasing fraud...'

Wilma's mouth stretched in a yawn. 'Boring.'

'Necessary. And it can't be overstated: firms like Innes Crombie and Harlaw Insurance are our bread and butter. And fraud is a growth sector. It brings in the fees.'

'Yeah, yeah.'

'Don't "yeah, yeah" me. We've been here before, Wilma, talking about sticking to routine casework. And it hasn't happened. Slow and steady, that's the watchword. We can't afford to lose clients. And I've had a couple of near misses: arriving late for meetings, rushing reports. Plus, we've become too reliant on those two firms. We need to broaden our client list.'

'Fair enough,' Wilma grudged, seeing in her mind's eye the stash of lock picks and other dodgy accoutrements she'd so painstakingly acquired gather dust in the wardrobe.

'We'll set targets. Weekly, to begin with: cases completed and billed, new clients signed up. Build from there.'

'Easier said than done.'

'Not if we put our minds to it,' Maggie said firmly. 'Haven't we shown we can turn our hands to anything?'

'Aye,' Wilma allowed. 'There is that.' Maybe she wouldn't have to retire her gadgets after all.

II

Annabel

The body lay sandwiched between a vast white leather sofa with angular chrome legs and a smoked glass coffee table. The woman was tall – five eight at a guess – a tangle of golden curls obscuring half her face. Slender. Long-limbed. Police constable Ian Souter took all this in as he entered the living space, an expanse of polished marble and plate glass. Well-heeled, too, evidenced by the designer furnishings and the red soles of her stiletto shoes. Souter was familiar with the Louboutin name, though he'd be hard-pressed to spell it.

'Christ!' PC Dave Miller was at Souter's heels. 'Want me to check for a pulse?'

Souter shrugged. 'No need.' Rigor mortis had already set in, blood pooling in the woman's calves. Mindful of police guidelines that death not be presumed, he went through the motions. A trail of yellow vomit dribbled from one corner of her crimson mouth onto the monochrome patterned rug. He took a sniff. Alcohol. At close range the skilfully made-up face suggested she was older than he'd first thought. The manicured magenta nails screamed high maintenance. Souter had seen plenty pictures of dames like her in the *Press and Journal*: dressed to the nines, hobnobbing with Aberdeen's high fliers at press launches or charity dos. He hadn't come across that many in real life.

He drew out his notebook. There was no obvious sign of injury, save for a bruise blooming on one temple. Nor had the clothing - skinny black jeans and cream satin shirt - been disturbed. He looked around. Floating shelves filled the opposite wall, carefully curated objects in glass and porcelain artfully displayed. At the far end of the space a black granite-topped island fronted a kitchen shimmering in snowy white laminate and stainless steel.

Minimalist. Not a thing out of place. Souter couldn't help but make a mental comparison with his own chalet bungalow in Bridge of Don, crammed to bursting with toys and Christ knows what.

'Better call it in.' Miller interrupted his train of thought, finger hovering over the call button on his Airwave radio. 'Looks like she took a turn, hit her head on the coffee table.'

'Aye,' Souter sniffed, giving the woman another once-over. 'Mebbe.'

Seaton School

The crimson stain pooled bright against the floor.

In the doorway, Maggie stopped dead.

'Am I glad to see you!' Lynsey Archibald crouched on the floor, a wad of paper towels in one hand. With the other she wiped a film of perspiration from her brow.

Maggie took in the twenty or so six-year-olds, who sat, eyes out on their cheeks, watching in stunned silence. The sight warmed her heart. Underpinned how vital it was to exert a moral influence while children were at an impressionable age.

Lynsey rolled her eyes. 'Not that I didn't get plenty offers of help. But I'd have got my head in my hands if I'd sent them home clarted. I've told them not to dare move until I get this cleared up.'

'Here,' Maggie said, crossing to her colleague's side. 'Let me finish up. You...' Lowering her voice, she yanked her head at the upended tub of paint which lay alongside. '...get rid of the evidence.'

'Thanks.' Lynsey grinned. 'You're a star.' Gingerly, she inverted the container and, holding it at arm's length, made for the door.

Don't know about that! Maggie had struck a blow for independence when she'd taken the job as a classroom assistant at Seaton School. In the early days, she'd found it hard going: the sometimes menial tasks she had to undertake little different from her domestic duties at home, the staffroom politics hard to swallow.

Changed days! She allowed herself a secret smile as, head down, she mopped up the mess. Maggie had suffered an erosion of confidence - the result of spending years at home and bowing to the opinions of others - but it had been strangely empowering to gradually find herself again. To summon the courage to challenge authority. Like when she'd bearded business magnate James

Gilruth in his den, when she'd got embroiled in the death of student Lucy Simmons, when she'd been torn off a strip by Inspector Chisolm. To stand up for what she believed in, even when she was quaking inside.

'Don't even think about it,' she admonished a small boy who had left his seat and was advancing on her.

Eyes like saucers, he turned around and scurried back to his place.

'Carry on with your reading,' Maggie instructed, tearing off another fistful of towels 'Once I'm done, you can *all* help me tidy the classroom.'

She smiled as she recalled the time she'd been clearing up and told a senior teaching colleague to sod off. It had been exhilarating at the time, and it didn't seem to have done their relationship much harm. These days, Maggie was accorded a measure of respect - albeit grudging from some quarters - in the staffroom. She still missed her friend, Ros. The young teacher had been in touch once or twice since she'd left her controlling husband and moved back to Edinburgh. Maggie even missed Glen, the personable supply teacher who had asked her on a date. Glen had moved on, and the school had a new supply teacher in place - an older woman with grown-up kids - but she didn't spend much time in the staffroom, volunteering instead to supervise pupils' jobs - library assistant, postie, plant waterer - assigned as part of the school house system.

Maggie gathered the sodden towels in a heap and dumped them in a waste basket, placing it safely on a shelf out of reach of the kids.

'Don't worry.' Lynsey, Ros's replacement, was at her back. 'I've brought a black bag for those. Don't want any more accidents.'

'I'll leave you to it, then,' Maggie said, one eye on the kids, who by now were scrapping amongst themselves.

'Fancy a drink?' Lynsey asked. 'My treat. I'll be done in half an hour.'

'Sorry,' Maggie coloured, embarrassed. 'I need to go straight home. Lot on my plate at the moment.'

'No worries.'

Maggie turned away, hoping her disappointment didn't show. It was at times like these she realised how isolated she'd become: widowed, shorn of friends. Real friends. Increasingly, she relied for company on Val's FaceTime calls. But FaceTime only went so far. There was Wilma, of course. Maggie had no doubt she'd be up for any number of social outings. But she'd let Wilma get too close. Maggie would have to be single-minded from now on. Keep a tight rein on her business partner. Gone were the dodgy escapades, the arguments over which cases to take on and which to turn down. Val's advice was sound. It was Maggie who needed to call the shots, no matter what Wilma said. And if she was paying Wilma, she'd get her pound of flesh. *Business is business*, Maggie told herself.

More of the Same

'When you're ready,' DI Allan Chisolm announced, holding up a cautionary hand.

Little by little, the chatter in the room died down, and detectives drifted, waxed paper cup or water bottle in hand, towards the table.

Chisolm's face creased into a tight smile. 'Let's see what the powers-that-be have in store for us this fine...' He threw a cursory glance towards the window, where a charcoal sky threatened rain. '...morning.' Flipping open the folder in front of him, he ran his eyes down the top page. Frowning, he observed, 'More of the same, wouldn't you agree, Brian?'

To the right of Chisolm, DS Brian Burnett scanned his notes and nodded assent. The catalogue of offences - theft, drugs, assault - was all too familiar. Depressingly so, for the combination of reduced police manpower and the increasing number of crimes committed online meant a high proportion hadn't a cat in hell's chance of ever being solved.

'Let's get these thefts out the way first. Where are we at?'

'Incident numbers have been issued and uniformed officers actioned to take statements. As time allows,' Brian added.

Bob Duffy threw him a dubious look. Victims would be lucky to see a uniform this side of Christmas. But he knew better than to get up his DI's nose first thing in the morning. Held his tongue.

'This assault in Craibstone Lane, get onto it, will you, Douglas?'

Douglas! Sitting alongside Duffy, Susan Strachan suppressed a smile. The boss must have got out his bed the right side, for it wasn't that long since her fellow DC, Douglas Dunn, had been in the doghouse for overstepping his authority by hacking into a suspect's computer on the Struthers case.

'Susan,' Chisolm's bark brought her attention back to the present. 'I want you to focus on...'

But before he could go any further the door burst open and a female PC, pink-faced from exertion, materialised at his side. 'Sir,' she puffed. 'Sorry to interrupt, but I've just had this through from...'

'Calm down!' Chisolm snapped, irritation written all over his face. He snatched the piece of paper from the girl's hand. 'Hmm.' Brows knitted, he studied the contents. 'Thanks.' Looking up, he mustered the ghost of a smile. 'Off you go.'

'We have a report just in of an unexplained death,' he announced once the PC had scuttled off.

Always first to get his oar in, Douglas pounced. 'Where?'

'Kepplestone.'

Dunn's eyebrows met his hairline. The high-spec flats in the city's West End were an unexpected setting for foul play. But, then, so was the plush Bieldside home of Douglas and Sheena Struthers. Douglas still got the squits when he recalled the buttoned-up accountant frothing at the mouth on the interview room floor. 'Right,' was all he managed.

'More bloody paperwork for nothing,' Duffy muttered. Every sudden death required the police service to tick all the boxes.

'Do we have ID?' This from Brian.

'IC-2 female: Annabel Imray, aged 36.'

'Never!' Susan gasped.

'You know her?' Chisolm queried.

'Know of her. She has her own PR business, operates out of an office in Chapel Street. Quite the celebrity. At least...' Susan said, her colour rising. '...she's forever in the news. Sees herself as something of a socialite.'

'Christ,' Bob Duffy chipped in. 'High-profile. The press will be all over us.'

Throwing a warning look, Brian asked, 'Who called it in?'

Chisolm checked. 'Cleaner, apparently.'

It was the cleaner who called in the Struthers case. From beneath lowered lids, Douglas surveyed the room. No one else seemed to have flagged up the further coincidence.

'Is foul play suspected?' Duffy this time.

'Can't say,' Chisolm answered. 'Scene's still open. From what I gather, the duty doctor has confirmed life extinct and SOCOs are lifting prints and trace evidence, so there's no point in speculating. But given the age of the deceased, there will have to be a post-mortem, so we'd best be prepared.' He jotted a note. 'Bob, I'm tasking you with the Craibstone Lane incident. Douglas and Susan, get yourselves along to Kepplestone. Get hold of that cleaner. Talk to the neighbours. You know the drill.'

Susan looked across at Douglas.

He shot daggers back.

Bugger! Prat still hadn't forgiven her for sabotaging the Struthers interview.

She straightened in her seat. 'Yes, boss.'

Henry

'Mrs Laird?'

'Yes?' Maggie eyed the male caller with suspicion. He looked respectable enough: early forties, tall, slim build, fair hair neatly combed in a side parting, she took in at first glance. Dark suit, black Oxfords, well-polished. He was even wearing a tie. Still, her mind jumped back to the two debt collectors who'd called after her husband died, there were so many dodgy people out there. Since being pitched headlong into the private investigation business, Maggie had developed a nose for trouble. She scanned the road behind. A brown Saab saloon sat at the kerb.

'Henry Dundas,' the man offered a nervous smile. 'Grossart MacNab.' Tentatively, he proffered a card.

Dammit! What with the business and the house and the kids, the estate agent's appointment had completely slipped her mind. She stepped back, holding the door open. 'Come in.' She ushered him through to the sitting-room. 'Take a seat.'

'Thank you so much.' He lowered himself onto the worn sofa and set a battered leather briefcase at his feet. 'Am I correct in thinking, Mrs Laird, that you are considering bringing your home to market?'

'Yes,' she replied, not meeting his eyes. In a despairing moment she'd contacted a couple of estate agents and arranged for them to call. 'It's early days. But...'

'I would suggest,' he offered cautiously, 'that one cannot be too well prepared.' Flipping open the briefcase, he extracted a brochure and held it out. 'You'll find everything you need to know in here.'

Maggie clocked the stump. He'd lost a forefinger, poor man. And from his right hand too. But before she could speculate as to the cause, he carried on. 'Any questions, I'm at your service.'

'Thanks.' Maggie clasped the glossy brochure. Found her hands were clammy with perspiration. She flicked through it. 'I'll have a proper read of it later,' she said, balancing it on the arm of the chair. George's chair. What she wouldn't give, now, to have a man at her back. *That's not going to happen!* she reminded herself sternly.

'Do you have a particular timescale in mind?' Henry enquired.

'Not, really. I mean, there's no hurry. Except...' *You don't have to do this!* a shrill voice sang inside her head. Then bills danced in front of her eyes: Colin's school fees, Kirsty's flat rental for the next university year, the mortgage, council tax, utilities, all jostling for precedence. Maggie's shoulders sagged. She knew she should take Wilma's advice and ask her parents for a loan. And they'd give it gladly. But she could imagine the exchanged looks. Rab and Netta McBain had been frugal all their lives, and desperate as she was, Maggie couldn't bring herself to swallow her pride.

'Selling one's home is a major undertaking.' Henry's voice interrupted her train of thought. 'And like all major transactions, it takes time. There's a lot of preparation involved: staging the rooms, commissioning photographs and floorplans, instructing a Home Report. You'll need an Electricity Performance Certificate.'

'Oh.' News to her. Maggie was already fainting with anxiety.

'But, don't worry,' he reassured her. 'I'll guide you through all that.'

I'll bet! From what she'd already seen, Henry Dundas was too smooth for words. And those vowels! Aberdeen? No way.

'Well,' he leaned forward. 'What do you think?'

Mind back on the bills, Maggie started. 'What about?'

'Retaining Grossart MacNab. We're a long-established...'

She cut him short. 'I understood Aberdeen Solicitors' Property Centre to be the main player.'

'They handle the largest number of property sales in the North-east, it's true. But, as I'm sure you'll agree, Mrs Laird, biggest isn't always best. Added to which, solicitors do, indeed, provide a valuable service, but they aren't property professionals. They have other things to deal with: probate, family breakdown. They can't specialise in the same way as an estate agent. Nor are they underpinned - as are we - by the Royal Institute of Chartered Surveyors.'

'No.' Maggie allowed. She would already have sought advice from her solicitor, had she not been fearful of incurring a fee. 'It's just...' A weight, like a huge concrete slab, settled in the pit of her stomach. '...To be honest, you've caught me at a bad time.'

Henry turned a stricken face. 'But, I thought...'

'I'd instigated this meeting? You're right. I did. Only...' Her eyes swept the room: the dated furniture, the frayed carpet, the faded curtains, the light fitting that had been cutting-edge when it was bought but now looked simply forlorn. Still, it was her home, hers and the kids. She scrabbled for an excuse - any excuse - to bring the visit to an end. 'You've made me realise I need to think this through before I can reach a firm decision.'

Henry Dundas forced a smile. 'I see. In that case, shall we agree another appointment for...' he brought his hands together, as if in prayer. '...Why don't we say, a week's time?'

In Your Dreams

Susan scribbled her name on the crime scene log. Ducked under the tape, Douglas at her heels. Just off the North Anderson Drive ring road, five minutes from the city centre and fifteen from Aberdeen Airport, the Kepplestone development was ideally situated for executive living.

The two walked through the hallway into the living space. The first responders would have checked for forced entry and any sign of a weapon and picked up house keys and personal identifiers.

'Wow!' Douglas exclaimed, crossing to the floor-to-ceiling windows. 'Get this view!' Turning, his gaze swept the room. 'Never mind the view. High-end, huh?'

Susan's attention was fixed on the coffee table: plate glass with sharp metal edging on x-shaped chrome legs. That and the forensic markers that dotted the floor. She didn't respond.

'When I make sergeant,' Douglas mused, 'I'm going to get a pad like this.'

In your dreams! Susan had done her research. Knew a duplex penthouse in Kepplestone would set you back near on a couple of grand a month in rent. What it would cost to buy she didn't dare think.

'Clock the integrated speaker system,' Douglas breathed, eyes out on stalks.

Susan had. Plus, the fact there were no radiators. The marble flooring that ran throughout must be warmed by underfloor heating. Streamlined, that was the look, so unlike her own modest place in Peterculter, where she'd gone for mid-century-modern. And failed. Susan sighed inwardly. She never had enough left over at the end of the month to splurge on extras. Still, she rationalised, her flat was lived-in. Unlike this place: so sterile, even the ornaments - a couple of sculpted marble figures and an etched glass octagon - were like something you'd see in a hotel lobby.

She skirted the kitchen island. Took in the high gloss units. The integrated appliances even ran to a stainless-steel Neff coffee machine. The gleaming black worktops were almost bare. The wall units held little other than coffee and a selection of herbal teas. The fridge bore testimony to a diet of salad leaves and white wine, a corked bottle of Chablis rubbing shoulders with what looked like vintage champagne. The freezer was stuffed with giant bags of ice cubes, nothing more.

'And get a load of this.' Douglas again.

Susan turned.

'Home entertainment system,' he marvelled, head buried in a cupboard.

'Will I take upstairs or will you?' she demanded, not bothering to hide her irritation.

He straightened. 'I'll do it.'

Thought so! Douglas never missed an opportunity to get one over on her. With his university degree, Susan feared he would leave her standing when it came to their sergeants' exam. All the more reason for her to shine in the field, she determined.

She wandered through to a bedroom fitted with custom-built mirrored wardrobes. A Juliet balcony opened off full-height windows. At the foot of the Queen-size bed, a desk held a computer monitor and not much else.

Susan dug into her pocket and eased on a pair of blue nitrile gloves. She riffled through one drawer after another. They yielded nothing of interest. The fitted wardrobe was empty. She was about to leave, when, 'Come and see this,' Douglas yelled.

Pulse quickening, she retraced her steps and sprinted up the stairs.

In the master suite, Douglas stood ogling an oviform free-standing bath.

'For God's sake,' Susan snapped. 'I thought you'd found something significant.'

He grinned. 'Gotcha.'

Susan eyed the thing. 'Waste of space,' she said, meaning the bath and Douglas both.

'There's a wet-room and all,' he added.

Susan threw a glance over his shoulder. Took in an expanse of black marble. Gave a peremptory nod. 'So I see.'

'And a roof terrace.'

She ignored this. Turning, she noted the wall of glazed cupboards. Pulled open a door. Found what looked like designer clothes, still shrouded in polythene dry-cleaning covers, hung in colour-coded order. She opened another door. And another. More of the same.

She followed Douglas into the wet-room. 'Anything?'

'Skin cleanser, moisturiser, foundation, perfume,' he rattled off, preening himself in a mirrored cabinet. 'Toothpaste, dental floss, alka seltzer, paracetamol. Pretty much what you'd expect. Oh, and sleeping pills: Zopiclone, 10 ml.' His head swivelled. 'No cocaine.' He offered a sly grin. 'Sorry.'

'You checked out the guest bedroom?'

Straightening, he gave a mock salute. 'Yes, ma'am. Nothing to report.'

'Right, then,' she said, swivelling on her heel. 'Neighbours next. And we better get our skates on.'

Anyone We Know?

Wilma gave Maggie a sharp dunt in the ribs. 'Clock that!'

'Back off.' Maggie snapped, inspecting her freshly-ironed blouse for creases. They were on the Number 19 bus bound for Bon-Accord Square, where they were to give a presentation outlining the agency's strategy for tackling a spate of insurance frauds.

'Newspaper.' Unabashed, Wilma jerked a thumb at the bald head two rows in front.

Taut with nerves, Maggie craned her neck. Crowning a full-length photograph, the banner headline read, 'Socialite Found Dead.' She turned in puzzlement to Wilma. 'Anyone we know?'

Jumping to her feet, Wilma thrust her head between the two wifies in front. 'Looks affa like thon Annabel Imray.' She sat down with a thud.

'Surely not.' Maggie hadn't got around to reading Wilma's magazine, but judging by the cover shot, Annabel Imray was in glowing health.

'Give us a mo,' Wilma said, shooting out of her seat. 'I'll go and check.'

Maggie watched her partner bend the bald man's ear, then wrest the paper from his grip. "You're a star", she heard Wilma exclaim, with a suggestive pucker of her lips. Maggie didn't know whether to laugh or cry. On the one hand, she had to admire Wilma's nerve. On the other, they were two professional women travelling to a business appointment and couldn't afford to get involved in a fracas. Plus, they'd been in the news more than once these past few months - and always for the wrong reasons.

'See,' Wilma hissed, regaining her seat.

Baldy man turned, stripping her with lascivious eyes.

Wilma threw him a stage wink. 'It says here she was found dead in her home.' She wrinkled her nose. 'Can't say I'm surprised.'

'What would you know?' The question was put before Maggie could stop herself.

Wilma squared up. 'Not posh enough to mix with the likes of her nowadays, is that it?'

'Not at all. I'm curious, that's all. I got the impression you hadn't met in years.'

'Annabel was brought into A&E not long since. Right bloody mess from what I heard. Claimed she'd been assaulted.'

'You saw her, did you?'

'You kidding? She was in a private room. Couldn't get near for folk dancing around her. But story goes, it was down to drink.'

'Who told you that?"

'One of the porters.'

'But,' Maggie protested, 'a porter, you said? How did he...?'

'Do I not keep saying,' Wilma cut her short. 'You can't judge a book by its cover, Maggie Laird. Hospital porters know every last fucking thing.'

'Shush.' One of the wifies in front whipped around. 'Mind your language.'

'If you don't mind.' her friend chipped in, affronted.

Wilma cast a sly look at Maggie, who had flushed pink with embarrassment. 'Scuse my French,' she said in an affected voice. 'Me and my friend...' She flashed the newspaper headline, '...have had bad news.'

'Oh,' the woman's eyes widened. 'I'm sorry.'

'Apologies,' her companion added.

'Don't mention it,' Wilma responded, poker-faced. Lowering her voice, she turned to Maggie. 'Eck – that's my wee pal's name – says they kept Annabel Imray in overnight as a precaution, her being high profile. Proper cow she was too. Had everyone running after her, consultants and all. Treated them like shite. Seems success went right to her head.' Eyes alight, she said, 'Wouldn't it be magic if some bugger's done her in? And the cops were toiling.

And we got to take on the case. We could...'

'That's not going to happen,' Maggie hissed, backing away. She'd had a bellyful of Wilma's flights of fancy. And, besides, it was difficult enough to moderate her partner's behaviour in a formal meeting without the added complication of Wilma arriving in a state of high excitement. 'If - and it's a big if - Annabel Imray has been the victim of foul play, that's none of our business.'

The animation wiped from Wilma's face.

'You may have a tenuous connection with the woman,' Maggie allowed. 'But there's no way we're getting mixed up in another police investigation. From now on, we're going to operate at a safe distance and strictly within our remit and level of competence. Slow and steady,' she enunciated. 'Didn't we agree?'

'Aye,' Wilma conceded, reluctance written all over her. 'Suppose.'

Just One Thing

Chisolm wasted no time. 'Imray case,' he barked, eyeballing Douglas. 'What did you get?'

Not a lot! Susan took a swig of her latte, wondering how Douglas would manage to big this one up.

'Wasn't much to see,' he replied, tugging at the button-down collar of his Charles Tyrwhitt shirt. 'Other than what the SOCOs flagged up. Place was pretty empty, as a matter of fact. Didn't look like Annabel Imray spent much time there.'

Chisolm harrumphed. 'Neighbours?'

'Not that many about. Wrong time of day. Suppose most of them would be out at work,' he broke off, stealing a surreptitious look at Susan.

'Plus,' she added her tuppence-worth, 'flats are mostly short-term rentals, so there's a high turnover of occupants.'

'The doors we did get an answer from,' Douglas came back in. 'Folk said they hardly saw her. She keeps...' He corrected himself. 'Kept odd hours. Out late most nights, often didn't surface until lunchtime.'

'Boyfriend?'

'There was someone, but he hasn't been seen for some time.'

'And,' Susan added, 'there was no sign in the flat. No toiletries, no male clothing in the wardrobe, nothing like...'

'Exactly.' Douglas cut her short with a dark look.

'Visitors?'

'One. Female. Same night every week.'

'Girl on girl?' Duffy interjected with a sly wink. 'Imray could have swung both ways.'

'Doubt it,' Brian remarked, joining the conversation. He'd been up half the night assembling an Ikea bookshelf and was feeling his age. 'Not if the press is anything to go by. All the photos I've seen, Annabel Imray has been hanging off the arm of some fat cat businessman.'

'No sign of forced entry?' Chisolm queried.

'Negative, according to Uniform's report.' Douglas responded. 'Nor did we find visible damage to the door or scratches around the lock.'

'Other points of access?'

'Balconies,' Susan chipped in. 'But they're too high up. Same goes for the roof terrace.'

'Not a botched burglary, then, by the sound of. The victim, does she own a vehicle?'

'Mercedes coupe. Still in its allocated parking space.'

'Which is where?'

'Secure underground garage accessed from the rear of the building. And before you ask, boss, entry is gained by means of a key fob.'

'Which Forensics are in possession of,' Susan added.

Chisolm nodded his understanding. 'Did you manage to talk to the cleaner?'

'Affirmative.' Douglas was quick to answer. 'Took a while, though. She was on the move the entire day.' He consulted his notebook. 'Nora Grassie, age fifty-two. Agency employee. Said she'd only worked for them a couple of months. According to Mrs Grassie, the client was – and I quote – "very particular". Gave instructions she was to be addressed as 'Ms' Imray. If anyone asked, Mrs Grassie was to say she was the housekeeper, not cleaner. Wasn't to arrive before eleven am, nor disturb the client if she was in bed or touch anything in the study.'

'Had she encountered any visitors?' Brian again. 'Male friends?'

Douglas shook his head. 'Not one.'

'She did mention Annabel took a lot of calls,' Susan volunteered. 'Either that or she'd be texting.'

'Par for the course,' Douglas observed. 'If she ran her own business.'

'Okay, you two,' Chisolm intervened. 'If you've nothing else to report let's crack on.'

Susan cleared her throat. 'There was just one thing...'

He raised an eyebrow. 'Yes?'

'The mugs in the kitchen.'

'What mugs?' The words were out before Douglas could stop himself.

Too busy eyeing up the boys' toys!

'The ones near the coffee machine: two of them.' Susan smirked at Douglas, enjoying his discomfort. 'Looked like Annabel had entertained a visitor. Either that or she was expecting someone.'

A Minnow

'I'm impressed by your submission,' Richard Carmichael said. 'But before I can put it to my board, I'd need to know more about your business. That's why I've asked you here today.'

Maggie felt a glow of satisfaction. She'd been on tenterhooks about this meeting, one of several scheduled in the hope of drumming up new business. 'Thank you,' she acknowledged with a smile.

'Harcus & Laird isn't a name I'm familiar with. Are you a recent entry to the market?'

'Relatively,' she conceded. 'It was established four years ago by my late husband. But,' she qualified. 'He had almost twenty years' service in the police force.'

'And did you also serve'?' Richard Carmichael enquired.

'No. My background is in the...' She broke off, feeling the colour rise in her face. '...legal field.'

'Ah,' he brought his hands together. 'You're a lawyer. Even better.'

'Not exactly,' Maggie rushed to disabuse him. 'I was a legal secretary. A PA, actually.'

'And how long, may I ask, did you do that?'

'Three years,' Maggie replied, her voice little more than a whisper.

'Mmm.' Carmichael studied her over half-moon spectacles. 'Coming back to your business, how many case managers do you employ?'

'Two,' Maggie confessed. 'Though we're a dynamic, fast-growing...'

'I'm sorry,' he interrupted. 'I can see from this...' He indicated Maggie's submission folder. '...You take a professional approach. But from what you've told me, you're patently too small an outfit to handle this company's caseload.'

'But,' Maggie protested. 'Small can be an advantage. We're more flexible than a large organisation. Can offer a more personal service.

And we're...' Cheaper, was on the tip of her tongue, though she knew Wilma would kill her.

'Let me stop you there,' he said, not unkindly. 'As things stand, you simply don't have the resources.'

He rose to his feet, bringing the meeting to a close. 'Feel free to make another approach, Mrs Laird, when you're more established.' He extended a hand. 'Meanwhile, I thank you for your time and wish you good day.'

*

Smarting, Maggie stood by a bank of lifts. Richard Carmichael's words brooked no argument: in comparison with other PI companies, Harcus & Laird was a minnow. But she'd spent hours working on that submission, and felt she hadn't had the opportunity to fully state her case. By this time, Maggie had mastered the spiel. Learned the bullet points off pat.

It wasn't the first occasion she'd made it to the interview stage and got no further. Aside from the fact the agency was small and had a limited track record, people didn't expect Harcus & Laird to be fronted by a woman, far less one of Maggie's diminutive stature. Inwardly, she cursed her lack of assertiveness. Wilma would have stuck in there, argued the toss. But she wasn't Wilma. If she was going to call the shots in future, Maggie would need to change her attitude. And fast!

Lift doors slid opened and shut, disgorging office workers and taking on others.

Maggie stood, a small figure buffeted by the constant activity.

'You lost?' A male voice asked.

She eyed the man, confused.

He grinned. 'If you're looking for the secretarial interviews, HR is down the corridor, second door on the right.'

III

Babies and Beasties

If Annabel Imray had been vibrant in life, death had drained her of colour as surely as had she been a photographic negative. Laid out on one of the stainless-steel cutting tables of the police mortuary, from her lank hair to her ashen skin she was monochrome as the rug upon which her life-force had ebbed away.

Susan joined the procurator fiscal, the two pathologists and DI Chisolm, who as Senior Investigating Officer was required to attend. The post mortem, a detailed examination of the body and its internal organs, would tell the story not only of the deceased's death but how they lived.

'Drawn the short straw?' Alec Gourlay asked, beady brown eyes twinkling above his facemask. The pathologist was a small man - no more than five foot seven or eight - with a hooked nose and thinning sandy hair combed in a neat side parting. Like a cartoon bird of prey, Susan thought, on their first encounter, the comic image only heightened by the addition of a rubber apron and welly boots.

'Pleased to see you, too,' she replied. And she was, for Gourlay had a commanding intellect, she'd learned, in addition to the requisite butchery skills. She wondered how long their easy relationship would last, for it was rumoured bodies would in future be transferred to the Queen Elizabeth mortuary in Glasgow, which had capacity for up to two hundred. Made sense, she supposed, The Forensic Pathology facilities at Gartcosh were the most advanced in Europe. Still, biggest wasn't always best. She dismissed the thought.

'Still line-dancing?' she addressed the petite mortuary assistant, who was bent to the task of weighing one of the internal organs, before listing the information on a wall-mounted whiteboard.

She'd already have opened the body, removed the chest bones and pulled out the organs from tongue to bladder.

'Too right.' A head came up, wisps of blonde hair escaping from under a protective cap. 'Fair gets rid of the cobwebs.'

Susan recalled her first visit to the police mortuary, when junior anatomical pathology technician Tracey had given her the tour: the cutting room, with its stark grey walls, the two stainless-steel tables in the centre, the extractor fans labouring overhead. The pervasive odour of formaldehyde and bleach had choked Susan of breath. And that's before she caught sight of the instruments: drills and saws and scalpels and pliers. She'd been chilled - literally - in the temperature-controlled space. Shivering in her white Tyvek bunny suit. And not a little afraid.

'What's the worst thing you've had to deal with?' she'd asked the young blonde assistant, then.

'Babies and beasties,' Tracey had replied without a moment's hesitation.

Those Susan could understand. She'd spotted a sad little straw Moses basket in the viewing area. Thankfully, she'd never yet seen it in use. She'd schooled herself to view maggots and other infestations of dead bodies dispassionately, the cadaver little more than a receptacle of information that might assist in an investigation.

Now her attention focused on the naked figure on the cutting table. Annabel Imray would have been stripped and washed before being cut open. Deep perforated channels held the blood and entrails that ensued from the pathologist's examination.

'Anything of interest?' she addressed Alec Gourlay, who was bent into the gaping incision that ran from the dead woman's breastbone to her groin.

He raised his head, breaking off from his running commentary. 'Aside from the obvious bruising to the temple, there are petechiae – tiny haemorrhages – to the face. Here.' he pointed. 'And here.'

Tyvek suit rustling, Susan bent to Annabel Imray's pallid face. 'Yes, I see.'

'There's also evidence of discolouration around the nose, consistent with pressure being applied.'

Susan's pulse raced. 'You're saying she was asphxiated?'

'I'm not saying anything of the kind,' Alec Gourlay replied.

'Could she have been strangled?' Susan persisted.

'There are no fractures of the laryngeal cartilages in the throat, nor evidence of bruising to the larynx. However, sometimes no marks are apparent in an asphyxiation.'

Susan knew better than to ask for an estimated time of death. Gourlay would need to take into account a number of different factors including the deceased's body temperature, weight and clothing, the position of the body and the ambient temperature where it was found, and the advance of rigor mortis.

'What are the odds?' she wheedled.

The pathologist voice was grave, but above the face mask his brown eyes twinkled. 'That's for you to establish.' he said.

Ursula

'Dr Evershed?'

The woman who answered the door fixed Maggie with an accusing glare. 'You're late.'

'My apologies.' The house - sitting side-on to the High Street behind heavy iron gates - had been hard to find. Added to which it was raining, a fine smirr that clung to Maggie's clothes and gave the ancient buildings and cobbled streets of Old Aberdeen an otherworldly air.

'Follow me,' Dr Evershed instructed, turning on her heel.

Maggie gave her a quick once-over. Tall, rangy, in ill-fitting fawn trousers and a long grey cardigan. Salt and pepper hair scraped into an untidy French pleat. Half-moon glasses hanging from a cord around her neck.

Eyes glued to the woman's back, Maggie negotiated a dark corridor and emerged into an equally gloomy sitting-room. A dark breakfront bookcase filled one wall, the others crowded with ponderous oil paintings. In front of a marble fireplace that didn't look as if it had seen a fire in years, threadbare rugs were layered on an equally worn carpet. The air was thick, permeated with the overweening smell of decay.

Out the ark, that's how Wilma would describe this. Maggie was thankful she'd come alone. Still, when Dr Evershed had called completely out of the blue, Maggie had set up a meeting with alacrity. If this turned out to be a meaty case, it might just be the answer to her prayers.

'Take a seat.'

She looked around. There were books piled everywhere: on side tables, on the floor, even on the hearth. Gingerly, she lifted a pile from an ancient overstuffed sofa and sat down, balancing them on her knee.

'Here,' Dr Evershed thrust out both hands. 'Allow me.'

'Thanks,' Maggie said, allowing herself be relieved of her burden.

Dr Evershed lowered herself into an armchair and deposited the books at her feet. 'The reason I asked you to call...'

Maggie waited. The putative client hadn't given much information on the phone. It was often the way, callers reluctant to go into detail. Plus, she'd learned from experience that people were prone to talk around the subject before they got to the point.

'...is I've suffered a grievous loss.'

Maggie's heart lurched. 'I'm so sorry.'

'My companion of the past sixteen years has disappeared, completely without warning.'

Husband? Lover? Maggie sneaked a glance at Dr Evershed's hands. No rings. This only served to confirm what she'd already guessed: the woman was what her mother would call "an old maid". Regardless, Maggie dispelled the thought. She'd been here before. Her stomach knotted. New business or not, no way was she going to take on a misper case again.

'The police,' Dr Evershed ran on, 'have taken no interest whatsoever. When I called 101, they passed me onto some jobsworth, who issued me with an incident number for insurance purposes. That's as far as it went.'

'Well,' Maggie extemporised. 'If I were you, Dr Evershed...'

'Ursula.' The stiff exterior relaxed, just a tad. 'Don't tell me to give it time. That's what the young woman in the call centre said: "He'll most likely turn up in a day or two".

So, a partner, after all.

'I've rung repeatedly, presented myself at the local station, even called into police headquarters, to no avail. Which is why, Mrs Laird, we are sitting here now.'

'I regret to say,' Maggie responded, 'I've come here today under a misapprehension. Missing persons' enquiries are outside my agency's remit. Aside from which...'

'Let me stop you there.' Ursula Evershed held up a bony hand. 'The companion to whom I refer is not a "person" but a cat.'

'A cat?' Maggie echoed, heart in mouth.

'A very...' Ursula's eyes assumed a faraway look. '...singular cat.'

Maggie was so gob-smacked, all she could manage was, 'I see.' Not that she did. She had no experience of household pets. The hours George worked, it had never seemed practical. They'd kept animals at the farm, of course: several dogs and a cat. But these were working animals: to shepherd sheep, keep the mice down.

'Malthus, we called him.'

'Interesting,' Maggie lied, her mind working overtime. She'd heard the name, but where?

'Bit of an in-joke. Daddy was Emeritus Professor of Political Economy.'

'Right.' Maggie didn't get the joke either. 'Well, as I said, this sort of investigation is not–'

'He was my mother's, to begin with,' Ursula interrupted. 'Daddy bought him for her before he passed away. Bowel cancer,' she leaned in, confidentially.

A spring was sticking through the sofa, jabbing Maggie's thigh. Surreptitiously, she rubbed the sore place and shifted position.

'Mummy died last winter,' Ursula ran on. 'Massive stroke, though it was pneumonia that did for her in the end.'

The old person's friend. Maggie made an appropriate murmur.

'I fully intended to find Malthus a good home. I'm fully committed, you see, what with the department and my research.'

'Quite.' Ursula had told Maggie on the phone she was Reader in Molecular Biology at the University of Aberdeen.

'But I couldn't bring myself. He was part of the family.' Her eyes welled with tears.

Poor soul! Maggie thought she was hard-done by – widowed in her early forties – but at least she had her children. 'Have you thought of putting a card in the newsagent's window?' she volunteered, in the hope of fobbing Ursula off.

'I did ask. And it's not that they weren't sympathetic, but the local Keystore is so short of space. I've combed the area, asked everyone I could think of, but there has been no sign. Not a trace.'

Maggie sneaked a peek at her watch. 'If you'll forgive me, I really must be going.'

Ursula leapt to her feet. 'Tell me you'll consider it, at least.'

Maggie steeled herself. 'I think not. There are other investigation agents who might be more suited to this sort of work.'

'I've already tried them. They're too corporate, don't you see? You, on the other hand, being women....'

Maggie felt a flush coming on at the mere mention. *PIs of last resort*! Wasn't that what Sheena Summers had claimed: that she'd hired them because they were so green?

'...and dare I say of a certain age, I should have expected to be more empathetic.'

She squared her shoulders. 'It's not that I don't have sympathy, Dr Evershed – Ursula – but I have to consider the practicalities. This sort of project can involve many man hours, and...'

Ursula crossed the room. 'I'm prepared to pay handsomely for your efforts. As you may observe...' She waved a hand in mid-air. '...I've been left very comfortable.'

Really? Maggie shifted her weight as another spring appeared out of nowhere. All of a sudden, her own home didn't seem quite so shabby.

'My needs are modest. I live frugally. My workload precludes much in the way of a social life. That's why...'

...your life revolves around a bloody cat, Maggie thought. She wondered if it slept on the bed.

Then, *Time I was out of here!* She rose and gathered her belongings.

'Don't go.' Ursula pleaded, laying a restraining hand on her arm. 'If I could only make you understand, Malthus isn't some pretty little puss. He's a handsome, virile...'

Randy?

'...highly intelligent individual. A real character. Everybody says so. And now,' she said, her voice cracking with emotion. 'Don't you see, if he doesn't come back, I've got nothing.' A tear wobbled in the corner of one eye, then made a snail trail down her cheek. 'Nothing at all.'

You Taking the Piss?

'How did you get on?' Maggie asked.

Wilma groaned. 'Not great: one surveillance job and a couple of depositions.' They were in her car heading for Peterhead to progress a historic fraud case.

'Thought we'd agreed to give surveillance a miss.'

'We did. But this would be a walk in the park: takeaway getting graffitied.'

'What about the police?'

Wilma snorted. 'What about them?' It was common knowledge the police force was so undermanned that petty crime had been downgraded. 'It's happening on a nightly basis. Fella's desperate. He's prepared to pay.'

'Still,' Maggie reasoned.

'It's most likely kids. All we'd have to do is put the fear of death in them.'

'That would take both of us,' Maggie argued. 'And these places keep long hours. We could be sitting there for nights on end before we get a result.'

Stuck in a tailback caused by a tractor, Wilma tapped her fingers impatiently on the steering wheel. 'It would be time better spent than driving this distance on a hope and a prayer. Black fish aside, Peterhead's not exactly the fraud capital of Europe.'

'Not so,' Maggie contended, though they were, indeed, making the trip on a hope and a prayer. 'Don't you remember that pair with the diet pills? Huge case. Claimed they'd burn fat and even treat cancer, but ...'

'...it was a swick,' Wilma supplied. 'I mind now: sisters weren't they? Made millions. But they weren't from Peterhead, they were from Fraserburgh.'

'I stand corrected,' Maggie said. 'But they were back up in court at Peterhead last year, served with confiscation orders.'

'That's ancient history,' Wilma grumbled. 'To get back to what we were saying, you do any better at drumming up new business?'

'Three background checks and a missing–'

'A misper!' Wilma exclaimed. 'I thought we were going to give that sort of thing a wide berth.'

'If you'd let me finish,' Maggie scowled. '...cat.'

'A cat?' Wilma echoed. 'You taking the piss?'

'I'm deadly serious. If you'll allow me to explain. This cat, Malthus it's called...'

'What?'

'Eighteenth century political economist,' Maggie rattled off. She'd Googled the name the minute she got home. 'Known for his work on population growth. His theory is that, left unchecked, a population will outgrow its resources.'

'Okay. But what has that to do with cats?'

'Family in-joke, from what I gather. Ursula Evershed, the prospective client, is a single lady. The cat in question male, and from what I gather, sexually promiscuous.'

'Oh,' Wilma nodded her head in understanding. 'Mebbe she should have called it Randy. Me and Darren went to Kos once on holiday, and everywhere you looked there were stray cats. Going at it, they were, like there was no tomorrow. Fair turned Darren on. We–'

'Quite so,' Maggie cut her short.

Flooring the accelerator, Wilma overtook three cars at once. The air freshener hanging from the rear-view mirror swung wildly. A horn blared as she cut back in.

'Try and not write us both off,' Maggie spoke through gritted teeth.

Wilma grinned. 'But you turned the dame down?'

'Actually,' Maggie began.

Wilma threw a warning look. 'You did, didn't you?'

'Keep your eyes on the road,' Maggie hissed. 'Didn't say yes. Didn't say no,' she equivocated. 'The woman wouldn't let me leave without promising to think about it.'

'Daft cow.'

'She's a poor soul.'

'Maggie,' Wilma admonished. 'We can't afford charity.'

'That's rich coming from you: the way you banged on about Debbie Milne's bairns.'

'There's a wheen of difference between a bairn and a fucking cat,' Wilma said. The tractor had turned off the main road and they were making short work of the Ellon bypass.

'*Touché*. All I'm saying is she offered big bucks, the first instalment upfront. Can't say I wasn't tempted. And, given the circumstances, we can't afford to be picky.'

'Picky? You're the one just turned her nose up at a wee bittie surveillance. And now you're asking me to chase some rampant cat all over the country.'

'It would be a whole load easier than sitting in a car half the night in front of a lousy chipper.'

'Did I say it was a chipper?' Wilma asked, as they passed Cruden Bay.

'No, but whatever it is, in the hope of nailing a bunch of toe-rags. They might not even be toe-rags. Have you never heard of the ice-cream wars?'

'It's a Chinese.'

'Triads, then.'

'A car would be warm, at least. And we'd be on our bums, not outside in the...'

'It's summer, Wilma.'

'Aye. On the Costa Del Granite.'

'If the case is straightforward and the client good for our fee, it will be easy money. We'll get paid for the hours we bill whether the cat turns up or not, whereas with a surveillance job we could end up with nothing. Less than nothing: a knife in the ribs.'

'Don't exaggerate.'

'All I'm saying is, the job would only entail a regular turn around Old Aberdeen, a trawl of Seaton Park...'

'Thought you were never going back there,' Wilma questioned. 'Not after...'

Maggie ignored this. 'Reckon that could be your remit.'

'Why me?'

'It would be good exercise for one thing. I know you're missing the gym, and...'

'Forget about the bloody gym,' Wilma snapped.

'There's no need to bite my head off,' Maggie complained. She wondered if Wilma had fallen out with Joe Grogan, the boxing coach, or was just feeling self-conscious about her weight. Decided she had enough to worry about.

'I don't know why you're so keen on taking this case, that's all.'

'I'm not,' Maggie insisted. 'I need the money, and it's all there is.'

'There's other ways.'

'Not right now. And the way things are... Women like us, we do whatever it takes to survive. I shouldn't need to tell *you* that.'

Wilma wagged a chubby finger. 'I get it. It's because this Ursula what's-her-name is a toff.'

'It most certainly is not. If you'd seen the place: springs sticking out the settee, threadbare rugs, everything thick with dust. Shades of Miss Havisham.'

'Who?'

'Never mind.'

'She *is* posh, though?' Wilma persisted.

'In a weird kind of way.'

'There you go again, Maggie Laird, getting taken in by appearances. Admit it, if thon dame been up the road in Tillydrone, you'd have been out of there like a shot.'

Maggie coloured. *Once a snob, always a snob.* She thought she'd come a long way in ironing out the worst of her prejudices since their paths first crossed, her and Wilma. Now, she wasn't so sure.

Footprints

'Thank God you've come!' Judith McNair raised an anguished face. 'It's been over two weeks since I phoned.'

'Yes, well...' Souter began. Along with fellow PC Dave Miller, he'd been detailed to follow up a series of petty thefts. But policing resources being what they were, this type of offence went to the bottom of the heap. Many a victim of minor offending would wait a month or more to see a police officer. If they saw one at all. However, an outbreak of thefts, resulting in a man being charged in relation to incidents in Thistle Street, Gladstone Place and Midstocket Road, had made headlines in the *Press and Journal*, putting the police on the back foot. 'Baby footprints, is that right?'

'Yes.'

'Footprints?' Dave Miller echoed. 'Isn't that a bit messy? My Chloe got handprints done first week at nursery. Red poster paint. Thought that was bad enough. Smudged like nobody's business. But ink?' Miller queried, his eyes out on stalks.

'They don't use ink,' Judith McNair replied. 'Not nowadays. Just a wipe and reactive paper.'

'That right?' Miller remarked, leaning forward in his seat. 'But how...?'

'To get back to what I was saying.' Souter interrupted with a warning look at his partner. Miller would do anything to put off time.

'The paper has a special coating,' Judith continued remorselessly. 'You wipe the soles of your baby's feet, then press them gently onto the paper and the image appears. It's miraculous, really. Almost as miraculous as...' She broke down in sobs.

'Don't upset yourself,' Miller said, leaping to his feet. 'It's only a print.' Ineffectually, he patted her hand. 'And the frame can't be worth much, so it's not as if...'

'That's the least of it.' With trembling fingers, she proffered a piece of paper. 'Look what the thief left in my bedroom.'

Miller peered at the crude drawing. 'Looks like a...' He scratched his head. 'Dunno.'

'It's a noose,' Judith insisted, eyes wide with fright. 'The thought that somebody could have been in my home, going through my things. Intimate things.' She shuddered in disgust. 'I found it in my underwear drawer.'

'Kids, most like,' Souter offered.

Judith ignored him. 'I haven't felt safe since it happened. Can't sleep in my own bed. I've been using the settee. The doctor has given me pills, but...'

'To return to your statement, Mrs McNair,' he interrupted. 'You said the framed item was on the mantelpiece on the Thursday and missing on the Friday. Couldn't your husband...?'

'We're separated.'

'And he didn't visit that week?'

'He doesn't visit. Full stop. We're getting a divorce.'

'Did you have any other callers?'

Judith McNair squeezed her eyes shut. Opened them again. 'Not that I can remember.'

'When you're in the house, do you normally keep your doors locked?'

'Always. Front and back. And the windows have security locks.'

'You couldn't have moved it?' Miller chipped in. 'My missus is forever shifting stuff around.' He rolled his eyes. 'Furniture and all. I'll come off shift and the settee...'

Judith looked daggers. 'I didn't move it.'

Miller shrugged. 'If you say so.'

Souter threw him a cautionary look. Bad enough they had a list of thefts as long as your arm to get through without whipping up a confrontation. 'We've circulated a description of the missing item. I should warn you, the chances of recovery are slim.'

'I knew you were going to say that.' This was followed by a further bout of weeping.

'But I can assure you, Mrs McNair, we'll do our utmost. Although without a photograph...' He looked to his partner for rescue.

Souter's senses pricked. His eyes roamed the room, searching for evidence. Found none. He took a surreptitious sniff. He'd have expected a vanilla smell: talcum, formula milk. Poo, even. He could still remember the horrific green slime that on occasion filled his own kids' nappies. Then he twigged.

'You can always make another set,' Miller was saying, now. 'I mean, it won't be the same, but near enough.'

Souter's eyes flashed alarm signals.

Miller ploughed on, oblivious. 'How old is the baby?'

'You just don't get it,' Judith McNair sniffed, brushing snot from her nose with the back of her hand. 'Archie...' She looked from one officer to the other. 'My baby... He passed away at five weeks. Cot death. I've never got over it,' she hiccupped. 'My marriage broke up on account of it. Those footprints are all I have left.'

What's Up wi You?

'Henry Dundas.' The estate agent stuck out his right hand.

Wilma clocked the missing digit. 'What's up wi you?' She eyed the stump askance. 'Caught with yer fingers in the till?'

'Childhood accident,' Henry mumbled, whipping his hand behind his back.

'That right?' Her blue eyes bulged. 'Tell me more.'

Maggie threw her a sharp look. 'Why don't we sit down?'

They were back in Maggie's front room. Following her abortive meeting with Henry the previous week, she'd felt bad. He seemed a decent enough fellow, a cut above what she'd expected, and she'd wasted his time. But there were searching questions to be asked, so to that end she'd enlisted Wilma's support.

'Okay.' Wilma plonked her backside down on the big chair, leaving Henry and Maggie to occupy either end of the settee.

Pig in the middle! Maggie thought. She seemed to be forever caught between a rock and a hard place.

Henry opened the conversation. 'As I've outlined to Mrs Laird...'

'Yeah, yeah.' Wilma was having none of it. 'How much do you charge?'

'That depends,' Henry answered with a tremulous smile.

'What on?'

'The valuation, principally. Then it's a question of how the property is marketed: schedule, video, online? Whether viewings are carried out by you...' He switched his gaze to Maggie. '...or by ourselves.'

'Give me a ballpark figure,' Wilma pressed.

'Well...' The middle finger of Henry's right hand tapped a rhythm on his knee.

Maggie and Wilma, both, sat with eyes riveted to the adjacent stump, which twitched in silent syncopation.

'...somewhere between one and two percent, plus whatever additional services are agreed.'

'How can you justify that?' Wilma demanded.

'We have twenty years' experience of selling properties in the Grampian region. Our staff are highly qualified and pro-active. We're properly regulated, unlike low-cost online sites. And...'

'The valuation?' Maggie finally found her voice.

'I'll need to do a full inspection. But judging by similar properties we've sold this year, I'd estimate your property to be worth in the region of £280,000.'

'Is that all?' Maggie gasped. She'd been scouring property sites online and had hoped for a figure upwards of £300,000.

'As you'll be aware,' Henry's voice didn't miss a beat. 'With the drop in the price of oil, the Aberdeen market has undergone a correction.'

'Accepted.'

'Of, I think it's fair to say, seismic proportions.'

Maggie nodded, mute. You only had to look at the selling agents' boards in front of the granite mansions along Queens Road and Carden Place to realise the bottom had fallen out of the property market. Still, she'd read that things were looking up. 'But,' she began hopefully.

'There's evidence of recovery, yes. But we've a long way to go. And...' He ran eyes over the room, gave a nervous cough. '...there's condition to take into account.'

From the big armchair in the window came a stifled snort. Wilma had been banging on to Maggie since they first got in tow the need to bring the latter's home into the twenty-first century.

'I'd propose coming to the market at £275,000 and seeing where that takes us.'

The bottom dropped out of Maggie's stomach. *Not far!* Only that week she'd seen two-bedroom flats in the West End advertised at £280,000. And by the time you added on the stamp duty and the Scottish Government's Land and Buildings Transaction Tax. Her mind worked overtime. The LBTT would add another few thousand pounds.

'You'll want to get other quotes,' Wilma came back in. 'Won't you?'

Maggie snapped out of her reverie. 'I suppose.'

The confidence vanished from Henry's face. 'Of course.' His head dropped and he fiddled with his shirt cuffs, looking for all the world like a five-year-old.

Maggie smiled an apology. 'Just for comparison.'

Henry regained his composure. 'May I keep in touch?' He looked up, a tentative smile on his face.

'Of course.' She turned to Wilma. 'Don't you agree?'

Wilma ignored her, giving Henry the full evils.

Maggie turned back. 'Give me a call in a week or so,' she said, her voice firm.

A Case File

'Listen up,' Allan Chisolm said, raising his voice above the ringing of the telephone and clatter of computer keys. 'Imray case. Preliminary forensic report has come back from the lab.'

In the big room, you could have heard a pin drop. 'What's it saying?' a voice called from the far window.

With a beckoning arm, Chisolm gathered his team. 'In brief, there are indications Annabel Imray's death may be suspicious.'

'What sort of indications?' This from Bob Duffy.

Chisolm consulted his notes. 'Suggestive evidence: furniture out of line, scuff marks on the floor. Might be indicative of a struggle.'

'Homicide,' Douglas Dunn muttered, as much to himself as anyone else.

'Not necessarily,' Brian chided. His constable had toned it down since he first came on the team, but still he had a way to go. 'Could have been happenstance.'

'She might have fallen and cracked her head on the corner of that coffee table,' Susan ventured. 'It had an angular metal trim. Would have been lethal.'

'Quite so,' Chisolm concurred. 'Death has all the hallmarks of a tragic accident: high degree of alcohol intoxication. Female had been sick, could have choked. However,' he glanced down at his file, 'the way the body was lying probably rules that out. Plus, as we know from the post-mortem, the victim had sustained an injury to the head. May have been accidental, but taken with the evidence of pressure to the face, we can't rule out foul play.'

Brian kept schtum. He'd been surreptitiously practising deep breathing, part of a new regime of diet and meditation. And, besides, he had nothing useful to add.

'Has the coffee table yielded any forensics?' Douglas enquired.

'Nothing other than a couple of fingerprints.'

'Bingo!' Douglas exclaimed, bringing his hands together in triumph. He knew it took only the tiniest piece of forensic evidence to yield a result. 'Have they thrown up a match?'

'Partial prints,' Chisolm said, grim-faced. 'You have a bad habit, Dunn, of jumping the gun. In case you've forgotten, let me remind you: the job of a detective is to go with the evidence. You don't guide the story, son. The story takes you.' He glowered. 'Got that?'

Douglas looked at the floor. 'Yes, boss.'

'Anything from those mugs?' Susan enquired.

'Victim's prints, nothing else.'

'Oh.' Her face fell.

Across the table, Douglas caught her eye. A hint of a smirk.

Susan turned her head away. Ever since he'd pulled a fast one on the Milne case by obtaining evidence on the sly, the pair had maintained a tacit stand-off. Still, ever the pragmatist, Susan hoped this case would furnish the opportunity to level the score.

'I've opened a case file,' Chisolm continued. 'We'll need to get hold of an incident room. See to that, will you, Brian?'

He snapped to attention. 'Yes, boss.'

'What about staffing,' Duffy grumbled. 'We're a man short already. What's the story on Wood's replacement?'

'In the pipeline,' Chisolm replied. 'So I've been informed.'

Duffy and Brian exchanged doleful looks. They knew what that meant: it could take months for Police Scotland's administrative machinery to grind into action.

'I've put a request in upstairs for more bodies and an extra block of overtime.'

'You should be so lucky,' Duffy muttered.

Chisolm silenced him with a stern look. 'We'll have to wait and see.'

Chalk and Cheese

'Gary Moir.' The young man introduced himself with a toothpaste grin.

Maggie gave him the once-over: mid-thirties, fitted light grey suit, buttons straining at the chest; short legs in narrow trousers; loafers, no socks. *Chalk and cheese!* She couldn't help but make a mental comparison with Henry Dundas. And it wasn't confined to his dress code. Gary Moir sported a tan that wouldn't have been out of place in the Caribbean. He'd obviously had his teeth whitened, and his dark hair dotted his skull in gelled peaks. *Italian meringue!* The words jumped, unbidden, into Maggie's head. She smothered a smile.

'Sorry I had to call off last week,' he added. 'Unforeseen circumstances.' He took a step forward, grin still in place. 'Can I come in?'

'Y-yes.' Grudgingly, she held the door open. If she'd been more clear-headed, she'd have cancelled the visit altogether. A wave of cologne choked her nostrils as she ushered him into the front room, where she was dismayed to see him make the big chair his own.

'Righty-ho!' He cut to the chase. Leaning forward, he proffered a laminated folder. 'This is your one-stop package to a successful sale. Don't waste your time, Mrs...' Another flash of teeth. 'Is it alright if I call you Maggie?'

From her perch on the end of the sofa, Maggie offered an affirmative nod.

'...Maggie, looking elsewhere. My company, Property Solutions, covers all the bases: pre-sale valuation, Home Report, EPC, marketing, viewing appointments. You won't need to do a thing.'

Except make a firm decision! Maggie thought with a qualm. The

Peterhead trip had been unproductive, and with little else on the horizon, the clock was ticking.

'Our offices are open 24/7,' he ran on. 'Our call centre around the clock. We've won major awards. We even have interpreters on hand. In short, Maggie...' He ran a hand through his quiff.

Oh, she thought, *he's ruined the meringue.* She was overcome by an irrational urge to giggle.

'...I'm your man.'

'Mmm,' she tried for non-committal. Hoped disappointment wasn't written all over her face. She had been expecting someone older. More professional. Still, if Gary Moir was good at his job, what did it matter what she thought? 'Before we start,' she asked, taking her cue from Wilma. 'How much do you charge?'

'There's a scale,' he replied with alacrity, dodging the question. 'Goes by the valuation. First impressions,' he looked Maggie in the eye, 'I'd value your property at £300,000. It's well-situated for schools. Would make the perfect starter home for a young couple looking to start a family.'

Maggie's heart lurched. That was exactly what she'd thought when she'd first viewed the bungalow with George.

'Or down-sizers' Gary continued. 'Quiet street. Good range of local shops. Handy for public transport.'

She nodded agreement. They'd thought that, too.

'Though, to attract the best offers, you might want to think about a quick outside paint job.'

Maggie's confidence plummeted. 'How much would that cost?'

'Few grand,' he said airily. 'Coat of emulsion inside while they're at it. Could be done in a week.' Then, seeing Maggie's crestfallen expression, 'Your choice, of course.'

'What if I don't?' she fretted.

'No worries, if you choose not to go down that road, I'll still get you a good sale.' He winked. 'Some folk love a doer-upper.'

'I suppose.'

'If you give me your business, Maggie,' he confided, eyes oozing sincerity, 'I guarantee you I'll give it one hundred percent.'

Of that she had no doubt, if only because Gary Moir was young and thrusting and - if appearances were to be believed - looked to have expensive tastes. He'd be paid on commission, she surmised. Probably spent it all on clothes.

'This is a lovely room,' he ran on. 'So bright with the bay window.' He leaned in confidentially. 'I bet you spend a lot of time here.'

Maggie shrugged. 'Used to.' In her mind's eye she could see George sitting of an evening, newspaper open at the sports pages, in the very spot Gary occupied now. She'd have her feet up on the sofa. The kids would be sound asleep in their beds. 'Now, not so much,' she responded, bringing herself back to the present.

''I'm sure the rest of the house is equally nice,' Gary asserted. He went to rise. 'Are you happy to give me a quick tour, just so I can be on the ball for when you instruct the Home Report?'

'Well, I...' Instinctively, Maggie was resistant to his hard-sell, and perhaps naively hadn't expected anything to be on show at this point. She made a mental whizz around, registering Colin's unmade bed, the mound of ironing awaiting her in the dining-room, the breakfast dishes still in the sink.

Getting to his feet, Gary said, 'Don't worry if it's a bit untidy. 'We're well used to that. Plenty time to present it for sale.'

'I suppose.' Maggie felt pressured to agree. Still, what harm was there? It would only take a few minutes. And she was hardly in a position to quibble. If she didn't address her financial problems, and do it soon, she was in danger of losing the family home.

A Fountain Pen

'Am I glad to see you,' the woman on the doorstep exclaimed. She beckoned the policemen into a formal front sitting-room. 'I've been worried sick.'

'Fountain pen, it says here.' Miller read, lowering himself onto a floral chintz settee. 'You reported it missing on 18th July.' He sneaked a glance at Souter, whose eye-rolling from the far end signalled they were wasting their time.

'That's right,' the woman answered. 'From over there,' she expanded, gesturing to the mahogany kneehole desk in the window. 'The pen belonged to my grandfather,' she confided. 'A Montblanc, one of the very few things I have to remember him by.' Her voice wavered. 'He was killed in the war.'

Which war was that? Miller wondered, for he'd be hard-pressed to put an age to the grand-daughter, whose pale moon-face was unlined and substantial figure camouflaged by layers of loose-fitting clothing.

'He was a journalist,' she continued. 'Rather a famous one, if I may say so. Showered with awards. He used to sit me on his knee when I was small. At that very desk,' she confided, smiling fondly at the memory. 'I was the youngest of three girls,' she ran on. 'Grandpa's favourite by a country mile. I like to think it was catching...' She broke off, registering the alarm on Miller's face. 'The gift for journalism, I mean, since I've followed in his footsteps.'

'You're a journalist?' Knowing the Fifth Floor's antipathy to the press, Souter was in there like a bullet.

Miranda Maitland lowered her gaze. 'Sadly, no. I never rose to the title of reporter. But I was employed for over thirty years as the agony aunt of a national newspaper. I'm not going to say which one, but I like to think I saved my loyal readers a great deal of heartbreak.'

Souter didn't want to go there. 'Vintage fountain pens… aren't they worth a bob or two?'

'They are. Only Grandpa's doesn't write all that well, a slight distortion in the nib I suspect.' Her lips thinned. 'One of my sisters probably. They–'

Miller smothered a yawn. 'You couldn't have put it down somewhere else?'

'Certainly not,' Miranda replied, her voice sharp. 'The pen never moves from that desk. It's something I'm very particular about. I've kept Grandpa's blotter too. And there's another thing. That blotter was pristine. Whoever took the pen defaced it. As if I wasn't distressed enough.' She waved a hand. 'Go on. Take a look.'

The two constables rose and crossed to the window.

'It's badly drawn,' Miranda observed. 'But it's clearly a noose. Gave me such a fright,' she wailed, hands twisting in her lap.

Miller looked to his partner, one eyebrow arched in a question. Souter acknowledged him with a nod. He'd had the husband collared for nicking the baby footprints. Family tragedies took a toll on a marriage. But two spooky drawings pushed coincidence too far. Turning to Miranda, he asked, 'Did you have any visitors that day?'

'Yes,' she responded. 'When the newspaper made me redundant, I re-trained as a psychotherapist.' She rose and, crossing the room, returned with a leather-bound desk diary. 'Let me see...' She leafed through several pages. 'July 18th, that was a Thursday, so I had my regular visitors: Mrs McIver at ten, Ms Thomson at eleven, Mr Fyfe at noon. Then I broke for lunch.' She looked up. 'A proper, cooked lunch. Vital to keep the old brain cells in good working order.'

Where did that leave him, Miller wondered, subsisting as he did on a diet of chocolate bars from the canteen vending machine and Greggs sausage rolls?

'Mr Niven came in at two. Then I appear to have a gap before

Mrs Marshall at four. They're new clients, both of them. Not a known entity.' She leaned in confidentially. 'As a lone woman one has to exercise extreme caution when inviting strangers into one's home. As you'll no doubt be aware, since Care in the Community came into operation, there are all sorts of people at large. Dangerous people. Take those London underground incidents, the Zito murder for one. The perpetrator was on medication for paranoid schizophrenia.'

'Incidents such as those are rare,' Souter said.

'Rare they may be,' Miranda retorted. 'But that doesn't help me. I depend on those clients for my livelihood, and I've been so frightened since the theft occurred, I'm terrified to let anyone over the doorstep.'

He moved to wrap the visit up. 'Did you have any other callers that day: tradesmen, window cleaner, delivery drivers?'

'No,' Miranda replied. 'Not even the postman,' I remember distinctly, because I was expecting a small package and it never arrived.' Her lips thinned. 'Changed days. When I was a girl, they–'

'In that case,' Miller said, regaining his cool, 'we'd better let you get on.'

'But...' Miranda began.

'We'll be back in touch...' He couldn't look Souter in the eye. '... the minute we have any news.'

A Chinese Takeaway

Wilma shifted in the seat of her car. Even fully reclined, she struggled to get comfy. She eyed the bottle of Irn Bru stashed in the door pocket. The portion of chips and curry sauce she'd eaten earlier sat like a stone in her stomach and had given her a raging thirst.

She checked the time on her phone. She'd been parked downwind of the Chinese takeaway for coming on three hours with not a sniff of the vandals, and had a desperate urge to pee. And there's no way she could wee in the street. She'd already gone against her senior partner's direct instructions, and a charge of offending public decency would, Wilma knew, kibosh her ambitions for good.

She weighed the option of nipping into the Chinese and asking to use their toilet, but didn't dare take the risk of the unit being vandalised whilst she was inside. Crossing her legs, Wilma wondered whether it was worth the effort, the private investigation business. Some days, it seemed the agency had as many failures as successes, and if she hadn't hung onto her jobs at ARI and Torry, she'd have been hard put to make ends meet. Then there was Maggie Laird. Wilma had developed a fondness for the wee thing. And God knows she had her troubles. But in Wilma's opinion, Maggie was fair up her bum much of the time.

This surveillance job was a classic example. Wilma had the PI skills, borne of experience and a hard upbringing. And she had the equipment. In her head, she ran through an inventory of the dodgy gear she'd purchased online. Why shouldn't she run a few wee ops of her own? But, no, Miss Methlick had laid down the law. Stymied, Wilma had run back to the owner of the Chinese takeaway and brokered a cash deal before he could place his business elsewhere. In their situation, a bit of cash in hand, she reasoned, wouldn't go amiss.

Her head was lolling when her ears pricked. Snapping to attention, she spied a clutch of youths huddled in front of the takeaway. In their early teens, her first thought was they were sharing a spliff or even dealing drugs. Then she clocked the cans of spray paint.

'Oi!' Wilma was out the car like a bullet. 'What d'you think you're up to?'

'None of your fucking business,' the tallest of the group, who she took to be the ringleader, shot back.

'Fat cow,' another chipped in. Deliberately, he raised an arm, discharging red paint onto the takeaway window.

Kitted out for the occasion in black leather trousers and biker boots, Wilma advanced upon them.

'Christ,' the leader exclaimed. 'If it's no Scully!'

'I'll fucking "Scully" ye,' Wilma snarled. Flicking open the tops of the Police Magnum Pepper Spray she held in each hand, she targeted the two nearest lads.

'Fuck!' They danced about, clawing at their faces, eyes and noses streaming.

'Any more for any more?' Wilma asked sweetly. 'There's UV dye in there an all,' she added. 'Jist in case ye wis thinkin o' comin back.'

The others fixed their eyes on the pavement.

'Here's the deal,' Wilma continued, hoiking her bra straps with two thumbs. 'Ye'll no trouble ma pal again. Gerrit?'

Vigorously, they nodded.

'An if ye wis tae be seen within half a mile o' here, there's plenty mair where that came from.' Her mouth curved into a malicious grin. 'A taser an all. So if ye want tae keep yer crown jewels, fuck off, the lot o' you.'

IV

As Long as it Takes

The incident room was jam-packed, every seat occupied, detectives, uniformed officers and civilian support workers ranged around the perimeter or perched uncomfortably on the edges of desks.

DI Chisolm motioned for silence. 'I've called you here this morning...' He paused to let the buzz of conversation die down. '... to inform you that Pathology have confirmed the death of Annabel Imray as suspicious. Estimate as to time of death is between the hours of eight and eleven in the morning, although as you know that may change when a full examination has been completed. Brian?' He looked to his sergeant.

Brian crossed to the whiteboard, where two photographs of the victim - full-length and passport head shot - were pinned side-by-side. He pointed. 'Annabel Imray. For those of you who don't read the newspapers–'

'Or can't read,' some wit called out from the back.

'...Annabel's body was discovered at her home on Tuesday morning.' He paused to let this sink in. 'What do we know about her? Age 36. Unmarried. Lived in rented property at Kepplestone. Self-employed public relations consultant. Maintained an office in Chapel Street and...'

'Although,' Douglas jumped in. 'Annabel worked from home much of the time. A search of her phone and laptop computer should yield any appointments on the day of her death. Or engagements the previous evening, come to that.'

Brian nodded. 'Thanks for your contribution,' he observed, with just a hint of irony. 'No doubt, as hacker-in-chief, you'll be offering your services?'

A ripple of amusement ran round the room. Almost all of them had heard the much embellished account of his Struthers' case cock-up, when Douglas had come close to compromising the prosecution case by covertly hacking into the suspect's computer.

'We're in the process of raising a warrant. Annabel must have left a footprint on the internet: Facebook pages, Twitter feeds, photos, comments, reviews. Working in PR, she'll have been active on all sorts of platforms: Snapchat, Tumblr, Pinterest, Instagram, YouTube, WhatsApp, Google, Linkedin, and no doubt umpteen more. I want you to find her close friends, run background checks, establish if anyone has a motive for causing her harm. But bear in mind, there's a balance to be maintained between moving fast and gathering too much information, so vital clues are missed. And we'll need to set up a timeline. In the meantime,' he continued. 'We have to establish who was the person - or persons - who last saw Annabel alive?'

'Who called it in?' one of the civilian officers piped up.

'The cleaner. Back of eleven. Didn't give us much.'

'How about the neighbours?'

'Same story. Seems she'd only lived there for a matter of months, and there weren't many around, so I'll need Uniform to get back there, conduct door-to-door enquiries outside office hours.'

'CCTV opportunities?'

'We're working on those.'

'Boyfriend?' A female voice questioned from the back of the room.

'None currently, at least that we know of. Annabel was frequently in the press, so newspaper archives might throw up recent business associates.' He cleared his throat. 'Which brings me to her financial status: how sound was her business? Was she in debt? Was she servicing a habit: drink, drugs?'

'How long before we get the toxicology report?' a uniformed officer asked.

'As long as it takes,' Chisolm said, stepping in. It would be weeks rather than days. 'So forget about that for now. Whilst we're waiting for the techies to get into Annabel's computer, I want you to get out there, do some solid policing, see what you can turn up.'

A Musketeer

'Three quotes,' Wilma said, slurping from a balloon glass of Merlot. 'That's what you're needing.'

'You would know,' Maggie retorted. She'd been strong-armed into a change of scene. 'Cheer you up', Wilma had insisted. Now the two were ensconced in a booth at a West End hotel.

'Because I lived in a caravan, is that what you're saying?'

'No.' Maggie was instantly contrite. 'I'm sorry. I didn't mean it like that. It just came out.'

'Aye, weel,' Wilma's tone sharpened. 'Didn't stop me learning off other folk's experience. Which is why I'm saying you need to get three quotes, minimum. Selling a house is a serious business.'

Maggie took a judicious sip of her Sauvignon Blanc. It tasted of green apples with an undernote of lemons, and took her back to a family holiday in the south of France: fields of lavender and sunflowers and lazy days and laughter. 'I don't doubt that's the received wisdom,' she allowed, putting the halycon memory to bed. 'But it's so unsettling having a total stranger trail through the house going over all the details. If I decide to go ahead with the sale...' The Harlaw Insurance cheque had come in, but there was still a shortfall. She resolved to chase up Scott Milne without letting on to Wilma. '...I'm happy to settle for the two I've got.'

'You're joking,' Wilma lisped through a mouthful of Merlot. 'Thon Henry's a waste of space.'

'I like him,' Maggie argued. 'He's a nice chap.'

Wilma sniffed. 'If ever I saw a useless...'

'I disagree.' Maggie's tone oozed defiance. 'Henry Dundas is a solid citizen.'

'You reckon?'

'I'd lay a bet on it: public school education, stint in the army. *Not Eton and Guards. Gordonstoun maybe.* Respectable career.'

Wilma hooted. 'An estate agent? Respectable? Who are you kidding?'

'Well,' Maggie back-tracked, 'they can't all be crooks.'

'No? Only ninety-nine point nine percent of them.'

'Don't exaggerate.'

Wilma's lower lip jutted. 'I'm not. As for thon Gary fella you got in, he sounds a right patter-merchant.'

'Gary Moir? He isn't my cup of tea, I must admit. Bit of a cheeky chappie. But he certainly is proactive. Plus, he reckons he can get me a good price.'

'Never met him.' Wilma reached for a handful of peanuts. 'Wouldn't know.' Mouth wide open, she tilted her head back and tossed them in.

Wondering if Wilma's nose was out of joint because she hadn't been included in the meeting, Maggie ignored this remark. 'To get back to Henry,' she said. 'I think you're being a bit harsh. The way you zeroed in on his missing finger, it must have put him on the defensive.'

'I thought that was the whole point of a private investigator: noticing things.' Wilma spoke with hamster cheeks.

'Yes. But not like that.'

'Like what?' She swallowed, brushed salt off her lips and reached for her wine.

'It was rude. Anyhow,' Maggie moved to defuse the situation. They were on a rare night out, after all. 'Let's agree to disagree on that one. But whatever his professional standing and physical disability, you have to concede Henry Dundas has nice manners.'

This was met with a loud snort. 'Manners, is it? Guy's a total throwback: Primary One haircut, clothes your dad wouldn't be seen dead in, and that's just for starters.'

'There's nothing the matter with his haircut.'

Wilma wrinkled her nose. 'Short back and bloody sides?'

'Better that than a Tweety Pie quiff or shaved up the sides like a felon.'

'Okay, okay, but how about that suit. Wouldn't look out of place in a museum.'

'He's maybe a bit old-fashioned,' Maggie conceded, 'but I like old-fashioned.' She took another sip of her wine.

'He's out the bloody ark. Minds me of thon Musketeer.'

'Who? D'Artagnan?'

It was Wilma's turn to look bewildered. 'Him took us out of Europe.'

'You mean Brexiteer?' For three years, opinions had been polarised by the 2017 referendum decision to leave the European Union and its potential to affect peoples' lives and incomes.

'Aye, that's it. Jacob bloody Rees-Mogg.'

'Wasn't it you that said you shouldn't judge a book by its cover? Just because...'

Wilma spluttered a shower of wine and peanuts onto the table in front of her. 'Talk about the pot calling the kettle black. Fella's a total construct: the outfit, the marbles in his mouth, "one" this, "one" that. You like him because he's pretend-posh, that's the long and the short of it.'

'It most certainly is not.'

Wilma's big blue eyes narrowed to slits. 'Don't think for a minute you can fool me, Maggie Laird. I know you through and through. Once a snob, always a snob.'

'That's not fair.'

'No? How about Sheena Struthers? You only took on that case because she was from bloody Bieldside.'

'Not true,' Maggie contended. 'And if you're hell-bent on going down that road, what about Debbie Milne? You conned me into thinking you were sorry for her kids, but the real reason was you weren't satisfied with solving bread and butter cases. Oh, no, that's too tame for you, Wilma Harcus. What you're after are cheap thrills.' She caught her breath. 'That's the difference between you and me: I'm in this business for the long-haul. You...' She stabbed a finger. '...see the role of a private investigator as one long...' Maggie struggled to find the word that would do her argument justice. Ended up mouthing thin air.

'Ancient history,' Wilma observed, draining her glass. 'But to get back to the subject,' she continued, a steely glint in her eye, 'you need at least three quotes before...'

'If it's two I want,' Maggie hissed. 'It's two I'll bloody have.'

'Get you!' Wilma exclaimed, eyes widening in naked admiration. 'Good to see you've got your mojo back.'

'What?' Out the corner of one eye Maggie could see Wilma's shoulders heave.

'If you could just see yourself,' she tittered. 'Laying it on. And you the size of a sixpence.'

'Size has nothing to do with it,' Maggie huffed.

'Aye,' Wilma's eyes glittered as she replayed her run-in with the Albanian people trafficker. 'Some days.'

She pointed to Maggie's half-full glass. 'You better drink up,' she said, lurching to her feet. 'I'm away to get another round in.'

A Medal

'I thought you'd have shown up sooner,' the woman complained. 'I've been scared out of my wits.'

'You reported the theft of a medal?' Miller queried. Mrs Ethel Troup looked to be in her late fifties. Permed hair, pink cardigan straining over a heavy bosom.

'That's right,' she replied. 'It was my dad's. Late father's.' she corrected. 'He passed away last month.'

'Sorry for your loss.' Miller mouthed, not looking up from his notebook. Hard to come across as sincere when death and trauma were part and parcel of the job. Aside from which, these reported thefts were becoming a pain and they'd hardly made a dent in the list. 'It says here it was silver. Awarded for long service.' He chewed the end of his pencil. 'What?' Took it out of his mouth. 'Like the George Cross?' Having second thoughts, he added, 'Only not.'

On the other side of the fireplace, Ian Souter smothered a sigh. Miller could be such a tool, sometimes. From beneath lowered lids he took in the room: swirly Axminster carpet, leaf-patterned wallpaper, three-piece Dralon suite. Father obviously hadn't re-decorated in decades. The arms of the settee had wooden tips. Even with his limited style-consciousness, Souter knew this to be a no-no. Or maybe it was that dated it had come back into fashion. A mirror hung over the tiled fire-surround. In the window, a drop-leaf table was flanked by two Queen Anne chairs. A modest TV set occupied the far corner. Nothing in the way of ornaments. That might account for the cardboard boxes in the hallway. The whole place stank of tobacco. It had caught his nostrils the minute he stepped through the door. Funny how when you gave up smoking - Souter had kicked the habit at the fourth attempt - other people's smoke irritated the hell out of you. 'You reckon you lost the medal sometime during the week before last?' he asked, jumping in.

'Correct,' Ethel Troup replied. 'I've been round here every day since, waiting for you lot to turn up. Whoever took that medal left a calling card. See!' She pointed to the mirror over the mantelpiece, on which the outline of a noose drawn in black was clearly visible. 'Put the fear of death in me, I can tell you. First thing I wanted to do was clean it off. If it came off. They must have used a sharpie. Some sort of marker pen anyhow. Then I thought I'd better not.'

Fuck! Souter cursed himself for not spotting it sooner.

'I've been terrified since it happened. I represent this ward on the council, you see, and my public profile could have made me a target.' Clasping a hand to her mouth, she spoke through spread fingers. 'I don't feel safe anymore, even outside. Somebody could be watching me. Waiting...' She broke off, eyes staring.

'I understand your concern,' Souter moved to reassure her. 'But...'

She cut him off. 'You don't know who's going about, not these days. And the political debate has become so toxic, threats against politicians and their families are commonplace. Take Jo Cox, for example. Dreadful business, that murder. And there was that MP was attacked with a samurai sword.'

'Those are extreme cases,' Souter observed, thinking all the while, *Doesn't happen in Aberdeen!* He reckoned his gut instinct - attributing the thefts to wayward kids - was right. 'You've told us you're in the process of clearing the house,' he changed the subject. 'It's a small item, a medal. Couldn't it have been packed away with other things?'

'Definitely not,' she insisted. 'And I didn't lose it. Somebody stole it.'

'How can you be sure?'

'Because I put it on the mantelpiece for safety.'

'What day was that?'

‘The Wednesday. Or it could have been the Thursday, I’m not a hundred percent sure. I’ve been in and out that often since Dad passed, there’s been such a lot to attend to.’

Miller roused himself. ‘This report doesn’t give a valuation figure. Scrap value, I’d better put.’

Mrs Troup drew herself up. ‘It was priceless to him. He was Glaswegian, my dad, a shipwright to trade. Worked at Fairfield all his days.’ She sniffed. ‘“Man and boy”, that’s what he used to say.’

Miller leaned forward. ‘That’s who gave him the medal?’

‘The shipyard changed hands a few times. He finally got laid off in 1988. My dad was devastated. He was in his late-fifties by then. Moved up here in the hope of work in the oil industry.’ A tear formed in the corner of one eye. ‘Never held down another job. Not a proper job.’ She rubbed a fist into her eye socket.

‘Have you been doing the packing yourself?’ Souter came back in, anxious to wind up the interview. The rate this was going, they’d never get out of there this side of Christmas.

‘Yes. Wouldn’t trust these removal firms you get nowadays. Bunch of cowboys.’

‘You’ll have had a few through the door, I daresay.’

Mrs Troup sighed, ‘Tell me about it. If it’s not the neighbours looking for a nosey, or removal companies wanting your business it’s folk do house clearances.’ She rolled her eyes. ‘Travelling folk, some of them.’

Souter and Miller exchanged knowing looks. A couple of years previously, two thousand litres of heating oil had been drained from the tank of a rural primary school, causing it to close at short notice, with major inconvenience. Some locals pointed the finger of blame at the travelling community. And travellers were notoriously difficult to pin down. They changed names, changed cars, a major headache in a police investigation.

‘That drawing on the mirror,’ Souter enquired. ‘Could one of the removal men have done it?’

‘No. First thing I did was check with them. But one thing’s for sure,' Ethel Troup spoke with conviction. 'I put that medal on the mantelpiece. One minute it was there,' her lips formed a thin line. 'The next it was gone.'

Souter's eyes signalled to Miller it was time they were gone, too. 'We'll make enquiries,' he reassured her, getting to his feet.

Fat chance! The likelihood of recovery was slim, the catalogue of petty thefts doing his head in. He wondered whether they'd established the cause of death in that call-out he and Miller had responded to at Kepplestone.

Malthus

'At our introductory meeting,' Maggie began. 'We didn't do more than skim the surface of your loss. Would you care to flesh out the details?' She was back in Ursula Evershed's sitting-room. Following the double whammy of the low house valuations, she'd come to the reluctant conclusion that any new business was better than no new business. Pulling out her notebook, she said, 'Let's start with a description.'

'Look no further,' Ursula responded, a note of pride in her voice. Rising, she crossed to the fireplace, above which hung an oil painting, heavily framed in gilt, of a cat.

Blazes! Inwardly, Maggie cursed herself for not picking this up on her initial visit. Had she registered the subject, she might have saved herself a return call. But the room was so stuffed with furniture, the walls so crowded, she hadn't taken more than a cursory look. Nor would she have remembered much detail, for the painting, like its surroundings, was dark, its subject swamped by a ponderous backdrop of crimson drapes.

'Malthus is a big chap,' Ursula said, lovingly stroking the painting's surface. 'Handsome. Long-haired. Big head. Snub nose. Toe and ear tufts.'

'Colour?' Maggie prompted.

'Marmalade. A tabby. Which, if you're a cat fancier, refers, not to the breed, but to the pattern on his coat.' Her face lit up. 'The name is believed to derive from the Arabic, Atabi, a type of striped taffeta that was manufactured in the Atabiah district of Baghdad, and which...'

'A pedigree, then?' Maggie interrupted, mid-flow. 'Must be worth a fair bit.'

'No,' Ursula repaired to her seat. 'That would have been outside an academic's budget, even sixteen years ago. When Daddy went to the cattery, they offered him a kitten that was, shall we say, mongrel: half Persian Longhair, the other half who knows?' Her chin quivered. 'Not that Malthus wasn't priceless to us.'

'Quite so. He's sixteen, did you say? That's a fair age for a cat.'

'Untrue,' Ursula responded emphatically. 'Many cats live into their early twenties. And of course indoor cats have a longer lifespan. The oldest reported lived to twenty-eight.'

'I stand corrected,' Maggie murmured, without conviction. The way she read the situation, the client could wax lyrical on cat attributes till the cows came home. *Cows, now...* An image of the old farm flashed in front of her eyes. *They were real animals.* 'Did he carry any identification?' she asked. 'Was he microchipped, for instance?' She'd been reading up on the subject.

'Good gracious, no.' Ursula's eyebrows shot into her hairline. 'I don't hold with such things.'

It might have saved you a lot of heart-searching, not to say expense. Maggie shifted on the hard seat. She'd opted for a side chair this visit rather than be attacked by the sofa springs. 'A collar, perhaps?'

'There was one. But since Mummy died, it seemed to annoy him. He'd put on weight, you see. And long-haired cats, their fur tends to get matted, so I took it off.'

'Couldn't you have bought a bigger one?' The words were out before Maggie had time to weigh their effect.

'Don't you think I've asked myself that question day and night since he went?' Ursula threw her an anguished look. 'If I hadn't been so wrapped up in my research. If I'd paid more heed. If I'd looked after him properly...' Her shoulders heaved. 'I promised Mummy on her deathbed.' Tears coursed down her cheeks. 'Promised.'

God Almighty! Embarrassed, Maggie turned away. Through the dirt-streaked window, the sky was a clear powder blue, which only served to heighten the gloom indoors. Added to which, there was a smell: damp, mould, soot. That chimney likely needed swept. And - overlaying all else - cat. Maggie wrinkled her nose. She rued the day she'd turned down Wilma's takeaway surveillance job, but that would have gone to some other firm by now.

Collecting herself, she enquired, 'You wouldn't have a photograph, would you?'

Brusquely, Ursula wiped her cheeks with her cardigan sleeve. 'Of course.' Rising, she crossed the room and ferreted in a cupboard.

Maggie checked her notebook. It showed a skeleton of entries and a mass of doodles. Her shoulders sagged. Far from being a walk in the park, this case promised to be an uphill struggle.

'Here we are.' Ursula appeared at her elbow bearing a weighty album. She flipped it open. 'That's him on his first birthday. Isn't he the sweetest thing?'

'Mmm,' Maggie murmured assent.

'And this...' Turning the page. '...Is him with his first mouse. And here he is on holiday with Mummy and Daddy in Nairn. And...'

'Something more recent? 'Maggie ventured.

'Oh,' Ursula's face fell. She upended the album. 'Will this suffice? It was taken last Christmas.'

Maggie's eyes followed the pointed finger. Malthus was, indeed, a large cat: square, with a huge head, pug face, malevolent amber eyes squinting out from a mass of orange fur. Quite the ugliest cat she'd ever seen, and that's if you didn't count the Santa hat perched on his head. The bottom dropped out of her stomach. How was she going to sell this to Wilma?

'May I borrow it?'

'If you're very careful.' Ursula said sternly, prising the photograph from its fixings.

'Thanks.' Maggie slipped it between the pages of her notebook. She changed tack. 'When did you first realise Malthus had gone?'

'August 13th. The date is etched on my memory. A Tuesday. Malthus went out to do his business, and...'

'Doesn't he use a litter tray?'

'Of course,' Ursula snapped. 'My boy is very particular about his toileting. When I said, "do his business" I meant precisely that. He is in the habit of doing the rounds on a daily basis. High Street shops first thing: Keystore, Ross the baker, Blackwell's Bookshop. Then he'll have a little lie down in the St Machar Bar before he makes a tour of the university: Edward Wright Building, then...'

Maggie cut her short. 'He sounds very sociable.'

'He is. Popular. Not that he doesn't have a temper. He's a full-blooded male. But nobody has a bad word to say against him. I would go as far as to say he is loved. Not just by me.' Ursula's voice cracked. 'That's why...' She rose and crossed to the window. '...I can't understand why he would go off like that, without a word.'

'And you've toured his usual haunts?' Maggie asked. She was bursting for the bathroom by now, wondered if this would never end. She crossed her legs, uncrossed them again. 'Spoken to everybody who...?'

'Umpteen times. I told you that already.'

'Enquired of the SSPCA?'

'I've rung them all: Cats Protection, Cat Action Trust, Mrs Murrays, Blaikiewell.'

'What about Facebook?' Maggie suggested. 'Have you thought of posting something there?'

'No,' Ursula harrumphed. 'I'm not a fan of social media.'

Figures! 'No, well...' Maggie flipped her notebook shut.

'Before you go...' Ursula held up a hand. '...can you give me your assurance you'll bring all the resources at your disposal to bear.'

'Of course. We'll start by combing the immediate area, distributing fliers, checking with veterinary practices, posting an appeal on social media, and take it from there.' Maggie stowed the notebook in her bag and made to rise. 'Trust me,' she said, inwardly quailing at the prospect of Wilma's reaction. 'My partner and I will give this our very best shot.'

Shane

'Are you going to arrest me?' the young man asked, half in jest.

'Maybe not today,' Brian replied. 'I have a few questions for you, that's all.' He picked up a folder from the table in front of him. 'Thanks for coming in.'

'No problem.' Shane Kelman sat back in his seat, a smile playing on his lips.

'Where were you on Tuesday, 13th August between the hours of 8am and 11am?'

'Dunno.' The smile wiped from Shane's face. 'I'll have a look.' Whipping out his phone, he frowned at the screen. 'Don't have anything down for that morning. But it was a Tuesday and I have a heavy training day on Mondays, so I'd likely still be in bed.'

'Can anyone vouch for you?'

'What? Like was I in the sack with somebody?'

Brian nodded.

'Doubt it.'

'Are you in a relationship?' Brian fished.

Shane coloured. 'Not at the moment.'

'You're a football player. The Dons, is that correct?'

'I'm signed with Aberdeen until the end of next season, but after that...' He smoothed his hair. '...who knows?'

'And you're saying you don't have a girlfriend?' Brian queried. It was common knowledge footballers earned big bucks and had no problem attracting top totty.

'That's right,' Shane asserted. 'Not that it's any of your business.'

'You're not...?' Brian began. Scotland hadn't yet an openly gay player, but it was only a matter of time.

'You fucking with me?' Shane demanded, visibly riled. 'Look,' he sat forward. 'Where the hell is this going?'

'Bear with me,' Brian said, cursing himself for letting the interview get out of hand. 'Your previous relationship...'

'I get it,' Shane interrupted. 'Annabel, that's what this is about. I heard on the news she'd topped herself.'

Brian pounced. 'What makes you think she might do such a thing?'

'She was off her head.'

'In what way?'

'Out of control: booze, parties, you name it.'

'Did you have any reason to wish Ms Imray harm?'

'Of course not,' Shane replied, exasperated. 'We were together for nearly two years. We...'

'That's not strictly true.' It was Brian's turn to interrupt. 'It is a matter of record...' He looked down at his notes. '...that Ms Imray levelled a serious accusation against you. Stalking, is that correct?'

'I wasn't stalking her.'

'What were you doing?'

'Trying to get back the money she owed me.' Shane's left knee performed a little dance. 'I explained it all at the time.'

'Humour me,' Brian said.

'She wanted to start her own business: public relations. She'd been temping in a PR agency, thought she could do it better. We'd been dating a while. Hadn't set up house together, but it was heading in that direction. I thought she was the one...' He broke off, face drained of colour.

Brian waited, impassive. Sex, money, a sudden loss of control, all, he well knew, contributing factors to homicide.

'She needed seed capital. Went to the bank. More than one. They didn't want to know. She had no track record, Annabel. No qualifications, nothing. She was really down about it, so I said I'd lend her the money. Fifty grand.' He shrugged hopelessly. 'What a mug. She no sooner had the business up and running than she gave me the bum's rush.'

Fifty grand! Brian's thoughts ran amok. Imagine having that sort of money in spare cash, never mind fifty thousand. In his reduced circumstances, he'd be lucky if he could summon five.

'Satisfied?' Shane's voice brought him back to the present.

Brian collected himself. 'Your word against hers.'

'Don't give me that. Case got thrown out.'

'Due to lack of evidence, it says here.'

'I got her to sign something,' Shane protested. 'I'm not that stupid.'

'A document which you couldn't produce in court.'

'She got it back off me.' he confided, colour flooding his face. 'Conniving bitch! Still haven't recovered, either financially or...' tapping his skull, '...up here.'

'When did you see Ms Imray last?'

He scratched his head. 'Six weeks, couple of months, maybe.'

'Under what circumstances?'

'Socially, that's all. We both attended a charity do at the Marcliffe, but we stayed well clear of each other the whole night.' He grimaced. 'We're not exactly on the best of terms these days. Christ!' His mouth dropped open when he saw Brian's face. 'That's what this is about! Somebody's done the bitch in.'

Good Timing

'Heartfelt apologies for dropping in like this,' Knees akimbo, Henry Dundas balanced on the very edge of Maggie's sofa. 'I was in the area and I thought...' Nervously, he wrung his hands, stump sticking up at an angle. 'To be frank, Mrs Laird,' he offered an apprehensive smile, 'I was rather hoping I might catch you.'

'Good timing,' Maggie said, trying not to look at the abbreviated forefinger. 'I've just this minute got in.' Caught off guard, she prayed her lazy eye wasn't giving her away.

A shadow crossed Henry's face. 'You don't mind?' 'If it's not convenient...' He made to rise, '...I can come back another time.'

'Not at all,' Maggie demurred. 'As a matter of fact, I was just about to call you.'

His face lit up. 'You were?'

'Yes. I...' She broke off. In that moment, Henry looked so eager, so guileless - like Colin when he first started school - she could have given him a hug.

He sat forward. 'You've reached a decision?'

'I have.'

'I trust it's in my favour.'

Just then, the doorbell chimed.

Maggie started. 'Excuse me.' She rose and walked through to the front door.

Two women stood on the doorstep.

'Good afternoon,' said the younger, an anaemic thirty-something in a padded jacket and clumpy shoes. 'May I ask you a question,' she posited, not quite meeting Maggie's eyes, 'Do you have faith?'

No I bloody don't, Maggie thought. Not anymore. She hadn't been in church since George's funeral. Couldn't see the day she'd ever go back. 'I'm afraid not,' she answered, working to keep the emotion from her voice.

'We can help.' the young woman ventured with a nervous glance at her companion.

Poor soul, Maggie judged. *Must be the trainee.*

'My personal beliefs aren't something I'd choose to share on the doorstep.' she said civilly.

'We can come in.' the girl persisted, her expression hopeful. 'If you can spare a few minutes.'

'I'm afraid not,' Maggie responded. 'I have someone with me at the moment. Now...' She made to close the door. 'If you'll excuse me.'

'May we leave you this?' The older of the two thrust a slim magazine into her hand.

'Thanks.' Maggie didn't even bother to look down. *The Watchtower* or *Awake*. Either way, it would go straight in the bin. 'Now if you don't mind.' Firmly, she closed the door and retraced her steps. 'Jehovah's Witnesses,' she announced. 'Doorstep callers. They're a proper nuisance, aren't they?'

Henry Dundas was standing by the fireplace, a framed photograph in his left hand. 'Oh!' His face fell.

'I didn't mean you,' Maggie said, rushing to cover her *faux pas*. 'Just...'

'Lovely photograph,' he remarked, placing it carefully back on the mantel. 'Your husband?'

'Yes. It was taken not long before he died.'

Henry gasped. 'I'm so sorry.'

'That's okay,' Maggie said, resuming her seat. 'To get back to what we were saying, you asked if I'd decided in your favour?' She took a steadying breath. 'I'm afraid the answer is no.'

'But,' Henry blanched, 'I thought you...' He floundered for some moments, then, '...liked me.'

'I *do* like you,' Maggie insisted. She had always considered herself a fair judge of character. Suspected that under the polished veneer Henry Dundas was a sensitive soul.

His shoulders drooped. 'I didn't put that very well. What I meant to say was, I thought I'd done a good job. In my professional capacity, that is.'

'This has nothing whatsoever to do with either your professional capacity or your personality, let me assure you.'

'You've retained another firm, is that it? If your decision is based on our commission, I'm sure there's room for...' He broke off. 'I could ask my manager.' Fumbling for his phone. 'I'll call him right now.'

Maggie held up a restraining hand. 'There's no need. To be perfectly frank,' she confessed, colour flooding her face. 'After giving the matter considerable thought, I've come to the conclusion that putting my home on the market at this time would be foolhardy.'

Henry put the phone down. 'You must think me pushy.'

'Not at all. A job like yours must be challenging, especially in today's market.'

'It's dog-eat-dog at the best of times,' he admitted. 'You wouldn't believe the underhand tactics some firms get up to. But to tell the truth, I haven't been in the estate agency business that long. Haven't done any job for long, to be honest with you. I'm shy, you see, and this...' He grimaced, waggling the fingers of his right hand. '...doesn't help.

Maggie eyed the truncated stump. She could imagine.

'I suppose you're wondering how my injury came about?'

'No,' she lied.

Henry's face darkened. 'My sister, Belinda. Binky I used to call her. She's four years older than me. Was.'

Questioningly, Maggie raised an eyebrow.

'Binky was killed in a road accident three months ago.'

'I'm sorry.'

'Don't be. She wasn't the most likeable of characters.'

'You didn't get on?'

'We did. When we were young, that is. I adored her. Looked up to her. We used to fall out, of course,' he qualified.

'It's always the way,' Maggie concurred. 'My two - a boy and a girl - are constantly at each other's throat. But offer the slightest criticism and they'll defend one another to the death.'

'Where are they, your children?'

'Kirsty's away at university. My son Colin's still at home.'

'Must be company for you,'

'Not really. We tend to pass in the night.' *Careful!* 'Do you have children?' She changed the subject, fearful of giving out too much personal information.

'I'm not married.'

Maggie's mind whirred. Well-educated, handsome, in an effete sort of way, Henry Dundas was an unlikely singleton. She speculated whether he was divorced?

He pulled a wry face. 'Makes for a rather solitary life.'

'I'd have thought you'd meet loads of people in your line of work.'

'I do, yes. Not all of them as charming, if I may say.'

Maggie felt a blush beginning to bloom on her cheeks. It had been a while since a man had paid her a compliment.

'But the acquaintance is transitory,' he continued. 'Once a sale is achieved, one moves swiftly on.'

Not unlike PI work, Maggie thought, though she wasn't going to say. 'I expect you live somewhere fabulous,' she ventured, trying to make conversation. 'You being in the business.'

'On the contrary,' he replied, his expression sombre, 'I haven't put down roots. Currently, I occupy a modest rented apartment in Prospect Terrace.'

Not the most salubrious part of town. Many of the single storey and basement Victorian terraced cottages had been divided and sub-divided and overlooked the huge Union Square shopping centre and the bus and railway stations. Maggie called to mind the ancient suit and battered briefcase Henry sported at their first meeting. He wasn't wearing a suit that day, but a baggy sports jacket, Tattersall checked shirt and cavalry twills with turn-ups.

Poor chap! Perhaps he's fallen on hard times.

And Henry Dundas was lonely.

Maggie smiled her understanding.

She knew the feeling.

A Box of Tricks

Wilma was on her knees scrubbing the lavatory when she heard Maggie's doorbell chime. She wondered who it could be. They didn't get that many doorstep callers in Mannofield: the postie needing a signature, maybe, the window cleaner wanting paid, Tesco or Asda with a grocery drop.

She determined to find out later. Meantime, she needed to concentrate on the job in hand. Her housekeeping had slipped this past while. Ian hadn't complained - not as such - but he'd made one or two passing remarks and Wilma was conscious of the need to keep her nose clean. After all, she reasoned, business might be thin, but who knew what juicy cases could be waiting around the corner?

Men! She scooshed another few squirts of green Toilet Duck under the rim of the bowl and redoubled her efforts. She'd wash the floor tiles later. Ian was faithful to her instructions not to leave the seat up. If he could only confine his piss to the pan as opposed to the floor, she'd be a happy bunny.

Exiting the bathroom, she fetched her Dyson from its cupboard under the stairs and was crossing the hall when Maggie's doorbell chimed again. Curiosity getting the better of her, Wilma propped the Dyson against the wall and crept into the sitting-room. Through the bay window, she could see two women standing on Maggie's doorstep, hear the murmur of conversation.

Wilma dropped to all fours and crawled into the far corner of the bay, so she was directly beneath the window nearest them. To her disappointment, the conversation tailed off. Raising her head, she hazarded a glance. She was just in time to catch one of the women hand something over, and hear Maggie's door shut.

Ducking, Wilma maintained her position in case the women

came to her door next. Nothing happened. Turning, she surveyed her sitting-room. Her suite was in need of a coat of leather cream, the chandelier was heavy with dust, and the purple cowhide rug she'd showed off to Maggie with such pride only a few months before was looking distinctly tatty.

Wilma hauled herself to her feet. She cast a glance at the sky. It was a fine day. If she got a move on, she could get a washing out. She was just about to move when something caught her eye: a car parked a couple of doors down from Maggie. It was a Saab. A brown Saab. *Bugger!* That first ring she'd heard must have been Henry Dundas. But hadn't Maggie told Wilma she'd decided against selling the house? So what was the estate agent doing there? Unless... Wilma gave her imagination full rein. It was obvious Maggie had taken a shine to the fellow. Could it be the attraction was mutual?

Over my dead body! She would need to keep a close eye. *But how?* Then Wilma had an idea. Running into the bedroom, she flung open her wardrobe and dug into her box of tricks.

Another thought occurred: if she passed Maggie's window, she'd most likely be spotted. Furtively, Wilma let herself out the back door, squeezed through the gap in the hedge and edged down the far side of Maggie's drive. Reaching Henry's Saab, she squatted on the pavement. Then, under the pretence of re-tying her trainers, she had a covert look around.

There was nobody on the street.

With one practised movement, she attached a GPS tracker to the car's undercarriage.

V

Tiffany

'Tiffany Reid?'

She was slight, but well-toned, fronds of dark hair framing an elfin face. Not at all how Susan expected Annabel Imray's BFF to be.

Eyeing Douglas, Tiffany struck a suggestive pose, her satin negligee slipping off one shoulder. 'Who's asking?'

'DC Susan Strachan,' she showed her warrant card.

'DC Douglas Dunn.' Giving the woman the once-over, Douglas mirrored the gesture.

'It's to do with Annabel, isn't it?' The come-hither look wiped from Tiffany's face.

'We'd rather not speak on the doorstep,' Susan said, with an apologetic smile. The landing of the second-floor council flat in the city's Kincorth district wasn't conducive to private conversation. 'Can we come in?'

With a shrug, Tiffany tugged at her negligee and swivelled on kitten heels.

Susan and Douglas followed her along a narrow corridor into an equally cramped living-room. A purple velvet sofa sat against a feature wall papered in black and silver. The wall opposite was dominated by an outsize television set, beneath which black-lacquered units held an array of what looked like sporting cups.

An unlikely pairing, was Susan's reaction, for the homes of Annabel Imray and her - allegedly - best pal couldn't have been more different.

'Have you arrested him yet?' Tiffany demanded, sinking into a squashy fuchsia armchair and crossing her legs above the knee.

'Arrested who?' Susan queried, Douglas having been persuaded she should take the lead.

'Shane Kelman.'

'Why would we do that?'.

'He's the one...' Tiffany's face crumpled. '...has most reason to do her in.'

'What makes you think foul play is involved?' Susan probed.

'It said in the papers...'

Douglas stepped in. 'You shouldn't lend too much credence to...'

'You telling me Annabel wasn't murdered?' Uncrossing her legs, Tiffany leaned forward, flashing a pair of milky inner thighs.

Susan saw Douglas's pupils dilate. 'Our investigation is ongoing,' she pronounced, shooting him a disdainful look. 'Nice flat,' she lied, steering the conversation back to safer ground.

'Thanks.'

'Yours, is it?'

'I wish. I'm paying off a mortgage.'

Susan threw her a conspiratorial look. 'Aren't we all?' She drew out her notebook. 'I've a few questions I'd like to ask you, Tiffany, in connection with Annabel's death.' She paused, then, 'When was the last time you saw her?'

'Monday night.'

'That would be Monday the twelfth of August.'

'That's right. We went out for a meal at The Silver Darling.'

'At the start of the working week?' Susan asked. 'Was that usual?'

'Annabel wasn't into cooking,' Tiffany replied. 'She ate out every other night, either that or she'd order food in.'

Susan had a mental picture of the pristine work surfaces, the near-empty cupboards in the Kepplestone flat. 'And afterwards?'

'We took a taxi back to her place.'

'What time would that be?'

'Dunno. We'd drunk a couple of cocktails, shared a bottle of fizz. I wasn't counting, to be honest with you.'

'Okay.' Susan jotted a note. 'Let's move on. When you got back to Annabel's flat, what did you do?'

'Had a few more drinks. Messed about.' She fixed Susan with a challenging look. 'What do you think?'

'"Messed about", you said. Doing what, exactly?' She wondered if Annabel and Tiffany were indeed an item.

'Sitting with Annabel's laptop, looking at her Twitter feed, WhatsApp, that sort of thing.'

'Did you stay over?' Susan probed.

'No way.' Tiffany answered emphatically. 'Annabel didn't like sharing her space.' She uttered a bitter laugh. 'Didn't like sharing anything, come to that.'

'Can you be a bit more forthcoming?'

Tiffany fingered her robe. 'Not really.'

Changing tack, Susan asked, 'When did you leave Kepplestone?'

'No idea.'

'Have a think.'

'Two? Two-thirty?'

'How did you get home?'

'Got an Uber.'

'You or Annabel?'

'Me.'

'Annabel, she was fine when you left, was she?'

Tiffany turned a troubled face. 'Well, I wouldn't say "fine", exactly. She was lying on the settee, pretty well out of it.'

'She was drunk?'

'You could say.'

'And you left her in that state?'

'Look,' Tiffany said, exasperated. 'We were tanked, the both of us.'

Susan consulted her notes. 'Coming back to Shane Kelman. He had "most reason", you said, for wishing Annabel harm. Can you expand on that for me, Tiffany?'

'Shane Kelman is full of himself,' she pronounced, jutting her lower lip. 'Couldn't accept Annabel had moved on.'

'She was in a new relationship?'

'No,' Tiffany answered, frowning. 'I meant she'd moved up in the world, business-wise.'

'In what way?'

'Annabel's company was doing well. She'd even won an award: Best Newcomer.' Tiffany's face glowed. 'Shane reckons he's a celebrity, him being a footballer and all, but this past while Annabel started mixing with top executives. She was always in the newspapers.' Her eyes went dark. 'Shane was jealous, simple as that.'

'But,' Susan countered, 'wasn't it Shane Kelman who loaned Annabel the money to start her business?'

'If he was daft enough to give it to her,' Tiffany retorted, 'more fool he.'

'Not "give"', Susan qualified. "Lend", according to our sources.

Tiffany pouted. 'Same difference.'

Douglas and Susan exchanged telling looks. Put Kelman's statement in a different light.

'Was it Shane put you onto me?' Tiffany demanded. 'It was.' Reading Douglas's guilty face. 'Wasn't it?'

'Why do you say that?' Susan asked.

Sharply, Tiffany turned her head away.

'Please answer my question.'

She turned back. 'He said I was to blame for them breaking up.'

'And were you?' Susan persisted.

'It wasn't just me,' Tiffany sulked. 'There was other things as well.'

Douglas broke off from cleaning his nails with the point of a pencil. 'Like what?' he asked.

'Shane told Annabel I was needy, that I was monopolising her, leeching off her. But it's not true. She was fed up of Shane pestering her: texting every five minutes, appearing at her door at all hours. She wanted to get on in life, broaden her horizons.'

Play the field? Susan wondered if there was another lover - or lovers - in the frame? 'These executives you mentioned, is it possible Annabel had formed a new attachment?'

Vigorously, Tiffany shook her head. 'No. She'd have told me. I was her best friend.'

So Much for Footglove

Maggie dropped onto a wooden bench. Her back was aching, her feet on fire. Especially the left. She eased off her shoe and pulled down her sock. Sure enough, an angry blister had risen on her heel. So much for Footglove! Marks and Spencer loafers had been her standby since she took on the detective agency. She resolved to invest in a pair of cushioned trainers. When there was money to spare. She sighed. Whenever that would be. True to her word, Ursula Evershed had paid a substantial retainer, but it had already been swallowed by the mortgage.

She'd started at the Spital, worked her way down the High Street, handing out fliers, quizzing folk as she went: asking householders and shopkeepers to check their outhouses, department secretaries their storerooms, students their hangouts and bike sheds. She'd crossed St Machar Drive, then, done a circuit of the Chanonry and Don Street and ended up in Wrights' and Coopers' Place. A haven of tranquillity amidst the bustling university campus, the MacRobert Memorial Garden commemorates the life and work of Lady MacRobert who, having lost three sons to the war effort, helped to fund a bomber aircraft named MacRobert's Reply.

How skewed the world, Maggie thought, when one woman could make a sacrifice of such magnitude, where another was prepared to throw good money after a blooming cat. Then again, who was she to judge? Hadn't her dad been upset for days when he'd had to shoot one of his sheepdogs, albeit the old thing had been replaced in short order? And by all accounts, Malthus was not just a cherished household pet, but a proxy child.

A knot of female students ambled past, chatting animatedly, oblivious to her presence.

'Here.' Maggie thrust a handful of fliers at them.

'No thanks,' their spokesperson, who must have been all of eighteen, batted her away. She must have followed up with some witticism, for they burst out laughing and continued on their way.

Maggie couldn't blame them. She must look a card, sitting on a bench with one shoe on and the other off. For the umpteenth time, she rued the chain of events that had reduced her to such circumstances.

The sky had darkened, rain clouds massing on the horizon. A sharp breeze was blowing off the North Sea. Shivering, Maggie dipped into her pocket, tore a corner off a tissue, made a small wadding cushion to protect her heel and pulled the sock back in place. She'd pierce the blister with a sterilised needle the minute she got home, put on antiseptic cream and a plaster. She checked her watch. She'd been pounding the pavements for almost four hours, and tomorrow would bring more of the same. Only less congenial. Her mind jumped to Seaton, with its towering high-rises and dismal four-in-a-block flats. Then to Tillydrone, on the nearside of King Street, where the hopelessness generated by lack of prospects and casual drug consumption was no less manifest.

Maggie wondered how Wilma was getting on. She'd been unusually quiet when they parted that morning. Perhaps Maggie's remark about exercise, though teasing, had hit home. But Wilma had undeniably piled on the weight again, the late nights and fast food consumption occasioned by their last investigation having taken its toll. As it had on Maggie. Her hair had lost its usual lustre, her skin its glow. And that left eye - the one that had dogged her for as long as she could remember - had been drifting again. Maggie cursed the fact she hadn't had the problem addressed in childhood, for the earlier amblyopia - or lazy eye - is treated the higher the chance of success. Now, she might have to wear glasses to realign her vision, block the stronger eye with a patch to retrain the eye-brain connection or even have eye muscle surgery. And with any of these the degree and extent of recovery would be greatly diminished.

With an effort, she brought herself back to the present. Once the cat was found...and the bills were paid...and Colin was settled into his sixth year...and Kirsty into her Honours year… she'd concentrate on number one.

Maggie struggled to her feet and limped on.

A Mobile Phone

'Ms Gilmore?'

'Yes?' The face that peered through the crack in the door was full of apprehension.

'PCs Souter and Miller.' Souter spoke for them both.

She didn't look convinced.

Clocking the security spyhole, they showed their warrant cards. Then, assuming what he hoped was a non-threatening expression., Souter asked, 'Can we come in?'

'I suppose.' The door chain rattled, unhooked by nervous fingers. Both constables had been here before: folk tended to react differently to a uniformed copper on their doorstep than they did plainclothes. Not so much what did they have to hide as what would the neighbours think?

The girl - she couldn't have been more than eighteen - was waif-like in ripped jeans and oversized jumper. She led them through a cluttered hallway into an open-plan kitchen/diner. Collapsed onto a corner sofa. Didn't invite them to sit down.

It was Souter's turn to lead. 'You'll know the reason for our call.'

'My phone,' she answered, voice little more than a whisper.

Ian Souter consulted his notebook. 'Was reported lost or stolen at 21.37 hours on Friday, 26th July.'

She nodded. 'Yes.'

'And, according to my notes, it was last in your possession earlier that evening?'

'That's right.'

'Can you be more specific?' Miller chipped in.

'Not really.'

'Why is that?' Souter again.

'I was out drinking, and...' She broke off, fingers clawing at her cuticles.

He noted the pallor of her skin, the hollows under her eyes. Wouldn't be surprised if drugs were involved. 'We're not here to judge you, Ms Gilmore,' he reassured her. 'We...'

'Cara,' she ventured. 'My name's Cara.'

'Alright, Cara,' Souter lowered his voice. 'As I was saying, we're not here to judge you. The sole purpose of this visit is to try to locate your phone.' *Fat chance!* Kids nowadays - his own included - were careless of their possessions. The reason being they didn't have to work for them, he thought with some rancour. *Easy come, easy go!* He could hear his own father, even now.

'You sure you haven't just mislaid it?' Miller asked, shattering Souter's train of thought.

'Quite sure. One minute it was at my elbow, the next...' She broke off, eyes wild.

'And that was...' He consulted his notebook. '... in the Students' Union on Elphinstone Road?'

'That's right. It was on the table. I'd been texting, then... I looked everywhere: on my seat, on the floor, in my handbag. I even went back to the loo in case I'd had a mental block and put it down when I was re-doing my make-up.'

'You definitely took it to the Union?'

'Yes. I needed it to...' Above her collar she flushed crimson.

'To what?' Souter prompted, his antennae twitching.

'Deal with...' Cara's knee, in judiciously ripped jeans, twitched. '...stuff.'

'What sort of stuff?'

She studied her fingernails. 'Private stuff,' she muttered.

'This phone,' Miller chipped in. 'Was it insured?'

Cara shook her head. 'No. I...' She shrank into the sofa. 'My parents will kill me.'

'Surely not,' Souter tried to reassure her. Kid looked scared to death. 'Accepted it's a significant outlay,' he said. *Nobody died,* is what he was thinking. 'But it's not as if...'

'You don't understand,' she wailed. 'There's stuff on that phone. Things I don't want anyone to see. Not my classmates, not my friends. And,' her eyes brimmed with tears, 'certainly not my parents.'

Revenge porn? For once, Souter was thankful his kids hadn't reached their teens. Though you never knew. Not nowadays. Still, common as phone thefts were, at least mobiles had real monetary value, unlike the rubbish he and Miller had been chasing up thus far. 'It might be worth contacting the University Counselling Service.' he suggested. 'If you find things are getting a bit too much for you, they...'

'My password,' she interrupted. 'I'm worried it's not secure. 'That's why I have to find it,' she turned a tear-stained face. 'Don't you see?'

Seaton Park

Wilma wandered along Cathedral Walk. Running downhill from St Machar, the avenue was bordered by mature trees and planted with formal flower beds. Wilma wasn't big on gardening. She'd never owned one until she married Ian, and he hadn't the time to do more than keep the grass tidy. She eyed a cushion of red and silver bedding plants. Begonias she recognised from a display outside her local Aldi, the others she didn't have a clue. There was a big spiky thing, like a cactus. She turned away. The flower beds were too low for a large cat like Malthus to hide in. As for the other, she reckoned cats didn't like jaggy things.

She pressed on, stopping now and again to peer into a low bush or under a hedge. Past the children's playpark, with its feature red brake van and railway wagons, where the tyre swings hung still, the climbing frames skeletal, the slides empty. The schools had gone back that week for the autumn term.

'Hey missus?' the voice came from nowhere.

Wilma swivelled on her heel. 'What?'

'Want me tae mak ye a mammy?'

'On yer bike,' Wilma charged at the small figure. 'Or I'll—'

The boy, who couldn't be more than seven or eight years old, jumped into the saddle and pedalled at speed down the path.

'Cheek!' Wilma muttered under her breath. Not that it was the kid's fault. He probably got it from his dad. If he had a dad.

She plodded on, heavy breasts thwacking against her ribcage, the crotch of her control pants cutting into her groin. "Good exercise", the words rang in her ears. It was alright for Maggie, not an ounce of fat on her. Wilma wished she hadn't polished off those three beers the previous night, them and the box of Maltesers. Then, so what? Ian liked her bigger, hadn't he said so?

Wilma didn't like to admit it, but maybe Ian was right about the other thing as well: Maggie Laird taking advantage. She'd been queening it, right enough: bigging up the 'senior partner' thing, hobnobbing with insurance executives and the like, while she, Wilma, was left to do the donkeywork. Wilma wondered where Maggie would be if she jumped ship? The time she'd spent with the agency had given her new skills and boosted her confidence. If she were to land a better job - one that didn't involve unsocial hours - her and Ian would be all set. Still, that wouldn't be fair. And if she was to get on... Really get on... Wilma saw in her mind's eye the sports car, the fancy detached bungalow. She resolved to stick in, whatever it took. Like this sodding cat. She cast her eyes skywards and ploughed on.

She passed the time of day with the occasional dog-walker, pressing a flier upon them, explaining that Malthus was not her pet, but that of a friend. His image had been photo-shopped, but where Wilma was concerned, he was one ugly fucker. She was overtaken by several runners, Lycra-clad, fitbits strapped to their wrists. Few students were in evidence, other than a stray Chinese. The others wouldn't be back until September. Even then, Wilma doubted they'd be prepared to walk through the park, when there were buses on hand. Taxis, too. She sighed. A whole other world.

By the time she reached the riverside walk that ran alongside the Don to the Brig o' Balgownie and the open sea, Wilma was bursting for a pee. The park toilets, she knew, were automated, and she'd left her purse in the car. There was a secluded walled garden at the far end. She made a bee-line. There was nobody in sight, and if she was quick... She nipped behind the high stone wall and, tugging her jeggings and pants to her knees, crouched in a planted border. Her urine, she reasoned, couldn't but help it thrive.

She was mid-flow, a hot puddle forming, steam rising, when, 'Got the time on you?' the voice came from behind. Feverishly, Wilma yanked her knickers back into place and pulled up her jeggings. He was a skinny runt: whey-faced in grey trackie bottoms and a grubby white hoodie. Wilma had come across plenty like him: druggies, schemies on the make. Instinctively, she thumbed her mobile. 'Three twenty-six,' she replied.

A veined hand shot out. Grabbed her phone. And he was off.

'Bastard!' Caught off-guard, Wilma cursed herself for falling for such an old trick. She charged in pursuit, catching the sleeve of his hoodie as he negotiated the exit.

The man turned.

Fist bunched, he raised his free arm.

But Wilma was too quick, kneeing him forcefully in the groin.

'Fat cunt!' Cupping his balls, he dropped to a crouch, keening like a bairn.

Wilma snatched her phone.

'I'll "fat cunt" ye, ya wee fucker.'

Still smarting from the blow to her professionalism, she finished him off with a hefty kick up the backside.

Friend Request

'Thanks for coming forward,' Susan said, with an encouraging smile.

'Nae bother,' Isa Dodd replied, though her face was guarded.

She was short: feet, clad in cheap trainers, barely reaching the floor. And as broad as she was long, stomach ballooning from beneath ponderous breasts. *Morbidly obese.* Susan noted the weeping sore on one cheek. *Probably diabetic.*

'Annabel Imray,' she began, flipping open the file in front of her. 'I understand you have information which might help us in our enquiries?'

'Someone done her in?' Mrs Dodd demanded.

'Ms Imray's death is the subject of an ongoing police investigation.' Susan replied evenly. She knew members of the public were usually co-operative, but when a fatality was involved, anxiety and reservation kicked in.

'It says so in *The Sun*.'

'If you could answer my question,' Susan persisted.

'We were at school together,' Isa Dodd volunteered. 'Kincorth Academy.'

'And that was when?'

'Late nineties. I didn't know her, mind, till we were in third year.' She picked at the wound on her face. 'You wouldn't have a spare fag on you?'

'Sorry.' Susan indicated the No Smoking sign above their heads.

'Oh.' Isa's face fell. 'Okay.'

'You were telling me about Annabel Imray.'

'Anne Imray she was, then.'

Susan jotted a note. 'Were you close friends?'

'No.'

'But you were in the same class, so you must have known her quite well?'

'Not really. She didn't mix with the rest of us. Thought she was a cut above, even then. Bit of a closed book, to be honest.'

Susan took a sneak peek at her watch. She hoped this wasn't going to be a complete waste of time.

'Knew what she wanted out of life, that one,' Isa asserted, her chins wobbling. 'Not like the rest of us.'

'She was a bright girl, then?'

'No more than anyone else in class. But we didn't have a clue. It was expected you'd leave school at sixteen, go into the fish. Shop work if you were lucky. Not that we were bothered, me and my mates. All we were interested in was clothes and make-up. The Top Twenty. I remember...'

Susan cut her short. 'Annabel, or Anne as you called her?'

'She had it all mapped out. Wasn't going to let anyone stand in her way.'

'Can you elaborate on that?' Susan leaned forward, all ears.

'Took up with an older guy, owned a hair salon. Married man. Not that she would think twice.' She pulled a tissue from the box on the table and blew her nose, bingo wings swinging from her upper arms. 'Next thing I knew, she was doing a hairdressing course, college and all.'

'And after that?'

Isa shrugged. 'Only what I've read in the papers.'

'You didn't keep in touch after you left school? Reunions, that sort of thing?'

'You kidding? They're knocking the bloody place down.'

'Yes,' Susan agreed. The building was well-known to the police, having been the target of vandals and firebugs since its closure in 2018. On one occasion, thugs damaged the school's fire alarm system, keeping nearby residents awake by making its sirens blare for hours into the night. During another, forty fire extinguishers were stripped from the walls and later discovered strewn across a nearby skate park. 'What I meant was, did you ever get together for a night out?'

Isa snorted. 'I've four kids. Haven't had a night out since I don't know when.'

'What about social media?'

'I sent her a friend request on Facebook. A good while back, it must have been.' Isa's mouth turned down. 'Bitch declined.'

'I see. Well,' Susan moved to wrap up the interview. 'is there anything else you'd like to add, Mrs Dodd?'

'Anne Imray was a conniving cow. Knew what she wanted and walked all over folk to get it.' With two hands, she hitched up her belly and tugged down her top. 'Wouldn't surprise me if she got what was coming to her.'

The Inversnecky

'How did you get on?' Wilma enquired. She was heading for her shift at the hospital and they'd rendezvoused at the Inversnecky cafe on the Esplanade.

'No joy.' Maggie answered, warming her hands on her cup. 'You?'

'Same. Spent bloody hours in Seaton Park. Total waste of time.'

'There's always something to be learned.'

'Aye,' Wilma scoffed. 'That, and get mugged for your trouble.'

'You didn't...'

'Course not.' She wasn't going to admit she'd been caught with her knickers around her ankles. She licked the froth off her hot chocolate. 'What's next on the game plan?'

'Seaton and Tillydrone.'

Wilma groaned.

'I'd best cover Seaton,' Maggie offered. 'Given prior knowledge.'

'Thought you'd say that.'

'Plus, I'm on the spot. I can put a couple of hours in after school, which just leaves Tillydrone.'

Cherry-picking again! Wilma stuck her nose in her mug. *Sod it!* 'Toss you for it?'

Maggie gave her a sharp look.

'Only joking.'

'Well, that's sorted. I've been in touch with all the cat rescue centres within a ten-mile radius, forwarded fliers, asked them to spread the word.' She took a judicious sip of her tea. 'Where are we at with social media?'

'Christ, you wouldn't believe there are so many cats in the world. Facebook's been swamped with moggies, none of them remotely like frigging Malthus. Twitter's awash with folk wittering on about how their own cat went missing, Snapchat and Instagram chock-full of ugly mugshots.'

Maggie's shoulders drooped. 'That's a blow. I thought we'd get a few leads, at the very least.'

'What's the client saying?'

'More distraught by the day.'

'She's paying up, though?'

'Yes. Money no object.'

'That's something. How about Scott Milne?'

Maggie coloured. 'Not yet.' She'd rung the home number repeatedly, but got no answer, and his mobile had gone to voicemail.

'I told you. If you'd let me go up to Belvidere Street, that money would be in the bank by now.'

'Always assuming there is any money.'

'You reckon?'

'I don't know. They'd just moved house. His job was at risk. What are the odds?' Maggie said a quiet prayer they hadn't done a bunk.

The woman at the next table caught her eye.

She lowered her voice. 'All I'm saying is...'

A chair scraped back. 'You thon quine was in the papers?' The woman stood at her shoulder: sallow, thin-faced, an inch of grey regrowth bordering a centre parting.

'Well...' Maggie's head jerked up, thoughts scrambling. More than once, the agency had made headlines, none of them complimentary.

'Your man wis thon copper on the take, wis he no?'

Colour flooded her face. At that moment, it seemed the aborted drugs trial in which George had been implicated would dog her till the day she died. '...I'm not sure,' she managed to get out, wishing the floor would part and swallow her up.

Wilma leapt to her feet. Planting herself in front of Maggie, she asserted, 'No bloody business but hers.'

The woman took a hasty step back. 'Just asking.'

Wilma squared up. 'And I'm just telling you.'

'Okay, okay.' Swivelling on her heel, she made a bee-line for the counter.

Wilma stood her ground until the woman had paid her bill and made a hasty exit.

'What on earth was that about?' Maggie demanded when Wilma re-took her seat.

She shrugged. 'Nothing.'

'It was a bit more than "nothing", Maggie contested, regaining her composure. 'You frightened the life out of that woman.'

'No more than she deserved,' Wilma retorted. 'Cheeky cow.'

Maggie pursed her lips. 'Really, Wilma, that's not on. We've a reputation to maintain, and...'

'Nee-naw, nee-naw.' Wilma aped the sound of a police siren.

'Seriously...'

"Seriously", she mimicked. 'I was doing what I've been doing since the day we first met, Maggie Laird. Watching your back.'

The Hell with it

'Chisolm.' The voice on the end of the line brooked no argument.

'Maggie Laird here.'

'Maggie!' he exclaimed. 'It's been a while.'

'Yes,' she replied, palms clammy on her cell-phone.

'To what do I owe the pleasure?' he asked, a note of amusement in his voice.

'Same old,' she responded. 'I wondered if there had been any word on Bobby Brannigan?' Since the drug runner whose perjury ended George's career had suffered a violent knife attack, Brannigan had dropped out of sight.

'Not a cheep.'

'Oh.'

Chisolm broke the ensuing silence. 'I wouldn't hold out for a result, not in that department. These druggies, as you know, have a rackety lifestyle. Brannigan could have met with another accident. Overdosed. He could be dead by now.'

'I understand,' Maggie conceded, though she didn't, not really. If there was any justice in the world, surely George - decent, long-serving police officer that he was - deserved better? She collected her thoughts. 'How about the Fifth Floor? Have you made any progress in persuading the powers-that-be to conduct a review?'

'Another negative, I'm afraid. Last time I raised the matter, it was dismissed out of hand.'

'They wouldn't...?' Maggie began hopefully.

'Look,' Chisolm's tone softened. 'I know this must be hard to accept, but not only has the Police Scotland structure changed, the whole ethos of policing has, too. Upstairs have other priorities. There's little to be gained from flogging what's seen as a dead horse, and...' He broke off, suddenly. 'I'm sorry. That was an unfortunate turn of phrase.'

'Doesn't matter,' Maggie said. She'd long since developed a thick skin in relation to her husband's premature death. 'I wouldn't want you to compromise your own position on my account.'

'That hasn't been a factor,' Chisolm replied. 'Until now it hasn't stopped me pursuing your case, but for both our sakes perhaps it's time to move on. My advice to you is concentrate your energies on your business. And your family, of course.'

'I suppose,' Maggie allowed. Hadn't Val said much the same?

'But James Gilruth,' she tried for one last throw of the dice. 'We both know he's engaged in a wide range of criminal activities. Surely you're not going to let him get away with...'

'We're on it,' Chisolm said firmly. 'Drugs and Fraud are building a joint case, but we're in it for the long game.'

'Oh,' Maggie said, all the fight gone out of her. James Gilruth might not have pulled the trigger, but in her mind he'd helped drive her husband to his grave. And he'd humiliated her. Maggie seethed at the memory.

'Leave that one to the professionals.' Chisolm added, his voice clipped.

'Okay,' Maggie conceded, stung.

'Meantime,' if I can help in any way, 'you know where I am.'

'Thanks.' Not for the first time, Maggie speculated about Allan Chisolm's background. Was he married? Divorced? He'd never opened up to her, kept things close to his chest. 'I appreciate the offer.'

Silence hung heavy between them. Then, 'Was there anything else?'

'N-no,' she stuttered. 'I'll let you get on.'

Maggie's eyes welled with tears as she set her phone aside. Angrily, she brushed them away. What a fool she'd been, clinging on to her crusade, only to have her hopes dashed again and again. And Allan Chisolm? She'd harboured romantic thoughts about the man. Flights of fancy, like a love-struck teenager.

Maggie steeled herself.

The hell with it!

She'd put all that bad business behind her.

Restore the Laird name by making the agency the best it could be.

Make her children a credit to their father.

Ticking the Boxes

'You are being interviewed under caution in connection with the unexplained death of Anne - known as Annabel - Imray,' Brian stated. 'You are entitled to have a lawyer informed that you have attended voluntarily to be questioned in relation to this offence and that you require their help. Do you understand?'

'Yes.'

Brian ticked a box on the form in front of him.

'You are entitled to a private consultation with a lawyer at any time while you are here. Do you understand?'

'Yes, again.'

Brian ticked another box.

'We have further questions regarding the unexplained death of Anne - aka Annabel - Imray. You are entitled to have a lawyer present with you while...'

'Yes, yes,' Shane interrupted. 'I get it. Can we crack on?'

Brian filled in his name and passed the form to Susan for corroboration. 'If you would like to sign here.' He pushed it across the table.

Shane scribbled his name. Then, tugging back his shirt cuff to expose a steel-cased sports watch, he asked, 'Will this take long? Only I've training to go to, and I'll get fined if I'm late.'

That's the least of your problems, Susan thought, eyeing the watch on his wrist. Armani, at a guess, or maybe Audemars Piguet? Either way, it would have cost the price of her flat. She sneaked a look at Brian. Doubted he'd have a clue.

As if he'd read her mind, Brian asked, 'Do you have a key to Annabel's flat?'

Shane snorted. 'You're joking. She took it off me when she dumped me.'

'Which was when?'

'Ages ago.' He knitted his brow. 'Must be a year, at the very least. And anyhow, the key wasn't for the Kepplestone pad, if that's what you're thinking. It was for the place she lived before that.' His lip curled. 'Couldn't settle for five minutes, Annabel. Always on the up and up.'

'And you haven't seen her since?'

"That's right. Not except for that one time at the Marcliffe. And as I said, we didn't speak.'

'And that was six to eight weeks ago?'

'Right again.'

'You must have moved in the same social circle, surely,' Brian insinuated. 'You being a celebrity and Annabel in her line of work. Are you saying your paths only crossed once in all that time?'

'Correct.'

'I find that hard to believe.'

'Believe what you like,' Shane looked from Brian to Susan. 'To tell the truth, we would have done. Crossed paths I mean. Aberdeen's not such a big place.' He ran a finger around the inside of his shirt collar. 'Only, whenever I'd rock up to something and see she was there, I'd chicken out. Do a runner.' His designer stubble quivered. 'Couldn't hack a re-run of that stalking business.'

'"Kepplestone", you said?' Susan came back in. 'How did you know Annabel was living there?'

'Isn't that obvious?' Shane demanded, regaining his composure. 'She's been all over the newspapers lately, and in the gossip columns before that. I couldn't not know, even I wanted.'

'Are you acquainted with Tiffany Reid?' Brian asked.

'Yes.'

'How would you describe her?'

Shane sneered. 'She's a devious bitch.'

'Why do you say that?'

'Woman wangled herself into Annabel's life, clung on like a bloody limpet.'

'Would you say they were close friends?'

'Close, maybe.' He gave a dismissive shrug. 'She's not someone I would want as a friend.'

'Last time we spoke,' Susan came back in, 'you told us you thought you were having a lie-in the morning of Tuesday, 13th August.'

'Yeah,' he scratched his head. 'I had a think. Couldn't come up with anything else.'

'But there's no one who could corroborate this?'

'Nope.' He offered a sarcastic smile. 'Not unless you want to put some knockout dame in my bed.'

Brian let this pass. 'Our officers have spoken to your neighbours. I understand, when you're at home, your car is usually parked in its designated space.'

'So?'

'It wasn't on that morning.'

'Oh,' Shane flushed, 'I remember now. It was away getting new wheel badges fitted. I'm forever getting them nicked.' He broke off, with a rueful grin. 'Occupational hazard.'

'Where was that?'

'Porsche Centre, Wellington Road.'

'When did you put the car in?' Susan asked.

He gave her a scathing look. 'I didn't. They picked it up first thing and had it back before I got up. Oh, and...' Anticipating the next question. '... one of their mechanics collected a spare set of keys the night before and posted them through the letterbox the next morning.'

'There's service for you,' Brian exclaimed, with false bonhomie. 'I expect that's what you're paying for.' Not that he knew the price of a fully-loaded Porsche but, things being as they were, it would be astronomical.

Shane stole another look at his watch, 'Is that it, only...?'

'One last thing,' Brian added. 'Are you willing to give fingerprint and DNA samples?'

'Sure,' he replied. 'No problem. But I better dash. Is it okay if I do it tomorrow?'

Catch 22

'Annabel Imray,' Wilma said, her face the picture of innocence.

They were having a coffee in Books and Beans prior to a business meeting in the city centre: more fraud. Maggie steeled herself. Needs must.

'It was murder right enough,' Wilma continued. 'Got it from two cops at ARI. Mebbe we could...'

Maggie silenced her with a stern look. 'Don't even go there.'

Changing tack, Wilma asked, 'You lined up another appointment yet?'

'In connection with what?'

'Putting the house up for sale.'

'You never give up, do you?' Maggie protested, feigning outrage.

Wilma grinned. 'I'm a determined woman.'

'That makes two of us,' Maggie countered, breathing in the heady aroma of her freshly brewed Americano. 'But, since you ask, Gary Moir is coming back to give me an updated valuation. I said he didn't need to come in person – a phone call would suffice - but he insisted.'

'Ooh,' Wilma bit into a glistening almond pecan Danish pastry. 'Maybe he fancies you.' Since putting a tail on Henry Dundas her mind had been working overtime.

'Don't be ridiculous,' Maggie snapped. 'He must be ten years my junior. And, besides, he's not remotely my type.'

'When did you say he was coming?'

'I didn't.'

'Oh, come on, don't be coy. If you really don't fancy him, what's the harm in me having a nosey?'

'Because...' She took a sip of her coffee. '...the minute you clap eyes on him, you won't be able to resist getting up to mischief.'

Wilma clasped a dimpled hand to her left breast. 'I won't. Honest.'

Maggie relented. 'He's coming tomorrow at four o'clock. If you want to check him out, I don't mind you sticking your head round the door. But no interfering, understand?'

'I get you.' Brushing crumbs off the acid yellow body-con frock she'd thought appropriate for their business meeting, Wilma nodded agreement.

'I'm serious,' Maggie insisted. 'This call is just a formality. I've decided not to go with either of the agents I've seen.'

'Told you,' Wilma whooped. 'You need to spread the net wider: three valuations at the very least.'

'Will you listen to yourself?' Maggie grumbled. 'You're beginning to sound like an old record.' She squared her shoulders. 'If you must know, I've given the matter a lot of thought and come to the conclusion selling the house is a no-go.'

'How come?' Wilma demanded.

'The property market's so depressed, it would only fetch a decent price if it was in tip-top condition. Which,' she pulled a tragic face, 'it patently is not. Truth is, I haven't maintained it since George died, and now it's so run-down it would take serious outlay even to do a paint job. Money I haven't got. So you see...' She took a comforting mouthful of coffee. '...it's Catch 22: borrow in the hope of recouping my outlay or sell at a knockdown price.'

'If you're serious about selling,' Wilma offered. 'A quick lick of paint needn't cost the earth. I know a fella would...'

'Plus, I've checked out more flats,' Maggie ran on. 'Ideally, I'd be looking for three bedrooms, so Kirsty and Colin could still have their own rooms, but even if I settled for a two bed, anything in a decent area would set me back well over two hundred thousand. I wouldn't have much left over, not once I paid an estate agent and conveyancing fees. And that doesn't take into account any furnishings I'd have to buy.' A tear formed in the corner of one eye and slid slowly down her cheek. 'I thought I had it all worked out,

Wilma. Turns out I was wrong.'

'Don't torment yourself,' Wilma urged, squeezing Maggie's hand. 'There's other ways.'

She pulled away. 'Like what?' Brusquely, she wiped the tear away with the back of her hand.

'You could go back to your folks. Ask them to bail you out.'

'I've already told you...'

'You could take out equity.'

'Not on your life. George always said that was a mug's game.'

Wilma's face fell. She stuck her nose in her cappuccino.

'Told you,' Maggie said morosely. 'It's a total no-win.'

Wilma kept her head down for some moments. Then, looking up, she brightened. 'You could rent out a room.'

'What?' Maggie threw up her hands, knocking over her cup in the process. She watched, aghast, as the contents dripped from the table onto her M&S grey suit.

'Here,' Wilma offered, thrusting out her paper napkin.

Maggie dabbed at the hem of her jacket, transferring sticky flakes of Wilma's Danish pastry to the stain. Feverishly, she tried to dislodge them, offering up silent thanks the suit was washable. Nonetheless, she'd have to hide the mess with her handbag when they went into their meeting.

'To get back to what I was saying,' Wilma continued, blithely unawares. She had been occupied in righting the cup and mopping the table.

'Rent out a room?' Maggie repeated, her voice wavering. 'Like have some complete stranger share the bathroom?'

'Doesn't have to be an adult.'

'Dear Lord,' Maggie spluttered. 'You've got me fostering kids now. I tell you, Wilma, you've totally lost the plot.'

'Not a kid. A teenager, more like.'

'As if I don't get enough grief from the two I've got.'

'A student, I was thinking. Someone keeps the same term dates as Kirsty. Then...'

Maggie interrupted. 'Semester.'

'Whatever,' Wilma ploughed on, undaunted. 'The lodger could have the use of her room. I mean,' she grinned, 'how hard can it be? Kirsty's never there. And the lodger, you'd hardly see them.'

Maggie chewed on her thumb, 'Mannofield's on the wrong side of town for Aberdeen Uni.'

'There's Gray's,' Wilma countered. 'The art school's just along the road, and we're not that far from Robert Gordon's.'

'I suppose.'

'Think on it.'

Maggie smiled weakly. 'Okay. But now...' Pushing her empty cup to one side. '...drink up,' she urged. She started to gather her things. 'We've more pressing business to attend to.'

A Piece of Work

VI

A Piece of Work

'Annabel Imray,' In the CID room, Chisolm addressed his core investigative team. 'What sort of picture are we getting?'

Brian was first to answer. 'Civilian support have had a ton of feedback off social media. As we predicted, she was highly proactive across a number of platforms. So much so, looks like it will take until kingdom come to sift through the information. Consensus is, though, Annabel may have been a social animal - her job necessitated that - but she was a bit of a loner. Had hundreds, perhaps thousands of acquaintances, but few close friends.'

'That was exactly my conclusion,' Douglas piped up, unbidden.

Suckering up as usual! Susan resisted the urge to comment.

'Seems she found her niche in public relations,' Brian ran on, unfazed. 'Everything for show. But from what's come out of social media plus statements from a former school classmate, ex-boyfriend and her pal Tiffany, Annabel's life was pretty superficial.'

'Out for what she could get,' Duffy growled. 'A piece of work, right enough.'

'Nominals?' Chisolm barked. 'Who have we in the frame?' He turned. 'Brian?'

'The ex-boyfriend, Shane Kelman, is still our number one suspect.'

'What have we got on him?'

'To be honest, boss, eff all. But he has motive, all fifty grand of it. And the stalking charge, it's only his word against hers.'

'Still and all,' Duffy contested. 'It wouldn't be the first time a woman has cried foul.'

Douglas jumped in. 'Case wouldn't have gone to court if there were no grounds.'

'It got thrown out,' Susan insisted. 'If I understand correctly, principally because of the alleged victim's unreliable testimony.'

'Whatever. Kelman saw himself as the injured party. He was carrying a great big chip on his shoulder.'

'So would you be,' Susan asserted, determined not to let Douglas get the better of her, 'if you'd been done out of that amount of money.'

'I'm not saying Shane Kelman deliberately set out to kill Annabel Imray,' Douglas countered. 'Might well have been an accident: they've both got drink in them, argument gets out of hand, he grabs her by the throat.'

Chisolm stepped in. 'You're making the story fit the circumstances again. Follow the evidence. What's indisputable is that Annabel received fifty thousand pounds from Shane Kelman. We've verified the transfer from her bank statements. Question is, was it a loan or was it a gift?'

'Tiffany Reid suggested it might well have been a loan,' Susan insisted.

'She's not exactly a reliable witness.'

'Maybe not.' Susan paused reflectively. 'Still, there could be something in her allegation that Shane was jealous.'

'Think about it,' Douglas picked up on this. 'He's lost a bomb, and now some dame has muscled in on his territory. Plus, Shane has no alibi: he says he was in bed that morning, but there's nobody can back him up. Outside of football training, his time was probably his own, so the opportunity was there.'

'He didn't have wheels,' Brian argued.

'We don't know that. Check with the Porsche Centre,' Chisolm instructed. 'Establish the exact time Shane's car was picked up and dropped off.'

'There's not many footballers nowadays manage with just one motor,' Duffy volunteered. 'He could have another four in a garage. Or borrowed one from a pal.'

'That's something else to follow up on,' Chisolm said. 'For now, we don't have any witnesses to his whereabouts between the end of training on Monday and Tuesday lunchtime, when he went to the gym.

'He may have had motive and opportunity,' Brian observed. 'But did he have the means?'

'Of course he bloody did,' Douglas replied, puffing out his chest. 'Fit guy like that? Even if he didn't stalk Annabel, there's evidence he pestered her. Probably put the fear of death into the woman, deserved or no. It wouldn't be a big step forward from there to finish her off.'

Chisolm quelled his ebullience with narrowed eyes. 'Do we have anyone else in the frame?'

'No one,' Brian responded. 'Unless you count Tiffany Reid. She was the last one to see the victim alive.'

'You're not suggesting she could have killed Annabel?'

'No, boss. Not when you consider the size of her. Plus, by her own admission, she was legless when she left.'

'When she left, yes,' Douglas stuck his oar in. 'But, speaking hypothetically, of course...' He threw a wary glance in Chisolm's direction. '...Annabel could have met her death earlier and Tiffany carried on drinking before she left the scene.'

The future of policing! One by one, Chisolm cracked his knuckles. *More geeks than plods.*

'Bottom line is,' Brian intervened, 'it doesn't square with Pathology's estimated time of death.'

'*Estimated*,' Douglas emphasised.

Chisolm silenced him with a black look. 'Have we got a trace on the Uber driver?'

'No. boss,' Brian answered. 'They're not that easy to pin down.'

'We could get lucky: pick him up on ANPR,' Duffy this time. 'There couldn't have been much traffic at that time in the morning.'

'We extracted entries from Annabel's bank statements,' Susan ventured hesitantly, not wanting to irk her boss further. 'Cash transfers to Tiffany's account, they–'

'Would have been payments for promotion work,' Douglas

interrupted. 'Tiffany told us that, don't you remember?'

'Yes, but...'

Douglas sniggered. 'Wouldn't be the first time someone didn't declare a bit of extra cash.'

'It's not so much the size of the payments,' Susan continued, undaunted. 'It's the frequency: every two weeks, regular as clockwork, with other - more random - payments in between.'

'A retainer?' Brian suggested. 'Something to keep Tiffany on the payroll, so to speak, supplemented by appearance fees?'

'Sounds plausible,' Chisolm observed.

'They're pretty large sums for a retainer,' Susan commented. 'And returning to Tiffany's statement...' She favoured Douglas with a smug look. '...she said Shane Kelman claimed she – Tiffany – was needy, was monopolising Annabel, leeching off her.' She paused for breath. 'Have you considered the possibility Shane was right?'

'Your hypothesis holds up except for one thing,' Chisolm replied. 'From what we've established, Annabel Imray was no pushover. She was a hard-nosed businesswoman. Ambitious. A woman who, by all accounts, would climb over anyone and anything to get to the top.'

'Do you think she'd shell out to some poor, wee, divorced hairdresser?' Douglas added, with a sneer.

'She might if Tiffany was useful to her.'

'In what way?' Douglas demanded. 'Not as event totty. It's easy money. She'd have had girls queuing up: younger, prettier girls. Even students earn pocket money that way.'

'Well, if Annabel was putting all that money Tiffany's way,' Susan ploughed on, 'she must have been looking for something in return. Is there a possibility...' She summoned what courage she could. '...that Tiffany was blackmailing Annabel?'

'How did you arrive at that?' Douglas pooh-poohed. 'Talk about making the story fit the facts? All we've got on Tiffany Reid are those bank transfers. Tiffany worked for Annabel. They go back a long way. End of story.'

Kirsty

Kirsty stomped down the stairs. 'Has someone been in my room?'

Maggie caught her breath. Her daughter hadn't been home five minutes, and already she was kicking up.

She looked up from a mass of paperwork. 'No. Of course not,' she said calmly. 'I've no reason. And, besides, you've made it absolutely clear you don't want anything disturbed. But now you mention it...' She laid down her pen, wondering how to broach the subject. Decided to tackle it head-on. '...I wondered how you'd feel about me taking a lodger?'

Kirsty eyed her with suspicion. 'Here?'

'Yes.'

'In this house?'

Maggie nodded.

Kirsty shrugged. 'How would it work? We don't have a spare room.'

'That's just it,' Maggie countered. 'With you away most of the time. And you'll soon be into your Honours year. And after that...'

'Not my room,' Kirsty screeched. 'No bloody way.'

'It was only an idea,' Maggie said, backtracking.

'Whose idea?' Kirsty demanded. 'I bet it was that cow next door.'

'Well,' Maggie began, not wanting to be caught in the lie.

'I bloody knew it,' Kirsty yelled, pink-faced. 'She can't keep her fat fingers out of any damn thing.'

'There's no need to get upset,' Maggie soothed, putting an arm around her daughter's shoulders.

Abruptly, Kirsty shook her off. 'How would you feel if your Dad died and your Mum wanted to move someone into your bed?' She asked plaintively, then burst into tears.

'I'm sorry,' Maggie said. 'I didn't know you cared that much. I honestly thought you were more invested in your flat than here, and very soon you'll be gone for good.'

'Is that what you want?' Kirsty snivelled.

'No, of course not. This is your home.'

Kirsty fixed her with an accusing look. 'You could have fooled me.' Then, turning on her heel she marched back upstairs.

*

Maggie was still mired in her paperwork when Kirsty appeared in the doorway. Smiling, she looked up. Time for them to make their peace.

Instead, Kirsty advanced on the dining table, a black look on her face. 'Have you had a dog in the house?' she demanded.

'A dog,' Maggie echoed, brows fused in bewilderment. 'No. Whatever gave you that idea?'

'There's hair on my duvet cover. Eugh!' She wrinkled her nose. 'Gross!'

'Well, I can't imagine how it got there.'

'You haven't...' Kirsty began, looking daggers. 'You wouldn't... have got a lodger in without even asking?'

'No,' Maggie replied, running out of patience. 'I would not.' Wearily, she rose from her seat. 'I'll come and have a look.'

'See!' Kirsty pointed an accusing finger when they were upstairs.

Maggie eyed the snowy duvet. Couldn't see anything amiss. Except, at the near edge there was an indentation. As if someone had sat down. Then it dawned. She flushed in embarrassment. 'You're quite right. I did come up. It was last week, I...' She broke off. How to come up with an adequate explanation after her earlier denial, far less to voice her fears for the future to a daughter who deemed life eternal.

'Don't bother making excuses,' Kirsty spat, her expression venomous. 'There's no point.'

'But...' Maggie protested.

She got no further. 'There!' Kirsty pointed a finger.

Maggie bent to the bed, couldn't see anything untoward.

Kirsty held up a hand. 'Don't move!' she ordered, running from the room.

Mind churning, Maggie stood rooted to the spot. She felt guilty at being caught in the lie, and at the same time angry that she'd allowed herself to be pushed around. If George was alive... She banished the thought. George would have defended his daughter. Hadn't it always been so?

Footsteps clattered down the stairs. Clumped back up again. 'Here,' Kirsty re-appeared, in her hand a roll of sellotape. She pulled off a strip, bit it off with her teeth and pressed it to the duvet. 'Now do you believe me?' she asked, brandishing the strip under Maggie's nose.

Maggie screwed up her eyes. Sure enough, there was a cluster of hairs attached. Dog hair? No way. Maggie hadn't been around any dogs and, besides, this hair was too fine. Not human hair either. She looked again. Then she realised. 'That bloody cat.' The words were out before she could stop herself.

'What cat?'

'A case I'm working on. When I was in the client's house I must have picked it up off the sofa.' For the umpteenth time, Maggie wondered what had possessed her to take the investigation on?

'Disgusting!' Kirsty exclaimed, with a poisonous look. She squared up. 'Still doesn't explain why you were in my room.'

'I couldn't sleep, so I got up to make myself a cup of tea. Then I thought I'd check on Colin. And while I was upstairs...'

'...you thought you'd have a nosey.'

'No,' Maggie protested. 'That's way off the mark. I just...' She broke off, in two minds whether to admit to missing her daughter desperately or to whack her over the head.

Kirsty made the decision for her. 'Save your breath,' she said brusquely, showing Maggie the door.

A Cream Jug

Dave Miller stood with his back to the door. He took the lead. 'You reported a theft.'

'That's right,' the old woman nodded, her tiny frame almost swallowed by a ponderous taupe recliner chair. I've had the shakes ever since. Had to call the doctor for my heart condition. My daughter got the locks changed, but it hasn't helped, not one bit. She says if my nerves don't settle I'll have to go into a care home. God's waiting room,' she sniffed. 'No way back.'

'Can I just check,' Miller asked, leafing through his notebook. 'A cream jug.' Chewing his lip, he added, 'Cream, as in off-white?'

Minnie Sinclair fixed him with a withering look. 'Cream, as in milk.'

'Oh,' Miller 's colour rose under his uniform collar. 'Righty-ho. A milk jug, then?' He knitted bushy eyebrows. 'I've got here it was shaped like a cow. Didn't know you got milk jugs like that?'

Trust Miller to go off at a tangent. From his stance by the far wall, Ian Souter tried to catch his partner's eye, conscious they'd still made scant inroads on their 'to-do' list.

'Oh, yes,' her face came alive, brown eyes beads in a patchwork of wrinkles. 'Cow creamers were common when I was a girl.'

'Antique, then, would you call it?'

Souter heaved a sigh. You couldn't swing a cat in the retirement flat, its sitting-room large enough to accommodate only the one easy-chair, a display cabinet, a glass-topped coffee table and a somewhat dated telly. And the smell: cooked food and cloying air freshener and piss. No wonder old folk lost the will to live.

'Well, it was old, certainly. But I wouldn't go as far...'

'Could you put a value on it?'

Minnie's face clouded. 'Oh, no. Not in today's money.'

Pencil poised. 'Rough guess?' Miller persisted.

The radiators were going full blast, the temperature in the room positively tropical. Souter felt a trickle of sweat run down his back. *Get on with it!*

'All I can tell you,' Minnie said, waving a gnarled finger, 'is that it was worth a king's ransom to me. It belonged to my mother, you see. My natural mother. I was adopted when I was only a few months old.' Her eyes welled with tears. 'How I came by it is a long story. Late in life - I must have been in my fifties by then - I managed to trace a half-sister. My mother had married and had another family. She was dead by then, and...'

Miller looked to his colleague for salvation.

Had they not been under pressure, Souter would have gladly left him to it, but by this time he was fit to faint. Plus, he'd developed a sudden urge to pee. He could ask to use the facilities, but didn't relish the prospect. The very thought of the bathroom, full of mobility aids and denture fixative, was enough to send him screaming for cover. He took a step forward. 'Can you think back to when you first noticed the jug was missing, had you had any visitors?'

'There's my daughter. She comes at the weekend. And I have a carer looks in every day.'

'Can you give me her name?' Souter asked. There had been a number of well-publicised incidents that year in which a carer had been accused of theft: a case in Prestwick where a care assistant was convicted of stealing from her brain-damaged 84-year-old client, another in Stevenston involving a 93-year-old female victim.

Minnie clasped a veined hand to her forehead. 'Can't remember for the life of me.' She threw him an apologetic look. 'Maybe if you ask me again later.'

'Doesn't matter,' he responded. 'Any other callers you can think of?'

'There were two strange men.'

His ears pricked. Only that summer a rogue trader had been

jailed for conning a Peterhead woman out of £45,000 for non-existent roof repairs. 'When was that?'

Minnie gave him a worried look. 'Who knows? I can recall the Queen's coronation clear as day, but ask me what I did yesterday and I haven't a clue.'

Souter's spirits sank. 'Can you describe them?'

She brightened. 'They were young. But everybody looks young to me nowadays. One thing I do know.' Fumbling in a rack beside her chair, she drew out a sheet of paper. 'This appeared after they'd left. Looks like...' Sparse brows knitted, she held it up close to her face. 'The name escapes me. One of them things you'd hang someone with.' She looked to the two constables for confirmation. Finding none, she said, 'They don't do that, now, do they: hang folk? More's the pity.'

'Do you think one of those men might have left that drawing?' Miller prompted.

'Maybe.' Minnie said. 'I couldn't be sure. There's that many wicked folk going about. You see these things on the television: old women raped in their beds. Hanging's too good for them, in my opinion. I remember the last man they hanged in Aberdeen, Burnett was his name. Murdered a merchant seaman. Shot him in the face, it said in the paper, and...'

*

'Bugger this for a pantomime!' Souter spat, as they made for the patrol car. 'I've had a bellyful of the job.'

Miller broke off from whistling through his teeth. 'Thought you enjoyed the challenge?'

'Aye.' Souter's focus had switched to where he could have a quick slash. 'Some days.'

'Seriously, though, pal,' Dave Miller was nothing if not dogged. 'Thon...' He yanked his head in the direction of the retirement flats. '...mebbe wisna a laugh a minute, but you can't deny there's variety: dead body one minute...'

Across the car roof Souter gave him the evils. 'And what?' he sneered. 'A clutch of attention-seekers, an over-indulged student and now a clear case of dementia.' He opened the door and slid into the driver's seat.

Miller got in the passenger side. 'Wumman gave us an explanation.'

Souter threw him a disbelieving look. 'She's a head case. Totally lost her marbles.'

Buckling his seatbelt, Miller said, 'We'll all be old someday. My Nana...'

Souter had no intention of going down that road. 'How are we meant to establish when the jug got nicked?' He jammed the key into the ignition. 'If it got nicked at all.'

'You think she's making it up?'

'Wouldn't be the first.'

'We could nip back and check with the neighbours. See if...'

'No way.'

'What about the drawing?'

Souter snarled, 'What about it?'

'Dunno.' When the old biddy had shown it to them, Miller had been convinced he was seeing a repeat of the other incidents. Now, looking at his partner's expression, he wasn't so sure. His resolve faltered. 'What are we going to do?'

'Precisely what was actioned: put in a statement like we were told.' Souter fired up the engine. 'Then forget all about it.'

'But...'

Souter turned. 'You got a better idea?'

'No,' Miller answered, checking his watch. 'Want to call it a day?'

'Better not chance it. We're in the sergeant's bad books as it is. But,' He turned, 'since you ask, what I really want...' A muscle worked in Souter's jaw. '...is a giant piss. After which...' The car shot forward. '...I suggest we get another couple of statements in the bag and get the fuck home.'

Think of the Money

'Thank you for your report.' Ursula said. 'But you've neglected to address one crucial question.'

'Oh?' Maggie was back in Dr Evershed's sitting-room. A squall of rain battered the window panes, the smell of damp more pronounced than ever. 'What's that?'

'Did Malthus leave me of his own accord?'

'You're not seriously suggesting,' Maggie began. Then: *you're being judgemental again.* Ursula Evered's distress was plain to see. She patently adored the animal.

'Indeed,' Ursula replied. 'If Malthus had simply gone walkies he'd have been home before now.' She lowered her voice. 'He likes his food, my handsome boy.'

Yes, Maggie eyed the bundle of fliers on the sofa beside her. *I can see that.* 'But to suggest someone has deliberately sneaked into your home and stolen him...' Her gut wrenched. Shades of Sheena Summers, who had alleged her husband was plotting to kill her. 'That's a whole other proposition.'

'And one that is not without merit,' Ursula snapped.

'Perhaps not.' Maggie's research had informed her dog theft was on the rise, due in part to the fashion for designer dogs. A walker in Kent had even been attacked with acid for refusing to hand over his pet. She wondered if it was the same with cats? Still, there was no way she was getting mired in another conspiracy theory. Time to nail this on the head. 'Did you have many visitors in the days leading up to Malthus' disappearance?' she asked, her expression wholly innocent. Dr Evershed had admitted to having a limited social life.

'Not more than a handful: PhD students, a couple of colleagues, that's about the extent of it.'

'Your colleagues are hardly likely to have stolen your cat.'

'Agreed. But students are prone to play the most wicked pranks, even post-graduates. And, besides, Malthus needn't have been snatched from the house, he could equally well have been abducted from the grounds. Or the shops. Or the pub. Or any number of places...' Her voice tailed off.

'But, surely,' Maggie reasoned, 'that would have attracted attention.'

'Not anymore. Time was, Old Aberdeen was like a village. We were all on first name terms: Moira at the Post Office, May Black at the grocer, Effie and Ida at the baker. The Old Town House was home to the local library. There was even a police station.' Ursula's lips formed a thin line. 'We looked out for each other. Nowadays, nobody gives you the time of day.'

Maggie nodded in sympathy, though she deemed Ursula's nostalgia misplaced. As Maggie recalled, Miss Black's shop was usually shut, and her window display comprised little more than a few tired tins and a scatter of thirsty geraniums, the Auld Toon Cafe had a few stands of dried-up scones, and the police office wasn't manned.

Spends too much time looking over her shoulder, she decided. *Let that be a lesson to you!* She wouldn't want to end up like Ursula, living like a hermit. Once she was on her feet financially, she'd get out there, re-connect with the world. 'I'm sure he'll turn up,' Maggie reassured her client. 'I'm told cats can go missing for months, years even, and return home. Indeed, there was a case in the paper a while back - Bristol, I think it was - where a family pet turned up after thirteen years.' What she didn't say was the cat died days later.

'You've had no success with your search of the area, you say?'

'No. But we propose to extend our enquiries to King Street and Kittybrewster. Then...'

Ursula cut her short. 'Or from social media?'

'Not so far. But...'

Her mouth turned down at the corners. 'Everywhere I turn, things remind me of my loss: his scratching post, his play tunnel, his crinkle ball. Even this,' she dug into a pocket. 'His special pet mouse.' She dangled the mangled thing by its tail. 'If you only knew,' she wailed. 'I can't bear it.'

In spite of her misgivings, Maggie felt genuinely sorry for the woman. 'As I said, I'm sure Malthus will turn up.'

'How about a television appeal?'

'TV?' Maggie spluttered, incredulous.

'The police do them all the time. Only last week...'

'I doubt their resources would run to...'

'I couldn't do it myself, of course,' Ursula continued, unabashed. 'Too upsetting. It would have to be you.'

'Me?' Maggie could imagine Brian's face were she to suggest such a thing. Not that Brian had been in touch. Her mind churned. Never mind Brian, what about Chisolm? Nervously, she cleared her throat. 'Local radio might be an option, though I can't promise...'

'Radio?' Ursula shrieked. 'What possible use is that?'

'Northsound 1 has very high listener figures.' Maggie had got this gem from Wilma. 'Almost a hundred and forty thousand a week.'

'That's as may be. But they can't see a picture of my boy, and no description in the world will do him justice.'

'Still,' Maggie countered. 'It would get the word out.'

'Like social media?' Ursula spat, her expression heavy with distaste.

Shifting her weight on the sagging settee, Maggie didn't respond. She could imagine how Wilma would have reacted to this last comment. She'd deliberately left her out of any face-to-face encounter with Ursula Evershed. Bad enough she'd committed to another unstable client without Wilma in the mix.

For a heady moment, Maggie was tempted to tell the client to get stuffed. She'd had a bellyful of Ursula and her bloody cat. Still, *think of the money.* Mentally, she totted up Colin's outgoings for the coming year, then drew a steadying breath. 'My partner and I will do our utmost to bring Malthus home,' she volunteered. 'Safe' was on the tip of her tongue. Then she remembered the dead cat in Bristol. Willow was its name. Thought better of it.

Wellington Road

The Porsche logo blazed scarlet on a sleek building clad in glossy panels of white laminate and smoked glass. To one side, a slender white column carried the Porsche Centre's name and an oversized gold, red and black Porsche badge.

Susan pulled into one of the visitors' parking spaces. She knew the Wellington Road area well enough - the police had plenty call-outs to Loirston and Kincorth - but had never visited the showroom. Apart from the obvious - even the pre-owned cars lined up on the forecourt were way beyond her detective constable's salary - flash cars weren't her style.

She pushed through the glass doors and made her way across the slate-tiled showroom floor, upon which the latest models of the marque were displayed to maximum advantage. Reception, a streamlined white counter decorated by an extravagant floral arrangement, was manned by a decorative young thing, whose name badge - displayed on a red body-warmer - identified her as Rachel.

Susan introduced herself and showed her warrant card. 'Can you check that this vehicle...' She flashed the registration number. '...was brought here for servicing on the twelfth and thirteenth of this month?'

'What's it in connection with?'

'An ongoing investigation,' Susan replied tersely.

'I'll have to check with my manager,' Rachel said, with a nervous upwards glance. 'Data protection.'

Susan followed her eyes. On a mezzanine, glass-fronted offices were occupied by executives. All male, she noted. 'Okay.'

Rachel vanished behind a screen. Within a few minutes she was back. 'He's on a call,' she shrugged an apology. 'If you'd like to wait.'

She indicated a seating area.

'Thanks,' Susan acknowledged. 'I'm fine here.'

*

'Is he going to be much longer?' Susan rasped. She'd been standing for fully ten minutes.

On the other side of the desk, Rachel's head jerked up. 'I'll go and check.' She scuttled around the screen and swiftly re-appeared accompanied by a man in his forties dressed in dark trousers and a detergent-white shirt.

'Sorry to keep you.' he said. 'You were asking about one of our vehicles?'

'That's right,' Susan replied, conscious of her own well-worn trouser-suit.

'I'm sure you'll understand, the vehicle in question belongs to one of our valued clients. A rather special client, in point of fact. So...'

'Look...' Susan made a show of checking her watch. '...we can do this the easy way, or we can do it the hard way.' She pulled out her phone. 'If you'd like me to ring DHQ...'

'Well, I...'

'In order to eliminate your "rather special client" from our enquiries, I need you to confirm that vehicle came in here on twelfth August. In addition, I require to establish how it got here, what work was done, and how long it took? Is that clear?'

'Absolutely. If you'll give me a few minutes, I'll check our records. Can I offer you a cup of coffee? If you'd care to take a seat, Rachel will...'

'There's no need. I'll also want to speak to the mechanic who carried out the work.'

'Right. I'll consult with our technical department and see if the *technician*...' He laid stress on the word, patently making a point. '...is available.'

Susan watched him dodge around the screen, Rachel at his

heels. She looked around her, taking in the hushed ambiance, the air-conditioning, the tracks of spotlights bouncing off the gleaming car bodywork, the smells of wax polish and leather. For all the noises about inclusivity, it was still very much a man's world.

She checked her watch again. She had a list of follow-ups as long as her arm and didn't have time to waste. Drumming her fingers on the counter, she wondered how Douglas was getting on.

Mata Hari

'Shit!' Maggie swore, stamping her foot in rage.

'Mum,' Colin looked up from his plate of stew. 'Swearing!'

'If I feel like swearing,' Maggie came right back, 'I bloody well will. I'm fed up with you two treating me like a doormat.'

'But...' He protested.

'Ever since you broke up with Ellie, you've done nothing but lie in your stinking bed fiddling with your phone, either that or play stupid computer games. The only time you surface is when you're hungry.'

'But...'

Maggie held up a hand. 'Don't argue with your mother.'

Ducking his head, he shovelled another forkful.

'As for you,' she said, turning her attention to Kirsty. 'I'm sick to death of you constantly putting me down.'

Kirsty pushed her plate to one side. 'I do not.'

'No? How about the way you criticise my clothes?'

'Only trying to help.'

'And make faces when I'm on the phone?'

Kirsty shrugged. 'Just a bit of fun.'

'And when I'm talking to someone, you barge into the conversation without so much as a by your leave.'

'Like who?'

Brow furrowed, Maggie deliberated for a moment or two, then, 'Wilma, to give you one example.'

'Ah,' said Kirsty. 'Now we're getting to it.' She put her head to one side. 'Have you two been at one another's throats again?'

'On the contrary, we're getting along just fine.'

'So everything's hunky-dory with the agency?'

'Of course,' Maggie lied.

'You drumming up all the business, while Wilma...' Kirsty's lip curled. '...swans around playing Mata Hari?'

'Mata who?' Colin queried.

'Never mind.'

Colin carried on eating.

'Wilma makes a major contribution,' Maggie insisted.

'Seems to me she calls the shots.'

'That's not how it is at all.'

Kirsty sniffed. 'So she doesn't follow her own agenda?'

'No,' Maggie said decisively.

Kirsty shrugged. 'Whatever.' She turned to Colin, who seemed intent on clearing his plate in the shortest possible time. 'What brought this on?'

'See,' Maggie's voice rose. 'I can't do a bloody thing - not even lose my temper - without someone casting aspersions either to my advanced age or my time of the month.'

'Is it...?' Kirsty began.

Maggie cut her short. 'No, it is not.'

'You aren't...' She eyed Colin's lowered head. 'You're not menopausal?'

'That neither,' Maggie answered, throwing up her hands in exasperation. 'What I am is...' She sank onto the nearest chair. 'Since your father died, I've worked hard. Tried to keep things together, for all our sakes. I don't want to burden you with my problems, but...' She broke off. 'Look at me when I'm speaking to you, Colin Laird.'

Colin's head shot up. 'Okay.'

'...I'm tired. I haven't had a day off since I don't know when. And you two don't help, the way you treat this house like a dormitory. Not just that.' She eyed each, in turn. 'The way your treat me.'

'Oh, Mum.' Colin reached out and patted Maggie's hand, to no great effect. 'I didn't think...'

'That's just it,' Maggie said. 'Your mind's on other things. And so it should be, at your age. But you could help by clearing the mess in your room once in a while. Coming downstairs for meals when you're called. Putting your stuff out for the wash. Save me trudging up and down the stairs. As for you...'

Kirsty turned a sullen face.

'I know you're an adult and want your independence, but you still owe me some respect. So in future you'll extend the utmost courtesy.' She shot a warning look. 'And that Includes Wilma. Got that?'

Sharply, Kirsty turned away.

Didn't hear you, was on the tip of Maggie's tongue. She'd had it up to here with Kirsty's attitude: the withering looks, the tart remarks, the total absence of support, far less empathy. At that moment, her impulse was to drag her daughter by the hair into another room, outline the hard facts of their precarious situation, present her with an ultimatum: either she changed her tune or she could move out and give up her room to a paying lodger.

Pragmatism got the better of her. 'Right,' she said brightly, though her heart was hammering in her chest. 'Now that's out the way, who's for afters?'

Ferryhill Library

Wilma sat with her head in a book. She'd been calling past Ferryhill Library once or twice a week for some while. Dating from 1903 and attributed to architect Arthur Clyne, the B-listed granite building - Gothic with Jacobean detailing - looked more like a gate lodge than a library.

Buoyed by the acquisition of her dictionary, Wilma had paid an exploratory visit to the Central Library in Rosemount Viaduct. But she'd found the imposing edifice, with its high ceilings and wide-open spaces, inhibiting. And besides, it was too close for comfort to Robert Gordon's. She wouldn't want to run the risk of being spotted. The wee local library on the corner of Fonthill Road and Hardgate had filled the bill. In addition to lending books and DVDs, it offered a range of useful services, she'd discovered: access to the Ferryhill Electoral Roll, newspapers, magazines and family history resources, and free Wi-Fi and PC access. If she bumped into anyone, she could claim to be doing work-related research.

'Shhh!' The woman in the seat opposite held a finger to her lips.

Wilma's head jerked up, unconscious of the fact she'd been repeating passages out loud. She was about to take the dame on when she thought better of it. Instead, she gave her the full evils.

She switched her attention back to her book: *Pride and Prejudice* by Jane Austen. Once she'd got the hang of the regulations, she'd hesitantly asked the librarian for some recommendations. At first, she'd found the folk in this particular book a bit weird, with their fancy manners and formal speech patterns. But she was beginning to get it, and could see that although the characters inhabited a different century, they weren't that far removed from her own situation. In fact, wasn't that Elizabeth Bennet, with her hasty judgements, a dead ringer for Maggie Laird?

Wilma felt a warm glow of satisfaction. Maggie could pontificate all she liked. 'Pon-ti-fi-cate,' she said aloud, rolling the syllables around her tongue.

'Shhh!' Glowering, her neighbour tried to silence her with a stern look.

Wilma stuck out her tongue.

Maggie Laird could call the shots to her heart's consent.

But there would be no stopping Wilma Harcus.

Pittodrie

'Some of them,' the football coach confided, 'they get a signing-on fee it goes right to their heads. They're given good advice. But do they take it? No. Come their first pay, they're straight out buying stuff - designer clothes, watches, cars - like there's no tomorrow.' The man, who identified as Gus, ran a fretful hand through his thinning hair. 'They're not long out of short trousers, that's the problem.'

Douglas nodded his understanding. When he'd parked the pool Vauxhall at Pittodrie, he'd clocked a stable of marques that would have made Jeremy Clarkson weep. Small wonder! A season ticket, even an Early Bird, ran to several hundred pounds, a single match ticket over twenty. Add to that the merchandise - shirts and shorts and baby clothes and souvenirs - the club must be raking it in.

It had been decided on the toss of a coin with Susan which one of them would pay a visit to the Porsche Centre and which to Pittodrie. He'd lost, much to his chagrin. Located on Golf Road, close to the Esplanade and beach and home to Aberdeen Football Club, he knew the stadium to be one of the largest in Scotland. Its main purpose was to host home matches for Aberdeen FC, but it was also used for Scottish international matches and had been the venue for a number of concerts. That, and the fact the new football season had started with a home game against Hearts, was as far as Douglas's knowledge went. He'd never done well at sport and his only visit to Pittodrie had been a Rod Stewart concert some woman had dragged him along to, but he would have given his right arm to cruise along the Esplanade in a flashy new Porsche.

'How about Shane Kelman?' he enquired.

Gus brightened. 'Shane? He's different. Came up the hard way.

Not like some I could mention.' He winked. 'Wouldn't do to name names.'

'No?' Douglas, fished, hoping to draw the coach out. A bit of juicy gossip would have gone some way towards. alleviating his boredom. 'Can you tell me a bit more about him?' he asked, when none was forthcoming.

'Keeps his head down and his nose clean. Not one of them divas, always kicking off about something or other. Shane's conscientious. Always turns up for training on time.'

'I wanted to ask you about that,' Douglas said. 'Was Shane at training last Monday?'

'Yes. Never misses a session.'

'Are you sure?'

'Absolutely. We spent a good ten minutes talking about next season.'

'Do training sessions take place here?' Douglas enquired.

'No. We'd bus the first team to Seaton Park,' Gus responded. 'Either that or they'd train on the beach. That's the drawback with this location.' He leaned in. 'Did you know we've new training grounds under construction?'

'No,' Douglas answered. Nor did he have the slightest interest.

'Out at Kingsford,' Gus ran on. 'If you're not familiar with the name, that's adjacent to the Aberdeen-Westhilll road and close to the new Aberdeen Western Peripheral route.'

'Really?'

'Yes. Purpose-built football academy and community sports hub. The Club raised over eight million pounds for the first phase of the project.'

'That's amazing.' Douglas remarked, without enthusiasm.

'New stadium is next on the list.'

'That so?'

'Don't get me wrong, this old place has done us proud. It has been home to the Dons since 1903, you know. Was the first all-seater stadium in the United Kingdom - it has a seating capacity of over twenty thousand - and Aberdeen the first club to use a dugout.'

Douglas's attention wandered. He wondered how much a Porsche Carrera would cost to lease.

'They've been talking about it for since I don't know when. It's the cost,' the coach confided. 'Billions. Plus, with a landlocked site like Pittodrie, development to UEFA standards has implications for local residents and traffic. So...'

'Getting back to Shane Kelman?' Douglas interrupted. 'How is he off the pitch?'

'No different. He had a blip. While back, it must be, now. Woman trouble. Oh,' he clapped a hand to his mouth. 'That's why you're here: the ex-girlfriend. I read in the papers she passed away. Maybe I'm speaking out of turn.' Gus turned to look behind him, nervous all of a sudden. 'I'd best refer you to the gaffer for anything like that, only he's not here at the moment.'

'Don't worry,' Douglas reassured him. 'I'm just conducting routine enquiries. If I need any more information, I'll make an appointment through the usual channels.'

'Fair enough.'

'You were saying?' Douglas prompted.

'I felt sorry for the lad when the thing blew up in his face. It's not the first time the Club has hit the headlines for something other than football, and it won't be the last. There was an incident...' He knitted his brows. 'Beginning of 2017 it must have been, when...'

'Shane Kelman,' Douglas hissed through gritted teeth.

'Oh, yes. As I said, I felt sorry for the lad. But he didn't let it affect his game. No, just got his head down and got on with it.'

'So?' Douglas snapped. 'To summarise?'

'As I said,' Gus responded with a broad smile. 'Shane Kelman is one of the good guys.'

VII

Westhill

The detached house in Meadowlands Avenue was much like the other ten in the cul-de-sac: red-roofed with an integral garage, Monobloc driveway and well-tended garden.

'Not another one!' exclaimed the householder, reading Maggie's business card. 'I've had two private investigators at the door already. And that's only this week.'

'I'm so sorry, ' Maggie said with an ingratiating smile. She took a small step forward. 'May I come in?'

'I suppose,' Lorna Petrie – in her thirties, with dark hair cut into a bob – answered, stepping back into the hall. 'If it won't take long. I'm working from home today,' she confided, indicating her black leggings and baggy T-shirt. 'But I've a conference call scheduled for eleven-thirty.' She led Maggie through to a spacious kitchen, where an open laptop sat at one end of a granite-topped island.

'I won't take up more than a few minutes of your time.' Maggie reassured her.

'That's okay, then. Have a seat,' she gestured towards a high swivel stool.

Maggie eyed it with trepidation. In the face of competition from other agencies, she was anxious to make a good impression, but her diminutive height made such things challenging. Steadying the stool with one hand, she placed a foot on a chrome rung and launched herself upwards. The stool turned forty-five degrees. Maggie just managed to perch her bottom on the edge before swivelling back to face Lorna Petrie. Pink-faced, she drew a folder from her bag 'As you know there has been an insurance scam operating whereby fake brokers offer cut-price car insurance tied to an address other than where the vehicle is actually kept?'

'You don't need to tell me,' Lorna retorted. 'Though why they've landed on us I don't know.'

'Says something about your choice of area,' Maggie remarked, trying to mollify the woman. 'This is a good postcode.' Meadowlands Avenue in the Aberdeen suburb of Westhill was, indeed, a hotspot for this, the fastest-growing type of fraud, according to the Insurance Fraud Bureau. Accounting for more than a third of cases of insurance application fraud, it had resulted in an 81% increase in investigations between 2015 and 2018. 'I'm acting on behalf of the insurer, and just need you to confirm...' Steadying herself with one hand on the worktop, she extracted a sheet of paper. '...that the vehicle listed on this insurance policy does not belong to you.'

Lorna Petrie scanned the document. 'No.'

'Have you ever owned or insured an Alfa Romeo?'

'No. My husband drives a company BMW and I run a Volkswagen Polo.'

'The policy-holder's name, do you recognise it?'

'No.'

'And are you happy to sign an affidavit to that effect?'

Lorna sighed. 'If it will help get this off our backs. My husband and I, we've been receiving several letters a week from a number of different insurers, a couple of hundred in total. They always seem to be about foreigners, too.'

Maggie nodded her understanding. 'So-called ghost brokers often target drivers of expensive marques or people who face high premiums: students, taxi drivers, and people newly arrived in Britain. But honest buyers looking for a bargain fall foul of the scammers too.'

'Look, I know I should feel sorry for the folk who took out policies in good faith,' Lorna contended. 'But remember the old saying: if something looks too good to be true, it probably is. And you wouldn't believe the stress all this has caused,' she sighed. 'I had a problem with my credit record at one point. Took ages to sort out. We've complained to the insurance companies. Got nowhere. I even had my knuckles rapped for opening letters that weren't addressed to me.'

'Sadly,' Maggie responded, 'the doctored documents are very convincing, and as you said the genuine documents were sent to you. The problem only arises when the policy-holder needs to make a claim, at which point they discover their cover is invalid and it's up to the insurance company whether to make a pay-out. What's more, the victims risk having their car seized and receiving a fixed penalty notice of £300 for driving without insurance.'

'I don't know why they can't catch them,' Lorna complained. 'The police said there was nothing they could do, but they didn't explain why.'

'It's difficult. The scammers advertise all over the place: on university campuses and social media, in pubs and offices and shops. Some use fake or stolen credit card details to pay for the policies themselves and then pocket the cash. Some are bought by criminals, who use the documents to open bank accounts.'

'Well, if the insurance companies ran proper checks when the application was first made...' Lorna posited.

'You're right,' Maggie agreed. 'But like everything else, it comes down to money. Running checks slows the application process and racks up costs before payment is made, and the fraudsters take advantage of this. The encouraging news is Aviva, for one, now screens all applications for motor insurance at the point of quote or sale. I'm sure you'll find...' Her voice was drowned by a ringtone from the laptop.

'That's my call,' Lorna exclaimed.

'Of course.' Maggie acknowledged, scooping up her paperwork and stowing it safely in her bag.

'Would you mind?' Lorna indicated the door.

'Not at all. Thank you for your time,' Maggie replied, sliding off the stool with as much dignity as she could muster. Inwardly, she sighed. Harlaw Insurance had furnished the agency with an exhaustive list of policies to be verified.

Wilma was right. Maggie thought, as she got back in the car: chasing fraud was a grind. Granted, the agency got Maggie out of the house. Plus, she met loads of people. Well, 'met' was something of an exaggeration. 'Encountered' more apt, since her experience was more often than not limited to a cursory greeting and a quickly closed door. Maggie sighed. She might as well update her computer skills and go back to being a legal secretary. Except computer training cost money, money she didn't have.

Neither Here nor There

'Am I under arrest?' Tiffany demanded, folding her arms across her chest.

'Should you be?' Douglas joked, getting an eyeful of small, but perfectly formed breasts. He wondered what she was like in bed. Fit, he decided, assessing her toned upper arms. Probably went like a rabbit.

'Ha, bloody ha!'

'We have a few questions,' he began.

She stifled a yawn. 'Do I have to? I told you everything last time.'

'Not quite everything,' Douglas asserted.

'That so?' she responded, brazenly leaning forward to give him a better look.

'Can I take you back to the monies you received from Annabel Imray?' Douglas opened his folder and slid across the table a clear self-seal A4 bag containing a bank statement and attached documentary production sheet.

'What about them?' Tiffany asked, her eyes blazing defiance.

'These amounts,' Douglas said, indicating several entries. 'Can you remind me what they were for?'

'Business promotions,' she snapped.

'Really?' he challenged. 'A couple of hundred every two weeks? You must be very good at your job.'

'I am,' she shot back. 'It's not just standing around looking decorative, you know. There's skill involved.'

Douglas raised an eyebrow. 'What, for example?'

'Social stuff. Interpersonal relations, you might say: assessing the clients' needs.'

Douglas shot a look at Susan. Saw that she was struggling to control her mirth.

'Knowing when to speak and when to shut up,' Tiffany continued. 'Seeing people's drinks are kept topped up, and...' Her voice tailed off.

'Okay,' Douglas said. 'We'll come back to that.'

Tiffany straightened. 'Is that all you've dragged me in here for?' she spat.

'You're here on a voluntary basis,' Douglas said equably. 'To assist with our enquiries into the death of Annabel Imray.'

'Well, you're wasting your time.'

'The benefits you're claiming,' Susan asked, entering the conversation. 'What do they amount to?'

Tiffany shot a nervous glance at the recorder. 'Can't remember?'

'How long have you been claiming?' Susan probed.

She shrugged. 'Not that long.'

'Would it surprise you if I told you three years?'

'Who said that?'

'We have our sources,' Susan replied, with a tight smile. 'So, going back to those regular payments you received from Annabel Imray, how would you respond if I were to suggest that you had some sort of hold over her?'

Narrowing her eyes, 'That's rubbish,' she asserted.

'Is it?'

'She had more money than me,' Tiffany protested. 'Loads more. A couple of hundred was neither here nor there to Annabel.'

'Perhaps not,' Susan conceded. 'But every fortnight?'

'You can't prove it,' she answered, her voice uncertain.

'Tiffany,' Susan insisted. 'We're talking about a very serious crime here. I'll ask you again, what were those payments for?'

She didn't respond.

'Were the two of you involved in something?' Susan probed. 'Was Annabel Imray murdered to keep her quiet?'

'No,' Tiffany wailed. 'It wasn't like that.'

'How was it?' Susan asked in a soft voice.

'It was Shane,' she insisted.

Susan and Douglas exchanged satisfied looks.

'When he gave her the money to start her business, he...'

'"Gave"?' Douglas jumped in. 'Or lent, which was it?'

Tiffany huffed. 'I was coming to that.'

He nodded acknowledgement.

'Shane made Annabel sign something; a document stating the money was a loan. Then when it came near to the trial, she asked me to help get it off him.'

'And you agreed?'

'Course.' Her voice rose. 'We were best friends.'

'Go on.'

'She kept it in the safety deposit box,' Tiffany ran on. 'It's at the back of her wardrobe,' she expanded. 'Anyhow, one night she was that drunk, she put some jewellery away and left it open. And I...' She broke off, her expression furtive.

'You're saying you stole the document,' Susan ventured. 'Is that correct?'

Tiffany's chin jutted. 'It's no different from anyone else would have done.'

Susan held a different view, but let this pass. 'Didn't Annabel notice it was missing?' she asked.

'Not until she sobered up.'

'Did she question you about it?'

Smirking, Tiffany said, 'What do you think? She was frantic. Took the place apart. Thought Shane might have got in somehow, that he'd produce it as evidence in court.'

'But,' Susan observed, 'the case was thrown out, as I understand.'

'Annabel lied her head off in the witness box. She was good at that. Only she went too far.' Tiffany sniffed. 'Never knew when to stop.'

'So, what was the benefit of that document to you?'

'Insurance!' she announced triumphantly.

'Can you expand on that?'

'We hadn't been getting on, me and Annabel. We used to be such mates. But the more successful she became, the more she queened it over me, put me down in front of people. I think she was tired of me, to tell the truth. We'd been together that long, one way and another.' Her eyes took on a wistful expression. 'Annabel liked to keep on the move. She had a short attention span.'

'So?' Susan prompted.

'If that piece of paper ever saw the light of day,' Tiffany ran on. 'She could have been done for perjury. Can you imagine what that would have done to her business, Ms fucking wonderful Annabel Imray?' She looked from one detective to the other. 'I could have ruined her.'

A Deal

'Two grand?' Joe Grogan echoed, grinding his back teeth. 'What the fuck have you been up to?'

'Sorry I haven't been in,' Wilma batted false eyelashes. 'Pressure of work.'

They were in Joe's Torry boxing gym. Black and scarlet leather punch-bags hung by chains from steel beams. Exercise mats were lined up alongside a mirrored wall. In the middle of the space, surrounded by huge barbells and other fearsome-looking pieces of equipment, two underfed youths were sparring in a raised boxing ring.

'You haven't answered my question,' Joe said.

'Asking for a friend,' Wilma replied, deadpan. She'd been gutted when Maggie had rejected her idea of taking a lodger. Decided the only thing for it was to take the initiative and raise the money needed to bail them out on her own.

Joe gave her a sly look. 'That so? I thought for a minute you'd fallen in with the bad boys. More evil than me,' he qualified with a leer.

Easier said than done. Wilma's first approach - to her boss in the Torry bar where she still worked a couple of nights a week - had met with a rueful dismissal. Since the introduction of the smoking ban and tougher drink-driving legislation, pubs were closing at an alarming rate - more than fourteen a week according to the Campaign for Real Ale - and he was already in debt to the brewery. He'd provided her with a couple of contacts, with whom she'd drawn a blank. Against her better judgement, Wilma had been about to phone an associate of dodgy ex-husband Darren when she'd remembered Joe.

'When are you needing the cash?' he was asking.

'Any chance of it now?' she came back in a flash.

'How long for?'

'Couple of weeks.'

'Don't move!' He crossed to have a word with the young boxers, then disappeared down a corridor.

Wilma followed him with her eyes. For all he was short in his boxer's boots, Joe Grogan was heavily muscled, and with his shaven head and multiple tattoos cut a threatening figure.

Re-appearing after a short interval, he brandished a fat brown paper envelope. 'It's all there, so you don't need to count it. And seeing as it's you I won't charge interest. But I'll be looking for you to bring in new members. You must have a helluva contact list, you being a PI.'

I wish! Wilma thought. She nodded her agreement.

'Two grand. Two weeks. Not a day longer. Not a penny less. Deal?' He thrust out a hand.

'Deal,' Wilma replied, wincing in pain as her fingers were crushed in a vice-like grip.

Joe handed over the envelope.

Giddy with success, Wilma hot-footed back across the Dee to Mannofield.

Good News and Bad News

'It's good news and bad news,' Chisolm announced, grim-faced.

Here we go! Brian thought, anticipating another tranche of directives from on high. Some days he'd as soon be back on the beat, itchy trousers and all, as glued to a desk drowning in a sea of paper.

'The good news is that Forensics have lifted a partial print off the glass trophy in Annabel's apartment.'

'They think it could be the murder weapon?' Susan asked, trying to form a picture of the object in her head.

'Let's not get ahead of ourselves,' Chisolm cautioned. 'It's only a partial, and Annabel Imray could have shown off that award to any number of people.'

'The bad news?' Bob Duffy piped up, never one to look on the bright side.

Chisolm cracked his knuckles, first one hand, then the other.

Bad sign! Brian ducked his head, avoiding any likelihood of eye contact.

'Those thefts,' Chisolm began. 'You'll have read the victim statements in your folders.'

Brian let out a relieved whoosh of breath. Couldn't be anything major.

'The analysts have picked up a pattern. Cases have been referred back to us.'

'But,' Douglas puffed out his chest. 'Petty theft? Isn't that a waste of resources?'

This was met with a cutting look.

'I mean,' he ploughed on. 'The stuff that got nicked, it's worthless, or near as. It will cost more to investigate than it's worth. Plus, we don't even have an accurate description of most of the items.

No photograph, nothing. We don't have a hope in hell of...'

Chisolm cut him short. 'Doesn't alter our response to criminality. An offence is an offence, and we've been tasked with investigating.'

'But,' Dunn protested.

His DI held up a silencing hand. 'I understand your concern,' he said, surveying his team. 'We're undermanned: a sergeant short...'

And no replacement in sight, Brian thought, but kept his opinions to himself. Dave Wood's bad back had eased sufficiently for him to turn up for his leaving do, looking hale and rested as he accepted a generous retirement gift and countless freebie rounds of drink. But finding a high calibre officer who'd be a good fit for the team was another story. These days, recruits to the police service sailed through their training, then realised the abuse they'd have to take - the lack of respect - and just as quickly bailed out.

'...and coming on top of what may turn out to be a homicide investigation,' Chisolm continued, 'it's all we need.'

'What sort of pattern?' Brian got to the point.

'No sign of forced entry. Thefts take place during working hours.'

Bob Duffy snorted. 'Takes in just about every opportunist theft you can think of. Plus, if you look at the locations: homes on the outskirts, in cul-de-sacs, dead-end streets, but close to a major thoroughfare. Plenty cover: trees, bushes, fences to scope the victim unseen. They're dead ringers for any thief.'

'Victims are all females living alone,' Chisolm continued.

'Exactly.' Duffy again. 'Who's most likely to be at home during the day but a woman?'

'Not necessarily,' Susan contended, jumping down his throat. 'Aside from which, according to Judith McNair's statement she's estranged from her husband, but he might well still hold house keys.'

'Okay, okay, but you get my point.'

'Plus,' Douglas came back in, 'if Uniform are to be believed,

Cara Gilmore isn't on her own. There was shaving kit in the bathroom and condoms by the bed. You're not telling me she isn't shacking up with someone?'

'And they told us Mrs Troup was only at Stockethill in passing. The house belonged to her late father.'

'As to old Mrs Sinclair,' Brian added. 'Who knows?

'Fair points,' Chisolm conceded. 'But they don't take cognisance of the crude drawings left at the respective scenes. If you care to look at the photographs, the intention would appear to be to instil fear.'

'A noose?' Duffy snorted. 'Looks to me more like the number six.'

'The drawings are not well executed, I'll grant you,' Chisolm came back. 'But the analysts reckon there's more to it: a repeat perpetrator following a distinct narrative.'

'A weirdo?' Duffy muttered.

'Could be a knocker,' Susan ventured. 'The thefts were all from properties in fairly affluent neighbourhoods. Even Cara's student flat is high-end, though according to her statement there was no drawing found at the scene.'

'"Found" being the operative word,' Douglas smirked. 'According to the plods, place was a tip. Even so, what I can't understand is thieves are generally looking for stuff they can sell: cash, jewellery, gold. So why leave quality stuff, antique furniture and that,' Douglas sneered, 'and nick any old tat?'

'The bottom has fallen out of the antique trade,' Susan countered. 'Didn't you know? 'It's all mid-century-modern these days. Could be they were looking for that, and when they didn't find it they just grabbed something for the hell of it.'

Duffy drew shaggy eyebrows together. 'Bastards. If it's not layabouts looking to make a fast buck, it's druggies thieving to feed a habit. And if it's not that, it's kids. Some twelve-year-old, most like, sitting up all night watching snuff movies. Time was, you saw a copper, you'd run a mile. Nowadays–'

'You're right,' Chisolm acknowledged. 'And we all know the biggest deterrent to criminal activity is a police presence. But that's unachievable, so we have to work with what we've got.' He gathered his papers together. 'It's unfortunate we've been landed with these thefts on top of what I know is already a heavy caseload, but I'm confident,' he asserted, eyeing each of his team in turn, 'you'll give every one of them your best shot.'

Taking Stock

'Clients billed?' Maggie demanded, pen poised over a spreadsheet.

'Two.' Wilma replied. 'You?'

'Same.'

They were seated across from one another at Maggie's dining-room table, two mugs of half-drunk tea at their elbows. Sun streamed through the front window, making the room with its fitted carpet and dated dining suite look shabbier than ever.

Carefully, Maggie entered the figures. 'New clients signed?'

'Three.'

'That all?' Maggie queried, disappointed. She'd been counting on Wilma's chutzpah and wide range of contacts to bring in more business.

'If I told you what it took,' Wilma began. 'Had to just about strip off....'

'Yes,' Maggie interrupted. 'I get the picture.'

'How many new clients have you signed up?'

'One.'

'See,' Wilma said, jabbing a finger.

Maggie held her tongue, not wanting to stoop so low as to argue her new client was corporate, and hence likely to earn the agency significant revenue. But it could be months before that helped their income stream.

'It's tough out there,' Wilma went on. 'A fucking jungle!'

'You don't have to tell me.' Since becoming a private investigator, Maggie had had her education. In more ways than one! A kaleidoscope of past cases formed a shifting pattern in her head. 'Work in progress?' she asked, snapping back to reality.

Wilma gave a loud sniff. 'If I had a pound for every fraud case I've chased, I'd be a bloody millionaire.'

'But you're working through them?'

'Aye.' She scrunched a fistful of blonde hair and pulled it up in a loose ponytail. 'You hot or is it my hormones?'

'It is a bit close in here,' Maggie said, rising from the table. 'I'll open the back door.'

'Now, if you had a nice wee conservatory,' Wilma offered.

'I can't afford a conservatory,' Maggie retorted, resuming her seat. 'Not until the business is on a sound footing. So...' She picked up her pen. '...you're working through the new fraud cases on your list?'

Wilma rolled her eyes. 'Them, and the fucking credit checks and the bleeding traces. I wonder, sometimes, if I'm right in the head.'

It was on the tip of Maggie's tongue to introduce the subject of an intern, then she thought better of it. Best not rock the boat.

'Your clients doing away?'

'Thankfully. Harlaw Insurance are happy with what we're doing. Ditto Innes Crombie, though the way fraud is going there's always the possibility they'll take investigating in-house.'

'Ach,' Wilma pooh-poohed. 'We'll worry about that when it comes to it.'

'Don't be so flippant. If we were to lose either of those accounts, we could wave goodbye to the business, and...'

'Before you say another thing,' Wilma stepped into the breach. 'Here,' she thrust out a battered brown envelope.

'What's this?' Warily, Maggie eyed it, fearful of uncovering another of Wilma's gizmos.

'Go on,' Wilma urged. 'Take it.'

Maggie extended a tentative hand. The package was an awkward shape. Not solid. She gave it a squeeze. More like... She lifted the flap. 'Wilma!' She gave a frightened squeal. 'Where on earth did you get this?'

Wilma tapped the side of her nose. 'Don't ask.'

'Seriously,' Maggie said, drawing out a fat wad of fifty pound notes. 'I've never seen so much cash in my life.'

Wilma swelled with pride. 'Two grand. You can count it.'

'That won't be necessary.' Maggie snapped, stuffing the notes back into their wrapping as if they were red-hot. 'Wherever it came from, you better take it back.'

'Can't.'

'Why not?'

'Cut a deal.'

'Who with?'

Wilma's eyes slid sideways. 'Not saying.'

Maggie's mind churned. Wilma had connections all over the place, most of them bordering on criminal. If she'd borrowed the money from one such, Maggie was in no doubt there would be conditions attached.

Wilma must have read her mind, because, 'Two weeks. No strings,' she supplied.

'How did you manage that?'

'Fella wants into my knickers,' she said, poker-faced.

'Don't be so crude,' Maggie responded, suppressing a smile. Who wouldn't fancy Wilma, with her sassy manner and china-blue eyes? Still, 'Give it back all the same.'

'Can't be done. Once you've cut a deal, that's it, so you might as well have the use of it.'

Maggie shrugged in resignation. 'We can talk about that later.'

'Suit yourself.'

'To get back to reality, that only leaves the Evershed case.'

Wilma snorted. 'If we haven't found that cat after all the hours we've put in, the fliers we've put out, there's zero chance the sodding thing is going to turn up now.'

'That's not true,' Maggie argued. 'Cats can go missing for years, and...'

'Yeah, yeah,' Wilma cut her short. 'Is the client still paying us?'

'Yes, but in all conscience...'

'We're still on the lookout, still ringing the cat rescue places?'

'Yes, but...'

Wilma folded her arms. 'Well, then.'

'We can't go on taking Dr Evershed's money forever.'

'She's plenty of it,' Wilma retorted. 'Didn't you say so yourself?'

'Yes. Only...'

'Look at it this way. We're doing her a service. Making her feel better, if you like.'

'That's not the point,' Maggie said sternly. 'We have our reputation to consider.'

'We couldn't pick up a bit of roadkill, stick it in a box, and–'

'Wilma!' Maggie exclaimed, aghast. 'That's a dreadful thing to say.'

She held up a hand. 'Hear me out. There's a pet cemetery in Cullen, complete with sea view.' It had been threatened with closure due to new EU regulations, but this was just a detail, in Wilma's view. 'We could give the client something towards a nice headstone. How's about...' Her eyes danced with mischief. '... Malthus, you left a paw print on my heart?'

The Devil You Know

The murder board was a mess: maps, diagrams, photographs; lists of actions and outcomes, lines and arrows criss-crossing one another. None of your hi-tech electronic gizmos here, just an old-fashioned whiteboard with wipeable pens.

'Disappointing news,' Chisolm announced once everyone had found a seat. 'We've exhausted our initial lines of enquiry. The Porsche garage has backed up Shane Kelman's story and the DNA and fingerprint samples he provided aren't a match with what Forensics have lifted from Annabel Imray's flat. Then there's Tiffany Reid. There's no hard evidence the payments from Annabel into her account were for anything other than promotional work. In short,' his lips compressed into a thin line. 'Looks like our investigation has stalled.'

Around the room there were murmurs of disappointment. They'd all – detectives, uniformed and civilian officers alike – been working flat out for days.

'Any word on the toxicology report?' a voice asked hopefully.

'Still waiting, I'm afraid, though I suspect it's only going to confirm what we already know, namely that the victim had consumed a fair amount of alcohol.'

'Any chance we could build a circumstantial case against Shane?' A voice from the back of the room. 'He's the one with the strongest motive.'

'I doubt it. We're evidence light. We can't place him at the scene. We have no witnesses. No definitive murder weapon. It would be a whole lot harder to prove, never mind convict.'

'We don't have grounds enough to seize his computer?'

'No chance, not as things stand. But one thing we can be sure of: as a professional football player, he'll have resort to the best possible legal defence.'

'I get you.'

'What about Tiffany?'

'All we have on her is a potential case of benefit fraud. If we used that to lean on her, we might get something more.'

'It's a long shot,' Chisolm observed. 'Still...' He turned to Brian. '...get back to Tiffany Reid, find out the story.'

'Boss.'

'The clock's ticking,' Chisolm continued, his face darkening. 'I'm already fending off enquiries from all quarters.' He paused to let this sink in. 'Upstairs are shouting the odds, newspaper and TV reporters fighting for precedence. Annabel Imray was high-profile, as you know. Our media department has put out a holding statement, but there's only so long we can keep them all at bay without releasing more information. We've been here before,' he went on. 'That point where an investigation loses momentum. What we need to do now is go back over the material with fresh eyes and see what comes out of it. Keep the ABC of policing at the forefront of your minds: assume nothing, believe nothing, challenge everything.' His eyes swept the room. 'You've done sterling work, sifting through what the techies turned up. Go over it again, see if it will throw up other connections: someone close to Annabel, someone who could have harboured a grudge.'

'That's just it,' one of the civilian officers complained. 'She had thousands of acquaintances. Woman seemed to know everyone in Aberdeen.'

'Still, it's hard to believe there wasn't a man in her life, looker like that.'

'Or a woman,' offered Susan. 'A love interest anyhow.'

'As for somebody holding a grudge,' another officer chipped in. 'She comes across as a nasty piece of work. Wouldn't surprise me if folk were queuing up to stick a knife in her back.'

This raised titters from some quarters, which were swiftly quelled by the SIO's black look. 'Whatever your personal antipathy to the victim,' Chisolm asserted, 'I expect you to conduct this investigation properly so that we can bring it to its rightful conclusion. And we need to do it PDQ. Otherwise...' He engaged each in turn, '...you can expect an MIT team from Strathclyde to parachute in.'

'Bad enough working with the devil you know,' Duffy grumbled. 'Not looking at anyone in particular.' He eyed Douglas, who was occupied in straightening his double shirt cuffs.

'Draw up a list of actions,' Chisolm signalled to Brian, 'and let's get to it. The answer is out there,' he declaimed, drumming a fist on the table. 'I'm counting on you to pull together and find it.'

A Change of Heart

'Val!' Maggie exclaimed, with a glance at the passenger seat, when her phone pinged. She grabbed it, registered a FaceTime call and pressed the Accept button. 'I'm in the car,' she mouthed in a stage whisper, although last time she checked her mirror the road was empty. 'Be with you in a mo.'

She was passing through Dinnet on her way to Strathdon. Another case of sheep-rustling, which, in Scotland, had escalated from opportunistic theft involving removing traditional tags and markings to organised crime, where dozens or even hundreds of sheep were loaded into trailers late at night. Insurers were increasingly alarmed, to the extent that coded paint and swallow-able tracking devices were being employed.

As she pulled into a layby, she was passed by a large, dark-coloured saloon. The male driver turned his head and their eyes met for a fleeting second. Maggie experienced a tremor of guilt. Who was he, and what had he seen? The police were known to mount unmarked traffic patrols, and the last thing she needed was to be reported for using her mobile while driving.

Switching off the engine, she shrugged the thought away. 'Hi. This is a nice surprise.'

'What are you up to?'

'Going to see a man about a sheep,' she joshed. 'Two dozen sheep, actually.' The case in hand was relatively small-scale: a neighbour suspected of altering colour markings for his own gain. 'Takes me back to my childhood.' And it did: the grass lush, the beasts replete, the sun ripening the crops to golden perfection under an almost cloudless blue sky.

'I'll bet. Be a challenge, though. They're not forthcoming, country folk, at the best of times.'

Maggie chuckled. 'Pays to be female. I can ask questions all day long. It's almost expected. Plus, it's good to get out of the city. Might help clear my head. But,' she broke off, 'are you ringing for a reason? I wasn't expecting you to call until next week.'

Val's face clouded. 'I'm worried about you.'

'Oof,' Maggie dismissed her with a shrug.

'Seriously. Since we spoke last, I haven't been able to get you out of my head.'

'I'm fine,' Maggie insisted. 'Must have been having a bad day.'

'Bit more than that,' her old friend responded. 'Have you found time to mull over my suggestion?'

'Dumping Wilma?'

Val wrinkled her nose. 'I don't know if I'd put it like that.'

'That's what it amounts to. But, yes, I have given the matter some thought.' In truth, Maggie had thought of little else.

'And?'

'I couldn't bring myself, Val. Not after all she's done for me.' Maggie had spent wakeful hours going over all the things Wilma had done for her since that first fateful lift to the mortuary. She'd been a source of strength and consolation during Maggie's first tentative steps towards rebuilding her life. She was more grounded than Maggie. For all her questionable dress code and dodgy wheezes, Wilma got quickly to the nub of things and made more rational decisions. She'd saved Maggie from serious injury by initiating her rescue from the Seaton tower block and the Palmerston railway arches. Above all, she was a true friend, someone who'd stick by Maggie whatever the circumstances, where Val – nice as she was – had shown herself to be a slave to convention.

'Oh.' Val's face was the picture of disappointment. 'I thought taking on an intern...'

'...is a great idea,' Maggie supplied. 'If she had an office to work out of. Maybe in the future,' she added hopefully.

'I had it in my head I'd convinced you.'

'You had. Pretty well,' Maggie added.

'What occasioned the change of heart?'

'A number of things.' *Not least a wad of cash!* Maggie was mortified she'd entertained for even a nanosecond the idea of letting her friend go.

'Whatever,' Val said, 'you can't go on like this, Maggie: putting out, working all hours, carrying the world on your shoulders. It's not healthy. You'll run yourself into an early...' She broke off.

'...grave.' Maggie finished. 'Like George?'

'I'm sorry.'

'Don't be. You're quite right.'

'However much Wilma contributes,' Val ran on, 'it's you that carries the can. You need to ease off, Maggie, be kinder to yourself. Get more out of Wilma, especially while you're still paying her a wage.'

'It's alright for you.' The words were out before Maggie could help herself. 'Look, I'd better ring off,' she added, checking the time. 'I need to crack on.'

'Of course,' Val said. 'Best of luck for today. And take my advice, be good to yourself.'

'I will.' Maggie replied. Switching on the ignition, she cut the call.

Last Known Address

Fighting for breath, Wilma leaned against the wall of the Torry tower-block stairwell. In her efforts to trace yet another insurance fraudster, she'd drawn a blank with Google, the electoral rolls and 192.com, but had picked up a photo off Facebook with a familiar block of flats in the background and was convinced she was on the right track.

She'd been knocking on doors for the best part of an hour, the lifts were out of order, and she'd had to take a breather at regular intervals on the way up. *Some way to earn a crust!* But Maggie had been insistent she wouldn't touch a penny of Joe Grogan's money, so there was nothing else for it. Wilma made a mental resolution to cut down on the booze and chocolate.

She looked out of the window towards Nigg Bay, where work was ongoing to create the new Aberdeen harbour. Much of the construction work was below the waterline: huge concrete blocks filled with water sunk into the North Sea to form the foundations of the new Castlegate and Dunottar quays. As a Torry native, Wilma knew the harbour had a long history. First established as a business concern in1136 by King David I of Scotland, it served as a major hub of fishing, shipbuilding and granite transportation. In 1909 it had made headlines when escapologist Harry Houdini dived into the freezing water in chains and handcuffs and emerged unscathed. Now, along with the one billion plus Aberdeen city bypass road and TECA - The Event Complex Aberdeen - it was among the biggest current construction projects in Scotland.

For a few minutes Wilma watched, as hard-hatted men in protective clothing bent to the task in hand and heavy machinery crawled - crab-like - back and forth. Then she continued her upward climb.

One hand on the wall to steady herself, Wilma rapped on the door of the seventh-floor flat.

There was no answer.

She tried again, using the flat of her hand.

Footsteps sounded down a hallway.

The door opened.

'Sorry to disturb you,' Wilma wheezed. 'Is Robert Rhind at this address?'

'*Nie rozumiem*,' said the young woman, a slim figure in jeans and T-shirt, her fair hair braided in a pigtail.

'Shit,' Wilma muttered under her breath. Since her teenage years in Torry, Aberdeen had become the most multicultural city in Scotland, with around one in six residents born outside the UK. Of these, the largest proportion are Poles, two thousand of whom live in the council ward of Torry and Ferryhill. 'Do you speak English?' she persisted, enunciating her words with care.

The girl looked blank. '*Nie*.'

Wilma tried one last time. 'Robert Rhind?'

'*Nie tutaj*.' Then the door closed in her face.

Wilma swivelled on her heel, and banged on the door of the flat opposite. She heard shuffled footsteps. Saw an eye pressed to the security spyhole.

The door edged open to reveal a thin woman dressed in track-suit trousers and vest top, well-worn slippers on her feet. Her spiky hair was dyed a lurid shad of pink and tattoos covered both arms from shoulder to wrist.

Bingo! Wilma recognised the tattoos from the Facebook photo. 'Mrs Rhind?' she asked.

'That's me.'

'Is your husband at home?'

'Fa's askin?' The woman lisped, not removing the roll-up that dangled from one corner of her mouth.

'Never you mind,' Wilma answered, trying not to breathe in too deeply. The reek of tobacco was overwhelming, that and the stink of deep-fat frying.

'You fae the council?' The woman demanded, moving to shut the door. The Torry high-rise blocks – Morven, Brimmond and Grampian courts – had been the subject of repairs to defective cavity barriers in the wake of the Grenfell Tower disaster. Some residents had denied permission for additional barriers to be installed in their homes, and council officers had been making targeted visits to enable the works to be completed.

But Wilma was too fast. She'd had it up to here with tracing con artists and getting doors slammed in her face. She wouldn't have minded so much if she could have seen the cases through to their rightful conclusion: a fine or jail sentence. But oh, no, *'Enforcement isn't our thing,'* Maggie had pronounced. *'We'll leave that to the professionals.'*

Wilma stuck a foot in the door.

She was fair bruising for a fight.

There was nothing more unsatisfactory, in her opinion, than a job half done.

Fuck This!

Fuck this! Maggie thought, stabbing at a turnip with a large kitchen knife. Then, emboldened by her use of the f-word, she said it out loud: 'Fuck this!' And again, louder still, 'Fuck this!'

She felt so weak at the knees she had to sit down.

'You alright?' Colin puffed, rushing into the room.

'Oh.' She looked up. 'I didn't realise you'd come in.'

'Obviously,' he said, throwing her a quizzical look. 'How are things?'

'Fine,' she qualified, 'As far as they go.'

He eyed the knife in her hand. 'Seriously?'

'I'm fine,' she repeated, setting the knife down. 'Go back to whatever you were doing.'

'Heading out again, actually,' he said with a grin. 'Keith's got hold of this new PC game. His mum said I could stay for tea.'

'Give her my best, won't you?'

'Sure will.' And with a clatter, he was gone.

Maggie heard the front door bang. She sat back in her seat and closed her eyes. She'd spent the best part of a fortnight following up motor insurance scams for Harlaw Insurance, and by the time she factored in her own car running costs, the agency's net profit per policy was tiny. Add to that, Harcus & Laird had to wait for their money. Not that Harlaw were late payers, simply that their accounting cycle meant if your fee-note just missed a payment date you might have to wait nearly two months for settlement.

She shook herself awake, and walked through to the bathroom, studying her reflection in the mirror. Her skin was dry, her mouth turned down at the corners and her eyes had lost their sparkle.

'Can I tell you something?' she screamed. 'I'm sick of being sensible. Sick of playing second fiddle. Up to here with being the poor relation.'

Maggie strode through to the bedroom and opened her wardrobe. She'd stowed Wilma's windfall in the bottom drawer where no one was likely to stumble upon it, under a few things belonging to George she hadn't the heart to throw out and which she sought solace from when the loneliness and the weight of expectation became too much. She'd checked on the cash every single day, but hadn't the courage to dip in. Knowing Wilma as she did, it could have come from any number of disreputable sources.

Her fingers closed around the fat envelope.

She drew it out and gave it a shake, letting the well-thumbed banknotes scatter over the carpet.

'Fuck this!' she said, again.

She might not have won justice for George.

But Colin would do his sixth year.

And he'd do it at Gordon's.

VIII

A Signature

'What if it's not so much the 'what' as the 'who'?' Susan voiced the thought more to herself than anyone else.

Slouched in their seats after a long week, Chisolm's team had gathered for their briefing.

'Such as?' Douglas sneered.

'Well, we know all the victims are women living alone, so...'

'You saying the perp was planning to shag them and couldn't get it up, so he took a souvenir? Bit old for that, are they not, some of them?'

'Don't be so bloody crude,' she retorted, eyes signalling her disgust. 'What I'm thinking is the items stolen are so random, could it be the thief has some other motive in targeting his victims? Maybe it's not about the theft itself, but the actual loss.'

Douglas smothered an extravagant yawn. 'You don't say. Theft Act 1968: theft in a dwelling from the person in breach of trust,' he quoted. 'Ergo loss ensues. So...'

She silenced him with a cutting look. 'Hear me out. It's not the monetary value. In most of these cases that's negligible. No, it's the act itself: depriving the victim of something they hold dear.'

'That's a reasonable enough hypothesis,' Chisolm observed. Turning to Brian, he asked, 'Do you agree?'

'Yes,' Brian said with alacrity. One consequence of his new eating plan was he felt near to fainting come five o'clock. He'd have agreed with anyone on any subject just to get out of there.

'Except,' Duffy added his contribution. 'I'm not persuaded that in every instance a theft has actually taken place.'

'Fair comment,' Susan acknowledged. 'But these women have one thing in common: they're all in distress. Grieving, if you like, from the loss of a father, a husband, a child, a natural parent, a...'

'Or,' Douglas interrupted, 'in the case of old Mrs Sinclair, their mental faculties.'

'You don't know that,' Susan snapped. The statement that had come back from Uniform's visit to the old lady had been a total balls-up, but she wasn't going to be the one to land PCs Souter and Miller in it. Wasn't that long since she'd been in their shoes. Plus, she was fed up with people treating anyone eligible for a bus pass as senile. 'Regardless, what appears at first glance to be little more than a misdemeanour could result in serious long-term consequences.'

'Can you expand on that?' Chisolm asked.

'Judith McNair, to take one example, has lost not only her baby, but her marriage and possibly all hope of having another child. Then there's Cara Gilmore. If, as she alleges, there is compromising material on her phone, just think of the fallout if it goes all over the internet. A ripple effect: her friends, her family caught up in it. Even her university studies could be damaged if it's not retrieved.'

'What's so special about Cara Gilmore?' Douglas argued. 'People lose their phones all the time. And there can't be many kids haven't taken a compromising selfie. Maybe someone should tell her to get over it.'

'Don't mock,' Susan took him on. 'You know full well how cruel social media can be. We've seen many a young person self-harm, even take their own life for less.'

'I still think they bear all the hallmarks of opportunist theft,' Douglas asserted. 'Cara Gilmore's phone is a prime example.'

'I disagree. Phones can be tracked. An opportunist thief is much more likely to steal something cash-able.'

'Which brings us right back to knockers,' Duffy complained, with a long face. 'Them. Or druggies. Or fucking kids.'

'But how about the drawings?' Brian came back in. 'They don't strike me as having been done as a prank. Too disturbing. As if someone is carrying out a vendetta.'

'Do you remember *The Godfather?*' Duffy grinned. 'The horse head in the bed?'

'I don't think this is in the same league,' Chisolm said, casting his eyes to the ceiling.

'There's no telling,' Duffy persisted. 'That guy, La Torre, ran the Sorrento Restaurant in Bridge Street is on remand in Italy for being a Naples Mafia kingpin.'

'Moving on,' he said firmly. 'Was the same paper used at Judith McNair's and Minnie Sinclair's?'

'No,' Douglas replied.

'And the nooses, did they look like they'd been drawn by the same hand?'

'Hard to say.'

'What about Mrs Troup's mirror?'

'We could get it dusted it for prints,' Brian offered dubiously. 'But the world and its wee sister will have been through that house.'

'Whatever,' Chisolm said, moving to wrap up the briefing. 'I want you to go back over those statements with an open mind.'

Brian squeezed his eyes shut. *The very thought!*

Chisolm fixed him with a laser gaze. 'Are you still with us, Sergeant?'

Brian's eyes snapped open. 'Yes, boss.'

'See if you can pick up a signature: what's distinct and relevant. And team...' He banged the table with the flat of his hand. '...we have serious work to do. So, let's crack on.'

Looks Okay to Me

'That's too neat on you,' Maggie said, eyeing the two buttons straining over Colin's chest.

He shrugged. 'Looks okay to me.'

'Try the next size up,' she said, unhooking from the fitting room wall a second navy wool blazer with the Robert Gordons' badge on the breast pocket.

Colin peeled off the first and handed it to her. He slipped into the second and fastened the buttons. 'This one's too big,' he grumbled, pulling a surly face.

'It's not,' Maggie insisted. 'Look,' she tugged at the front. 'There's scarcely room in there for a pullover. And come winter, if you were wearing a thicker jumper...'

'It's all fitted jackets these days,' Colin interrupted. 'I don't want the thing hanging off me.'

'It wouldn't be "hanging off" you. And I'm not going to spend almost a hundred pounds–'

Colin sighed. 'There you go. Everything always comes down to money.'

'That's not what I meant,' Maggie replied, though the reason they were in John Lewis, where they'd have to try on a sample and order online rather than Stevensons, the school outfitter in Union Street, was for its proximity to the Civil Justice Centre, where Maggie had been called as a witness in a fraud case. 'All I'm saying is you're still growing, and...' All the while a voice niggled inside her head, *Where the hell had Wilma got that money from?*

'It's not as if it has to last.'

'No, but...' Uncertain as to Colin's future, Maggie had missed out on the Parents' Association second-hand school uniform sale in June. Still, a good blazer might serve some other lad whose family had to keep a close eye on the purse strings.

'In fact,' Colin tugged off the blazer. 'The way things are going I won't need a blazer at all.'

Maggie started in alarm. 'What do you mean?'

There was a tap on the door. 'How are you getting on?' A smiling John Lewis partner stuck her head into the cubicle.

'Oh,' Maggie said, distracted. 'Fine.'

'Can I bring you anything else to try?'

'No,' she retorted, rather more sharply than she'd intended.

'I'll leave you to it, then,' the woman said, patently offended. She beat a hasty retreat.

Maggie turned to Colin. 'You were saying?'

'I've decided not to do a sixth year.'

'But,' she protested, pulse racing. 'We've already been through all that.'

Colin looked at his feet. 'I've changed my mind.'

'Well, you've left it too late,' Maggie countered, heart in mouth. 'I've already paid a chunk of your fees.'

He raised his head. 'I'll pay you back.'

'How?'

'Get a job.'

'Doing what?'

'My pal Stuart is working at the Multiplex.'

Maggie sniffed. 'That's not much of a job.'

'He says it's good fun.'

'Maybe for a month or two,' she allowed. 'But after that...'

'He's going to save up and move into a flat.'

Her eyebrows shot up. 'On minimum wage?'

'Don't be such a misery, Mum. I could do something like that. Study in my spare time. Go to uni next year.' Brightening, he added, 'Save you a load of money.'

'That's not the point.'

He cocked his head. 'Isn't it?'

'I don't want you working in some dead-end job. You could get stuck there, and...' She sneaked a glance at her watch. 'Look, I have to go. I'm due at court in twenty minutes.'

'Whatever.'

'Will you take these blazers back to the desk and say thank you very much?'

'Okay.'

'We'll continue this conversation when I get home.'

A Wee Arrangement

'Our wee arrangement,' Wilma simpered, batting inch-long false eyelashes 'Will you give me a bit more time?' She'd been in two minds when Maggie had changed her tune about taking the loan: pleased she hadn't gone to all that trouble for nothing, and at the same time terrified as to how - if their cash flow didn't improve - she'd pay it back. Now her worst fears had been realised.

A hardened face stared back. 'Two weeks, that was the deal.'

They were in the back office of the Torry boxing gym, though in truth with its cement flooring, breeze block walls and pervasive odour of stale sweat, it was little more than a glorified storeroom.

She bent over the scarred wooden table that served as a desk, giving him the full benefit of her cleavage. 'I know. I'm only talking a couple of days, three at the most.'

The stare didn't waver. 'A deal's a deal.'

'But, Joe,' she puckered her lips in a provocative pout. 'We're friends.'

In slow motion, he flexed tattooed biceps. 'Friends don't come into it.'

'Please?' she wheedled, licking her lips with the tip of a moist pink tongue. Joe Grogan was almost a foot shorter than her but, Wilma knew, as strong as an ox.

His eyes fastened on her breasts. 'It'll cost.'

'How much are we talking?' In her head, she did a lightning run-through of likely percentages. Joe would quote an outrageous figure, she was sure, on top of the money she'd already borrowed, but it would be worth it to keep Maggie worry-free and the business afloat.

'Two hundred. A day.'

'But, Joe...'

'Take it or leave it.'

'But...'

'I'll make an exception' He rose from a torn vinyl chair. 'Seeing as you and me go back a way, I'll take it in kind.' Nimbly, he skirted the table. Then, grasping Wilma's chin in one calloused hand and tilting it downwards.' You better make it worth my while.'

'Joe,' Wilma mouthed through clenched teeth. 'I'm a married woman now.'

The vice-like grip eased a tad. 'You were, before.'

'In name only,' Wilma argued. 'We were separated, Darren and me. I was waiting for the divorce.'

He shrugged. 'All the same to me.'

'But, Joe...' Tugging his hand away. '...I'm not asking for much.'

'Reneging on a deal?' he sneered. 'There's nobody does that to Joe Grogan and gets away with it.'

Wilma tried another tack. 'I understand that. And it's not as if I'm not grateful, but...'

Behind her, the door burst open.

She turned to see a skinny youth in vest top, satin shorts and boxer's boots.

'What?' Joe barked, not moving.

'Liam's decked Gaz.'

'So?'

'Reckon he's concussed.'

He sighed. 'Give me five.'

Nodding his understanding, the youth beat a hasty retreat.

Joe ran a hand over his shaven head. 'As I said, you want more time, it'll cost.'

'I couldn't.' Wilma pictured Ian the night he'd given her an ultimatum - the agency or her marriage - the cold fury on his face. 'Not now.'

'No?' Grabbing the flesh of Wilma's backside with one hand, Joe ran the stubby forefinger of the other down her cleavage. 'Would it be so hard?' He pulled away. 'If you get my meaning,'

Wilma followed his eyes. Registered the bulge in his tracksuit trousers. She drew a calming breath. She'd thought this would be a walk in the park. Now, she felt a sudden urge to pee.

'Come on, Joe,' she forced a laugh, though it came out as more of a squeak. 'Let's not fall out over this. It was a good try.' Decisively, she removed his hand from her buttock. 'And I'm flattered, truly I am.' She batted the other hand off her front.

His face turned to stone. 'You're turning me down?'

Wilma tried one last time. 'I'd love to, really I would.' She crooned, making cow-eyes. 'You're some fella, and it's not as if I don't fancy you ...'

'That pal of yours,' he interrupted. 'Tidy wee redhead.'

She froze.

'Widow, isn't she?'

'Yes.'

'Your choice: you or her.'

'But...' Wilma began, nearly fainting from fright. It was one thing her landing herself in deep shit, but she'd die before she involved Maggie.

'And don't think you can duck out of sight. If you don't come up with the goods, I'll come looking. And it won't be pretty,' he leered, stabbing a finger. 'There's nobody messes with Joe Grogan.'

'N-no,' Wilma stuttered, wishing she'd never thought of the idea.

'Two days you're asking?'

'Two or three,' she said, chancing her arm. 'Week at the most.'

'Okay. Two days I'll grant you. But if you're not willing,' Joe threatened, his face cracking into a lascivious grin. 'She'll do.'

A Family Drama

'Do me a favour, will you?'

'Like what?' Kirsty raised her head from the book she was reading.

'Talk some sense into your brother?'

Kirsty yawned. 'What's he done now?'

'It's not so much what he's done as...' Maggie worried the chain at her neck. 'He's refusing to go back to Gordon's.'

'Christ,' Kirsty rolled her eyes. 'I come home for some peace and quiet and land in the middle of a family drama.'

'It's not a drama,' Maggie lied. She'd made more than one attempt at changing Colin's mind since their session in the John Lewis changing room and was at her wit's end. 'I'd like to know what's behind his decision, is all, and he's more likely to open up to you.'

Kirsty's lip curled. 'You reckon?'

Maggie's eyes signalled her understanding. Getting more than two words out of Colin this past while had been like getting blood out of a stone.

'Whatever.' Kirsty said, setting the book aside. 'Where is he?'

'Upstairs.'

Languidly, she peeled herself off the settee and padded, barefoot, from the room.

Maggie collapsed into the big chair and let her eyelids droop. All that worry and effort to come up with the fees, and for what? She tried to second-guess the school's reaction if she were to ask for a refund. They'd be sympathetic, she was sure. And yet... She did a quick mental calculation of bills outstanding, fee notes pending settlement. Head swimming, she tried to make sense of it all, but her brain wouldn't play ball.

*

'Sorted,' Kirsty announced, flopping back onto the settee.

Maggie rubbed her eyes. 'Really?'

Kirsty reached for the book she'd been reading. 'Yup.'

'That was quick.'

'Didn't feel quick to me.'

Maggie sneaked a glance at her watch. 'Oh,' she realised three-quarters of an hour had elapsed. 'Sorry. Didn't realise I'd dropped off.'

'That's okay.' Kirsty shot her a concerned look. 'You must have needed it.'

'I suppose.' She'd had another full day, grinding her way through a soul-destroying series of depositions, as well as trying to drum up new business and keeping tabs on her existing case-load. 'What's the story?'

'Oh.' Pulling a sympathetic face, Kirsty put the book down. 'Turns out it's all down to love. Colin finished with Ellie.'

'I know that,' Maggie said. 'But...'

'Seems he saw her cosying up to one of his mates. Stormed off. But not before he'd said some horrible things. Then she stopped speaking to him, and...'

'Poor lamb.' Maggie's heart went out to her only son. He was young, yet, and she could still remember how wounded she'd been when a boy at school dropped her after one date.

'"Poor lamb" nothing,' Kirsty retorted. 'He's behaved like a total dick, and he knows it. That's why he doesn't want to go back to school. Ellie's doing a sixth year, and he can't face her.'

'And?' Maggie ventured.

'Took a lot of persuasion. He wasn't for backing down. Men!' she exclaimed. 'What is it about them? Anyhow, I finally persuaded him to call her. Stood over him while he apologised.'

'How did Ellie react?'

'She asked to speak to me when they were done. Poor girl was in floods of tears. Seems she and the classmate were only conferring over some essay or other. Colin was jealous, jumped to the wrong conclusion. Then he dug his heels in. Didn't want to lose face.'

So like his father, Maggie thought. It was at times like these that she missed George's support more than anything. She pressed her back into the chair, imagining herself in her husband's embrace.

'Boys,' she said with a grimace. 'They take a long time growing up.'

'Tell me about it.'

It was on the tip of Maggie's tongue to ask if Kirsty had someone.

She'd been quiet on the subject of boyfriends since earlier that year when they'd given that lad Shaz a bed after he'd discovered a body in a Dundee builders' skip. Then she thought better of it. No point in making waves in one direction when they'd just settled in another. Maggie sighed inwardly. The joys of motherhood! She was weary of the constant push and pull between one thing and another, one person and another, the overwhelming guilt.

She resolved to act on Val's advice: be good to herself, take control of her life.

Thistle Street

'Ow!' Wilma shrieked, as the waxed strip came off with a noise like a thunderclap.

'Sorry,' the beautician said, her face a mask under a tight ponytail.

Cow! Wilma swore under her breath. She shifted on the couch, trying to find a more comfortable position. Though how you were supposed to relax with one bent knee sticking up in the air and the other lying flat at an angle of ninety degrees she couldn't fathom.

She'd lain awake the night before, agonising over what to do. Sleeping with boxing trainer Joe Grogan would be a one-off. And Joe wasn't one to shoot his mouth off, so who would ever know? But every time Wilma looked at Ian, out for the count in bed after yet another late shift working his butt off to give them - give her - a brighter future, she realised Joe's ultimatum had the potential to wreck her life.

'Ow-ee!' she screamed as another strip of muslin was ripped from her groin. She raised her head. 'I said tidy up, not fucking skin me alive.'

The girl didn't respond, but instead bent to the task in hand.

Wilma hadn't thought twice about taking Joe's money. Desperate circumstances demand desperate measures, and Maggie Laird was a deserving case if ever there was one. She'd been gutted when she had to go back and plead for more time. And the clock was running down. Wilma's own words rang in her ears, *Couple of days.*

Grudgingly, she acknowledged Joe Grogan was right: a deal was a deal. And he wasn't a man to cross. Wilma might have winged it if Joe hadn't brought Maggie into the frame. She could picture, still, how he'd eyed her neighbour up that first time Maggie had gone to his gym. But Wilma hadn't covered Maggie's back all this time to hand her on a plate to a hard nut like Grogan. What was it Maggie said? "Women like us, we do whatever it takes..." Too right! When the chips were down you just got on with it. Like she had that first day at the fish processing. Like when she'd got shot of Darren. Like when - against all Wilma's expectations - Maggie Laird had acceded to her wild proposal that they go into business together. Wilma resolved to keep Maggie out of the picture, and if that meant a quick fumble with Joe, so be it.

The beautician was using tweezers, now, to tackle stray hairs. Wilma wished she'd had the time to take a couple of Ibuprofen, but she'd made the appointment at the last minute, determined to follow through while she still had the nerve.

Ah, weel! As the tweezers nipped and tugged, Wilma said a quiet prayer it would all come good.

Not for Public Consumption

'Been a while,' Brian said, setting down two cups of coffee on the parquet-topped table.

'Yes.' Maggie replied, toying with the scarf at her throat.

They were in Sweet Mumma's Kitchen. His suggestion. Their old haunt, The Wild Boar in Belmont Street, might stir up memories that were best left dormant.

'They've made a good job of converting the place, don't you think?'

Her eyes took in the streamlined glass display counter in one corner, the lime green banquette seating, the artful clusters of pendant lights. She nodded her agreement.

'Thought it would amuse you.'

Men! The cafe, with its corrugated iron curved ceiling, would have been Maggie's very last choice of meeting place. Arch 11, Palmerston Road, resurrected painful memories of the Milne case, when she'd been trapped overnight in a disused railway arch not that far away. She speculated Brian had chosen the venue to make himself look good. It was he, after all, who'd liberated Maggie from her ordeal, seen her safely home, tucked her up in bed with a hot water bottle. *You're over-thinking things again!*

'How are you?' Brian's voice broke here train of thought.

'Fine.'

'Agency picking up?'

She pulled a doleful face. 'I wish.'

'Seriously?' he persisted.

'I'm keeping my head above water,' she replied. But it's hard: too many outfits, that are better resourced, competing for a dwindling amount of business.'

'But, surely, you'd survive on fraud cases alone. I mean, the way things have been going...'

'You'd think so. But, increasingly, insurers take a view.'

'They'd rather settle?'

'All too often. Saves time and hassle.'

'I shouldn't worry. If it's not insurance fraud it will be something else.' He grimaced. 'Human nature.'

Maggie didn't respond, wishing she had his confidence.

'How's your pal, Big Wilma?'

Bristling, Maggie said, 'Don't call her that.'

'She is big, though, isn't she?'

'Not as big as she was.' Maggie retorted, rushing to Wilma's defence.

'Whatever you say.' Brian conceded, with a grin. 'Kids doing okay?'

'Kirsty has a summer job in Dundee. She'll be starting her Honours year in September. Colin...'

Brian couldn't resist. 'Keeping out of trouble?'

'Fingers crossed,' Maggie said, joining in the joke. It seemed another life away that her son had been caught with weed in his school trousers. 'He's heading for a sixth year,' she added.

Brian furrowed his brow. 'Will you manage?'

'Just. That's if there aren't any surprises. I've been stretched these past few weeks. So much so...' She resolved to take Brian into her confidence. He was an old friend, after all. '...I've been seriously thinking of selling the house.'

Brian's face lit up. 'That's it,' he exclaimed, looking like he'd just experienced a eureka moment. He jumped to his feet, almost knocking over his flat white. 'Forgive me,' he said, whipping his phone from his jacket pocket. 'I have to make a call.'

'You can make it here,' Maggie said, bemused.

'No.' Brian insisted. 'Has to be somewhere I can speak without being overheard.'

Maggie's lip jutted. 'I don't see…' she began. But she was talking to his back as, punching in numbers, he weaved his way through the tables and out onto Palmerston Road.

She'd been pleased when Brian rang out of the blue. More than pleased. Maggie had felt the warm glow of familiarity when she heard his voice. And an unexpected frisson of excitement. Could it be he wanted to breathe life into their relationship? If so, she wouldn't be so resistant, not this time.

'Sorry about that,' he breezed, sliding back into his seat.

Maggie raised a questioning eyebrow.

'Not for public consumption,' he joked, picking up his cup and taking a hasty swallow.

'"Public consumption"?' She bristled, hurt to the quick.

'Look, I'm really sorry, I have to go.'

'But,' Maggie spluttered, 'you've only just got here.'

'I know.' He drained the last of his coffee. 'Something has come up.' Scraping back his chair, he rose. 'Can we do this some other time?'

'Well...,' Maggie began, slack-jawed. In her head she'd rehearsed how it would play out, her first solo encounter with Brian since the dinner date in Poldino's that had ended in acrimony. '...if you really have to, I suppose....'

But with a smile and a wave he was gone.

Nose thoroughly out of joint, Maggie took a sip of her - now lukewarm - latte, wondering what could have caused Brian to leave her in the lurch? They went back such a long way. And it's not as if she'd breach his confidence, not after... She flushed, recalling the brazen way she'd milked his insider knowledge in the fledgling days of the agency. Must be police business, she concluded, somewhat mollified. Hadn't it been the same when George was alive: the children's birthday parties he'd turned up late to, the school concerts and parents' evenings missed? But what could be so pressing, she fretted, pushing her cup aside, that he couldn't have stayed even ten minutes?

In her head, she heard his voice again:

Not for public consumption.

Something private, then.

So private that...

Then she twigged.

Brian had a new girlfriend.

It'll Keep

'Have you won the lottery?' Ian asked, cutting into a juicy sirloin steak.

'No,' Wilma replied. 'You've been looking tired these past couple of weeks is all. Reckoned you need feeding up.'

'Wondered what it was in aid of,' he remarked, chewing with relish. 'And you're right, I've been grabbing all the overtime that's going. We'll put the extra money towards that new kitchen you've set your heart on.'

Wilma's conscience pricked. With an effort, she banished her guilty thoughts. She was doing this for the greater good.

Ian swallowed. 'How about you? Have you eaten already?'

'Cutting down,' she replied. 'I'm off to the gym. I've been piling the weight back on. High time I did something about it.'

'I like you the way you are,' he said, sneaking a feel of one sturdy buttock.

'Get off,' Wilma pulled away. 'You'll crease my skirt.'

Grinning, he eyed her up. 'There's hardly enough of it.'

'All the same,' she grumbled, smoothing it over her belly. She picked up her car keys and headed for the door.

'You're not going to the gym dolled up like that!' he exclaimed.

Wilma turned, bristling. 'What if I am?'

'In a leopard miniskirt and six inch heels?'

'Is there something the matter with the way I look?'

'No,' he marvelled. 'It's just, I thought you usually wore them legging things.'

'Fancied a change.' Wilma asserted. 'That give you a problem?'

'No. Only...' He looked at his watch '...isn't it a bit late in the day for the gym? You usually go before dinner.'

'They've changed the times,' Wilma lied, hoping Ian would

never have cause to check.

'Shame,' he said, setting down his knife and fork. He rose from the table and took her in his arms. 'You look fit to eat.'

'Your food will get cold.' Wilma wheezed, struggling to break free.

Ian's grip tightened. 'It'll keep.'

'I've got to go,' she insisted.

'No,' he countered. 'You don't. You can go to the gym any day.'

'But...' she protested, feeling his cock harden against her.

He nuzzled her neck. 'How about we go upstairs?'

Wilma panicked. There was no way she could stand Joe up. Who knows what he would do to her? Worse, what he might do to Maggie?

'Pack it in,' she said, managing to disengage. 'I didn't cook you that muckle steak for it to end up in the bin.'

'Mebbe not,' Ian retorted, his face hardening. 'But I wasn't born yesterday. There's no way you're going to any gym dressed like that.'

'I told you,' Wilma began.

"Fancied a change" is it?' he mimicked? 'Fancied a fuck elsewhere is what I'm thinking.'

'No,' Wilma lied. 'I wouldn't...'

'Too right you wouldn't.' He grabbed her by the wrist and snatched the car keys from her hand.

Wilma squared up. 'Don't you dare!' If she played it right, she might still make it.

But Ian was in full macho mode. 'Dare what?' he taunted, dangling the keys under her nose, whilst simultaneously putting his other hand up her skirt.

Wilma let out a soft moan. She was wet, by now, between her legs. 'Give me my car keys,' she breathed. 'I'm needing to get out. I've been in all day and I'm going stir crazy.'

'I'll give you "stir crazy",' he grinned, slipping the keys into his trouser pocket.

Wilma sighed. Maybe the choice had been made for her.

And Joe and her went back years.

Maybe he wouldn't press the matter.

Or would he?

A Calling Card

'Settle down,' Chisolm instructed.

His team had been called in at short notice: Bob Duffy from court, Susan Strachan from checking statements, Douglas Dunn from picking up his suits from the dry-cleaner.

'There has been a development. Brian, over to you.'

Brian cleared his throat. 'These thefts...'

Everyone groaned.

'There has been something niggling at me since the cases were assigned to us, but I couldn't put my finger on it.'

They waited, expectant.

'We've been looking for a signature – a calling card if you like – where the repeat perpetrator follows a narrative, or...'

'Shoot,' Duffy growled. 'Some of us have homes to go to.'

'The analysts are right,' Brian confirmed. 'There is a link, and it's staring us in the face: all these female victims are homeowners. I only made the connection when I saw a sale board going up at my block of flats,' he fibbed. There's no way he was going to let Maggie Laird muddy another investigation.

'So?' Douglas queried. 'What does that...?'

Brian cut him short. 'They're all looking to move house.'

'I get it,' Susan spoke up. 'Janet McNair is getting divorced, so she'll have to sell up.'

'Or,' Douglas slipped in, 'buy the husband out.'

She ignored him. 'Mrs Troup is planning to sell her father's house.'

'She might be moving in herself.'

Susan looked daggers. 'That's not what she told me. She'd had the place valued. Was waiting for probate before she could proceed.'

'Mrs Sinclair may be moving into a care home,' Brian observed. 'If so, her house will be going on the market.'

'What about Cara Gilmore?' Douglas persisted. 'She doesn't show any sign of moving. Quite the contrary, she has just started uni.'

Pompous wee shite! Susan saw red. 'It was her parents who shelled out for that flat. How do you think they're going to react when whatever's on that phone goes viral? I'd bet they'll whip her back home to bloody Gloucestershire before you can...'

'Enough,' Chisolm barked. 'We're all tired, so I won't keep you much longer. Brian, can you sum up?'

'In every one of these instances, the victim has - or potentially could have had - a visit from an estate agent, or been in contact with one, even if they didn't follow through. They could have given out personal details over the telephone, or been invited into the home and established the householder's circumstances. Then...'

Susan finished the sentence. '...used the opportunity to perpetrate a theft: whatever was most precious, a minor item in monetary terms, but the loss of which has a disproportionate effect on the victim.'

'Someone sick in the head?' Brian queried.

'A perv?' Duffy added his tuppence-worth.

'You're suggesting the perp targets women on the basis of their vulnerability, then gets off on twisting the knife by leaving those drawings?' Douglas interjected. 'He'd have to be a real sicko.'

'It's not beyond the realms,' Susan countered. 'No different from an arsonist jacking off in the bushes while the fire takes hold.'

'How do you get to that?' Douglas again. 'The perp would have to stick around, or at least re-visit the scene. And there's no evidence to suggest...'

'If it was a perv,' Brian reasoned, 'we'd most likely have caught him by now. Like arsonists, they tend to want to enjoy the results.'

Douglas yawned. 'Might just be somebody bored out their skull.'

Chisolm threw him a sharp look. 'It's not a bad hypothesis. But it's all very well delving into the psychology of the thing – what we need to concentrate on is hard evidence.'

'And we've precious little of that.' Duffy said, re-establishing his role as the team's naysayer.

Chisolm let this go. 'I need you to make follow-up calls on those victims, double-check they haven't forgotten to tell us about an agent's visit.'

'In the case of Mrs Sinclair,' Douglas observed, 'that might be difficult.'

Wee Jobbies

'Fraud, fraud and more fraud,' Wilma moaned through a mouthful of Mexican chicken.

'It brings in the fees,' Maggie insisted.

They'd grabbed a sandwich from Greggs and were sitting on the grass in Union Terrace Gardens, a sunken green space in the middle of town, where after years of heated debate work was underway to transform the Victorian park into an inclusive 21st-century space. The ambitious plans incorporated pavilions, a walkway from Union Street, lift access, landscaping and lighting, whilst the central lawn would be retained for gatherings and events. Overlooking the gardens, the Central Library, St Mark's Church and His Majesty's Theatre – known locally as education, salvation and damnation – cast a granite shadow.

'Speaking of which, is the Evershed dame still paying us?' Wilma demanded, swilling down her wrap with a swig of cloudy lemonade.

'Just. But she's not happy. She's been making noises about taking the case back to the police.'

'Chance would be a fine thing,' Wilma muttered, her mouth full.

'Yes, well if there are no developments in the next week or so, I'm planning to resign the case.'

'That wee idea I mentioned...'

'No,' Maggie said emphatically. 'You were saying...'

'Fraud,' Wilma pronounced. 'It's so bloody boring. If we could just get one decent case instead of all these piddling wee jobbies....' She broke off, her shoulders starting to heave.

Maggie's lips compressed. 'What's so funny?'

'Wee jobbies,' Wilma tittered. 'Get it?'

Maggie sighed. 'I'm not in the mood for playground humour. I get enough of that in Seaton.'

'What's wi the long face?' Wilma challenged. 'I was only saying, if we took on a few big cases instead of all these wee ones, life would be a whole lot easier.' She added, 'The cops have gone affa quiet on Annabel Imray. Mebbe it would be worth our while to...'

'I've told you already,' Maggie retorted, taking a bite of her tuna and cucumber sarnie. 'We're not getting involved in stuff like that.'

'But, we could just...'

'Not even at arm's length. We stick to what we know.'

'Okay,' Wilma sulked. 'Just saying.'

'From small acorns...' Maggie began.

'Yeah, yeah. Don't start on your sermonising...' she caught her breath, then slipped in '...rhetoric.' One of her 'new' words. Since 'subliminal' had captured her imagination, Wilma had steadily filled her secret box of new vocabulary. The paper squares, each with a word carefully spelled out, now had the makings of a game of paper chase. She could as easily have found the definitions online, but there was something thrilling about the furtive thumbing of her charity shop Chambers Dictionary. And she'd found some real beezers: 'discombobulate' her current favourite. Plus, she wouldn't want Ian to catch her with something on screen. He wouldn't understand.

'The point I'm trying to make,' Maggie persisted, seeming not to notice Wilma's expanding vocabulary, 'is that fraud often starts small and escalates into something much more serious.'

'Give us a for instance,' Wilma countered, her expression dubious.

Maggie shrugged. 'Can't think of one off the top of my head.'

'See,' Wilma said, smirking.

'Give me a minute,' Maggie railed. She drank from her bottle of water, then, 'There was a case a good few years back. Oil company: Subsea Offshore if I remember right. Senior cashier defrauded them of hundreds of thousands over a long period. She was convicted and sent to jail.'

'Fae Ballater, that quine,' Wilma chipped in, her cheeks bulging. 'Sent down for five years.'

'How do you know that?'

'The reason I remember is she ended up in Cornton Vale, working in the library. Had the neck to complain about the company.' She rolled her eyes. 'It was in all the papers at the time.'

'Just goes to prove my point.'

'Okay,' Wilma conceded. 'But how often does that happen?'

'Infrequently, I admit, but the trend is...'

'And while we're waiting,' Wilma interrupted. 'We'll likely die of boredom.' She yawned. 'I'm beginning to think we're not cut out for this lark.'

'You don't mean that.'

'Think about it,' Wilma insisted. 'What do we do all day? Sit on our arses digging up dirt, either that or go looking for shite on dirty scumbags.'

'Well, if you put it like that...'

'What other way would you put it? Small wonder there's no women in the PI business.' She winked. 'Aside from us.'

'That's not true.'

'It bloody is. If you think of the companies in our line of work, you'd be hard-pressed to...'

'You're wrong,' Maggie argued. 'All the big organisations employ both male and female case managers. Why wouldn't they, when they do such a lot of matrimonial work: infidelity, internet dating checks? Women are more discreet, and...'

'They're bloody invisible.'

'My point entirely. Female private investigators may be in the minority, I admit, but they have a long history. As far back as 1905, Maud West set up a detective agency in London and ran it for more than thirty years.'

Wilma huffed. 'Must have been off her head.'

'She was pretty imaginative, from what I've read. Adopted all manner of disguises.'

'Ooh!' Wilma exclaimed through the last of her lunch. 'Now, there's a thought!'

XI

Back to Square One

'Theft cases,' Chisolm announced. 'What have we got?'

'It's not good news,' Brian responded. 'Susan, can you expand?'

'When we called on Mrs Troup, the place was like a bomb site, boxes and rubbish everywhere. She couldn't spare much time. Said she was rushing to meet a deadline at Milne's saleroom.'

'Antiques and Collectibles sale,' Douglas expanded, putting his oar in. 'Milne's hold auction sales weekly, but their specialist sales only happen once in a while.'

'Thanks for that,' Chisolm said, his face expressionless. 'Good to know.'

'The upshot is,' Susan resumed, 'Mrs Troup is now saying she might have put that medal somewhere else.'

'Typical woman.' Duffy muttered.

Douglas favoured Susan with a smug grin. 'So much for your theory of depriving people of their most treasured possessions.'

'I think that medal *was* important to her,' Susan insisted.

'Either that or it turned up before the auctioneer's valuation chap came to the house,' Duffy added, 'and she's put it in the sale.'

'Wouldn't be the first time,' Brian remarked with a wry smile. They'd all come across fraud cases where goods had been spirited away and reported as theft.

'There's already a question mark over the reliability of Mrs Sinclair's account,' Susan continued. 'And it now turns out that of the agents who called on her, at least one dealt with Mrs Sinclair's daughter, who holds Power of Attorney. Then to muddy the water even further, Miranda Maitland rang yesterday, full of apologies.'

'She's found her fountain pen?' Brian queried.

'No, Sarge. Still insists it has been stolen, but thinks she might have got the day wrong. She's a psychotherapist,' Susan explained.

'In great demand, if she's to be believed. Has a pretty full diary of clients.'

'Silly buggers,' Duffy muttered. 'Putting good money after bad.'

Susan smiled. 'Takes all sorts. Anyhow, out of all the statements we checked, we've only come up with two names that are common to all: Henry Dundas and Gary Moir.'

Henry Dundas? The name tugged at Chisolm's memory. He couldn't place it. *Sign of old age!* When he'd looked in the mirror that morning, he'd seen silver glinting through his sideburns, greying stubble on his chin. Then it came to him: Melville monument in Edinburgh's St Andrew Square. The figure on the column was Viscount Melville, Scottish advocate and Tory politician. Chisolm raked his memory. All he could remember from distant school history lessons was that Melville was the first Secretary of State for War, though he had an inkling there was scandal lurking somewhere. Sounded a complex character. He wondered if his namesake was in the same mould? Decisively, he dismissed the thought. Experience had taught him not to judge by appearances.

'Mmm,' he said, bringing his attention back to the job in hand. 'Looks like we may have to accept your hypothesis...' He turned to Brian, who was seated on his right, his ears on fire. '...that the common thread the victims were homeowners was mistaken. But in the absence of other leads, ask those two gentlemen to attend on a voluntary basis, will you, Brian, and let's see what comes out of it?'

'Boss,' Brian acknowledged, avoiding his colleagues' eyes.

'And while you're at it, you might as well establish where they were on the morning of thirteenth August.'

Anything Wrong?

Maggie's heart sank when she saw the car in the drive. 'Anything wrong?' she called, letting herself in the front door.

'Your dad's just fixing something,' her mum answered. 'We'll be out your way in five minutes.'

Maggie followed the voice into the sitting-room. 'What are you doing up there?' she asked anxiously.

'Fixing this curtain rail,' her father smiled down from atop a set of wobbly wooden steps. 'End has been hanging off for I don't know how long.'

Another thing Maggie hadn't got around to. She started forward. 'Be careful. Those steps aren't safe.'

'I've been telling you that for years,' her mother spoke through pursed lips. 'That's why I'm standing here holding them now.'

Screwdriver in one hand, her dad grinned. 'Never mind. They'll do the job. And next time we're at Bridge of Don I'll pick you up a set of aluminium ones at the DIY store. They'll be a lot lighter, and...'

'Don't be daft,' Maggie cut him short. 'These will do me fine.'

'They're dangerous,' her mother insisted.

'Which is why,' Maggie countered, 'I rarely use them.'

'Well, if that's your attitude,' her mum began.

Maggie took a deep breath. If there was one reason she wouldn't go running to her parents for a loan, it was staring her in the face right now. 'Look,' she reasoned, 'I know you're trying to help. And I'm grateful, really I am. But the arrangement was you'd do a bit of home cooking, Mum, help keep the freezer stocked, and Dad would tidy the garden, that's all.'

'We didn't think we had to stick to a set of rules,' her mum said stiffly.

'You don't,' Maggie responded. 'It's just...' She broke off, exasperated. '...I've been planning on getting someone in. I've a mountain of jobs need doing, and Wilma knows a man who...' She stopped, mid-sentence. She didn't want to let on she'd been thinking of selling and needed to smarten the place up first.

'What has that woman–?' her mother began, shoulders stiff with affront.

'Forget it.' Whatever Maggie said, now, she was on a no-win. 'Fact is, Dad shouldn't be up there, not after...' A flashback of her father prostrate on a hospital bed filled her head. Her dad's heart scare had shaken her to the core. Made her realise how precious her parents were, despite their frequent differences.

'You saying I'm not up to it?' her dad chuckled.

'No, but...' She checked her watch. '...isn't this your bridge night? You're way later than usual. I'm worried you'll get stuck in traffic, leave yourselves tight for time. And stress isn't good for you, Dad, you know that.'

Isn't good for anyone, is what she was thinking. She'd been on her feet all day: knocking on doors, trying to tie up cases. What Maggie wouldn't give for a cup of tea.

Her dad ignored this. 'Doctor says I'm fit as a flea.' He fixed a final screw into place and hooked the curtain back onto the rail. Gingerly, he descended onto the carpet. 'There.' Taking a step back, he added, 'Isn't that better?'

Maggie smiled her thanks. 'It is, indeed.'

'If we hang on,' her mum ventured, 'is there any chance we'll catch Colin? Just in passing,' she added hurriedly, seeing the crestfallen look on Maggie's face.

'Sorry,' Maggie replied. 'He's round at a friend's tonight.'

'Oh, well,' her mother said with a wounded expression. 'Doesn't matter. We'll catch him another time. Won't we, pet?' She looked to her husband for confirmation. 'How are the children, anyhow?'

Guilt nibbled at Maggie's conscience. She couldn't remember the last time they'd all been out to her parents' retirement home in

Oldmeldrum. 'Both fine. We'll make a point of paying a visit next time Kirsty's home,' she promised with another pang, knowing full well it was unlikely to happen.

'They're not children anymore,' her father chuckled. 'Young adults, more like.'

Wish they'd behave like adults, Maggie thought mutinously.

You've Had Your Tea

'Hello,' Allan Chisolm said. He'd had it up to here. The investigation into Annabel Imray's death was moribund, and his officers were chafing at being lumbered by the string of trivial thefts. Plus, he was overdue a duty visit, so had decided to clear the cobwebs by taking a day away from his desk.

'Oh.' The man turned in his high-backed chair, face devoid of expression. 'It's you, is it?'

'Seems to be.' Chisolm replied, occupying the seat opposite. 'How are you, Dad?'

'How do you think?' Richard Chisolm waved a hand at his surroundings. 'Stuck in a place like this.'

Chisolm looked around. The room was spacious, a few well-chosen pieces of furniture from the family home ranged around the walls. Picture windows looked out upon a well-tended garden. Only the bed, with its hydraulic controls and pull cord alarm gave lie to the fact this was other than a care facility. 'It's the best...' he began. '...*money can buy*,' he was about to say. Thought better of it. No point getting in an argument.

'There's nothing to look at, nowhere to go. They...' Richard jerked a thumb at the exit, where a full-length glazed panel revealed a broad corridor punctuated by identical doors. '...don't even bother to answer half the time when I call.'

Same old! Chisolm wondered why he bothered. He and his dad had never been close. Richard's job as a civil engineering consultant had taken him away from home for long periods during Allan's formative years, and it was his mum who'd nurtured and encouraged her only child, guiding him through school and on to university. Richard had railed at his son's career choice, and Allan, hell-bent on thwarting his father's desire to steer him towards a profession, had ultimately severed ties. A lump rose in his throat. It was his mother's death that had reconciled them. Helen Chisolm had died of breast cancer shortly after Allan had finished police training.

'That's what I'm paying for.' His dad's voice interrupted Chisolm's train of thought.

You're paying? He stiffened. After decades of rattling around in the family home, Richard's diabetes had forced him into twenty-four-hour care, funded in part by the house sale. Not that Allan had been counting on his inheritance, but it might have eased things at home, where his marriage was crumbling under the double whammy of unsocial hours and a hefty mortgage. 'I expect they're busy,' he said.

'Busy?' Richard's voice rose. 'Busy doing damn all.' He plucked at the cuff of his oatmeal cardigan. 'Have you noticed how fat nurses are these days?'

'Care assistants,' Chisolm corrected, before he could stop himself.

'Nurses, care assistants, they're all the same to me. Fat, idle slobs the lot of them. And do you know why?'

Chisolm held his breath.

'Health and Safety,' Richard announced triumphantly. 'Buggers aren't allowed to lift a thing. And that's not all. They...'

Chisolm stared into the middle distance. He'd heard it all before.

His silence must have done the trick, because next time he looked, his dad's head had lolled onto his chest.

Chisolm closed his eyes. It hadn't been dramatic, the end of his marriage: a gradual loosening of threads as opposed to a theatrical stand-off. A series of high-profile cases hadn't helped, the final straw when he rolled up two hours late to his younger daughter's graduation.

'This can't go on,' Clare had said, then. And she was right. She was always right. That was part of the problem: how she quietly coped with all the crap the job threw at them, didn't give him grief, just got on with it. She was an intelligent woman, one of the reasons he married her. That and the classy looks, the throaty laugh, the... Chisolm didn't want to go there. Not that they'd had a relationship - not in any real sense - for years. His fault. He was the one was always too tired for sex.

After that, it had all been downhill. They'd limped along. Until the moment came he couldn't stand the pained look on her face, the weight of guilt in his heart. When she asked him to leave, he put in for a transfer - somewhere, anywhere - never thinking the first thing that turned up would be outside the central belt.

Aberdeen was unknown territory to Allan Chisolm, the north-east a foreign country to a Glaswegian born and bred. He'd done his homework: one of the oldest cities in the UK with the area around the current city centre having been populated at least 8,000 years ago, Aberdeen was nicknamed the Granite City due to the use in its Victorian buildings of granite – a material that is very long-lasting and makes the 19th century buildings seem surprisingly new. What Aberdeen is also famous for, he'd learned, is its extensive flower displays, for which the city had won the Britain in Bloom award a record amount of times. Chisolm had jumped at the chance. It could be a good career move. Although violent crime had fallen, oil money had brought other problems: prostitution, people trafficking, drugs. Gangs from the north-east of England dealing in mainly Class A substances operated county lines radiating from Aberdeen further north.

Alice was twenty-three, now, working as an accountant in London. Her sister, Hannah, eighteen months older, lived in New York. To start with, Chisolm FaceTime'd on Sundays. Then that fell away. Either the girls were out doing things with their friends, or he was on duty, or he simply forgot. He harked back to when they were small: the sticky hands pressed in his, the soft limbs, the wet kisses. He missed all that, and more.

He'd let time run through his fingers, immersed himself in one case after another at the expense of a social life. His team was beginning to pull together. Now was the moment to forge new relationships. He might even get lucky, find someone to share his bed. *Fat chance!* Dating websites weren't for him, and there wasn't a woman in the world would put up with his work hours. Not unless she was in the job herself. And he hadn't come across many of those. His opposite number, Melanie Coutts, was in a lesbian relationship, Susan Strachan, his DC, too young. And, besides, as her DI, he needed to keep her at arm's length,

Behind him, the door banged open, rudely interrupting his reverie.

Richard Chisolm's head jerked up.

'Cup of tea?' The woman pushing the trolley could have been mistaken for a tea cosy, so triangulate was she: small head with scraped back hair crowning a pear-shaped trunk, culminating in the thickest ankles Chisolm had ever seen. 'Thanks,' he said, gratefully. 'Milk. No sugar.' He'd hit heavy traffic after Stirling and hadn't eaten since his early morning start.

'What kind of biscuits have you got today?' his dad barked.

'Custard creams.'

'Again?' Richard grumbled. He turned to Chisolm. 'They make them out of the leftovers from other production lines. Bet they didn't tell you that in the police.'

Chisolm shook his head. He took one anyway. The tea was too milky and not overly hot. Still... He took a welcome sip.

'Can't even get a decent biscuit in this place,' his dad droned on. 'Charge the earth and cut costs to the bone.'

Maggie Laird, now, Chisolm's thoughts ran away – she would understand. She'd been married to a policeman. And they had chemistry. Chisolm could feel, still, the compact heat of her in his arms. And that hair! Like beech leaves in autumn. Called to mind one rare day out in Perth, when he and Clare had enjoyed a leisurely lunch at a fishing hotel on the banks of the Tay. Afterwards, they'd marvelled at the Meikleour beech hedge. A third of a mile long and soaring to a hundred feet in height, it is thought the men who planted it were called to fight in the Jacobite Rebellion and killed at the Battle of Culloden. In tribute, the trees were allowed to grow. The hedge remains a living landmark to them.

Chisolm snapped back to reality. Although his last meeting with Maggie Laird in Aberdeen's Ardoe House Hotel had been cordial, he doubted the aloof private investigator would hold much truck with another approach. He resolved to get out more: join a gym, perhaps. That might be a good way to get to know people. Anything rather than end up lonely and embittered like his dad,

'I suppose you'll want to be going,' Richard Chisolm said, slopping liquid into his saucer. 'Seeing as you've had your tea.'

My Pleasure Entirely

'Good of you to come in,' Susan said, opening the conversation. She'd noted Henry Dundas's injury when they'd met in Reception and hadn't attempted to shake hands. 'Take a seat.'

'My pleasure,' Henry replied, lowering his lanky frame onto a chair. 'Although it's a new experience, I must admit.' His eyes roamed the room's sparse furnishings, the public information posters on the wall. 'I've never been in a police station before, and I did wonder...' His foot tapped a staccato on the floor.

'As I said on the phone,' Susan reassured him, 'you're here on a purely voluntary basis. 'We've a few questions. You may be able to help with our enquiries into an ongoing investigation.'

'Happy to.'

Get the subject relaxed and talking. 'You're an estate agent, is that right?'

'Yes.' He offered an apologetic smile. 'We don't get a good press, I know, but...'

'You must meet a lot of people.'

'I do.'

'Can you confirm you called to these addresses?' She slid a sheet of paper across the table. 'On these dates and times, with a view to being retained to market the properties?'

'I'd need to check.' Henry said. He fumbled in his suit pocket. Drawing out his phone, he thumbed it for a few moments. 'I can, yes,' he said with a concerned expression. 'I do hope there isn't a problem,' he added, putting the phone down.

'I'm sorry to say each of the ladies in question subsequently reported a theft.'

'A theft?' Henry echoed. 'How very distressing.'

'Quite.' Susan observed. 'Can you throw any light on the matter?'

'No. Indeed,' Henry protested, 'I can assure you I left my potential clients in rude health.'

'Can I ask you, now, whether in the course of your employment you have encountered a woman by the name of Annabel Imray?'

'No. Doesn't ring any bells.' He threw her an earnest look. 'Should it?'

'She's well-known in the city. Could it be you've met Ms Imray socially?'

With a grimace, he answered, 'Not a chance. I haven't lived here that long. And I'm a crusty old bachelor, I'm afraid. Don't have what you might call a social life.'

'Where were you on Tuesday, 13th August, between the hours of 8am and 11am?'

'I'd be at work,' Henry answered.

'You're quite sure?'

'Absolutely. Haven't had a day off since I started. Competition's cut-throat for one thing. And the idea of taking a sickie, as they call it...' He wrinkled his nose in distaste. 'I was brought up differently.' He straightened in his seat. 'Backbone, stiff upper lip, all that.'

'You say you were at work on that day,' Susan stated, bringing the interview back to the subject in hand. 'Would that be in the office or...?' She left the question wide open.

'In the office first thing, then out on client appointments if I had valuations to do.'

'And on that particular morning?'

'Mmm,' he mused, reaching for his phone. He opened an app. 'August 13th, did you say?'

Susan nodded.

'That's odd,' he remarked, furrowing his brows. 'There's only one entry showing for that morning: at 11am.' He leaned in conspiratorially. 'I'm not supposed to say, but business isn't exactly buoyant. And as I recall, the meeting was unproductive, sadly.'

'Why was that?'

'I'd have to consult my files, but there are any number of reasons why potential clients don't proceed: they've retained another agent, they've used an online service. Sometimes they call us on a whim and then decide not to sell.'

'We'd want to verify the details of that appointment,' Susan insisted.

'Of course. My office manager will be able to assist you. I'll write down her contact number.'

Susan pushed a pen and pad across the table.

Henry grasped the pen awkwardly between his thumb and forefinger, his stump waggling as he wrote. 'Don't worry,' he caught Susan's eye as he looked up. 'Doesn't hurt.'

'Thanks.' Susan said quickly, to cover her embarrassment. She closed her notebook. 'You've been very helpful, Mr Dundas. We appreciate your co-operation.'

'My pleasure entirely,' Henry answered, with a courtly bow.

Good Underpinnings

'Thought you were skint,' Wilma observed, eyeing the clutch of carrier bags on the dining-room table.

'I am,' Maggie replied. 'I came upon a voucher Val sent for my last birthday. Put it somewhere safe and forgot about it.'

'Val!' Wilma echoed, her tone scathing. 'With her money, you'd think she could have come up with something a bit more...' She wrinkled her nose in distaste. '...special.' She'd been agonising over how - and when - Joe Grogan would get his money back. It hadn't escaped her that Maggie had made no mention of Val offering her a loan. Grippy, was Wilma's verdict. That's how folk like her got rich and stayed rich, in her opinion.

'It's difficult for her,' Maggie rose to her friend's defence. 'Trying to organise anything from Dubai.'

'She doesn't have the internet?' Wilma asked, trying it on.

Maggie flushed. 'Don't be so sarky. I'd as soon have a Markies voucher as anything. The reason I put it away was... probably... because in an emergency I'd be able to use it for food.'

'It's not groceries you've got in there,' Wilma said archly.

'No.'

'Come on, then,' she persisted. 'Show us.'

'None of your business.'

'Ooh,' Wilma cooed. 'Secrets?'

Maggie reached for the bags.

Wilma snatched one from her grasp and upended it onto the table. 'Well,' she eyed the lacy black bra and Brazilian knickers. 'What are you up to?'

'Nothing,' Maggie responded, a little too quickly. 'I need new underwear, that's all.'

Wilma picked up the bra. In her best posh voice she read, 'Nina

Balcony Bra, underwired and padded to lift and separate.'

'It's all right for you,' Maggie grumbled. 'You've got plenty up top. Some of us...' she contemplated her own small breasts, '...need a bit of help.'

'Come on then,' Wilma grinned. 'Let's see the rest.'

'There's not much to see: another bra, a pair of knickers, and some bits and bobs.'

Wilma took a sideswipe at the bags and delved in. 'Twenty-two quid for a bra!' she exclaimed. 'Can't see past Primark myself.'

'That's as maybe, but my things have to last. And, besides, Marks is a whole lot cheaper than Rigby and Peller.'

'Who?'

'Corsetières to the Queen.'

'You learn something every day.' Wilma rolled her eyes. 'I'm sure that will come in handy.'

'Good underpinnings are important' Maggie insisted.

'Aye,' Wilma said. 'Black lace. I can see practicality is the thing.'

'Black doesn't show the dirt,' Maggie shot back. 'Or discolour.'

'What about these?' Wilma waved a pack of stay-up stockings. 'They for work?'

'Don't be facetious,' Maggie said, pink spots of colour on her cheeks. 'I fancied them, that's all.'

'Like you fancied pushing your boobs together,' she dangled a plunge bra. 'And trying out a thong?'

'I don't see what you're getting so worked up about. They were supposed to be a birthday present after all. So what if I was a bit extravagant?'

'Depends who's going to see them,' Wilma fished. Could it be Maggie had found a man? Dropping the bra like it was red-hot, she asked, 'You haven't been on Tinder?'

'Don't be ridiculous.'

Then her heart almost stopped. Had Joe Grogan followed up on his threat when Wilma had stood him up? He hadn't been in touch, but that didn't mean he'd forgotten. Biding his time, more like. His parting words rang in her ears: "If you don't come up with the goods, I'll come looking".

Assuming an innocent expression, she said, 'If you do have a date, you will tell me, won't you?'

Maggie smiled contentedly. 'Of course.'

Gary

'Thanks for coming in.'

Gary Moir shrugged. 'Did I have a choice?"

Douglas offered a placatory smile. 'We've a few questions you might be able to help us find the answers to.'

'In connection with what?'

'If you'll bear with me,' he said, pretending to read through an entry in his file. With Susan Strachan breathing down his neck, these days Douglas was meticulous in doing his interview prep. 'I see you've been in trouble before, Mr Moir.'

Gary's tan paled. 'That was ages ago.'

'2013, it says here. Money-laundering, wasn't it?'

'I was a lot younger then,' Gary protested. 'Impressionable. Someone took advantage of me.'

Probably why you managed to dodge a prison sentence, Douglas thought. 'That someone being?' he enquired.

'Mark Aitchison.'

'Who - correct me if I'm wrong - colluded with you to launder money by making a large number of small deposits through your friends' bank accounts.'

'I didn't think I was doing any harm, not at the time.'

'You were in a position of trust: a bank employee.'

Gary's chin dipped onto his chest.

'Moving on,' Douglas said, beginning to enjoy himself. 'You currently work as an estate agent, is that correct?'

Gary looked up. 'Yes,' he brightened. If you could call it "work". Bit of a skive, actually. Mainly chatting up birds.' He gave a sly wink.

'Your employer is?'

'Property Solutions, one of the fastest-growing...'

'Which is owned by?' Douglas interrupted.

Gary chewed his bottom lip. Then, 'Mark Aitchison,' he muttered, a sullen expression on his face.

'Bit of a coincidence, that,' Douglas said disarmingly. He went for the jugular. 'Can you confirm that you called on these householders on the dates and at the times specified?' He slid a sheet of paper across the table.

Caught unawares, Gary frowned. 'Dunno. I'd need to check my diary.'

Douglas nodded. 'Be my guest.' Watched as he drew his phone from his inside suit pocket, thumbed it for a few moments.

'That's right enough,' Gary confirmed. 'Look, what's all this about?'

'By another coincidence, all the clients you visited subsequently reported thefts.'

'You saying I nicked stuff?'

'Did you?' Douglas asked.

'No,' Gary spluttered. 'What do you take me for?'

'That's what I'm asking you,' Douglas persisted. 'We've already established you're a fraud and a liar.'

'You're barking up the wrong tree,' Gary complained. 'I didn't nick anything from those houses. It would be more than my job is worth.'

'Okay,' Douglas conceded. 'Let's leave that for now. Can you tell me where you were on Tuesday the thirteenth of August between the hours of 8am and 11am?'

Gary smirked. 'Business appointments,' he replied, quick as a flash.

Cocky bugger! 'The appointments, where were they?' Douglas asked, deadpan.

'Let me see,' Gary said, thumbing his phone again. 'Cults and Mannofield.'

'Can anyone vouch for you?'

'The punters, obviously. Anyone else, I'd have to think.'

'Can you tell me their names?' he asked, pen hovering over his notebook.

'Mr and Mrs Shepherd and Mrs Lippe.'

'Give me their phone numbers, will you?'

'Checking up on me, are we?' Gary quipped.

Too right! 'Please do as I ask, so we can eliminate you from our enquiries.'

'Okay.' Sighing, he rattled off the numbers.

Douglas jotted them down. 'And you were there how long?'

'Nine o'clock to just before ten with the Shepherds. Waste of time, if you ask me. Reckon they just wanted to pick my brains. Get an expert opinion, if you know what I mean. Probably end up going to some shite franchise. Online even. False economy.' He threw Douglas a scornful look. 'I got to Mannofield for ten. Stayed a bit longer there. Look...' He made a show of checking his watch. '...is this going to take much longer, I'm a busy man.'

In this market? Douglas thought. *I very much doubt it.*

'Can you confirm for me whether you know a woman by the name of Annabel Imray?'

Gary's orange tan morphed into a sickly shade of yellow. 'That dame in the papers? Christ! You don't think...' His eyes bulged. 'I've absolutely no idea. I've never even met the quine.'

'That right?' Douglas said silkily. 'Then can you explain this to me?' He extracted a press photograph from his file.

Gary peered at the black and white photo: a group of dinner-jacketed men and dressed-to-the-nines women seated at a circular table.

Douglas pointed. 'Is that you?'

Gary nodded.

'Do you recognise anyone else in this photograph, Gary?'

He took another look. 'My boss, obviously.'

'And that would be?' Douglas prompted.

'Mark Aitchison.'

'Ah, yes.' Douglas was having fun. 'He of the money laundering scam and...'

'It wasn't like that,' Gary contested. 'It was an agency bash. One of many. Mark is very into networking.'

'So I understand,' Douglas said, with a sly grin.

'Not the way you're implying. It was just a meal. A few drinks. Bit of a long night, to be honest with you.'

'Never mind. Let's move on. Is there anyone else you know?' He pointed, again, at the photograph.

'No,' Gary insisted.

'What about this woman?'

His eyes slid to the left. 'Don't think so.'

'Take a closer look.'

Gary lowered his head. Then, 'Christ!' he exclaimed. 'It's her, isn't it, the quine in the papers?'

'And this event is where you met Annabel Imray?'

'I never met her.' Gary responded, wild-eyed. 'We were sitting at opposite sides of this muckle great table. Plus, there was a bloody great flower arrangement in the centre, candles and all.'

'And you didn't try to chat her up,' Douglas insinuated, disbelieving? A looker like her?'

'Why would I? She was too old for me.'

'And that would stop you having a go?'

'You've got to believe me,' Gary said, looking close to tears. 'We never exchanged two words.'

Kevin

The sun was out, but the elevated site of the Altens breaker's yard exposed it to the worst of the north-east weather. A snell wind stung Wilma's ears as she tugged open the door of the Portakabin that served as an office. She'd been running credit checks the whole morning and was going stir-crazy. *Slow and steady?* It was alright for Maggie Laird, out dressed to the nines drumming up business. Wilma resolved to find some action of her own.

She pushed through a second door. 'Andy,' she greeted the sallow weasel of a man who sat behind the desk. 'Fit like?' Lapsing into her native Doric, she offered the standard greeting.

HIs eyes darted from her to the desktop and back again. 'Aye chaffin awa,' came the stock response.

She brightened. Since the day she'd raced the fraudster in the souped-up Mondeo along the Lang Stracht, Wilma had forged an acquaintance with Andy McManus, the chop shop owner. In her view, the PI business couldn't have too many connections, dubious or otherwise.

'You busy? Her gaze lighted upon the hooded figure seated opposite, head lowered. She took a couple of swift steps forward. 'What the hell are you doing here?'

Kevin raised his head. 'What do you think?' he mumbled. 'Looking for spare parts.'

'What for?' Wilma demanded.

'A car.'

'You don't own a fuckin car.'

'Not my car.' He threw her a shifty look. 'Somebody else's.'

'Who else's?' She clocked the black and silver object lying on the desk. 'I get it,' she identified it as a device used in keyless car theft. 'You been nickin motors again?'

'Naw,' her younger son protested. 'Ah'm here doin a wee job for a mate.'

'That you?' Wilma turned on Andy.

'Leave me outta this.' Palming the device, he rose and headed for the door.

Wilma stuck her face in Kevin's. 'What sort of job?' From her background research, she was well aware that keyless car theft had spiked by almost fifty percent over the past few years. Using equipment sourced on the internet or from Eastern Europe, a thief can detect and amplify a car key's signal through a house door or window and send it to the transmitter of his accomplice, who can then open the vehicle and drive away.

'Come on, Ma.' he fingered the peak of his Adidas baseball cap. 'Stop giving me grief. Me an ma mate, we wis jist hangin oot.'

'Don't you "grief" me.' With the back of one hand Wilma landed a stinging blow. 'Wee fucker that you are.'

'Ow!' Kevin rubbed his right cheek. 'That hurt.'

'Aye,' Wilma observed drily. 'It was meant to.'

He took his hand away from his face to reveal an angry red splodge.

'So,' she set her jaw, 'ye've been nickin motors.'

Kevin looked at the floor. He didn't reply.

'On yer own, wis ye?'

The silence lengthened, then, 'Aye.'

Wilma landed another crack. 'Dinna give me that shite.'

Kevin's hand flew to his face once more. 'But, Ma...'

'Takes twa tae tango.' Wilma knew the scam was operated by thieves working in pairs and could be executed in seconds. 'Wan tae hold the transmitter, the ither tae check oot the hoose wi the amplifier.' She pinched Kevin's other cheek. Hard. 'Dae ye think ah wis born yesterday?'

He scuffed the sides of his trainers together until they squeaked.

'Ye workin' wi Wayne?'

'Naw.'

'Who, then?'

No answer.

'The gear,' she continued.

'It's legal,' Kevin muttered.

'Legal tae buy, mebbe,' Wilma shot back, aware police can only arrest someone using a scanner if they can prove intent to steal. 'Canna be yours,' she added, frowning. The last time she'd looked online, the scanners had been advertised at around ten grand. She grabbed Kevin by the scruff of the neck. 'Is that the deal: you an yer mate nick the motors. Andy moves them on?' Stolen cars, she knew, were shipped abroad, given a new identity or broken for spares.

'Never mind.' Wilma's eyes narrowed. 'Ah'll mak it ma business tae find oot.'

A Complaint

'What's this?' Detective Chief Inspector Edward Scrimgeour demanded, waving a sheet of paper in the air.

'No idea, sir.' Across the desk, Allan Chisolm shifted in his seat. A summons from his superior was always unwelcome, doubly so given the added pressure his team was under.

'Don't come the smart Alec with me,' Scrimgeour barked, moon-face the colour of pickled beetroot. He thrust the paper under Chisolm's nose.

'It's a Complaints Form,' his DI observed.

'Full marks, Detective Inspector. You didn't get those pips for nothing.'

'Sir,' Chisolm acknowledged. He waited for what was coming.

'Shame you haven't put them to better use.' Scrimgeour spat, stabbing a fat forefinger at the form. 'Read what it says here.'

Below the Police Scotland crest and the heading, 'Personal Information', Chisolm read, 'Dr Ursula Evershed.'

'Quite so.' Scrimgeour snapped. 'And the date of the incident?'

Chisolm ran his eyes down to, *Details of your complaint.* His mood darkened when he saw the names of the officers involved. *Souter and Miller. What the hell had they done now*? Clearing his throat, he answered, '13th August.'

'You get my point?' Scrimgeour barked.

'Yes sir.' His stomach knotted. They were near enough into September.

'This cat,' Scrimgeour ran on.

Jesus Christ! Chisolm wasn't one for swearing, but this took the biscuit. He scanned down the form to the box where details of the complaint were entered. Sure enough: tabby cat by the name of Malthus missing from High Street, Old Aberdeen.

'The complainant - Doctor Evershed - heads a research team at the University of Aberdeen. A critically acclaimed research team, attracting very significant inward investment.' He broke off, fixing Chisolm with a hard stare. 'You see where I'm going with this?'

'Affirmative,' Chisolm said, feigning humility.

'It transpires the animal is Dr Evershed's...' Scrimgeour looked up to the yellowing ceiling tiles for inspiration. '...what one might call constant companion.'

Child substitute. Chisolm sighed inwardly, picturing the reaction of his already overstretched team. 'In my defence, sir,' he responded. 'We've had a spate of reported thefts this past couple of months. My team are working their socks off, but we're a sergeant short and there's a limit to...' He broke off, judging it imprudent to remind his DCI around forty thousand man-hours had been lost by Police Scotland the previous year due to stress-related illness.

With a wave of the hand, Scrimgeour batted his excuses away. 'It's not good enough, Inspector, for a member of the public to be fobbed off with a reference number and then not hear another thing.'

'But, sir, with all due respect,' Chisolm said, choosing his words with care. 'Uniformed officers followed up with a house visit and took a statement, which—'

Scrimgeour cut him short. 'The complainant has made a number of enquiries of us since, both by telephone and in person. We're already getting a bad press: petty crime downgraded, no police presence on the streets.'

Chisolm could have told him the reasons why. They included the escalation in 999 calls for minor incidents – including as a taxi service – and the need to look after vulnerable people suffering from drugs or alcohol dependency or mental illness. 'Forgive me, sir,' he said. 'But I don't understand what CID...'

'For your further information, DI Chisolm, Dr Evershed happens to be the chief constable's sister-in-law.' Eyeballing Chisolm, he asked, 'You get my drift?'

Now, Chisolm knew where this was going. 'Sir,' he said, thoroughly downhearted.

'The Fifth Floor are leaning on me,' Scrimgeour confided, pulling a folded linen handkerchief from his tunic pocket and dabbing at his bald pate. 'I can't stress how important it is we bring this to a satisfactory conclusion.'

'Understood.'

'And Inspector,' Scrimgeour barked, snapping his fingers.

'Sir?'

'Get me a result.'

Beach Babes

'Whose idea was this?' Maggie huffed, as the rain started to spit.

'I hold my hands up,' Wilma replied with a sheepish grin.

They were power-walking along the beach before breakfast to kick off a new regime of diet and exercise. It had taken all of Val's strictures and Maggie's new underwear to bring home how out of condition she was.

'I still don't understand why we couldn't have gone to your gym?' she complained, her ancient plimsolls gritty with sand.

'Too dear,' Wilma snapped, with rather more force than she'd intended. She was kitted out for the occasion in snakeskin-print leggings and gold trainers topped by a day-glo lime mesh tee, strands of bleached hair escaping from a red baseball cap worn back-to-front on her head.

'Can't be that expensive.' Maggie retorted, stung, 'if all those unemployed lads can afford to go.'

'Kids get a discount,' Wilma snarled, side-stepping to avoid a puddle of seawater.

'Still,' Maggie pondered. 'Surely we could get season tickets?'

'A season ticket's not cheap,' Wilma countered. 'And the beach costs sweet Fanny Adams. Work it out. You're the one needs to balance the books.'

'I get that,' Maggie acknowledged. 'But you have to weigh it against the fact it would be a whole lot more amenable to work out under cover than subject ourselves to this.' Throwing her hands in the air, she looked up at the sky, which offered a palette of unremitting grey.

Wilma followed her gaze. 'Fifty Shades,' she quipped. 'Only not.' Then, registering Maggie's thunderous look, added, 'It won't rain for long. The forecast says...'

'They never get it right,' Maggie interrupted. 'And we won't be able to do this all year round, whereas we can at the gym.'

'This is far healthier.'

'If you say so,' Maggie grumbled, wiping her forehead, whether of rain or sweat she had no idea. 'And another thing, you can box in any old clothes, you don't need special kit. '

'You don't need special kit to do this.'

'Yes, you do.' Maggie protested, waving an arm at a straggle of joggers. 'Look at those folk. I bet their outfits are breathable and their trainers cushioned. And get those things they wear on their wrists.'

'That's jogging,' Wilma muttered obstinately. 'Walking's different.'

'Plus,' Maggie persisted, fighting for breath, 'the gym's closer to home.'

'No, it's not.'

'Yes, it is.'

Wilma answered through clenched teeth. 'Depends what road you take.' Scowling, she took off her cap and turned it right way round, tugging the brim down over her eyes.

The rain had come on in earnest: fat drops blown sideways by a sharp wind off the North Sea.

'I still don't see,' Maggie said, turning up the collar of her fleece, 'why we can't go to your boxing gym? Surely Joe would–?'

On the nail, Wilma thought morosely. She didn't dare dwell on what Joe Grogan would do. To either of them. Or both.

Grabbing Maggie's jacket by the collar, Wilma stuck her face in hers.

'Drop it,' she said.

X

Slick Willie

'How did it go with the estate agents?' Chisolm enquired. He turned to his constable. 'Douglas?'

'Gary Moir is a bit of a Slick Willie, in my opinion,' Douglas responded.

Takes one to know one, Susan thought.

'He also has previous. From way back. A chancer, I'd say. But insists he never stole anything from those houses nor met Annabel Imray, although we can place him sitting across the table from her at a social event.'

'Couple of years ago, wasn't it?' Brian countered. 'She might have looked different then.'

'Not that different. Plus, she's been in the newspapers day in and day out. He'd have been hard-pressed to miss her. He's supplied details of a couple of client appointments for the morning of 13th August, which we're in the process of checking out.'

'Moving on to you, Susan,' Chisolm said with an encouraging look. 'Henry Dundas, how did it go there?

'Turned out to be a toff. One of those old-school types: privately educated, presentable, if a bit down-at-heel. Perfect manners. He professes to be single.'

'Bet he's a poofter,' Duffy muttered. 'Them boarding schools are breeding grounds for that sort of stuff.'

Susan ignored him. 'Dundas says he's innocent of those thefts and has never met Annabel. He only had one appointment on the morning of the thirteenth. However, he happily volunteered his office manager's contact number for verification, although I haven't managed to get hold of her yet.'

'What was your overall impression?' Chisolm pressed.

'Hard to say. He has that veneer of self-confidence you get with his sort, but although he's a tall guy, quite good-looking in an old-fashioned kind of way, he came across as a bit lost.'

Douglas sniffed. 'My heart bleeds.'

'Lost as in?' Chisolm prompted.

'Distant,' Susan replied.

'It's not a crime to be introverted,' Brian reminded her.

'No,' she acknowledged. 'That's probably it. He wasn't evasive, more... ' She hesitated. '...fey, I suppose is the word I'm looking for. Probably not helped by the fact he had half his right forefinger missing. Inoffensive, I'd say, overall.'

'Looks like my theory is dead in the water,' Brian said morosely.

'Not entirely,' Chisolm observed. 'The victims of these thefts are all householders, some of them indeed looking to sell.'

'But we haven't got anything useful out of Gary Moir or Henry Dundas,' Brian grumbled. 'And we've established both were in at least three of these houses on the day of the theft.'

'Have we, though?' Susan queried. Of the victims we've taken statements from, Mrs Troup, is now saying she might not have lost the item after all, Miranda Maitland isn't certain about the time frame. Judith McNair had a number of agents through, but she's so strung-out she can't remember one from another.'

'And don't forget Mrs Sinclair,' Douglas piped up. 'She doesn't know the time of bloody day.'

'I reckon the analysts have ballsed up,' Duffy growled.

'Always a possibility,' Chisolm acquiesced. 'But until we're told otherwise, we'll have to press on. Follow up on those appointments, you two. Meantime...' He paused for breath. '...let's go back to the beginning: what do we know for sure?'

'The victims are all female,' Susan volunteered.

'Living alone,' Douglas added. 'Or near as, in Cara Gilmore's case.'

'Which raises the question,' Chisolm continued. 'What else might link them apart from their homes?'

'Their past?' Douglas again. 'They all went to the same school or uni?'

'Doesn't work,' Brian came back in. 'Too broad an age range.'

'Social media?' Douglas persisted. 'They're all Facebook friends, whatever?'

'Unlikely.' Susan shot him down. 'They're a pretty random bunch.'

'Or members of the same club,' Douglas pressed on doggedly. 'Gym, book group, bridge four?'

'How about same GP?' Bob Duffy suggested, coming to life. 'Women, if they're not pre-menstrual they're pregnant. And if they're not pregnant they're menopausal. And if they're none of those they're fucking depressed.'

'That's the most ignorant, most–' Susan launched at him.

'It's a valid point,' Chisolm observed. 'We can't rule anything out, and I'm a firm believer on drawing on our collective experience. Before we go chasing off in different directions, I suggest we trust our first instincts. Talking of chasing in different directions,' he said, cracking his knuckles so forcefully Susan feared he might break them. 'We've been tasked with another... Ahem!' Loudly clearing his throat, he enunciated, '...project.'

'You have to be joking,' Duffy spluttered. 'I'm already long overdue for a sickie.'

'Something more rewarding than sodding theft, I hope,' Douglas opined.

'I hate to disappoint you,' Chisolm said, deadpan. 'But it appears a cat has gone missing from Old Aberdeen.'

'So?' Duffy challenged. 'Where's the crime? And how come it landed on us?'

'For one, the owner is now alleging it was stolen.'

'Oh, come on,' Douglas said, unable to help himself. 'Cats go missing all the time. So I'm told,' he added, catching his sergeant's warning look.

'That's as may be,' Brian remarked, trying to divert Chisolm's attention. Dunn should know better by now than to question the chain of command. 'What makes the owner think it was stolen?'

'Out of character,' Duffy quipped.

'Very funny.' Brian muttered. He had been up since dawn trying to get the hang of his mantra and was in no mood for jokes.

'Belongs to an academic,' Chisolm responded. 'Single lady. Child substitute...' He looked down at his notes. '...the way this reads.'

'What does the woman want?' Duffy chipped in. 'Fucking police helicopter?'

Chisolm ignored him. 'You should be aware the lady in question is related to the chief constable.'

'I get it,' Duffy said, ducking his head.

'And given what we've already got from our criminal intelligence analysts about this unusual string of thefts, we'd better make doubly sure this isn't connected. Douglas,' addressing his constable, 'since you seem to be the authority in the room, I'm tasking you with this.'

'But...' Douglas began.

'If there are any gaps in your knowledge, Susan will keep you right.'

Douglas gave her the evils. 'Sir,' he muttered.

Suppressing a laugh, Susan fixed her eyes on the floor.

Worried About Mum

Kirsty was in the university's main library on Small's Wynd when her phone signalled an incoming FaceTime call from Colin. Sighing, she declined. She was just getting to grips with a particularly obtuse piece of case law when another call flashed up. Putting a marker in her book, she grabbed her phone and ran down the stairs to the PC internet cafe on the ground floor.

'What?' she said when Colin answered.

'I'm worried about Mum.'

'What about her?'

'She's behaving oddly.'

Kirsty snorted. 'That's unusual?'

'Seriously,' Colin said. 'She's started wearing high heels. Mum never wears heels. Not to work, anyhow.'

Sighing, Kirsty said, 'If that's all you're ringing about, I've an essay to write. And it has to be in for tomorrow, so...'

'Plus, there's all this new stuff in the bathroom. Smelly stuff. She was in there for hours last night, and when she came out she was clarted in make-up.'

'You think she's dating someone?' Kirsty asked, her voice heavy with suspicion. She still hadn't got over the sight of her mum cosying up to creepy Brian.

'Dunno. She's been out drinking with Wilma, though.'

'No!'

'I'm telling you.'

'Bloody woman. Did Mum come home drunk?'

'Not drunk. But tipsy, definitely.'

'You think they were out on the prowl?' Kirsty was familiar with the cougar phenomenon: women of a certain age chasing after younger men.

'Mum was dressed to the nines, that's for sure. Agency business, she said, but...' He broke off, uncertain. 'She's had a couple of men at the house, as well.'

'When?'

'During the day. Not that she said, but I heard Wilma slagging them off.'

'And you think they were...?'

'I don't know what to think. Plus, it's not just the heels and the lippy and stuff, I caught her swearing yesterday.'

'So?'

'Properly swearing. Effing and blinding. Plus, she was talking to herself.'

'Mmm.' Last time she was home, Kirsty had registered a change in her mother, but hadn't thought more of it.

'D'you think she's having....' Colin hesitated. 'You know...the thing?'

'What thing?' Kirsty repeated testily.

'The women's thing,' he ventured.

'No,' Kirsty snapped. 'I don't. Now, if you don't mind, I'm supposed to be studying.'

'Sorry.'

'And, Colin....'

'What?'

'Don't call me again.'

Formula One

Susan exited the DHQ building by the back door, where a scatter of fag-ends on the tarmac testified to the smokers' station. She crossed the Rear Podium Car Park to where a pool car sat, engine idling, Douglas impatiently tapping his fingers on the steering wheel.

'Sorry,' she said, slipping into the passenger seat. In truth, she was fizzing at being caught on the back foot.

'Pain in the arse, this.' Douglas spoke through clenched teeth, manoeuvring the Vauxhall saloon down the ramp and round onto Queen Street.

'You said it.' For once, Susan was in wholehearted agreement. Coming on top of the Imray case and the burgeoning list of thefts their team been tasked with investigating, a missing cat was all they needed, even it was related by proxy to the chief constable.

Douglas swung right onto Broad Street, right again at Littlejohn Street, crossed West North Street into Mealmarket Street and turned left onto King Street, the main artery between Union Street and points north.

Long road for a shortcut. Susan could hear her Gran's voice. She'd have nipped up the Gallowgate past Mounthooly roundabout and taken The Spital, then College Bounds before it became the High Street. 'There's no point in moaning,' Susan countered. 'We've been tasked with it and that's that.'

'I mean,' Douglas moaned, not letting up. 'Who would nick a bloody cat?'

'Allegedly. According to the boss, complainant only said it was missing on the Complaints Form.'

'That's what it says,' Douglas corrected. 'But according to Steady Eddie...'

'Don't call him that,' Susan chided. 'One of these days you'll get caught in the act, and then where will you be?'

'If you'll let me finish,' Douglas turned, scowling. 'DCI Scrimgeour told the boss victim is now adamant the cat has been stolen.' He turned back. 'Waste of police resources, if you ask me.'

'People are very protective of their pets,' Susan observed, trying to lower the temperature.

'Dogs, I could imagine. But, cats?'

'Have you never heard of the Cats Protection League?'

'Nope.'

'They're a charity,' Susan explained, with as much patience as she could muster. Sometimes, being stuck with Douglas was like caring for a small child. 'Offer advice on caring for your pet, arrange adoptions, provide a grief support service.'

'Grief support? You're having me on.'

'Straight up. I Googled it after we were handed the action. Some of the listings on the Memory Wall would reduce you to tears.'

'You, maybe.' Douglas said scornfully. 'Wouldn't faze me.'

Susan wondered what it *would* take? Thus far, her fellow DC had exhibited emotional Teflon armour. But everybody had a weak spot. Susan prided herself on keeping her cool, but once in a while she'd managed to soldier through the day, only to break down in tears the minute she got home.

'Seriously. "Sent to rainbow bridge yesterday" – that sort of thing.'

'Bloody hell!' Douglas spluttered. 'Who'd have believed?'

'All I'm saying is it's obvious from my research that people who're into cats are utterly devoted to them. Spend a fortune on them, too. You must have seen the ads for natural foods. And don't get me started on the gear. There are companies online offering contemporary cat stands at near on seven hundred pounds, I'll have you know. You can even get cat prescriptions.'

'Yeah, yeah,' he yawned, not bothering to cover his mouth. 'The only thing I'm interested in right now is getting a result. The sooner we find the frigging thing, the sooner we get it back to its owner. And the sooner we do that, the sooner we return to serious policing.'

Susan didn't respond. When he wasn't behaving like a spoiled child, Douglas could be a pompous prick.

'Did you see that?' Changing down a gear, he gunned the car through a set of traffic lights.

'What?'

'Thought I spotted the cat.'

'Where?'

'There,' he pointed, swerving around a corner into Orchard Street. Sure enough, a striped marmalade cat streaked from the road ahead onto the pavement.

'You're breaking the speed limit,' Susan yelled, one eye on the speedometer.

'Hang on!' Douglas responded, speaking through clenched teeth.

'But...' Susan protested.

'Shut up and hold on,' Douglas commanded, flooring the accelerator. 'Christ,' he swore. 'This thing's clapped-out.'

You would know! Douglas saw himself as a bit of a Lewis Hamilton. He was forever bumming off about the modifications he'd made to his own Audi. Susan watched as the cat zig-zagged up the pavement before squeezing through a privet hedge and disappearing out of sight. 'Calm down,' she urged. 'You've lost it.'

Easing off the gas, Douglas turned, pink-faced. 'And whose bloody fault is that?'

'Don't blame me,' Susan countered. 'I...' She stopped short, as a giggle started in her throat and worked its way out.

'Don't know what you're finding so funny?' Douglas snapped. 'We could have had this thing wrapped up and be back at DHQ.'

'Did you even look at the photograph?' Susan asked, her shoulders heaving.

'Course I did,' he insisted. 'Orange. Black stripes.' His eyes narrowed. 'Same as that frigging thing you've just made me lose.'

Except,' Susan retorted. 'That cat wasn't long-haired. It didn't bear the least resemblance to Malthus. Can you imagine what would happen if we went back with the wrong cat? You can forget your sergeant's exam, and that's just for starters.'

She watched in smug silence as the colour drained from Douglas's face.

A Flier

'Sarge?' Susan called, running Brian to ground in the canteen.

Cramming the last of a Kit-Kat into his mouth, he looked up. 'What?'

'A word?' she said, advancing on his table.

Brian covered the chocolate wrapper with one hand. 'I can give you five.' Scrunching it up, he stuffed it into his trouser pocket, not wanting to be caught breaking his much-vaunted healthy eating plan. Especially by Susan. She'd been unimpressed when he told her he'd invested in a juicer. Said he'd be far better eating a balanced diet and cutting back on junk food and booze. Brian sighed. He knew his young constable talked sense, but sometimes she sounded like his bloody mother.

Now, Susan dropped onto the seat opposite. 'Thought you should see this,' she confided, extracting a folded sheet of paper from her shoulder bag.

'What is it?" Brian asked.

'See for yourself.' She slid it across the table.

Brian unfolded the A4 sheet. 'Christ,' he exhaled noisily. 'Where did you get this?'

'Old Aberdeen,' Susan replied. 'Picked it up in Ross the baker when Douglas and I were tasked to follow up that Dr Evershed's complaint.'

'The baker?' Brian queried.

'Yes, Sarge. I checked with all the local shops: up the High Street, down St Machar Drive onto King Street.'

'What was Douglas doing?' Brian asked pointedly.

'He was driving.'

'And I don't suppose he sent you into the Auld Toon Cafe for a fine piece?' Brian teased.

'Sarge?' Susan exclaimed, her innocent expression belied by the two bright spots of colour in her cheeks.

Brian shrugged. 'Never mind.' Cocky wee bastard was probably sitting on a double yellow, treating Strachan like his personal skivvy. He made a mental note to task his constable with something especially tiresome the next opportunity he had. Talk about tiresome! With an effort, Brian brought his mind back to the present.

'Harcus & Laird' he read. How in hell had Maggie Laird got herself mixed up in this one? The Seaton business he could understand. She'd worked in close proximity to those kids. Struthers and Milne - the other two major police investigations she'd almost scuppered - her agency had been retained to handle. But a missing cat? Either Maggie was on her uppers or she'd lost it completely. Come to think, when Brian had seen her last, she had looked a bit spaced-out.

'What are you saying to it?' Susan asked, breaking his train of thought.

Shit and fuck! That's what.

Brian wondered how in hell he was going to break the news to Chisolm.

'Leave it with me,' he said.

A Bidey-In

'Do you understand why we've brought you back in,' Douglas asked, with a glance at the lawyer who sat by Gary's side.

'Haven't a monkeys,' Gary replied, with a flash of Colgate Max. 'But if you're still on about me nicking stuff, you're on a hiding to nothing.'

'Tuesday, 13th August. You may recall the last time we met I asked you to explain your whereabouts between the hours of 8am and 11am on that date.'

'Which I did,' Gary insisted, his toothpaste smile barely faltering.

'You did, indeed.' Douglas confirmed, fixing him with a hard stare.

'Is there a problem?' Gary queried, fingering the lapels of his Prince of Wales suit.

'Should there be?'

'I don't know.'

He looked shifty, thought Brian, sitting alongside.

Douglas decided to play a while longer. 'You told me you attended an appointment in Cults at nine and stayed until approximately ten o'clock Is that correct?'

Gary nodded.

'Please answer for the tape,' Brian interjected.

'Yes.'

'That's not quite true, is it, Gary?'

'It is true,' he protested. 'My appointment was arranged for nine o'clock and...' He stopped, floundering.

'Let me help you out, ' Douglas said. 'You did, indeed, turn up to your appointment at nine o'clock. But once it became obvious that the Shepherds were wasting your time, you made your excuses and left.'

'What did you expect me to do?' Gary muttered. 'A good chunk of my wages is made up of commission.'

'You then proceeded by car to a second appointment in Mannofield?' Douglas again.

'That's right,' Gary replied. 'My ten o'clock.'

He consulted his notes. 'You stayed at that address, and I quote, "A bit longer".

Gary threw a glance at Brian. 'Yes.'

'How much longer?'

Gary shifted on the hard seat. 'Can't remember.'

'Rough guess?' Douglas prompted.

'An hour. Hour and a quarter, maybe.'

'Mmm.' Douglas let the ensuing silence lengthen into one minute, then two, the only sound in the room Gary's foot drumming a small tattoo under the table. 'Then, will you explain to me why the householder said you rang up and asked to postpone the appointment until the following week?'

'I...'

'Which I've no doubt will be verified by a search of your phone records.'

Gary balked. 'You can't touch my phone.'

'We'll see,' Douglas said archly.

'Maybe this is a good time to take a break,' Brian intervened. He eyeballed Gary. 'So you can have a think about things.'

*

'When we spoke earlier,' Douglas said, after coming back into the room and running through the preliminaries. 'I asked you to explain the discrepancy in your statement regarding your whereabouts on the morning of Tuesday, 13th August? Now you've had time to consider your position, is there anything you want to add?'

Gary gave his lawyer the nod.

'My client wishes to intimate that he did, indeed, postpone his meeting with Mrs Lippe due to a last-minute change in priorities.'

'A change in priorities?' Douglas echoed. 'And what would that be?'

'Another call came in, so I asked the Lippe woman if she was happy to leave it until the following week?' Gary jutted his chin. 'Is that a problem?'

'Not if you can explain your whereabouts during the time frame in question.'

'Well,' he shifted in his seat. 'That's the thing.'

Douglas feigned puzzlement. He guessed what was coming.

'I was with someone.'

'Would you care to elaborate?'

'A woman.'

'On business?'

Gary's face flushed scarlet. 'What do you think?'

'Can anyone vouch for you?'

'No.'

'We'll need a name and address,'

'Do I have to?' Gary protested. He turned to his solicitor, who gave a curt nod. 'I mean...' He appealed to the detectives in turn. '... it was in the firm's time. And she's married. If it came out...'

''Fraid so,' Douglas said, putting the boot in. 'If you'd like to write the details down for me.' He pushed a pad and pen across the table.

With a shaky hand, Gary wrote in wonky capitals.

Douglas retrieved the pad without comment. 'Moving on, do you recall from out last conversation I asked you about this woman.' He slid a photograph across the table. 'For the tape, I'm showing the suspect a photograph of the victim, Annabel Imray.'

'So what?' Gary replied, his tone defiant.

Douglas made a show of consulting his notes. 'At that time, you denied having ever spoken to the deceased.'

'That's correct.'

'You maintain you knew Annabel Imray by sight, but had never engaged in conversation?'

Gary sighed. 'I told you at the time. She was too old for me. Too tall. And, anyhow...' He pulled a dismissive face. '...she wasn't my type.'

'So, how come,' Douglas insinuated, 'you were photographed sharing a meal. A rather intimate meal. For the benefit of the recording, I'm showing Mr Moir a photographic documentary production.'

Gary stared at the photograph, his face bleached of colour.

'That is you, Gary, isn't it?' Douglas prompted.

He nodded, mute.

'Sharing a table with Ms Imray? A table for two?'

'I can explain.'

'Please do.'

'It was a business meeting.'

'About what?'

'I can't say.'

'Why not?'

'She was a client.' Gary mumbled into his shirt. 'It's confidential.'

'And is it usual,' Douglas continued, 'for your so-called business meetings to be accompanied by champagne?'

'Mark...' He broke off. 'My boss likes the firm to make a good impression.'

Douglas rolled his eyes. 'I'll say.' He stabbed a finger at the photograph. 'Taittinger, if I'm not mistaken.'

'Annabel likes the best,' Gary retorted.

'It's Annabel now, is it?' Douglas challenged. 'I put it to you you've told us a bunch of porkies regarding your movements on the morning of Tuesday, 13th August.'

'I haven't,' Gary snivelled. 'God's honest truth.'

'You expect me to believe that?' Douglas responded, affecting incredulity. 'When I've documented evidence...' He banged a hand on the file in front of him. '...that you're a crook and a liar, and...'

'If you'll give me time,' Gary wheedled. 'I'll talk to the bint I was with on the 13th. Tell her it's important.'

'Persuade her to perjure herself?' Douglas insinuated.

'No.'

'What, then?'

Gary's head slumped onto his chest. 'I don't know.'

The Bervie Chipper

Handily situated beside a bus stop in the Cowgate, the fish and chip shop in the village of Inverbervie – otherwise known as The Bervie Chipper – was a legend. Wilma had been sitting in her car outside for the best part of twenty minutes, her stomach growling, as a raggle-taggle group of workmen and schoolkids assembled, waiting for opening time at four-thirty.

She'd been stuck in the house again that day, sitting at her computer trying to run down defaulters. Hacked off, she'd a notion to take a run down the coast. She'd a trace outstanding on a man whose last known address had been a farm cottage in Arbuthnott.

It was a fine day, the sea shimmering below the cliffs at Catterline. As she drove through the Howe o' the Mearns, fields of barley and wheat stood tall on either side of the road, and oilseed rape glowed butter-yellow in the sunshine.

'Sit-in or take-away?' the whey-faced lass behind the counter asked when, finally, Wilma got to the head of the queue and placed her order. The choice was too seductive. 'Sit-in,' she replied. Ian was working a late shift that night. And, besides, he'd valeted her car a couple of days before, clearing out the accumulated crisp packets and Diet Coke bottles and general debris. She'd best not take it home reeking of fish and chips.

The downstairs seating area – simply furnished with grey laminate tables and pink faux leather seats – was quiet: one old man in a cloth cap and a granny with a couple of teenagers silently thumbing their phones while they waited for the fish to fry. Wilma installed herself in a seat facing the window and placed her handbag by the chair-leg. Her gut rumbled. With an effort, she drew in her stomach muscles. Her control knickers had been fighting a losing battle for months. She made a mental note to invest in a new pair.

Wilma watched as a streamlined coach drew up at the door, and decanted its passengers onto the narrow pavement. They filed through the door and up the stairs: Club 80-90, the majority female, in polyester slacks and shapeless cardigans. The living dead.

The auld mannie caught her eye. 'Fit like?' He touched a gnarled hand to the peak of his bunnet.

Wilma ducked. She was bloody starving by now, and not in the mood for conversation. She reached for the menu. She'd ordered haddock and chips, but now she was here... Her saliva ran as she read the dessert selection: sticky toffee pudding, syrup sponge, chocolate pudding with chocolate sauce. '...she might as well have a proper dinner.

'Braw day!' The old man appeared at her elbow. Clad in faded blue dungarees and baggy tweed jacket, he bore the weathered complexion of a farm worker. 'Fit's a bonnie quine like you doin...?' He made to sit down.

'Fuck off,' she hissed under her breath. Not quietly enough, for the granny at the next table tutted loudly. The situation was saved by the arrival of Wilma's order. 'Whoarr!' she let out a long whoosh of breath as she eyed the plate of food: a fat haddock encased in crispy batter was crowned by a sharp lemon wedge. Alongside, a small pyre of chips begged to be doused in salt and vinegar. The whole was accompanied by a dense morass of mushy peas.

She picked up her knife and fork. Speared a chip. Chewed. She seasoned the chips with salt and a generous sprinkling of vinegar, then cut into the fish, watching the firm white flesh flake apart. Wilma had raised a greedy helping halfway to her mouth when a large ginger cat jumped onto the table, a paw shot out and swiped the fish from under her nose.

With a blood-curdling yell, she dropped her cutlery and whacked the animal on the nose.

Skittering to the floor, its fur went up, almost doubling its size. Then it turned on her, teeth bared, hissing and making an almighty din.

Wilma leapt to her feet. Reluctant as she was to forgo her fish supper, the cat roughly fitted the description of Malthus. But what was he doing in Bervie? And did she bloody care?

Wilma took a last, lingering look at her fish supper.

Then she turned on the cat. Ugly fucker! She'd bloody show it who was boss.

But before she could make a move, with a disdainful backward glance, it shot across the restaurant and out the open door.

Story of My Life

'Boss?' Brian said, edging the office door open. 'You wanted to see me?'

Chisolm raised his head from a sea of paperwork. 'Yes. Have a seat.' He gathered files into an untidy bundle and set them aside. 'I wanted to have a private word.'

Brian's heart pumped. This might be the news he'd been waiting for: a summons to go before the board for inspector.

'DC Dunn,' Chisolm began, wasting no time.

Brian's chest deflated. He'd built up his hopes, only to see them dashed. And not for the first time. *Story of my life!* he thought morosely, waiting for what was coming next.

'We've received a complaint...'

'Yes,' Brian acknowledged. 'The cat. I've tasked—'

'If you'll let me finish.'

Brian dipped his chin. 'Yes, sir.'

'...from a pedestrian in connection with a speeding car.'

'Sir?'

'Which transpires to be one of our pool cars, signed out by DC Dunn.'

'Was Dunn in the driver's seat?'

'Appears so. The complainant identified the vehicle's occupants as a male and a female and stated the male was at the wheel.' Chisolm drummed his fingers on the desktop. 'It goes without saying, Sergeant, coming on top of a homicide, a spate of bizarre thefts and a disgruntled university luminary, the last thing we need is for one of our already undermanned team to be suspended.'

Brian felt nauseous. He'd drunk a green juice at 6am and precious little since. 'The complainant?' he croaked, eyeing the half-empty glass of water sitting at Chisolm's elbow.

'Number withheld, and wouldn't leave her name. Could be a curtain-twitcher. Nonetheless, I expect you to put the fear of death into Dunn.'

'He's had it coming,' Brian acknowledged. 'Him and Strachan have been at one another's throats.'

The corners of Chisolm's mouth twitched. 'Not always a bad thing. Keeps the pair of them on their toes.'

'That's all well and good, but the way the lad's always putting himself out there,' he contended. 'He'll probably do well.' Said with a bitter smile.

'Douglas thinks I don't know what he gets up to,' Chisolm confided. 'More fool he. But enough of that. Whilst you're here, Brian,' he said, his voice mellowing. 'I haven't forgotten about the promotion board.'

Brian's heart turned a somersault. 'Boss?'

'Susan is an intelligent and committed officer,' Chisolm went on. 'And I've little doubt – when the time comes – she will do well in her sergeant's exam. As to Douglas...' He raised his eyes to the ceiling, '...I think you'll agree he's nowhere near ready.'

Brian felt sick to the stomach. Said a silent prayer he didn't throw up.

Steepling his fingers, Chisolm continued. 'That only leaves the cat.'

'*"Only"?*' Brian's heart missed a beat. Ever since Susan Strachan had shown him that flier, he'd lived in fear of Chisolm's wrath. His first instinct had been to ring Maggie Laird and demand to know what the hell she was up to? Then he'd had to retrench. If Harcus & Laird had been hired to find a missing cat, it was no concern of his. Still, he wondered if the agency was in trouble, when she had to stoop so low?

'Are you listening to me?' Chisolm's voice brought him back to the here and now.

'Yes, sir.'

'Dr Evershed's complaint. If we don't get a result soon, upstairs will start kicking up.' He paused to let this sink in. 'And we don't want that, do we, Sergeant?'

Brian took three deep breaths and three quick ones in succession in a vain attempt to slow his pounding heart.

'No, boss,' he replied.

Wasn't Meant

'What happened to you?' Maggie exclaimed, coming into Wilma's conservatory.

Wilma's eyes dropped to her bandaged hands. 'Had a wee...' She struggled to pick the right piece of paper from her word box. '... al-ter-ca-tion,' she said.

'Who with?'

Wilma spoke into her chest. 'A cat.'

'Our cat?' Maggie queried, her pulse quickening.

'Most likely. But how would I know for sure, when all I've got to work from is a rubbish photo?'

'There's no need to bite my head off,' Maggie admonished, lowering herself into one of Wilma's cane chairs.

'Well,' Wilma grumbled, 'wherever I bloody turn there's cats. Effing things are everywhere. How I'm meant to tell one fat ugly one from another I don't know.' She sniffed. 'Told you we were on a hiding to nothing taking on that case.'

'Let me remind you.' Maggie retorted. 'We were jolly glad of it at the time. Ursula Evershed's bounty has kept the wolf from our door.'

'Aye,' Wilma muttered. 'That and other things. She'd jumped through hoops to raise that money, and in the face of Wilma's grandiose gesture Maggie had shown scant gratitude. Worse, she was yet to confirm when it would be paid back, and Wilma lived in daily dread of Joe Grogan's wrath.

'What did you say?'

'Nothing.'

'To get back to the cat.'

'I was in the Bervie Chipper, minding my own business, when...'

'Inverbervie?' Maggie queried. 'What were you doing there? I thought you were supposed to be...'

Wilma waved her away. 'Tell you later. As I was saying, I was in the Bervie Chipper, and...'

'On your own?' Maggie interrupted.

'What do you think? I had a hot date with George Clooney?'

'Okay. I was only asking.'

'I was away to eat my dinner when this muckle big cat jumped on the table and nicked it right out my hand.'

'What did you do?'

'Gave it a skelp. Then I went for my phone to take a photo. It was in my handbag. I'd put it at my feet in case it got chip fat on it. That bag was brand new an' all. Leopard-skin. Pony-skin,' she corrected, 'but it looked like the real thing. I only bought it last week. TK Maxx. They've got a load of new stuff in. Next time you're down Union Square you should...'

'The cat?' Maggie prompted.

'It turned on me, hissing and spitting and clawing at my hands. The noise, you wouldn't believe!'

'And you think it could have been Malthus?'

'It looked like Malthus, sure enough: right colour, long-haired. Only a bit chewed, like it had been in a fight.' With a wry grin she held up her hands. 'Figures.'

'What did you do then?'

'The minute it backed off I tried to grab it again, but it was too quick for me. The chipper door was wide open, and by the time I hit the street...'

'You never let it get away?' Maggie asked, raising her eyes to the ceiling.

'I did chase after it,' Wilma protested. 'But it ran down an alleyway and jumped over a wall.'

Maggie's lips thinned. She didn't respond.

'What?' Wilma demanded.

'I thought you would have shown more initiative,' Maggie sniffed. 'After all, weren't you the one said you were bored with fraud cases?'

'I found the fucking thing,' Wilma snarled. 'That not do you?'

'Oh, well,' Maggie said, back-pedalling furiously. 'Wasn't meant.'

Wilma bridled. 'I get torn to bits and my dinner stone cold and all you've got to say is, "Wasn't meant"?'

'Well...' Maggie began.

'Don't start,' Wilma interrupted. 'You've torn me off a strip, and now you're trying to make up. Well, it won't wash.'

'I apologise,' Maggie said through gritted teeth.

'Okay,' Wilma allowed. 'Maybe it wasn't Malthus. The chances of him landing up in Bervie are zilch.'

'On the contrary,' Maggie contended. 'Cats can stray for miles, and...'

'Yeah, yeah. But then they head home.'

'Yes, but what if someone was feeding it? And where better than a fish and chip shop?'

'I get you,' Wilma conceded. 'Still, it's a long shot.'

'You reckon? There was a cat in St Andrews: a ginger tom called Hamish. Belonged to a local woman, but led a nomadic life, sleeping anywhere that took its fancy from student flats to shop windows. As I recall, there was an estate agent Hamish was particularly fond of. He became such a cult figure, he even had his own 'Hamish recommends' section in the town's Waterstone's bookshop.'

'Jings!' Wilma exclaimed. 'Would you credit that?' She paused. "Was", you said. Where is Hamish now?'

'Dead. Lived to the age of fifteen, but passed away from a chest infection. The townsfolk have put up a statue to him.'

'You're having me on.'

'No. It's in Church Square. I read in the paper.'

'All very informative,' Wilma observed, 'but what's your point?'

'According to Dr Evershed, Malthus followed much the same pattern in Old Aberdeen. It's not beyond the realms of possibility he could have pitched up in Bervie and found a comfortable billet there. It's not a big place. Might be worth asking around.'

'Well, don't look at me,' Wilma retorted, waving her bandaged hands. 'I've had Bervie up to here.'

XI

A Six-Foot Oiler

'We meet again.' Gary joked, with a touch of the old insouciance.

Douglas was about to put him down when he caught a warning look from Brian. He drew a steadying breath. Gary Moir was lawyered up. This was no time for wisecracks.

'During your last interview,' he said, diving right in. 'You furnished the name and address of a party with whom allegedly...' He let the word hang in the air. '...you had relations between the hours of 10am and 11am on the morning of Tuesday, 13th August.'

'That's right,' Gary replied, folding his arms across his chest.

'Un-for-tun-ate-ly,' Douglas stated, stringing out the syllables, 'the lady in question denies all knowledge.'

Gary uncrossed his arms. 'Well, she would, wouldn't she?'

'Oh?' Douglas said, dissimulating. 'Why would she do that?'

'The husband's a six-foot oiler. He'd have her guts for garters. Mine, too, if it ever came out.'

'Maybe you should have thought of that before you...'

'I shagged her, okay?' Gary admitted, leaning across the table. 'You probably know that. You're just trying to wind me up.' He looked over his shoulder at his lawyer. 'Isn't he?'

'Let's stick to the facts,' Brian intervened.

'There's no law against shagging someone,' Gary said. 'And that's a fact.' Grinning, he sat back in his seat.

'Can you further explain,' Douglas continued, unmoved. 'Why your initials were found against an appointment that very same morning in the electronic diary of Ms Annabel Imray?'

With a nonchalant shrug, Gary replied, 'I've absolutely no idea.'

'You didn't have an appointment to visit her that morning in a business capacity?'

'I've already told you my appointments that day. And...'

'Let me stop you there,' Douglas interrupted. 'You've given us two sets of client details that don't stand up and a third that doesn't exist.'

'It does,' Gary insisted. 'Bitch is lying.'

'And was Annabel Imray fantasising when she wrote your initials in her diary?'

'How should I know?'

'That wouldn't have been the call you took? The - and I quote - "change in priorities" that caused you to cancel your original appointment?'

'She never called me.'

'You didn't arrange to nip over there for a quick shag?'

'No. And how do you know those initials were mine? There must be tons of folk in Aberdeen with the same ones. Not even Aberdeen. Annabel knew loads of people.'

'But not on an intimate basis, Gary. And you do admit you were intimate with Annabel Imray?'

'No comment.'

'It's too late for "no comment",' Brian interjected. 'I put it to you, this is a serious crime we're investigating, with very grave consequences. You need to consider your answers carefully.'

Gary took a furtive look at his lawyer, whose eyes were fixed firmly ahead. 'I fucked her once, okay?'

'When was that?'

'The night I took her out to dinner.'

'And then?' Douglas probed.

'Then, nothing. She threw me out in the early hours. Couldn't get rid of me fast enough, if you ask me. After all the money I spent on her,' he snarled. 'Fucking cow.'

Wayne

Wilma was driving along Carnegie Crescent on her way to Rosemount when she spotted a familiar figure.

Brakes screeching, she pulled into the kerb and lowered the passenger-side window. 'Oi?' she yelled, leaning across the front seats.

The hooded figure slowed, turned. 'Ma?' Wayne said. 'You're a surprise!'

'Surprise my arse,' Wilma spat. 'What the fuck are you doing over here?'

He jerked his head away.

'Well?'

'Going to visit a pal.'

'Must be loaded, your pal,' Wilma shot back, 'when he can afford to live in Rubislaw.'

'Aye,' he mumbled.

Her eyes narrowed. 'What have you got there?'

'Where?' he asked, looking into thin air.

'In that hand?'

'Nothing,' he replied, hastily slipping something into his jacket pocket.

Wilma bristled. 'D'you think I was born yesterday?'

He gave a shrug. 'Fags.'

'Thought you'd given up.'

'I had. But...'

'What number?'

'Eh?'

'What's the number of yer pal's house?'

Wayne stuck his pinkie up his nose and wiggled it about. 'Hoose disna hiv a number.'

'Show me, then,' Wilma insisted.

Wayne waved a vague hand. 'It's up there.'

'Get in.'

'But...'

'In.' she hissed. 'I'll give you a ride.' She smiled grimly. 'Save yer wee legs.'

With the utmost reluctance, Wayne opened the car door and folded himself into the passenger seat.

'You'd better fasten your belt,' Wilma spoke through clenched teeth. 'Canna be too safe.' She put the car into gear and pulled away, watching out of the corner of one eye as her son fidgeted in his seat.

They hadn't gone far when his head swivelled.

'Getting close?' she asked, with a show of guile.

'Naw,' his right knee in Adidas trackie bottoms drummed a steady beat. 'Good bit further on.'

'That right?' she said, eyes sweeping the pavement left and right. 'Weel, I never!' she exclaimed, jumping on the brakes. 'Who have we here?'

'Naebody.' Wayne muttered.

'I'll give you "naebody",' she bawled, red-faced, as Kevin emerged from the shrubbery, an amplifier held in both hands. 'Nickin motors, wis ye?'

'Naw,' Wayne insisted. 'We wis jist hivin a bit o' fun.'

'I'll give you fun,' she screamed, swiping the flat of her hand across Wayne's right ear.

'Ow!' he yelped.

Wilma opened the car door. 'Get in!' she commanded Kevin.

Meekly, he opened the rear door and slid onto the seat.

Wilma turned. 'I'll say this once. And once only. What you two idle fuckers make of your life is up to you. But I've made mine. And there's no way you're going to screw it up. So clean up your act. And do it RIGHT NOW!'

There was no answer.

'Capisce?' she hissed.

Wayne and Kevin nodded in unison.

An Abduction

'Do you understand why you're here?' Susan asked.

'Not really,' Henry Dundas replied, his face creased with concern. 'But of course if there's anything more I can do to assist I should be happy to.'

Susan took note of the shine on Henry's suit, the frayed points of his shirt collar. She wondered how much he took home. There must be slim pickings for estate agents in Aberdeen these days. Or maybe he was just eccentric. 'Tuesday, 13th August.' She got straight to the point. 'When we met last, you told me you had only one business appointment that morning.

'That is correct.'

'But when we checked with your office, they told us you'd been asked to squeeze in a second.'

'That does surprise me,' Henry remarked, ostensibly unruffled. 'Did they say where?'

'Perhaps you can tell me,' Susan said, dodging his question. When she'd rung Henry's office, it transpired the office manager had gone on holiday. She'd been put through to an assistant, who said she remembered a last-minute enquiry on the day in question, but had no idea who it was from.

'Let me have another look.' Henry said. He pulled his phone from an inside pocket and tapped away for a few moments. 'No. I was right the first time: one appointment at 11am.'

'And that was with?'

Henry's eyes dropped. He didn't respond.

'A Dr Evershed, according to your office. Is that correct?'

He raised his head. 'Yes.'

'How did you travel to the meeting: car, bus, on foot?'

'By car,' Henry replied. 'One can't rely on public transport.' He looked from Susan to Brian and back again. 'And it wouldn't do to arrive late. No. No. No.' He waggled a finger in the air. 'That wouldn't do at all. I was taught always to be punctual.'

Susan didn't want to go there. 'Returning to Dr Evershed,' she said, one eye on her notes. 'She was planning to sell, was she?'

Henry grimaced. 'So she said. I'd been there before, after the mother died. We were all set to proceed, then Dr Evershed changed her mind, said she had too much invested in the place. This time, she said the house was getting on top of her and she was finally looking to downsize. I wanted to believe her,' he confided, looking to Susan for understanding. 'I'd have earned a good commission. Place must be worth a fair bit, even with the downturn. In that location, buyers would be swarming all over it. You've no idea...' He broke off, eyes filled with mute appeal.

Susan waited, knowing silence to be her ally.

'She was beginning to wind me up, the way she kept rabbiting on...' Henry broke off, head dropping into his hands.

Susan sat very still, listening to his laboured breathing. *Let them talk and keep talking,* she'd been told, way back. The advice had stood her in good stead.

'...about her blessed cat.'

Alarm bells jangled in Brian's head. Had Uniform missed something? Or was it him at fault? He sat up, ears twitching. 'Tell me more.' Might as well run with it.

'I don't know what made me do it.' Head bowed, Henry Dundas spoke through cupped hands.

Brian's pulse quickened. He hadn't expected a confession to the thefts, not at this stage.

'She was a time-waster, to be frank with you, a dreadful woman. I was already discomfited when I got there, and she made me worse. The more she droned on, the more agitated I became. I was anxious I might say something out of turn and scupper my commission for good, so I made my excuses and left. But when I saw the cat, I thought, that's one way of redressing the balance, making up for all that time she'd wasted, for no reason at all. I don't think she has the least intention of selling that house.'

Brian's pulse rate soared. What the hell was going on? He shot a glance at Susan, who was sitting bolt upright in her seat, as though transfixed. 'The cat?' he prompted.

'It was in the garden. Crouched under a bush. Shooting spite at me with those horrible yellow eyes.'

God Almighty! Brian had heard many a tall tale in the job, but this was bordering on the bizarre. He drew a deep breath, 'So, what did you do?'

'Grabbed the bleeder under one arm and covered it with my briefcase.' Henry replied. 'It wriggled like Billy-o. Weighed a ton, too. But I hung on until I reached my car - I'd parked around the corner - and deposited it in the boot.'

A cat abduction? Brian deliberated. He wondered how he was going to explain this one to Chisolm? His stomach sank into his boots. Never mind Chisolm, how in hell would it go down with upstairs?

'Unusually, my afternoon appointment was in Dundee,' Henry continued. 'There has been an upsurge of activity in the property market in the wake of the V&A. So, I drove down the coast, the cat all the while yowling and scratching and throwing itself off the boot lid.'

Brian sighed. He wasn't a cat lover. But, still.

'You didn't stop to think it might be hungry?' Susan demanded, jolting back to life. 'Thirsty? Short of air?'

Henry gave an apologetic shake of the head. 'I'm sorry to say I didn't care. All that was in my head was the wasted morning. The old bag never stopped moaning, and her sitting on a fortune. Some people don't know when they're well off.'

'Mmm,' Susan murmured, Shane Kelman coming into her mind. 'What did you plan to do with it?' she asked half-heartedly. Nasty as it was, stealing a cat wasn't a treasonable offence, and Henry Dundas not the only one who'd had his morning wasted.

'I honestly had no idea,' Henry answered politely. 'After I passed Stonehaven, I toyed with the idea of tossing it over the cliffs at Catterline. I'd have enjoyed watching its paws flailing in mid-air. Might even have taken a photograph on my phone.' His face creased into a lopsided smile. 'But there was heavy traffic, so I didn't have the time.'

'Go on,' she persisted.

'I thought I could do it on the way back. But the thing was making such a racket,' he explained. 'And I was trying to listen to the radio: Classic FM. There's an excellent programme on at midday.'

'Yes, yes,' Brian interrupted. 'So, what did you do?'

Decorously, Henry folded his hands on the table. 'Tossed it into a field at Laurencekirk.'

Stalemate

'What's it going to take,' Duffy moaned, biting into his morning jam doughnut, 'to crack these bloody cases? We've got the embittered ex-boyfriend,' he expanded, speaking through a full mouth. 'The so-called "best friend" and a couple of dodgy estate agents, none of them talking. In my day...'

'You can't string them up by their heels,' Susan remonstrated.

Duffy took a swallow of his builder's tea. 'I wish.'

They were huddled around a table in the canteen, grabbing a restorative cuppa.

'On a positive note,' Brian qualified, salivating at the sight of Duffy's doughnut. 'Shane Kelman and Tiffany Reid aren't out the picture. They've both got motives for wishing Annabel Imray harm: Shane because she's done him out of fifty grand, and then - to add insult to injury - set the law on him. With Tiffany it's a clear case of the green-eyed monster. And it's not true the estate agents aren't talking. Gary Moir has admitted to having sex with Annabel and being sent on his way.'

Douglas jumped in. 'Which gives him a motive as well.' He took a careful bite of his Danish pastry. 'So that's three individuals who demonstrably bore Annabel a grudge. What are the chances one of them decided to get back at her? It's human nature. And not one of them can properly account for their movements on the morning she died. Shane Kelman, for one. We haven't been able to prove or disprove his whereabouts that morning.'

'I'd take Tiffany out the equation,' Duffy added, licking a smear of jam from the corner of his mouth. 'Why kill the goose that lays the golden egg?'

'She could have caused Annabel's injuries by accident,' Douglas countered, taking a mouthful of coffee. 'Conversely, Annabel might have called Tiffany's bluff over that piece of paper and they had a cat-fight.'

'And you're not seriously fingering Gary as a murder suspect,' Susan argued. 'If our reading of him as a ladies' man is correct, getting the heave from Annabel Imray wouldn't put him up nor down.'

'You saying Gary doesn't have a motive?'

'I'm saying we have to keep an open mind.'

'Whatever,' Douglas sulked.

'To get back to what I was saying,' Brian commented, changing the subject. 'Henry Dundas has put his hands up to nicking the cat.'

'Thank Christ for that!' Duffy exclaimed, sending a shower of damp crumbs onto the table-top. He wiped them away with his sleeve. 'We've put in more man hours on that bloody cat than any animal is worth.'

'Did he say why he took it?' Douglas asked.

'Spur of the moment,' Susan replied, taking a sip of her sparkling water.

'Daft bugger!' Duffy again.

'Oh, I don't know,' Susan said. 'I think he's just a bit of an oddity. So much so, I'm seeing parallels between him and Dr Evershed.'

'The mad scientist?' he grumbled. 'Pair of nutters, I'll wager.'

'Eccentric, maybe. But they're two lonely people.'

'Maybe you should set them up with a blind date,' Duffy joked.

'It would have to be blind,' Douglas came back in. 'He's repressed by all accounts, and you want to see her: dry old stick. Wouldn't want to go there.'

'Not funny,' Susan retorted. 'But I'm beginning to understand why Dr Evershed is so distraught. That cat has been her constant companion since her parents passed away. Perhaps she has her head stuck in a book or glued to a microscope the whole day, and it's no fun coming home to an empty house.'

'You would know,' Douglas jeered. 'Didn't take you for sentimental.'

'I'm not,' she lied.

'Did your estate agent take the cat home to cuddle, then?' Duffy asked.

'Dumped it in a field down the coast.'

Douglas whooped. 'Didn't I say? That kind of scuppers your argument.'

'What do you reckon the chances the cat turns up?' she pondered.

'In the Mearns?' Duffy asked, chewing with his mouth open. 'Zero, I'd say. There's crops three feet high this time of year.'

Brian stared into his cup. More than once, he'd cursed Maggie Laird for cutting across police business. If ever he wished her well in her endeavour it was now.

'Any chance we could finger Dundas for the other thefts?' Duffy mooted, polishing off the last of his doughnut.

'Not a hope,' Susan replied. 'Wouldn't have the bottle. Much more likely to have been Gary. He's the one already has form for theft.'

'Wouldn't have taken much,' Douglas countered. 'The cat was in the driveway, out of sight of the house.'

'If Dundas was man enough to take that muckle cat,' Duffy added. 'Wouldn't it have been a doddle to pocket a few small things?'

'Let's give it a go, anyway,' Brian suggested. 'It's not as if we've anything to lose.'

Susan nodded, half-heartedly. 'Whatever you say, Sarge.'

Cats Everywhere

'Your cat has gone missing, did you say?' Janet Buchan enquired, fussing over a tray laid with bone china cups and saucers.

'Not my cat,' Maggie responded wearily. She'd had a full day of meetings in Aberdeen, and the drive south in heavy commuter traffic had only exacerbated her tiredness. Add to that, she'd had to kill time at the Bervie Chipper until the queue dissipated and staff were free to speak, and then fruitlessly knocked on doors for a further hour before she'd hit on Mrs Buchan.

The old lady ignored her, pouring from a teapot clothed in a knitted crinoline cosy. 'I lost my Simba last Christmas. We were together fourteen years. Left such a huge hole in my life.' Her eyes ranged the room, as if expecting a vision.

'You were telling me about the stray,' Maggie reminded.

'Oh, yes,' she said, passing Maggie a cup of tea. 'It was when I went to pick up the post. Not that I get anything but fliers, but at my age you live in hope. And there he was, sitting on the doormat. Like a gift from God,' she exclaimed, her face alight with pleasure.

'Mmm,' Maggie acknowledged, carefully setting down on a side table the teacup and saucer: Royal Albert, decorated with florid roses, the cup handle crusted with gilt. She recognised it from the old farmhouse, where from one year to the next it had sat imprisoned in a glazed china cabinet.

'I'd have found another, only...' Janet Buchan lapsed into a contemplative silence.

'Must be expensive,' Maggie observed. Anything to move the conversation along. 'What with vets' bills and...'

'A small price to pay for companionship,' Janet retorted sharply. 'Not your cat, did you say?' Rheumy eyes squinted at the flier Maggie had furnished. 'I take it you're not a cat person or you'd realise what wonderful creatures they are.'

'Well,' Maggie began. There was no doubting Janet Buchan was a cat lover. The front room of the terraced cottage was awash with cats: a row of china ornaments lined the windowsill, a huddle of soft toys hugged cat needlepoint cushions on the settee. Over the fireplace, the pendulous tail of a cat clock ticked away the seconds. Still, she couldn't help but compare Janet Buchan's pin-neat cottage with the shambolic living conditions of Ursula Evershed.

'Cats don't take up a lot of space. They're not a lot of bother: don't have to be walked or bathed or let outside to do their toilet.'

'I didn't mean...' Maggie started to apologise, then gave up.

'It's not the expense so much as...' Janet Buchan ran on. '...I'm ninety-five, and I'm not going to live forever. My family are all gone, and I don't want to be a bother to my neighbours. Cats have a huge capacity for receiving affection, but they're not demanding. They can be left alone for long periods.'

'So I believe,' Maggie said, stifling a yawn. She'd heard quite enough from Dr Evershed and wasn't in the mood for another exposition.

'And they keep the mice down. They're the cuddliest, most...'

'The tabby?' Maggie prompted, trying to steer the conversation back to the topic in hand.

'I took him in. Looked like he'd been in the wars, poor thing. Set a nice dinner down to him. Made up a bed. Let him sleep.'

'You didn't think to ring an animal shelter? There might have been someone missing him?'

'That's the thing. I called the Stonehaven branch of the Cats' Protection, but the phone rang and rang, and nobody answered. They're underfunded,' she confided. 'That's why I've decided to leave my house to them. It's written into the will, and...'

'What did you do then?'

'Nothing,' she insisted. 'It just went out of my head. Hector - that's what I christened him - settled in quite the thing. Got to know his way around the village, and...'

'You didn't try to report him found to anyone else, the police maybe?'

'He wasn't tagged,' Janet Buchan said defiantly. 'Wasn't even wearing a collar. You'd think if he was precious to somebody, they'd...'

'Where is the cat now?' Maggie asked.

Janet's lined face sagged even further. 'No idea. One moment Hector was here, the next he was gone.' Her chins trembled. 'That's the thing about cats. They're independent. Come and go as they please.'

Sorry Is as Sorry Does

'Let's start with the cat's...disappearance,' Brian began. He didn't think he'd manage to call it an abduction with a straight face.

'Yes.' Henry Dundas spoke from beneath lowered lids. 'I really am most terribly sorry.'

Sorry is as sorry does. Brian couldn't look at Susan, who sat alongside him in Interview 2.

Henry raised his head. 'Have you found it?'

'Not yet.'

'I could help,' Henry volunteered, leaning across the table, his expression eager as a child's. 'I have a car. I could...'

'That won't be necessary,' Brian cut him short. 'Our local stations in Laurencekirk and Stonehaven have been alerted, and will take all necessary steps to recover the animal.'

'But what if it strays onto the road,' Henry countered. 'It could get run over.'

'Shouldn't you have thought of that,' Brian retorted, not without satisfaction, 'before you abandoned it in the middle of nowhere?'

Henry's head slumped onto his chest. 'What's going to happen to me?' he mumbled.

'That depends.'

He looked up. 'Dr Evershed, I didn't mean those things I said about her. I was having a bad day. A bad year, if I'm honest with you. I depend on my commission, you see,' he looked for succour to Susan. 'And the market being as it is, my income has dwindled, at much the same time as rents are increasing. Added to which, the fact is clients don't like me. I'm not local. And this...' He waved his stump. '...doesn't help. Puts them off, and...' He broke off, visibly distressed.

'Can I get you a drink of something?' Susan volunteered. 'Tea, coffee, water?'

'A glass of water, if you'd be so kind.'

Susan made her declaration for the recording and left the room, returning with a disposable cup of tepid water.

Henry drank greedily, his face flushed.

Susan waited until he was finished, then, 'Moving on,' she said. 'We are investigating a number of other thefts which have occurred in similar circumstances.'

'No,' Henry shrilled. 'I'm not a common thief. That cat...' Blood infused his face. '...was a one-off, a spur-of-the-moment reflex. I've never done anything like that in my life before.'

'Then how do you explain that in every instance, the victim of the thefts to which I refer is a homeowner looking to retain a selling agent.'

'I have no idea,' Henry answered. 'None at all.'

'And that in each case the agent was in or around in the property when the items went missing?'

'There are dozens of estate agents in Aberdeen,' Henry countered. 'Why pick on me?'

'Because you were one of only a handful whose movements placed him at the scene.'

'You can't be seriously suggesting,' Henry contended, managing, at last, to compose himself. 'That just because I had a momentary brainstorm, I might be implicated in something like that?'

'Were you?' Susan looked him straight in the eye.

'No,' he replied in a steady voice. 'I was not.'

A Free Agent

'Seems men are like buses,' Maggie joked. 'You don't see one for ages, then two come along at once.'

'Two?' Wilma's china blue eyes stood out on stops. They were in the Aberdeen Civil Justice Centre and Commercial Court Building on Queen Street, waiting to be called as witnesses. 'How did you manage that?'

'Not sure,' Maggie said coyly.

'Who are they?' Wilma demanded. 'No,' she clapped an excited hand to her mouth. 'Let me guess: your old lapdog Brian Burnett and thon miserable Inspector Chisolm.'

Maggie giggled at her descriptions. 'Wrong on both counts.'

'Ooh,' Wilma trilled, 'someone brand new!'

'Twice over,' Maggie corrected, her mouth curving into a happy smile.

'Come on, then,' Wilma nudged. 'Give us the lowdown.'

Maggie looked away. 'I'd rather not.'

'You can't wind me up and not follow through.'

'Why not?'

'We're pals, aren't we?'

'Yes,' Maggie agreed. 'But this is personal. I don't want you muscling in.'

'Would I do that?' Wilma asked, her face the picture of innocence.

'You know perfectly well you won't be able to stop yourself.'

'I will. That's a promise.'

'Well,' Maggie confided, 'Gary Moir rang on Tuesday. He asked me out to dinner, and...'

Wilma snorted. 'That wee scumbag? You don't want to get involved with him.'

'How would you know? You've only seen him in passing.'

'I saw enough to know he's bad news.'

'He's good fun.'

'Fun, is it?'

Maggie pursed her lips. 'You're the one always telling me to lighten up.'

'There's ways and ways,' Wilma countered. 'You didn't say yes, did you?'

Maggie jutted her chin. 'What if I did?'

'I've come across plenty like him: chancers, the lot of them. Only one thing on their minds: getting into your knickers.' She wrinkled her nose. 'I suppose you'll have on your new underwear.'

'Don't be so coarse.'

'I'm serious. If you're not careful you could catch something. There was a nightclub down Windmill Brae, Happy Valley it was called. Before my time, mind you, but in Torry they used to call it Clappy Valley.'

'Don't be disgusting.' Maggie said, screwing up her nose. 'What I'm talking about out is completely different: just a bit of fun, something to take me out of myself for an hour or two. Where's the harm in that?'

'I suppose,' Wilma grudged.

'And it *is* only dinner I'm talking: nice meal, somewhere quiet. Gary's probably still hoping if he hangs in he'll persuade me to sell.'

'That's no reason to go out on a date.'

'It's not a date. It's... Look, nothing's going to happen,' Maggie rushed to reassure her friend. 'We'll have a meal, bit of a laugh, then he'll bring me home.'

'You won't invite him in?'

'Course not. I'll likely get him to drop me at the end of the road. I've the neighbours to think of.' She cast a sideways look at Wilma. 'And there's Colin to consider.'

'Still, could you not have found somebody more...?'

Maggie bristled, Val's advice to shake off Wilma's influence ringing in her ears. 'You want to be my chaperone now?'

'No, but...' She changed the subject. '... two, you said. Who's the other lucky fella?'

Maggie covered her face with her hands. 'You won't believe this,' she mumbled through her fingers.

'Try me.'

Maggie lowered her hands. 'Your friend, Joe.'

'Joe Grogan?' The colour drained from Wilma's face.

Maggie laughed. 'Took me by surprise, too. His call came right out the blue.'

'He asked you on a date?' Wilma mouthed, her voice hoarse.

'Did I say that?' Maggie teased. 'Don't get excited. It was a business call.'

'Business?' Wilma echoed, ashen-faced.

'Yes. He said he hadn't seen me back at the gym, and would I like a free training session? One-to-one.'

'I hope you turned him down.'

'Why would I? Someone offers me something for nothing? Might cheer me up.'

'If it sounds too good to be true,' Wilma countered. 'It probably is.'

Maggie ignored her. 'As well as do me good. Joe said high-density exercise would lower my stress levels and help me sleep better. Sounds just what I need.'

'No,' Wilma spat. 'You are not letting Joe Grogan anywhere near you.'

'Why not? It would be a whole lot better than walking on the beach in the pouring rain.'

'He's got fingers in all sorts of unsavoury pies.'

'Doesn't stop you,' Maggie argued. 'Last time I saw you two together, you were all over him, as I recall.'

'That's different. We go back a long way. I know him through and through. But you don't want to get close to someone like that.'

'Too rough and ready, is that it?' Maggie posited. 'Wasn't that what you called Kirsty's boyfriend, "her bit of rough"?'

'What if I did?'

'I might just learn something.'

Wilma turned a distraught face. 'That's just it. If I were you I'd run a mile.'

'Well,' Maggie said evenly. 'You're not me.'

'Gary I get,' Wilma persisted. 'Though personally I wouldn't touch him with a bargepole.'

'And you're a good judge of men?' Maggie couldn't resist a dig.

'Fair dos. But Joe? Handle him the wrong way and he can turn nasty.'

'Look, I'm under no illusions,' Maggie said with a dismissive shrug. 'He probably just wants to sign me up. Added to which, I'm perfectly capable of looking after myself.'

'Aye? Like you did in the high rises, and the railway arches, and...'

'Wilma, we're talking a training session, okay?'

'Okay. Go and have a meal with your horny estate agent if you must, but ring Joe Grogan back and say you can't make it.'

'I'll do nothing of the sort.'

'Trust me, Maggie. You don't know what that man is capable of.'

'You're not suggesting he'd try something on?' she said. 'Now you've really lost the plot.' She drew herself up, though her eyes were only level with Wilma's cleavage. 'You're a huge support, Wilma, when it comes to the business.' Her voice wobbled when she realised the *double entendre*. 'But you can't control my life.'

'Humour me, Just this once.'

Maggie shook her head. 'I'm a free agent. It's time I took my life back. And that's exactly what I'm going to do.'

Old Blackfriars

'Nightmare!' Douglas exclaimed, agitating the stirrer of his large gin and tonic.

'You said it,' Brian nodded, in agreement for once with his DC. 'Cheers!' With a grimace, he raised his hi-ball glass of lime juice and soda. Healthy living was all very well, but after the day he'd had he could have sunk a bottle of whisky.

'Cheers!' Douglas said. He picked up his glass and took a greedy swallow.

'Cheers, guys!' Susan replied, taking a ladylike sip of her vodka and tonic.

The three were seated in a corner of the Old Blackfriars on Castle Street, a favoured hangout of Chisolm's team, either that or The Illicit Still on the Netherkirkgate. Duffy was under strict instructions to be home for his dinner, and had shot off when their meeting broke up.

'Some day!' Susan observed.

'Bad enough we're not getting anywhere with the murder case without these sodding thefts,' Douglas opined. 'They're doing my head in.'

'And there's more,' Brian remarked.

'You're winding me up.'

'Hand on heart,' Brian said, clamping his right hand to his Asda suit pocket. 'Uniform are working their way through the list. Boss got another batch of statements through this afternoon. But that's enough of that.' Swiftly, he changed the subject. 'Not driving tonight?' He worked to keep a note of envy out of his voice. He'd give his right arm for a large Glenmorangie, but that would undo a week of careful diet.

'Nope,' Douglas brightened. 'Car's in for its MOT.'

They relapsed into a companionable silence, the two detective constables letting the alcohol gradually take effect, Brian trying - and failing - to observe mindfulness amidst the buzz of a packed pub.

'Do you think there could be a connection?' Susan broke the silence.

With precision, Douglas set his glass on a beermat. He cocked his head. 'What are you on about?'

'Those thefts and Annabel Imray's murder.'

Douglas leaned across the table. 'What have you got in there?' He asked, making a show of examining Susan's drink. 'Neat vodka?'

'Don't be cheeky.' With the back of one hand, she batted him away. 'I'm being serious. If our theory holds true and the thefts are targeted at lone women, wouldn't that include Annabel Imray?'

'We talking about the same woman,' Douglas joked. 'Annabel, the party girl? She of the trillions of Facebook friends and Twitter followers?'

'Bear with me,' Susan countered. 'It must have been isolating, keeping up appearances like that. Pretty well around the clock, too, the entertaining she had to do.'

'I wouldn't my waste time on...' Douglas began.

'I'm not,' she argued. 'I'm putting a valid point of view. According to Tiffany, after Annabel Imray changed her name, she severed connections with her family. Took days to get a formal identification. And it wasn't just the parents she was estranged from, but siblings, grandparents, cousins. Cut all ties with her past.'

'It's not against the law,' Douglas retorted.

Susan ignored him. 'Running your own company, you're at a remove. You have to maintain a certain distance if you're to be effective. Plus, the way people flitted in and out of her life...'

'Where are you going with this?' Douglas asked pointedly.

'The victims of those thefts are vulnerable, and so was Annabel Imray, for all her posturing. Think about it, what was she all about? Image.'

'There at least one huge hole in your argument.'

'Which is?'

'Annabel Imray hadn't reported a theft.'

'Doesn't mean she hadn't lost anything?'

'Like her cherry?' Douglas leered.

'Don't be so crude.'

'Plus, she doesn't have a house to sell.'

'Fair enough.'

'And how about the cat?' Douglas loved to stir it up, 'There's no bloody way that's connected.'

Susan squared up. 'Sez who?'

'Come on, you two,' Brian intervened, hands making a parting gesture. 'No more talking shop for tonight. Who's for another drink?'

Ellie

With a heavy heart, Maggie turned her key in the lock. She doubted she'd ever get used to this, the feeling of coming home to an empty house. It wasn't only that it reinforced her widowed status. More that the loss of her husband had rocked her very foundations. She'd lost her role in life: as wife, lover, the glue that held the household together. Kirsty had moved out in all but name. *You've Colin, yet,* she reminded herself. But for how long? Lacking his sister's adventurous streak, her son might be content to stay in Aberdeen at the end of his sixth year, but he'd soon be looking to move into a flat.

She closed the door behind her and kicked off her heels. She'd been closeted all afternoon in an airless office at solicitors Innes Crombie, and her feet were hot and swollen.

Her sombre mood lifted when she heard a familiar voice.

Footsteps clattered down the stairs.

'Mrs Laird!' The girl's face lit up in surprise.

'Hello Ellie,' Maggie said. It had been weeks since Colin's girlfriend had last visited, and she was relieved they'd settled their differences. And yet, she wondered what they'd been up to, two healthy young people in an empty house?

'Colin,' she asked. 'Is he upstairs?'

'Yes. We've been working on a homework project since we came in from school. Just taking a break.'

A door banged and Colin appeared at the top of the stairs. 'Hi Mum,' he said, lolloping down. 'You're just in time to make us a cup of coffee.'

Maggie drew herself up as far as she could manage in stockinged feet. 'Don't think for one minute, Colin Laird...'

He winked. 'Just joking.'

Maggie turned to Ellie. 'I'd ask you to stay for tea, only...' She hadn't had time to do a shop and had planned to rustle up some pasta.

'Don't worry,' Ellie said. 'Coffee's fine.'

'Well,' Maggie murmured. 'Another time.'

'I could phone out for something,' Colin offered. His face fell. 'Can I borrow your phone, Mum? I've lost mine.'

'Not again,' Maggie said angrily. 'That phone cost an arm and a leg. I'm forever telling you not to be so careless.'

'It's somewhere in the house,' he muttered.

'Still,' Ellie said, backing Maggie up. 'Your Mum's right, A girl at my spin class lost her phone recently, and it had such serious repercussions she's had to withdraw from her course.'

'Yeah, yeah,' Colin argued. 'You told me already. But that was because...' He broke off, throwing Ellie a covert look.

'She sent compromising photos to a boy,' Ellie supplied. 'And when they broke up, he threatened to send them to the whole class, all her friends, and...'

Maggie was up to speed on revenge porn. Indeed, ever since Kirsty had broken up with Shaz, she'd lived in fear of something similar happening to her own daughter. 'Somebody at school?' she asked.

'No, uni. My dad works there, so I get to use the sports facilities.'

'Of course.' Maggie knew that, but had forgotten. 'Let that be a warning to you,' she said, wagging an admonitory finger at Colin.

'As if,' he came back. 'I just came down to make us a coffee,' he added, changing the subject. 'Can I get you something?'

'Coffee? No thanks, I've been drinking that all day, but I'd love a cup of tea.'

'No probs.'

Ellie trotted after him through to the kitchen. As if nothing had happened between them: no words said in anger or falling out.

Maggie had a vague recollection of herself at that age. The drama: up one minute, down the next. *What it is to be young!*

She sank onto a chair. Her mind churned: that afternoon's meeting, the agency's financial woes, the missing cat.

'Mum?' Colin's voice startled her into awareness. 'There's no milk.'

'*Damn!* Maggie had written a to-do list, but it had gone right out of her head. 'Will you run to the shop?'

'That will take ages.'

'No. it won't.' The small parade of shops on Great Western Road wasn't more than a few minutes' walk.

'Ellie has to be home by half-past-six,' he volunteered. 'I'll nip round and ask Wilma.'

'No,' Maggie said vehemently.

'Why not?'

'Because...' *Because her dad had patched up the hole in the hedge again. Because Val had cautioned her to be less reliant on Wilma. Because Wilma would give Colin the third degree about her dinner date.* She gave a weary shrug. 'Just because.'

Colin put his head on one side. 'Have you two fallen out again?'

'No.' Maggie replied. 'It's not that, it's–'

'That's okay, then.' Turning on his heel, he opened the back door. 'Won't be two ticks,' he said cheerfully.

'Colin,' Maggie called to his receding back.

'What?'

'Don't let Wilma engage you in conversation.'

XII

A Connection

'Annabel Imray,' Chisolm announced, opening the case conference. 'Where are we at?' He directed the question to Brian.

'No further forward,' he replied. 'Any word from Toxicology?'

'Report came through this morning. High alcohol reading. Doesn't tell us anything we didn't know.'

'Drugs?'

'Negative.' Opening a folder, he said, 'Moving on, any progress on the thefts?'

'We've tried to link them to Henry Dundas, but he denies all knowledge. Admits to being at the scenes, and to being short of cash, but insists he's not so skint he would stoop to taking trinkets off old ladies.'

'They weren't all old,' Douglas piped up. 'Some of them – I'm thinking Judith McNair and Cara Gilmore – are quite attractive.'

'What's your point?' Susan demanded.

Douglas winked. 'Just saying.'

'Bottom line is,' Brian observed. 'We've absolutely nothing on Henry Dundas other than his admission to taking the cat and that he – along with others like him – was at the scene of those thefts.'

'With the exception of Cara's,' Douglas was quick to point out.

'We don't even know that was connected,' Duffy again. 'Sodding students.'

'How about we bring the fella back in,' Duffy suggested. 'Lean on him?'

'We don't have grounds,' Susan argued. 'Stealing a cat, what's that in the scheme of things?'

Chisolm turned back to Brian. 'Has the cat turned up?'

'No, boss.'

'Christ,' he put his head in his hands. 'What a can of worms.'

'Maybe we'll get lucky with Gary Moir,' Duffy volunteered. 'He's the only one with form, after all.'

'Well you'd better get them both back in,' Chisolm said through splayed fingers. 'And obtain DNA samples while you're at it, if Gary didn't have his taken for the prior. And make it quick. The press are baying like wolves. Upstairs are breathing down my neck.' He raised his head. 'I've been summoned to a meeting this afternoon. It would save all our hides if I had something to give them.'

The detectives exchanged looks, then lapsed into an uncomfortable silence.

'Anything?' Chisolm prompted. 'Bob? Brian? Douglas? Susan?' He eyed each in turn.

'The only thing I can think of...' Susan said, breaking the impasse. '...is, it's been niggling away at me, and I'm not sure there's anything in it, but...'

'For God's sake, woman,' Duffy snarled. 'Let's have it.'

'Those coffee mugs,' Susan ventured.

'In Annabel's apartment?' Chisolm queried.

'Yes. I was kind of assuming she had a visitor. A man friend, I mean.'

'Go on,' Chisolm encouraged.

'Then, when we found Gary Moir's initials in her diary, he's the only caller we know for sure she was expecting.'

'Except he's managed to get himself an alibi,' Douglas said, with a curl of his lip.

'Stands up, does it?' Chisolm asked.

'Appears so,' Brian answered for his constable. 'Moir's bidey-in was admitted to ARI early yesterday with two cracked ribs and multiple bruising. Seems the husband came back off the rigs a day early, and...'

Chisolm interrupted. 'I get the picture.'

'That doesn't mean Moir's alibi is solid,' Duffy argued. 'Quine could have been sleeping around.'

'Quite.' Chisolm concurred. 'One of you get up to Foresterhill and check that out.' He turned to Susan. 'You were saying?'

'Well, the more I thought about it,' she said, chewing the end of her pen. 'The more it made me wonder whether Annabel was expecting Gary in, you know, a personal capacity, or...' She broke off, pink in the face.

'Yes?' Chisolm said, clearly irritated.

'...in his role as an estate agent?'

'Annabel's flat was rented,' Brian said, in an attempt to stop his constable digging herself into an even deeper hole.

'I know,' Susan said. 'But didn't Shane Kelman tell us Annabel couldn't settle anywhere for more than five minutes?'

'So?' Douglas asked. 'How is that relevant?'

'She'd moved around. Her business was doing well. It's not beyond the bounds she was looking to buy.'

'So she called in a selling agent?' Douglas came back. 'Doesn't make sense.'

'Estate agents don't just sell property,' Susan argued. 'You can register with them so they keep an eye out. They even get retained to sell properties off-market.'

'Okay.' Douglas dipped his chin, chastened.

'There's just one other thing,' Susan ventured. 'Those initials: GM.'

Brian's eyes flashed warning signals. He said a silent prayer she'd get to the point. And make it quick. He could see the boss was fit to explode.

'You might think this is clutching at straws.' Doggedly, Susan pressed on. 'But as you know there's a discrepancy in Henry Dundas's account of his movements on the morning of 13th August. I've been trying to verify his statement. Except his office manager is on holiday. Somewhere obscure. Anyhow, she can't be reached. I hadn't been reading a great deal into it. But, Henry's agency is called Grossart MacNab. So, in theory of course...' She cast an apprehensive glance towards her sergeant. '...those initials could relate to either Gary Moir or Henry Dundas.'

'What!' Chisolm's exclaimed, his voice rising in a crescendo. 'And we've only just made the connection?'

Seaton School

'Maggie!' her head teacher exclaimed. 'What are you doing here?'

'Thought I'd stay on,' Maggie replied, colour rising in her face. 'Give the equipment store a good clean out.'

'On a Friday afternoon? That's over and above the call of duty, wouldn't you say?'

Maggie shifted from one foot to the other. 'Thought it might make up for my lapses last term.' In truth, she'd told her date she was working late and had arranged to meet at Bridge of Don, lest Wilma get wind of her outing.

Anne Shirreffs laughed. 'Water under the bridge. How is your Dad? I hope he made a full recovery.'

'He's fine,' Maggie replied, recalling the day she'd been summoned to the head's room and served with a verbal warning for poor timekeeping. Not that it wasn't warranted. She'd been burning the candle at both ends, trying to service her caseload whilst holding down her Seaton job, when the call had come that her dad had been rushed to hospital. But the experience had pulled her up short. Made her realise how much she valued what the Seaton kids brought to her life. They grounded her, put the often seedy aspects of her investigation business into perspective. 'He has to take things easy. No heavy lifting, that sort of thing. And they're both getting older, him and Mum.'

'You see a fair bit of them, do you?'

A wave of guilt washed over her. 'Not as much as I would like.' She made a mental note to pin Kirsty down next time they spoke and make a date to go out to Oldmeldrum.

'It's the way of the world,' Anne observed. 'All of us rushing around chasing our tails. You have to wonder where it will end.'

Maggie nodded her agreement.

'You're looking well, anyhow. The summer holidays must have done you good.'

I wish! Maggie thought. Colin had started his sixth year on 22nd August. Since then, she'd lain awake at night worrying about whether he'd settle down, make a fist of it. She wasn't holding her breath.

'Have you changed your hairstyle?" Anne's voice snapped her out of her daydream.

Instinctively, Maggie raised a hand to her head. 'Yes. I mean, no,' she corrected, 'I've had it cut, that's all.' She'd managed to get a cancellation the previous day at the local salon that sat in a small parade of shops at the foot of Countesswells Road. The stylist wasn't someone she went to regularly, but she'd made a good job, taming Maggie's fiery curls so her hair sat in a smooth, shiny cap. Maggie had to admit it did look good.

'Going out somewhere tonight?' Anne was asking, now.

Maggie smiled. 'Yes,' she said in a confident voice. 'As a matter of fact, I am.'

Foresterhill

'Shannon Ogg?' Susan enquired, approaching the bed.

'What's it to you?' the woman lisped through swollen lips.

Susan showed her ID. 'I need you to answer some questions.'

'What about?'

'Your...' She hesitated. '...mishap.'

'Why do you want to know?'

'Don't worry, it's just routine, so we can eliminate someone from our enquiries.'

'It was an accident,' Shannon protested.

'So I understand. Do you mind if I sit down?'

'Suit yourself,' she scowled, making the ends of the stitches in one eyebrow twitch.

Susan lowered herself onto the orthopaedic chair that sat by the bedhead. 'Can you tell me when the incident happened?' she asked, recalling the last time she'd occupied such a chair: her vigil by the comatose Sheena Struthers' side, whilst she waited for her to regain consciousness. The domestic violence Sheena had endured for decades was sexual in nature, and hadn't involved the sort of brutal assault Shannon had fallen victim to. But what the two women had in common was that both had been violated. Anger rose in Susan's breast. Another all too common incidence of control and consent.

'Thirteenth. Wasn't a Friday,' Shannon said, attempting a feeble joke.

'What time?'

'I can't see what that's got to do with it,' she glowered through bloodshot eyes.

'Answer the question, please.'

'Tuesday morning. Can't remember the exact time, but it would have been the back of ten I suppose.'

'And when your husband...'

With a grimace of pain, Shannon elbowed herself upright. 'I'll not be pressing charges.'

'No.' Inwardly, Susan sighed at the all-too-familiar refrain. 'But that's not the reason for my visit. I want to ask you about Gary Moir.'

'That wee fucker,' Shannon spat.

'Can you confirm you are in a relationship with him?'

'Is that what you'd call it?' Shannon scoffed. 'More like a fast fuck, I'd say.'

'But you are involved with him?' Susan persisted.

'Was.'

'Were you in bed with him that morning when your husband came off the rig unexpectedly?'

'No,' Shannon cried, wincing in pain. 'That's not how it was at all.'

Country Drive

As they left Bridge of Don behind and drove through the picturesque village of Potterton, Maggie relaxed into her seat. The arrangements for their meeting had been convoluted. Hogtied by her lie about working late at Seaton School, in the end Maggie had changed outfits in Asda's toilet and left her car in the Bridge of Don supermarket car park.

Her date had asked if she was happy to take the country route? After a heavy week in the city, nothing could have pleased her more. The sky was bright, the fields dotted with fat sheep and bordered by tidy drystane dykes. As they passed Newmachar, Maggie's thoughts turned again to her parents in Oldmeldrum. She had a sudden pang of nostalgia for the old farmhouse: its solid stone walls, the slate roof pierced by twin dormers. One of these had been her childhood bedroom, a comforting nest of dimity flowered wallpaper and soft down quilts, though in truth life on the farm had been hard, the north-east climate unrelenting.

She sneaked a glance at her companion, who sat upright, hands clamped to the steering wheel. He was humming softly, a tune she didn't recognise. And she thought - once again - how unlike they were, how thoroughly unsuited. *Don't be so picky*, she chided herself. Hadn't that been her undoing with Glen? Not to mention Brian. She flinched at the memory of their dinner date, when she'd ordered him out of her house. Their latest meeting, when he'd gone charging off, hadn't gone much better. Which led her to Allan Chisolm. Maggie wouldn't go as far as to admit she carried a torch for the man, but the Glasgow DI aroused feelings in her - uncomfortable feelings - she hadn't experienced since she was courted by her dead husband. Not even then. She'd been a schoolgirl when George and her got together. Now, she was...

what? A forty-something widow with stretch marks and a mortgage. Some prospect! No, she resolved, she wouldn't make the same mistake twice.

The ping of her mobile phone snapped her out of her reverie.

Dammit! She reached for her handbag.

'Everything okay?' he asked.

She put her bag back in the foot-well and turned, smiling. 'Of course.'

It pinged again.

Maggie ignored it. Colin was having a sleepover at Ellie's. And it was Friday night. Whatever it was could wait until Monday.

Yes, she reminded herself, it was high time she got a life.

Cat and Mouse

'You driving?' Wilma whispered.

'What do you want?' Maggie demanded. She'd determined to turn her phone off if it pinged again, but the temptation was too great. It might be new business, after all. Or one of her children. Something she could deal with and still have a pleasant evening.

'Tell me,' Wilma insisted.

'Can't hear you,' Maggie said angrily. She thought she'd made it clear she was going her own way. Couldn't believe, after all that had been said, Wilma was trying to muscle in.

'Keep your voice down and your answers short.'

'Why?'

'Don't argue. Are you in a car or not?'

'Yes.'

'Your car?'

'No.'

'Who are you with?'

'None of your business.'

'Maggie?' Wilma's voice rose a notch. 'I wouldn't be phoning you if it wasn't important.'

'I can't imagine what's so–'

Wilma cut her short. 'Where are you headed?'

'I don't know.'

'Maggie,' Wilma said, her tone more urgent, now. 'Stop playing cat and mouse.'

'I'm not.'

'Listen to me, this is serious. Make out like it's someone calling on agency business. Say as little as you can.'

'I understand,' Maggie acknowledged, though she hadn't the foggiest.

'Now, tell me who you're with?'

Maggie sneaked a glance at the figure in the driving seat. His eyes were fixed on the road, his posture relaxed.

'Come on,' Wilma encouraged.

Maggie didn't reply.

'It's Gary Moir, isn't it?'

'I couldn't really say.'

'Tell me it's not Joe Grogan?' Wilma persisted, her voice heavy with dread.

'Not without knowing the facts,' Maggie replied. 'And for that we'd have to set up a meeting.'

'Maggie!'

'That's unfortunate. Why don't you call me when you get back?'

'Don't you dare hang up on me,' Wilma threatened.

'No, there's no great urgency.'

'Either way,' Wilma hissed. 'You've got to get out of there!'

'Really?' Maggie said, her voice rising. 'Why would that be?'

'Just do it,' Wilma repeated. 'NOW.'

'Is there a particular reason?' Maggie enquired.

'The police are at my door,' Wilma said, her voice shaking. 'And I'm fucking standing here in the altogether. Whoever you're with in that car, Maggie Laird...' she paused to let her words hit home, '...is either a murderer or a rapist.'

A Murderer or a Rapist

A murderer or a rapist. Wilma's whispered words echoed in Maggie's ears. They rose in volume, shrill, clamouring, until they filled every space in her head.

Through the passenger window, the countryside flashed past. If she could only find an excuse to stop the car she could summon help. But where? There wouldn't be a petrol station, not out here. Nor a shop. Or a tearoom. Not even a farmhouse. Those tended to sit back from the road at the end of a rutted track. If there was even a forested area, Maggie's mind ran ahead of her, she could make a run for it, lose herself in the undergrowth. But the fields rolled, gently undulating, as far as the eye could see.

She made her decision. Turning to him, she said, 'I'm terribly sorry, but I really need to pee.'

He grimaced. 'Hold on. It's not far, now.'

'But,' she conjured up, 'I've an awful feeling it's my...' She let the word hang briefly. '... you know. I'm worried I'll spoil my dress.'

'That so?' he said, clearly unconvinced.

'Yes. I suffer from heavy periods,' she ad-libbed. 'And...'

Irritably, he cut her short. 'I'll look for somewhere to stop.'

After half a mile or so, 'There's a good place,' Maggie pointed ahead. The copse of trees was sparse, but might afford some cover.

He pulled onto the verge, but kept the engine running.

'Thanks,' she said, bending to rescue her bag from the foot-well.

'You don't need that, surely.'

'I do,' she hissed.

Grabbing hold of one handle, he made to tug it from her.

'Let go,' Maggie insisted, yanking the bag away. 'It's got my...' Phone, was what she was thinking. '...stuff,' she said.

'Okay,' he conceded. 'But don't get lost. will you?'

Enlighten Me

'You're not looking too chipper,' Douglas said.

'Neither would you be,' Gary replied, 'if you'd just lost your job.'

'Lost your job?' Douglas echoed. 'That's a shame. Any particular reason?' He chanced a look at Susan, who returned a filthy scowl.

'You know bloody well,' Gary muttered.

'No,' Douglas pretended surprise. 'Give me a clue.'

'Shannon Ogg,' Gary sniffed. 'Cunt landed me right in it.'

Douglas put a hand to his forehead. 'If my memory serves me right, wasn't it Shannon you said you were in bed with the morning of 13th August?'

'That's right.'

'Only that was a lie.'

'Okay,' Gary admitted, sneaking a glance at his lawyer. 'I had a thing going with Shannon. But it wasn't her I was in the sack with that day, it was someone else.'

'So why,' Douglas demanded, 'did you give us Shannon's name and address.'

'I had to give you something. Hers was the first name came into my head.'

'Really?' Douglas exclaimed, a smirk on his face. 'That wasn't too clever, was it, given you've told us the husband is a giant oiler.'

'No.'

'Have you heard Shannon was subsequently assaulted?' Susan enquired, tiring of her colleague's play-acting.

'Yes.' He nodded, shame-faced.

'So I'll ask you, Gary, who were you with that morning if it wasn't Shannon Ogg?'

He looked to Douglas and back to Susan, then his head fell

forward.

'I put it to you,' Susan said, her face expressionless. 'You were with Annabel Imray that morning.'

Gary's head shot up. 'No,' he bleated, 'you've got it all wrong.'

'Your initials were in her diary,' Susan stated, keeping up the pressure. 'You'd had a fling with her. She'd humiliated you. You wanted to get your own back.'

'No,' he shrilled, tears welling in his eyes.

'I further put it to you that you deliberately set out that morning to cause Annabel Imray harm.'

'That's not what happened,' Gary sobbed.

'Enlighten me.'

'I was with Mark Aitchison's partner,' he stuttered. 'Sorry. Wife,' he corrected. 'They got married three weeks ago.'

'Mark Aitchison being your boss?' Susan asked.

'Ex-boss,' Gary sniffed, wiping his tears. 'Why do you think I got the sack?'

Safe Enough

Under the canopy of trees, it was dark, the air heavy with moisture. And decay. Squatting on a bed of damp moss, Maggie scrabbled feverishly for her phone. As her fingers fastened around the solid weight of it, she let out a long whoosh of breath.

With shaking hands, she opened her contacts and hit redial. It was only when she punched through the call she registered the bars on the top left of the screen. *Fuck!* Why hadn't she thought of that? It was blindingly obvious that in the middle of nowhere she'd struggle for a signal.

'You alright?' The voice came from nowhere. Followed by a hand, clutching a wad of tissues.

Hastily pocketing her phone, Maggie peered through the branches.

'Found these in the glove compartment,' he said.

'Too late,' Maggie replied, struggling to her feet. She affected to re-arrange her clothing, unsure how much he had seen.

'Take them, anyway. You never know when you might need them.'

'For what purpose?' Maggie's mind ran away with her. Reluctantly, she took the tissues and stuffed them into her bag.

'Here, let me help you back to the car.' He guided her through the trees and held the fence wires apart so she could squeeze through onto the grass verge.

Covertly, Maggie scanned the road in both directions. There wasn't another vehicle in sight.

He opened the passenger door and helped her in, slamming it behind her with an ominous clunk.

She heard the dull click of the central locking, then they set off again. For a few moments she sat stock still, all the fight gone out of her. Then, drawing a deep breath, she asked, 'Where are we going?'

'It's a surprise.'

'So you said when we arranged to meet. But if we're almost there,' she wheedled, watching him out the corner of one eye, 'can't you tell me now?'

He didn't reply.

Maggie groped for her phone. If she could send a text, then...

He turned his head.

Then hit the brakes.

Maggie's upper body jerked forward, causing her phone to fly from her hand.

The car swerved violently, then righted itself.

'Sorry about that,' he mouthed an apology. 'Pheasant. Stupid birds. Should have stopped and wrung its neck, put it out of its misery.' There was a long pause, then, 'Hope you didn't get a fright.'

Maggie sat, mute. She knew from the farm that he was right. Still, she couldn't possibly be more terrified than she was already. Her eyes slid sideways. He was sitting bold upright, trunk straining forward, knuckles white on the wheel. He wasn't humming any more.

Her thoughts charged like a steam train. If she could only get him to tell her where they were headed. *Then, what?* a small voice demanded inside her head.

She resolved to give it another try. 'Where did you say we were going?'

'I didn't.'

'Please?'

'Don't push your luck, you might regret it.'

'Pretty please?' she asked, her voice plaintive, now.

'Oh,' he laughed, a high reedy laugh. 'I suppose I'm safe enough.'

"Safe"? Maggie's mind raced. *From what?* Her head filled with wild imaginings. Like when she was incarcerated under the railway arches with only rats for company. Like...' *Stop it!* she checked

herself. *Stop it right now!*

'Look,' he pointed ahead. 'We're approaching the village. Udny Green. The restaurant here gets good reviews.'

'Oh!' The tension in Maggie's body eased. She knew the place by reputation: Eat on the Green, a fine-dining establishment serving Scottish cuisine located in a converted Post Office.

'I didn't want to say, just in case.'

She smiled. 'That's okay,' though she was seething inside. *Bloody Wilma!* What did she think she was doing, winding Maggie up like that? *Typical!* Maggie fumed. Woman couldn't keep her sticky fingers out of any damn thing. She supposed it was Wilma's idea of sport: sabotaging Maggie's dinner date by inventing an emergency.

Her heart was beating fit to burst by the time they approached the restaurant, a two-storey granite building with attic dormers situated opposite the village green. What could be more tranquil?

And, yet? Something nagged at the back of Maggie's mind. Hadn't Wilma said the police were on her doorstep?'

As they turned into the car park, Maggie spied the comforting blue and yellow hatching of a patrol car. She stole a glance at her companion. Saw he had followed her eyes.

He stood on the brakes.

Threw the car into reverse gear,

The last Maggie saw as they screamed out of the car park was a flurry of Hi-vis vests.

XIII

A Coincidence

Maggie held on for dear life.

Taking a corner at high speed, the car lurched to one side.

Her spine jolted as it righted itself.

She lunged for the door handle.

Found it wouldn't open.

Hazarded a look.

He was hunched over the steering, his head whipping this way and that, eyes flicking as he checked the rear and side mirrors.

Desperately, Maggie listened for the sound of a police siren.

None came.

They left the village and gained open country, fields and farm buildings flashing past. The sky had darkened, suddenly, and Maggie remembered when she'd been deciding what to wear and checked the weather that thunderstorms had been forecast.

'This is your fault,' her companion yelled, as the tyres tore up the tarmac.

'No,' she gasped.

'Little point denying it. You're a private detective, aren't you?'

'Yes, but...'

'You've been spying on me.'

'No,' Maggie said with all the force she could muster.

'Then what were the police doing at that restaurant?' His eyes narrowed to dark slits. 'Bit of a coincidence, wouldn't you say?'

Maggie's thoughts scrambled. 'They must be looking for me,' she said, trying to sound convincing. 'That call I took earlier, it was about my son. He's injured himself playing rugby,' she improvised, saying a fervent prayer he wouldn't remember what she'd said earlier. 'I'm sorry to say I brushed it off. The age he's at, they're forever taking knocks. But it must be more serious than I thought.

So...' she broke off, running out of puff.

'How did they know where to find you?'

'I...I...'

He turned, a malicious look on his face. 'They didn't, did they?'

'No,' she mumbled into her chest.

'You didn't honestly believe I'd swallow that load of tosh?'

Maggie didn't reply.

'Women,' he raged, 'you're all the same: lying, cheating...'

Maggie heard the low rumble of thunder.

A jagged bolt of lightning lit the horizon.

'Please let me out,' she pleaded.

'I thought you were my friend,' Henry said, his voice devoid of emotion.

'I was,' she responded. 'Am.'

'Don't waste your breath,' he hissed. 'You're no better than she was.'

'Tell me about her,' Maggie said in a soft voice.

'Binky?' he asked.

'Your sister?' Desperately, Maggie mined her memory for detail. Came up with damn all except she was dead. 'You were close?' she hazarded a guess.

'Were,' he spat, keeping the accelerator floored. He waved his stump in her face. 'Until this.'

'Do you want to tell me what happened?' Maggie prompted, in the hope of drawing him out. If she could get him talking and keep him talking, she might be able to distract him.

'I was ten at the time,' Henry answered. 'She'd have been fourteen, a beauty even then. She took after my mother. Mama had what you might call a nervous disposition. She was nervy, excitable. Suffered from mood swings: up one minute, down the next. When she was in good humour, she'd be such fun: playing the piano, singing arias from opera - she had a lovely voice - always with a cigarette at the corner of her mouth. Then...' He assumed a wistful expression. '...she'd take to her bed for days.'

Maggie wondered where this was going, but held her breath. 'Binky bossed me about. You'll say that's normal: big sister syndrome. But there was more to it. Controlling, that's the word I'd use. She was at my shoulder from morning till night. '*Do this, Henry. Do that.*' Not that I minded, not at first. I was a timid child, easily led. I looked up to Binky, hung on her every word. It was lonesome, rattling around that great big house on our own, Papa absent for long periods, Mama upstairs. There was Nanny, of course, but she'd be well into her seventies by then, let us do pretty much as we pleased. Then...' His face crumpled. '...Mama went into hospital - I learned later she'd been sectioned - and we were sent off to boarding school.'

'Poor you,' Maggie remarked. And she meant it. In her eyes there wasn't that much to choose between men who abandoned their kids and those who dumped them like a piece of lost luggage. Then, remembering her predicament, she stole a glance in her wing mirror. Saw the road behind was empty.

'I missed my sister so much,' Henry wailed. 'She was like a little mother to me. Everybody said I'd get used to it. But I didn't. It was an ache that never went away.' He looked to Maggie for understanding. 'Like bad toothache. I did my best to blank it out. Other boys threw themselves into sport. I found consolation in music. I must have inherited my mother's talent for the piano - I'd been having tuition from the age of five - and hoped to make it my career. I was ecstatic when we came home for the holidays. Nanny had retired, and Papa would be closeted in the library for much of the day, so Binky and I had the house to ourselves. We used to run wild, chasing one another up and downstairs, playing games.' He gave a hopeless shrug. 'Binky always won. She'd set me challenges, dare me to do crazy things. If we got into trouble, I was the one always got the blame.'

'My two are much the same,' Maggie said, forcing a smile, though her fingers were glued to the edge of the seat and her teeth clamped together.

Henry ignored her. 'One day, we were in the woods, and we came across a snare: nothing sophisticated, just a noose formed out of chicken wire attached to a stake. There was a rabbit in the trap. 'The wire had tightened around its head and it was struggling to free itself, paws digging frantically at the soil. I screamed, as I recall, and backed away. But Binky crouched, fascinated and wouldn't leave until we were due home for tea. She dragged me back to that spot until the rabbit was dead, by which time...' He shuddered at the memory. '...its head was almost severed from its body and the poor thing had chewed off its front leg.'

'That must have been a traumatic experience.'

Henry turned, eyes blazing. 'Not nearly as traumatic as what happened next.'

'Go on.' Maggie soothed. If she didn't manage to talk him down, she could end up dead.

'We went back into the woods a week or so later,' Henry supplied. 'I wasn't keen. I'd been having nightmares, wetting the bed. But Binky insisted, and she always got her way. The snare was empty, not a sign there had been an animal anywhere near. It looked so innocuous - like a hoop you'd throw over a prize at the fairground - and Binky said...' He broke down in heaving sobs.

Terrified he would lose control of the car, Maggie lunged for the glove compartment. Hadn't Henry said there were tissues? She snatched a handful and passed them to him.

'Thanks,' he snuffled, causing the car to weave back and forth across the road.

'Shouldn't you stop?' Maggie suggested.

'No,' Henry cried. 'They're not going to catch me.'

'Just until you compose yourself,' she cajoled.

In response, he took a shifty look in the rear-view mirror and gunned the engine.

'You were going to tell me what happened next,' Maggie said hopefully.

'Was I?' he asked, eyes glued to the road ahead.

'Yes,' she said, trying to conceal her terror. 'You were in the woods with your sister. You found a rabbit caught in a trap. And...' She left the sentence unfinished.

Henry turned a tear-streaked face. '...Binky said, "I dare you to stick your hand in."'

'Is that what you did?' Maggie asked gently.

'I was scared. I put one finger in, and pulled it out fast. Then she said, "You're a little shit. Worse than that, you're gutless, and I hate you."'

'That must have wounded you dreadfully.'

'I was shocked. We bickered all the time, but when the chips were down, we'd defend each other to the hilt.' He drew a steadying breath. 'I knew why she was angry: she'd broken a glass - a Georgian lead-crystal flute - and blamed it on me. But I told on her, and Papa sent her to bed with no supper.' He lapsed into a contemplative silence.

'Was that unusual?'

'Highly. She was the golden girl. In every sense: heart-shaped face, baby blue eyes, that mass of blonde curls.' Henry offered a wry smile. 'Where Papa was concerned, she could do no wrong.' He sighed. 'I suppose she decided to get her own back.'

'And did she?'

He waved his stump. 'What do you think? I wanted to show I was as strong and brave as her, although I knew it wasn't true. So I thrust my finger into the noose, and...' He broke down once more.

Maggie held on grimly as the car braked hard, skidded on mud tracks left by a tractor, and regained its forward momentum.

'...at that very moment she yanked on the wire so my finger was caught.'

'What happened then?'

'She ran off?'

'To get help?'

Henry shrugged. 'Seems not. I must have passed out, and when I came to my finger was snagged above the knuckle. There wasn't any blood, but it was blue and swollen to twice its normal size.' He looked down at his injury. 'They didn't find me until next morning, and by the time they got me to hospital it was too late to save it.'

'I'm very sorry,' Maggie said. 'That must have been...'

'She cheated me,' Henry screeched. 'Robbed me of my education, my music, my entire life.'

'But surely...?' Maggie began, checking the wing mirror again.

'Ever since my accident, I've been looking for a way to get back at my sister. But we were estranged, situated far apart, and I had to scrape a living. There was time, that's what I told myself. All I had to do was wait. But she robbed me of the opportunity...' His face contorted. '...by getting herself killed.'

'Couldn't you have...?' *Where were the bloody police when you needed them?*

'And when I saw that woman, it all came flooding back.'

What woman? Maggie wondered, faint with fear. If Henry had harmed someone, she could be next.

'How she looked. How she lived: pampered, debauched. I saw such parallels with my sister. Everything to excess. No sense of propriety. They pick people up and drop them, women like that. Use them. Like Binky used me: to be her lap-dog, her little slave. Cast me out when I could be of no more use. It offended her to have a brother with an affliction. Embarrassed her. She couldn't bear to be in the same room, never mind introduce me to her social circle.'

'And the other woman?' Maggie hardly dared ask.

'She looked the part.' Henry said. 'But it was all on the surface.' His eyes narrowed. 'Underneath, she wasn't a nice person. I can tell,' he confided, lowering his voice to a whisper. 'I get to see a lot of people in my job, you know.'

'This was someone you met through work?' Maggie fished.

'Yes. I shouldn't have been there, but they take advantage, all of them.'

'And did something happen, Henry?' she pressed. 'Something that's been worrying you?'

'She looked so like Binky, that awful Annabel Imray. And all I could think of was that I finally had the chance to get my own back: take something from her, something precious.'

'I understand,' Maggie said, laying a gentle hand on his arm.

'How can you?' Henry cried.

'Because we have a connection. You've felt it, I'm sure you have.'

'Well...'

'And so have I. Look,' she gave his arm a squeeze, 'we're both blighted by our respective quirks: your missing finger, my lazy eye.'

'I did notice,' he commented with a quick sideways glance. 'But didn't like to say.'

'Too well brought-up,' she came back, trying to keep her voice light. 'But I'm glad you confided in me, because I am your friend.'

'Then why...' His voice hardened. '...didn't you give me your business?'

Maggie's thoughts scrambled. If she gave the wrong answer, it could mean the difference between life and... *Don't even go there!* 'Because...' She drew a calming breath. '...I'm trying to keep a roof over my children's heads. Like you, I'm on my own, trying to make ends meet. Selling their home is a last resort.' She was about to further develop their connection when something caught her eye.

She leaned forward to take a closer look.

Was relieved to see a blue light winking in her wing mirror.

Henry must have caught it, too, because the car picked up speed.

'I want to help you,' Maggie blurted, desperate, now. 'You have to believe me.'

'Don't think I haven't spotted them,' Henry answered, grim-faced. 'You're in cahoots. Don't try to tell me otherwise.'

'We're not,' Maggie stuttered. 'I'd no idea...'

'Your husband was a policeman, I found that out.'

'Yes, but–'

'Then don't treat me like an idiot. The minute I stop this car they'll arrest me. Throw me in jail with a bunch of perverts, just like boarding school. And then what?'

'It's not like that at all,' Maggie protested. 'Trust me, Henry, they'll be able to help you.'

'They won't get my finger back,' he said, jutting his lip.

'No, but...slow down,' she admonished, putting a hand over his on the wheel. 'You've unburdened yourself. Maybe you even feel the better of it. Now all I'm asking is you tell the story once more.'

Henry let out a long sigh. Then the tears began to fall, slowly at first, sliding down his cheeks and onto his shirt front, then in a torrent of wet and snot.

'There,' Maggie soothed. 'There,' softly massaging his hand.

Henry eased his foot off the accelerator.

Slowly, the car began to lose speed.

A Clear Case of Paranoia

'It was an accident,' Henry protested. He'd been brought from a Kittybrewster custody cell to the interview room, where Susan - under the supervision of her sergeant - had been tasked with leading the questions.

They all say that, Susan thought. *To start with anyhow.*

'Do you understand why you've been arrested?' she asked. She'd already stated the time, date, persons present and read the caution.

'Yes,' Henry replied.

'And are you aware this interview is being recorded?'

'Yes,' he said again, his voice barely audible.

'Louder, please, for the tape.' Susan said, glancing at Brian, seated beside her.

'Yes.'

'She was winding me up,' Henry wailed.

'So you said,' Brian remarked with all the patience he could muster. His morning green juice was playing havoc with his innards, and his attempts at meditation getting nowhere. If he heard one more word about Ursula Evershed and her bleeding cat he'd throw up on the spot.

Henry raised his head. 'She reminded me of Binky, that's the thing.'

'Binky?' Brian queried. What sort of bloody name was that? They were all the same, these upper-class twits: living in another world. The last one he'd cautioned - a solicitor with penchant for nappies - had, at the age of fifty-three, still been fixated on his nanny.

'You were telling us about Ms Imray,' Susan prompted.

'Okay,' Henry snapped, clearly annoyed. 'She even looked like

Binky: same build, same heart-shaped face. And those golden curls!' Henry's hands flew to his face. 'Took me right back to my childhood. When I first clapped eyes on Annabel Imray, I felt as if someone had walked over my grave.' His hands dropped to his lap.

'Go on,' Susan prompted, noting her sergeant's discomfort.

'She was drunk,' Henry said, his gaze flickering from the two detectives to the duty solicitor and back again. 'At that time in the morning! Rambling incoherently about her business: how much it was worth, the millions she'd rake in when she sold it. Then the car she drove, the designer clothes and handbags and shoes. She sounded just like Binky crowing about her divorce settlements: the things she'd buy, the places she'd go. She was on her third husband,' he added. 'Jetted between homes in Chelsea and New York and Monaco. Although we were estranged, I followed her on social media,' he confided, throwing the detectives a sly look.

'And Annabel?'

'The Imray woman told me she'd won an award. She was unsteady on her feet, but she insisted on showing it to me: an angular glass trophy that was as crass and shallow as she. I watched her lurching across the room when all I could think about was getting out of there. But she went on and on about this trophy: how prestigious it was, how she'd won it against UK-wide competition, how her photograph had appeared in the national press. Transpires she only had possession for a year, then she had to hand it back. I remember making polite noises about leaving – Ms Imray had approached my agency with a view to securing an off-market apartment in Rubislaw, but the state she was in, I was patently wasting my time – when she said, "No, you seem a nice man."' He broke off, a faraway look in his eyes.

Susan's shin registered a kick under the table. She turned to look at Brian, whose own eyes were open, now, and signalling... Well, she'd no idea what he was trying to convey. 'Can you expand on that?' she asked.

'"You seem a nice man", that's what she said. "Let me make you a coffee". I couldn't have cared less about coffee, but I didn't want to cross her. Drunks can be unpredictable.' He shot a look at Brian. 'And, besides, I thought it might sober her up and there might still be a chance of getting her instructions.' He lapsed into silence.

'And?'

'She was in the kitchen when I had the idea. Not a separate kitchen. That's the way new-builds are nowadays: open-plan to the living area. She had her back to me, fiddling with her fancy coffee machine. And I thought, it's not the way I would want to live: everything on show. Must be hard work keeping it clean, not to mention the cooking smells.' He pursed his mouth. 'I'm more of a traditionalist. Then, I thought, imagine one had friends in for supper. Assuming one had friends,' he qualified. 'And something got broken. How embarrassing would that be?'

Susan nodded an acknowledgement. They weren't far in, and already her interview strategy had flown out the window.

'And all the while I was sitting there, thinking of my commission, looking at that horrible trophy. It was sitting on a shelf, right in my line of vision. And I thought, what if it got broken? It was glass, after all. She'd be devastated, she was so proud of it. Then I thought, no, if it gets passed on it's probably insured. She'd have to lose it.' His eyes darted back to Brian. 'Think about the loss of face, of reputation. Isn't that what public relations is all about?'

A sharp elbow caught Susan in the ribs. Furious, she turned to Brian, whose hands, she saw, were cupping his crotch. *For God's sake!* Her eyes flashed question marks. *Men!* 'So,' she struggled to resume her line of questioning. 'What did you do?'

'I decided to take it.'

'Can you be more precise?'

'Steal it, if you insist.'

'Mmm, ' Susan observed, distracted. She wondered what in hell was going on with Brian.

'I crossed the room and picked it up. Carried it back to where I'd been sitting. My briefcase was on the floor. I had just stooped to open it when Annabel staggered back out of the kitchen. I straightened. Made as if I was going to put the trophy back. But she came at me, kicking and scratching. Like a madwoman,' he said, outraged. 'She screamed at me, asked me what the... She used an obscenity which I won't repeat. ...I was doing. Tried to wrestle the trophy out of my hands. We struggled, and...' His shoulders heaved with dry sobs.

'I think,' Henry's solicitor interceded. 'This might be a good time to take a break to allow my client to compose himself.'

'Agreed,' Brian concurred. *A clear case of paranoia.* He had heard enough. Aside from which, his bowels were threatening to erupt.

Susan threw him a sharp look. They were just getting to it, whatever 'it' might be. Her sergeant did look a bit green about the gills, mind you.

'Shall we say twenty minutes?' Susan asked.

She looked up at the red light in the corner of the room.

Stated the time.

'Interview suspended,' she said.

*

Brian knelt on the cubicle floor of the men's toilet. 'Aargh!' he retched an arc of bilge-green liquid into the bowl, where his stomach contents formed a suppurating layer, not unlike the surface of a stagnant well. A trail of mucus slithered from the corners of his mouth and dangled, swaying slightly, from his chin. Straightening, he brushed it away with the back of his hand, then - unthinking - wiped his hand on the leg of his light grey trousers.

Shite! Tugging sheets off the toilet-roll dispenser, he scrubbed at the dark stain, but only succeeded in rubbing the mucus in.

'Sarge?' Susan's voice called from the direction of the corridor. 'You okay?'

Brian held his breath. All he needed was his constable saying, *Didn't I warn you?*

He heard the door open, the sound of stealthy footsteps. 'Anything I can do?'

'Go away,' he groaned.

'Whatever you say.'

As her footsteps faded, Brian was overcome by another bout of retching. *Christ!* he vomited again, cursing his idiocy in thinking a diet of juice and precious little else would sustain him through the rigours of a major investigation.

At his back, someone tapped on the cubicle door. 'Sarge?'

He turned, to see, at floor level, a hand clutching a wodge of green paper towels. 'Thanks!' he growled. 'Now, will you bugger off? I'll be out in a minute.'

'No worries.'

Brian used the towels to dry his face and hands, then wipe around the rim of the bowl. He gave the toilet a good flush and waited until he saw it was clear. Using the cubicle walls for support, he rose groggily to his feet and unlocked the door. He emerged to see Susan leaning back against the washbasins, a bottle of water in one hand.

'Thought you could use this,' she said, holding it out with a wry smile. 'We're due back in fifteen minutes.'

Brian accepted it with as much grace as he could muster, uncapped the bottle and took a welcome swig. 'I'd be as well to give the boss a quick update. Give me a sec to get cleaned up,' he said in a shaky voice, setting the bottle at the side of the basin. He ran the cold tap and splashed his face, shaking the drips off his hands before inserting them into the Dyson drier.

'Here,' Susan said, spotting the stain on his trousers. 'You can't go in there looking like that.' She dampened a paper towel under the tap. 'Stand still,' she commanded, rubbing the mark in circular movements and patting it dry with a fresh towel.

Brian stood, feeling like a kid out of school.

The colour rose in his face at about the same time as his cock hardened.

So much for Susan sounding like his mother.

Doesn't Make It Right

'Told you.' Wilma hissed before Maggie was even through her back door.

'What?'

'Henry Dundas,' she spat. 'I had my doubts about him from day one.'

'He's a poor soul.'

Wilma drew herself up. 'Will you listen to yourself, woman? Man's a bloody murderer.'

'You don't know that.'

'No? Then why, tell me, is he sitting in a custody cell at KIttybrewster right this minute?'

'I don't know,' Maggie replied, eyes welling with tears. 'He's a gentle person. Damaged, maybe, but...'

'And,' Wilma waved an admonitory finger, 'you could have been next.'

'Don't exaggerate.'

Wilma ignored her. 'And you thought to keep it from me,' she went on, her face the picture of hurt.

'I'm sorry.' Maggie extended a consoling hand.

Wilma recoiled, as if she'd been stung. 'I don't know which is worse: the fact your judgement's in your big toe or that you lied to me.'

'I didn't.' Maggie protested. 'All I said was that someone had asked me out. I didn't say I'd accepted.'

'Not an outright lie, then. But you fair led me up the garden path. Made me believe whoever was in that car with you could only be Gary Moir.'

'I thought telling you I was going out with a working-class guy would prove I'm not the snob you think I am.'

'You turned him down and he didn't push it?' Wilma said, incredulous.

'I'll come clean,' Maggie admitted, pink spots of colour appearing in her cheeks. 'I was all set to go out with Gary, but he rang me up at the last minute. Said he couldn't make it, something else had come up.'

'I'll bet,' Wilma gloated. 'But how about Joe Grogan? It's not like him to take no for an answer.'

'I fobbed him off,' Maggie replied. 'Told him Colin wasn't well and I had to stay home. Promised to drop past the gym another time.'

'You'll do nothing of the kind, you hear me?' Wilma threatened. They'd managed to scrabble together the cash to repay the loan, Wayne and Kevin press-ganged into acting as couriers. Wilma had quailed at the thought of sending her sons into the lion's den. But there was safety in numbers. And they owed her, after all.

Maggie lowered her gaze. 'Loud and clear.'

'That's okay,' Wilma grudged.

'I'm sorry,' Maggie said, again.

'Doesn't make it right.'

'No,' Maggie acknowledged, her chin quivering.

'Come here,' Wilma said, throwing open her arms.

Gratefully, Maggie crept inside.

'Daft cow?' Wilma admonished, hugging Maggie tight. 'What are you?'

'A daft...' She broke off and started to cry.

*

'Better?' Wilma soothed, stroking Maggie's tousled hair.

'A bit.' She raised a tear-stained face. 'How did you know it was Henry?'

'Process of elimination. When you refused to tell me who you were with, I phoned Joe. Got him at home. Having an argy-bargy with the wife by the sounds of, her screaming blue murder in the background.' She grinned. 'I still have his private number. Then I called your pal Brian. The police were already zero-ing in on Gary Moir and Henry, and got your name, amongst others, from their respective offices. Then the cops ran down Gary. "Working late", according to him. However, he had a seventeen-year-old blonde in the office and the blinds drawn, so you can draw your own conclusions. But when questioned he let on he'd cancelled a date with you.'

Maggie didn't know where to look.

She was saved by Wilma rattling on. 'It was your pal, Brian, you've to thank for putting two and two together.'

'But,' Maggie persisted, 'how on earth did they find me?'

'ANPR.'

Maggie's blood boiled. 'Don't bullshit me.' She knew Advanced Number Plate Recognition cameras would probably only track a vehicle on the main arterial routes in and out of the city. 'We were in the middle of bloody nowhere.'

Wilma's eyes slid away.

'Wilma?' Maggie insisted. 'Look at me.'

Slowly, Wilma turned her head.

'Well?'

She raised a forefinger to her face.

Tapped the side of her nose.

'Peezers,' she said, deadpan. 'I'm a private eye.'

A Solid Case

'Brian!' Chisolm exclaimed, looking up from a sea of paper. 'What are you doing here?'

'Interview's been suspended.'

The DI's face registered alarm.

'At the lawyer's request. Thought I'd keep you in the loop.' *Earn myself Brownie points,* was what he was thinking. He hoped he didn't look too dishevelled.

'Good man. The suspect, is he talking?'

'And how,' Brian replied with a sigh. 'Problem is getting him to stick to the narrative.'

'Are we ready to charge?'

'Not yet.'

'We haven't reached the evidence threshold?'

'Pretty much. Forensics have given us a twelve-point match on that print. Taken together with a confession, which I'm hopeful of...'

Chisolm harrumphed. 'Yes, but will it stand up in court. Confessions have been retracted before now.'

'Granted. But they've also lifted a couple of hairs, some fibres, and flakes of skin, and they're testing for DNA on the fingerprint residue. If they can tie that in with the suspect's DNA, I think we're home and dry.'

'Thank God for that,' Chisolm said, running a weary hand across his brow.

'Your meeting upstairs.' Brian ventured. 'It didn't go well?'

'Don't ask.'

Brian offered a sympathetic smile. 'Bad as that?'

'There's some hotshot young investigative reporter moved up from Manchester, obviously wanting to make his mark. He's looking to run a series on police cock-ups. Approached the media department for comment on our investigation. Upstairs are running scared if we make a bog of this it will reverberate all the way to Gartcosh.'

Brian frowned. 'I don't see what that's...'

'He's sniffing around the death of Henry Dundas's sister.'

'Thought she was killed in a car accident.'

'She was. But this guy alleges there are question marks over the whole thing.'

'That it wasn't accidental?' Brian queried. 'He can hardly lay that at our door.'

'No, but you get the inference: if Henry Dundas was implicated in his sister's death, and the police had fingered him at the time, Annabel Imray - shining light of Aberdeen's social scene - might still be alive.'

'Oh,' Brian nodded. 'I get where you're coming from.'

'You've raised a search and entry warrant for the suspect's flat?'

'Should be happening as we speak.'

'Good. You never know what we might turn up.'

'No,' Brian grimaced. The last house search he'd been on, they'd uncovered a life-size, fully operational sex doll and a mind-blowing stash of porn.

'Speaking of which,' Chisolm continued. 'Any progress on those thefts?'

Brian shook his head. 'Sorry, boss. Gary Moir is out the frame for Annabel's death. Mark Aitchison has confirmed his story, but that doesn't rule him out for the thefts. We're working through the list of appointments we got from his office to see what we can tie in.'

Thoughtfully, Chisolm stroked his chin. 'You think the analysts are barking up the wrong tree?'

Brian shrugged, 'Who knows?' He sneaked a glance at his watch, 'If that's all for now, boss, I'd better get back down there.'

'Before you go,' Chisolm said. 'A couple of quick questions.

First, that pesky cat. Any news from Laurencekirk or Stonehaven?'

'Afraid not.'

'Second,' Chisolm fixed Brian with penetrating look. 'What about the tracking device that was found on the suspect's car? Any idea who could have put it there?'

Big Wilma! Brian felt the heat rise under his collar and start to creep up his face. 'No, sir.'

'Very well,' Chisolm said, clearly disbelieving. 'Get yourself back in there.'

'Yes, boss.'

'And, Brian?'

'Sir?'

'Build me a solid case.'

Ma Cameron's

'What I don't understand,' Wilma puzzled, 'is how you landed up in that car?'

'Henry rang me. Said he had a dinner booking and the client had called off. It was too late to cancel, he said, and could I help him out by stepping into the breach?'

'And you swallowed that?'

'He caught me on the hop,' Maggie offered in her defence.

They were in Ma Cameron's in Little Belmont Street, the oldest pub in Aberdeen. Dating back three hundred years, and originally known as the Sow Croft Coaching Inn, it had been taken over in 1937 by Amelia 'Ma' Cameron and was reputed to be haunted. Its warren of adjoining rooms was warm and inviting, popular with a mixed crowd, from mums with pushchairs and shoppers to football supporters, who favoured the rooftop beer garden. Maggie and Wilma had opted for the Snug, which along with the Whisky Bar occupied the original building. Virtually untouched, with wood-panelled walls, it housed original portraits of the Cameron family.

'I'd just come through the door,' Maggie continued, nursing the large gin and tonic Wilma had thrust upon her. 'I had a shop to unpack and Colin had rung to ask if he could stay over at Ellie's.' She wasn't going to admit she felt an affinity with Henry Dundas.

'And after I called, why didn't you just make an excuse and get out?'

'To begin with, I thought it was a wind-up: one of your cock-eyed schemes to stop me getting involved with someone dodgy.'

Wilma angled her head. 'No kidding?'

'Plus, we were in the middle of nowhere. No phone signal, nothing but fields for miles.' Raising her glass to her lips, she savoured the sharpness of the ice-cold liquid in her mouth and thirstily gulped it down.

'Thought you were brought up on a farm. You could have used your initiative.'

'I was. But that doesn't teach you how to disable central locking.' Or...' She broke off, spluttering. 'Golly, this is strong.'

Wilma ignored her. 'You didn't even try?'

'Of course, I did.' Maggie protested. 'I even managed it. But he came after me.'

'And you didn't think to do a runner?' she demanded, taking a hungry swallow of her Bacardi and Coke.

'His legs are longer than mine.'

Wilma sniffed. 'Hasn't stopped you before.'

Maggie's mind jumped back to the early days of the business: the two Alsatian dogs that had been let loose on her. 'I suppose.' she conceded. 'I had in my head if I could only find some trees, I could hide. Wait until it got dark, then...'

'What?' Wilma scoffed. 'Make yourself a tent out of fallen branches? Rub two sticks together to start a fire? Brew yourself a cup of tea?'

'I'd have managed fine,' Maggie retorted. I was a Queen's Guide I'll have you know.'

'One of them guys that takes folk up mountains?

'A sherpa? Don't be daft. Queen's Guide means top dog in the Girl Guide movement. Somebody who's done all the badges, learned how to survive in the wild. Woodman was one of mine,' she announced proudly. 'Bet you didn't know I can wield an axe?'

'That will come in handy,' Wilma observed, deadpan.

'Didn't you do anything like that: Brownies, Guides?'

'Where I come from,' Wilma said, taking another swig of her drink, 'you didn't need to join a club to learn survival. You got that in the street. But, getting back to Henry Dundas...'

'What will happen to him now?'

'I'll lay a pound to a penny he gets done for murder.'

'Not manslaughter? He claims Annabel Imray's death was an accident.'

'And you'd believe that?' Wilma asked, her voice rising. 'You should have listened to me, Maggie. I told you he was bad news from the start.'

'You could be right,' Maggie allowed. 'Brian said...'

'Don't tell me he's back on the scene?'

Maggie drew herself up. 'That's neither here nor there. We were never an item in the first place.'

'Never said you were. Though after what you've been through, you'll mebbe be a bit more careful in future about your choice of men.'

Maggie ignored her. '...that Henry is also implicated in a string of thefts.'

'Jeez!'

'Personal items.'

'Knickers, you mean? I knew a guy used to steal them off washing lines. And another fella, he had a fetish for smelling dirty panties. Liked the ones with menstrual blood the best, and...'

'That's enough!' Maggie exclaimed. Through a haze of alcohol, she pictured Henry standing in her front room, George's photograph in his hand. Had he been about to steal it? She'd never know. But of one thing she was sure. In future she wouldn't measure her worth by her relationships with men. Rather by how she lived her life.

Nothing of any Consequence

'"Struggled", you said earlier,' Brian directed at Henry when the interview resumed. 'Will you expand on that?'

'Annabel tried to wrestle the trophy away from me,' he replied. 'I'd have permitted her do so,' he asserted, looking fleetingly at Susan. 'I am not a violent man. But when she flew at me, such cold venom in her eyes, all I could see was Binky, that time in the woods. And I thought, *You're not going to win, not this time.* So, I hung on for dear life.'

'Can you describe to me what happened next?'

'We wrestled the trophy back and forth. For an inebriated woman,' Henry said, eyes wide, 'Annabel was surprisingly strong. I thought I had possession when she lunged at me again. It slipped out of my hands and struck her a glancing blow on the temple.'

'Then?' Brian prompted.

'Then,' he said, voice quivering, 'she staggered and fell to the floor.'

'How was your emotional state at that time?'

Henry's eyes slid to the left. 'I wasn't thinking straight. In a red mist, you might say.'

'Let's go back a little. "Slipped", did you say?'

Henry looked at the lawyer. Looked back at Brian. 'That's correct.'

'I put it to you,' Brian challenged, 'that you deliberately hit Annabel Imray over the head with a heavy glass object with a view to causing her harm?'

'No!' Henry protested, leaping to his feet.

'Sit down, Mr Dundas. I need to remind you that you are being interviewed under caution. Do you understand?'

'Yes,' Henry nodded, resuming his seat.

'So,' Brian posited. 'Annabel was lying on the floor, injured. What did you do next?'

'I picked the trophy up and looked for something to clean it with. I found a tea towel in the kitchen, wiped off my fingerprints and put it back on the shelf.'

Susan came in. 'Why didn't you call for help?'

Henry cast around, his eyes unfocused.

Susan gave him a moment. Bad enough she'd had to stand outside a toilet cubicle during her break while her sergeant puked, without being side-lined. Then, with a glance at Brian she said, 'Carry on.'

'There wasn't anyone around. No neighbours. The apartment occupied the entire top floor.'

'You could have phoned for an ambulance. You had a phone, had you not?'

He gave a barely perceptible nod.

'Please answer for the tape.'

'Yes.'

'I'll ask you again, why didn't you seek help?'

'Panicked, I suppose. She didn't look that bad. There wasn't any blood. It was only a bump on the head,' he qualified, his face set.

'Hardly,' Susan countered. 'I put it to you that a forceful blow with a faceted glass trophy is more than a "bump".'

'I thought she'd mostly passed out from drink,' Henry responded, lowering his head.

For long minutes, there was silence.

Somewhere, a door banged.

Henry's head jerked up. He stared straight ahead, unseeing.

'Henry?' Susan said, her voice urgent.

He blinked. 'I told you,' he shouted, with such ferocity she flinched.

'Remind me,' she pressed.

'Lying there, Annabel looked the image of Binky: the shape of her face, those golden curls. And it all came flooding back: the woods, the trap, the wire cutting into my finger, the searing pain....' He broke off, his body racked with sobs. 'She turned her back and walked away. Left me there all night in the cold and dark.' He looked from Susan to Brian. 'I was only a little boy.' He appealed to his solicitor, who sat, impassive.

'Then what did you do?' Susan asked.

'I left.'

'You walked away,' Susan said, incredulous. 'And left that woman lying fatally injured?'

'She cheated me,' Henry said stubbornly.

'Who did?' Susan enquired, seeking clarification. 'Annabel?'

'No,' he answered, riled. 'Binky.'

'Would you care to elaborate?'

'She cheated me,' he repeated, his face twisting into an ugly grimace. 'By robbing me...' He waved the stump of his finger under Susan's nose. '...of this.' He drew a ragged breath. 'I wanted to make her pay. But she robbed me of the opportunity...' His face contorted. '...by getting herself killed.'

'Your sister died in a road accident,' Brian said, coming back in.

'Correct.'

'When was that?'

'A few months ago.'

'Under what circumstances?' he enquired.

'Her car collided with an articulated lorry.'

'What were the road conditions like at the time?' Brian persisted, his conversation with Chisolm at the forefront of his mind.

'Very poor. Heavy rain, as I understand. It was night-time. The lorry braked suddenly. She didn't see its lights until it was too late.'

'Her vehicle didn't malfunction?' Brian fished.

'I shouldn't think so,' Henry replied. 'It was only days old: a Lamborghini. The police said she was driving too fast, went into a skid. Car went straight under the lorry. Binky was decapitated,' he said, matter-of-factly. 'Rather apt, don't you think?'

'How did you react?'

'I felt cheated,' Henry replied, 'my sister dying like that. Bitch cheated me twice over: once when she cut off my finger, then again when she wrote herself off.'

'So, you decided to kill Annabel Imray instead?' Susan ventured.

'No,' Henry replied, agitated now. 'It was an accident. I wasn't even meant to be there. She called the office. Demanded they send someone straightaway. I was the only one free.' Wild-eyed, he looked, again, from one detective to the other. 'You can check. They'll back me up.'

'So, what motivated you to try and steal that trophy?'

'I wanted to deprive that ghastly creature of something she treasured. So, when I saw the way she looked at that hideous object...' He broke off.

Bells rang in Susan's head. 'Have you done this before, Henry?'

'Pardon me?'

'Stolen something that was precious to someone?'

'No.'

'Are you quite sure?' Brian came back in, fixing Henry with a hard stare.

'I haven't stolen anything,' Henry insisted. 'Not ever.'

'The cat?' Susan jogged his memory.

'Of course,' Henry conceded. 'But that was completely different.'

'Why was that?'

He pondered for a moment, then, 'It was alive, for one thing.'

'Alright. We'll come back to that. But, for now, I'll ask you again, have you stolen anything else?'

'No.'

His eyes roamed the room.

'Nothing of any consequence,' he said.

XIV

Oldmeldrum

'More meat?' Netta McBain offered from her place at one end of the table.

'No thanks,' Maggie replied.

'Kirsty?'

'Not for me.' Said with a shudder.

Her gran's mouth turned down. 'You're not on a diet?' she asked. 'There's not a spare ounce on you.'

Maggie eyed the crescents of lard that sat at the side of her daughter's plate. Kirsty's diet these days was bordering on vegan. She'd done well to get through two slices of beef.

'No. It's just...'

'Come on,' Netta cajoled. 'You could do with fattening up.'

Kirsty eyes flashed.

Maggie stepped in. 'I think Kirsty's full, Mum,' she said in a firm voice. It had taken all her powers of persuasion to engineer this visit. The last thing she needed was a confrontation.

'Well, if you're sure,' Netta snapped, clearly offended. She turned to Colin. 'You be a good boy and help me out.'

'Sure thing!'

'Rab?'

Her husband reached for the carving knife and expertly cut a fat slice. 'There you go,' he deposited it on Colin's plate.

They'd driven out to Oldmeldrum for Sunday lunch, Kirsty complaining all the while she should be on the bus back to Dundee, Colin in a sulk because he wouldn't see Ellie. Maggie felt for them both. The event would be all too predictable: roast beef and all the trimmings while her mother threw quick-fire questions about the business and the kids' education and prospects. Then a welcome hiatus whilst the grandparents dozed, and an afternoon cuppa before they could respectably escape. Still, she reasoned, wasn't the extended family a bedrock? And weren't her children lucky to have grandparents at all?

'Could you manage a pudding?' her mother was asking, now.

Kirsty shook her head.

'It's trifle,' her gran encouraged. 'I made it myself.'

Surprise, surprise! Maggie had already clocked the bottle of Bailey's Irish Cream sherry sitting on the kitchen counter. It would have been pulled out of the cupboard for the occasion, having languished there since the previous Christmas. Which was the last time the three of them had been there together, she recalled with a stab of conscience.

'Great!' Colin exclaimed, polishing off the last of his beef. He put his knife and fork down with a clatter. 'Mum never makes trifle.'

Along with all the other things! With her mother's home cooking keeping the freezer stocked in Mannofield, mealtimes had been less erratic of late. Nonetheless, Maggie sometimes had to send Colin out for a fish supper from their local chipper - named tongue-in-cheek Oor Wullie's Braw Fish 'n Chips - or order in a pizza.

Her eye was caught by the pair of La-Z-Boy recliners lined up in front of the TV. She was stung by a pang of envy. The tranquil companionship of old age would never be hers.

'...clear the table.' The words jolted her into action. From force of habit, Maggie jumped up and began to stack plates.

'Leave that.' Kirsty was at her side. 'You sit down, rest up. You've had a long drive.'

'But...'

'Go on,' her mother ordered. 'Sit in my chair. Kirsty and I will have a natter in the kitchen.'

Maggie sank gratefully into the big chair. Colin had followed her dad into the garden, to be shown some prize specimen, no doubt. She watched as Kirsty carried crockery and cutlery into the kitchen and wiped down the mahogany pedestal table. That and the matching balloon-back chairs had come from the old farmhouse. Maggie had urged her mother to put them in the displenish sale. Her mother had been adamant:

'That table belonged to my mother, and her mother before her.'

'I know. But it's far too big for a modern house.'

'The new living-room's large enough to accommodate it.'

'But it will look out of place.'

'I've had to let so much go: things that have done me well for years and years. I'm not parting with my table, and that's the end of it.'

Now, Maggie had to admit her mother was right. She might well have sat at that table with her own grandparents. Shared many family occasions: christenings, birthdays, Christmases, even funerals.

Through the open window, she could hear her dad expounding some cultivation theory or other to Colin, her son making appreciative noises. From the kitchen, came the clatter of plates being put away and the sound of her mother's laughter, as Kirsty related funny stories about student life.

Maggie closed her eyes and counted her blessings.

She had her health, and her children were set on the right path.

Malice Aforethought

'Henry Dundas,' Chisolm enquired. 'Have we got the story?'

'Not the whole story,' Brian replied. 'But we're starting to piece it together.'

They had come out of DHQ for a change of scene, and strolled past Marischal College and up Schoolhill to the Kirk of St Nicholas where, at Chisolm's suggestion, they were taking the air on a bench in the graveyard.

'He's confessed to killing Annabel Imray,' Brian continued. 'Accidentally, of course.'

Chisolm sighed. 'Don't they all? What's the background?'

'Seems, since he lost that finger, Henry has harboured a grudge against his sister.'

'For all this time?'

'He claims what Binky did was deliberate: an act of spite to get back at him for landing her in trouble.'

'Nonetheless,' Chisolm argued. 'Any normal person would have come to terms with it.'

'Her actions had serious repercussions: the index finger on the dominant hand is a major contributor to small precision acts, I've learned. Henry's schooling slipped when he had to learn to write all over again, and he left with no qualifications. He lost the chance of a musical career. Lost his home. He's been estranged from his family since he was in his late teens. Lost his future, really.'

'Accepted. But that doesn't explain his behaviour.'

'I can only think the childhood grudge became an obsession,' Brian suggested. 'That someday he would be in a position to exact revenge. Only it didn't happen, and his sister's sudden death probably tipped him over the edge.'

'Which begs the question: is he fit to plead?'

‘Hard to say.’

‘Mmm,’ Chisolm mused, eyes feasting on his surroundings. Dating from 1157 and enlarged in the 15th century, the ‘Mither Kirk’ was a favourite haunt: somewhere he could spend a few minutes of quiet contemplation in the middle of a busy day. That day was a prime example. Chisolm couldn’t remember when he’d had a case so convoluted. His thoughts jumped to Lucy Simmons, whose body been found in the kirk-yard of St Machar Cathedral amidst the sort of weathered stone effigies he was looking at now. ‘Chances are, he finds himself a good lawyer, he’ll plead some form of mental illness,’ he observed, bringing himself back to the here and now.

‘If he can afford one,’ Brian said. ‘Henry Dundas has no qualifications. He’s moved from one dead-end job to another. Lived in a succession of rented flats. Doesn’t strike me as flush.’

‘Regardless, no doubt the defence will ask for a whole range of tests. How did the search go?’ Chisolm asked, changing the subject.

‘We got a result. Well,’ Brian qualified, ‘a partial result. Turned up some of the items from those thefts: the baby footprints, the cow creamer, the fountain pen.’

‘The creamer?’ Chisolm marvelled. ‘Now, there’s a surprise. How about Mrs Troup’s medal?’

‘No sign.’

Chisolm smiled wryly. ‘Figures. Woman probably put it into the saleroom, right enough. And Cara Gilmore’s phone?’

‘Handed in a couple of weeks later. Another student picked it up by mistake and promptly forgot about it.’

‘Kids,’ Chisolm said, wondering what his girls were doing that very moment. Then, remembering that Brian’s marriage had been childless, he quickly added, ‘That wee girl will have learned a hard lesson.’

‘Tell me about it. She might have got the phone back, but not before the damage had been done. But talking of damage, there was other stuff in that flat: nothing of any value, but who knows the knock-on effect its loss could have caused. We'll have to check back through reported thefts and see if we can get a match.'

'So, the two investigations are linked?'

'Looks like it. Same signature written all over them. And there were the drawings. We found more of those in his lodgings. The parallels between those and the snare that caused Henry's injury are uncanny.'

'You're saying there was a degree of planning?' Chisolm asked. 'That Dundas deliberately targeted his victims on the basis of their vulnerability?'

'Arguably the first theft was spur-of-the-moment, then when Henry's firm was retained and he was sent back for a second visit, he saw the effect the loss had on the victim. Must have given him a perverse sense of satisfaction. and his activity escalated from there.'

'It would be an aggravating factor when it comes to sentencing, that and his attempt to conceal the evidence. But, coming back to Annabel Imray...'

'I think Henry saw his opportunity to deprive her of something she held in particular regard. Only he got too ambitious. That trophy was too big to fit comfortably in his briefcase. And when she tried to get it from him...' He broke off. 'Who'd have believed his sister's small act of spite could have resulted in such far-reaching consequences?'

'Question is,' Chisolm added, 'under that bland exterior, does there lie there a deviant personality? Was Henry Dundas acting out a fantasy or is he a poor soul who just lost it?'

'He's on a crusade, that's for sure. We found a scrapbook in his flat full of press cuttings of the sister. Seems she was quite the party animal.'

'Like Annabel Imray?'

'Yes, only on the international circuit. Plus, according to Henry, Binky used people then dropped them as a way of life.'

'Charming.'

'Thing is,' Brian added, 'all the photographs were defaced.'

'Man sounds unbalanced, right enough. But we can't take any chances. Make sure there aren't any mistakes when it gets written up.'

Brian nodded morosely. If it was just a case of catching the bad guys, his life would be a doddle. But the amount of paperwork involved in policing was enough to stifle the most avid copper's zeal.

'What I don't understand,' Chisolm mused. 'Is where that damned cat comes into it?'

'By his own admission, Dundas was in a state of panic when he left Annabel. He planned to say there had been no answer when he called - perfectly plausible when you consider her state of inebriation - but thought it would raise suspicion if he didn't turn up to his next appointments. In his mind, he'd already been cheated twice: once by Binky's death, and again by Annabel. So, when it appeared Dr Evershed was going to deprive him of his commission, he looked for something to steal. Only he realised she held so little regard for possessions there was no point.'

'So, he settled on the one thing that meant the world to her?' Chisolm posited.

'I don't think it was as cut and dried as that. Dundas may not even have laid eyes on the cat, or dismissed its theft as impractical. What we do know, is he had left the meeting when he came upon it, so he might be telling the truth when he says he simply had a rush of blood.'

'Doesn't ring true to me,' Chisolm argued. 'Those thefts were callous in the extreme. As to whether Annabel Imray's injuries were inflicted with malice aforethought or accidentally, we'll leave that to a jury to decide.'

Robert Gordon's College

'You asked to see me?' Maggie said.

'Yes,' Will Mackie replied. 'Come on through.' He led her into his room. 'Take a seat.'

Maggie lowered herself onto the high-back chair. Clasping her bag tightly on her lap, she planted both feet on the floor. The last time she'd been in this room, it had been with Colin, and the guidance master had been the bearer of bad news. She said a silent prayer. She'd invested so much in her son's sixth year studies, she'd be devastated if they went wrong.

'Thank you for coming in at such short notice,' Will Mackie was saying, now. 'It's difficult when you're trying to hold down a job.'

Two jobs, Maggie corrected in her head. 'Never too busy,' she said.

'As you are aware from our last meeting, although Colin made a commendable effort to buckle down in the latter part of S5, his earlier absenteeism meant he left it too late to make a significant difference.'

'Yes,' Maggie concurred. 'That came as quite a shock, I must say. To us both,' she attempted a feeble joke. 'However, I'm hopeful he'll make up time this year.'

'That's what I wanted to discuss with you,' Will Mackie said.

Maggie pressed her knees together, such was her nervous need to pee.

'Colin has entered S6 with the right attitude, but...'

Maggie held her breath.

'...there's still work to be done. Much will depend not only on what he achieves in class, but his after-school projects. I'm talking here about the amount of time he spends on the sports field, and even the company he keeps.'

'He has a girlfriend,' Maggie volunteered. 'I'm hoping...'

'Ellie, isn't it? At least it was Ellie last time I looked. These young folks,' he chuckled. 'Can't keep up with them.'

'That's right.'

'Lovely girl. She's a prefect this year.'

'Oh,' Maggie said, her nerves easing a tad. 'She didn't say.'

'She'll keep him on the right track. But he may still require extra tuition if he's to achieve the grades he needs for university.' He paused. 'Always assuming you want him to go on to higher education.'

'Yes,' Maggie said fervently. She hadn't come all this way and scrimped and saved for nothing. Then she had a sobering thought. 'The tuition you mentioned, would it incur extra fees?'

'I'm afraid so. But you wouldn't be the first parent to sit here after paying out for five years and baulk at spending another farthing. So, what I suggest is we continue to assess Colin's strengths and weaknesses and meet again before the September holiday to agree a plan of action.'

'Good idea,' Maggie said, though her heart was hammering in her chest. She doubted she'd have the strength – mental or physical – to address a further round of fees.

'Any additional tuition,' Will Mackie qualified, 'would only be for the subjects Colin is particularly weak in. And there are always graduates looking for extra income, if you'd find it more convenient to have a tutor come to the house.'

Tactfully put! Maggie thought. Her heart rate slowed. 'I appreciate your advice and support,' she said, with all sincerity.

Patisserie Valerie

'I've been thinking,' Kirsty said, picking at the tricolore salad Maggie had forced upon her as a substitute for breakfast.

Maggie stuck her nose in her latte. She knew better than to second-guess her daughter's mood.

They were in Patisserie Valerie in the city's Union Square shopping centre, putting in time until Kirsty's bus for Dundee departed from the adjacent Guild Street bus station. Kirsty's choice. Since the Struthers case, Maggie had given the place a wide berth.

'You know how we were out at Gran and Grandpa's yesterday?'

'Yes,' Maggie replied, her voice guarded. She'd leapt at the chance to sit down with Kirsty and have a proper conversation. The rented flat had been secured for the next academic year, but she hadn't had the opportunity to ask how Kirsty's studies were going, nor to establish whether there was a boyfriend on the scene?

'Don't you think we should go out there more often?'

Maggie bit her lip. She'd been on at Kirsty for weeks, trying to arrange just that.

'Mum?' Kirsty prompted.

'Good thinking,' she ad-libbed. 'They'd like that.'

'The grandparents used to be such grumps when they had the farm,' Kirsty continued, through a mouthful of salad leaves. 'But Gran and I had a good laugh in the kitchen yesterday, and Colin gets on well with Grandpa, so maybe we should make more of an effort.'

'We'll do that,' Maggie agreed.

'After all, they're not going to be around for much longer,' Kirsty pondered, taking a mouthful of mineral water.

'What makes you say that?' Maggie asked, frowning.

'Grandpa's heart condition for one.' Kirsty speared a fat globe of mozzarella and chewed hungrily. 'Plus, they're looking a lot older.'

Maggie chuckled. 'Aren't we all?'

'Not you,' Kirsty countered. 'You look just the same as you've always done.'

'You think?' Maggie preened.

'Yes.' Kirsty digested a wedge of avocado and put down her fork. 'Boring.'

The wind went out of Maggie's sails. 'Well, if that's what you think,' she said stiffly.

Kirsty covered her hand with her own. 'Only joking. I think you look great.'

'Really?'

'Well,' Kirsty qualified. 'A lot better than you did. That short haircut suits you, and it's nice to see you in heels some of the time instead of those horrible old Footglove things.'

'I need comfy shoes for work,' Maggie protested.

'I know. But you don't have to go around looking like a throw-back to the last century. It's as well I persuaded you to bin those baggy old trousers. The jeans you have on are a much better fit, show off your figure. Next time I'm home, I'll update your makeup, then you'll really knock them for six.'

Maggie quailed, thinking of Wilma's primary-coloured eye-shadow and killer lashes. Surreptitiously, she checked her watch. Kirsty's bus would leave in twenty minutes. 'How are things going, otherwise?'

'In Dundee, you mean?' She balanced a slice of tomato on her fork and lifted it to her mouth. 'Okay.'

'Sarah well?'

'Looks like it.' Kirsty's flatmate had been abroad for the summer. 'From what she's posted on social media. We'll catch up properly when she gets back.'

'Anyone else on the scene?' Maggie fished.

Kirsty threw her a quizzical look. 'Honours is an important

year, Mum. If I'm going to get a good degree, I'll need to keep my head down. So, if you're asking do I have a boyfriend, the answer is no.'

Bloomin Heck!

'We need to have a conversation,' DI Chisolm said, from his seat on the edge of the sofa.

Here we go! Anticipating another lecture on putting herself in danger, Maggie studied the pattern on the carpet.

'The case of the missing cat,' he began.

'If that's why you're here,' she retorted, from the relative safety of the big chair. 'You can leave right now. That cat has nothing whatever to do with you. My agency was retained to investigate its disappearance.'

'That may be so,' Chisolm replied. 'But Dr Evershed, the cat's owner, reported it missing to the police in the first instance.'

'And if you had done your job,' Maggie spat, 'the case would never have come to us.'

'You've found it, then, the cat?'

'No,' she admitted, her cheeks aflame. 'But that's not the point.'

'Maybe we should join forces,' he said, his face a mask.

Maggie's mind worked overtime: her first thought that were she to cede control, Harcus & Laird would likely lose revenue. Then her better nature took over. That poor woman was bereft. And Maggie could see why. She'd developed a sneaking admiration for the feisty Malthus.

'Well,' she responded, at last. 'if you really think...' Abruptly, she broke off, seeing the corners of Allan Chisolm's mouth twitch. 'You're making fun of me,' she railed. 'Are you happy, now?'

'Would I do that?' Chisolm asked, a broad smile on his face.

Bells rang in Maggie's head. Those were Wilma's exact words when Maggie had broached the subject of her dinner date with Gary. They couldn't be in cahoots, could they?

Leave the paranoia to Henry, she told herself. And yet...

She leapt to her feet. 'You're the most officious, humourless, buttoned-up man I've ever come across,' she yelled, arms flailing.

'And you're the most dogged, cussed, infuriating woman I know,' he shot back, levering himself off the settee.

She faced him down.

He eyed her gravely. Then, 'I've missed you, Maggie.'

Heart in mouth, she whispered, 'I've missed you, too.'

For what seemed like forever, they eyed one another across the room.

Maggie took a bold step forward.

Chisolm spread his arms wide.

She took another step...

And another...until his arms closed around her.

He dropped a kiss on the top of her head.

Maggie tilted her face.

His lips found hers, gently at first, then with increasing urgency.

'Maggie,' a voice bellowed.

She started, breaking free from Chisolm's embrace.

The door burst open.

'Bloomin heck!' Wilma stood on the threshold, open wine bottle in hand. Her eyes darted from one to the other and back again. 'Sunshine's got something on his face,' she observed drily. 'You been making jam?'

'N-no,' Maggie stuttered. Then, getting the joke. 'Hold still,' she reached up and brushed a smudge of lipstick from Allan Chisolm's cheek.

'I'll leave you to it,' Wilma grinned, turning tail.

Maggie snuggled close to Chisolm's chest, the steady thump-thump of his heartbeat outpaced by the frantic racing of her own.

She held her breath...

Scarcely believing this was happening...

That she might be safe at last.

Three Weeks Later

'Where did you find him?' Ursula demanded, as she and Maggie came through the door.

'Cove Bay,' the SSPCA inspector replied. 'Farmer's wife phoned it in. Cat was terrorising her chickens.'

They were in Drumoak, the local rehoming centre of the Scottish Society for the Prevention of Cruelty to Animals.

He led them into a space lined with glass-fronted enclosures. 'This your man?' he asked, stopping halfway down.

'Oh,' Ursula gasped, one hand clasped to her mouth.

From the back corner of his enclosure, Malthus fixed his owner with a haughty stare.

Ursula tapped on the glass. 'Malthus?'

The cat stretched languidly and closed his eyes.

'It's often the way,' the SSPCA inspector said, with a knowing chuckle. He unlocked the glass door and reached in.

Maggie watched from a respectable distance.

The inspector held out the cat.

'Come to Mummy,' Ursula cooed, arms spread.

Paws scrabbling, Malthus wriggled in the man's grasp.

'Give him a minute or two,' the inspector said. Stroking the cat, he set him down.

Malthus gave himself a shake, then head erect he padded towards Maggie. Tail standing rigid as a flagpole, he pressed his flank against her calf.

Maggie froze, uncertain. Her first instinct was to stoop, scoop the cat up and hand him back to his owner. And yet...she'd developed a growing respect for the animal: his independence of mind, his total disdain for the opinions of others.

Ursula's voice interrupted her thoughts. 'Sweetie,' she simpered.

'Mummy's here.'

The cat ignored her, rubbing himself against Maggie's leg and nudging her with his cheek.

'Malthus!' Ursula commanded.

For a moment the tabby stilled, amber eyes alert, then it resumed its attentions.

Maggie cast around in alarm. When she'd collected Dr Evershed from the university and driven her out to Banchory, the atmosphere in the car had been frosty: not a word of conversation, far less thanks. The client wasn't happy, that much was obvious. And she'd been a good source of revenue. Unlike some. Maggie experienced a fleeting moment of *deja vu*. Wilma was right. She should have done something sooner about Scott Milne. Happily, he'd finally responded to her increasingly urgent phone messages and - full of apologies - settled his bill.

She looked down at the cat, drawing comfort from its closeness, a comfort that was lacking in her life. Her anxieties eased. And she understood, for the first time, why Ursula Evershed was so attached to the animal, and why she'd been so devastated by her loss.

Looking up, she caught the inspector's eye.

He winked.

Then she saw the funny side.

Maggie's shoulders shook, then she started to laugh.

Acknowledgements

To my publisher, Sara Hunt, heartfelt thanks.

For patient and skilful editing, Russel D. McLean.

For specialist input, Professor James Grieve of Aberdeen University, Sergeant Teresa Clark of Police Scotland and former Detective Sergeant Bill Ogilvie.

For local knowledge, Pauline McBain and Sheila Reid.

To my family and friends, with special mention to Chris Blair, thank you for your unwavering support.

My sincere appreciation goes to the reviewers, bloggers, booksellers, festival programmers and librarians who have brought Maggie and Wilma to a wider audience, and to the many readers who have taken this unlikely crime duo to their hearts.

To the good folk of Aberdeen and the dedicated staff of Seaton School, my apologies. I have taken liberties with both in the pursuit of a good story!

The events in this novel are entirely fictional and inaccuracies wholly mine.

Also in the Harcus & Laird series

LONGLISTED: MCILVANNEY AWARD FOR SCOTTISH CRIME BOOK OF THE YEAR
When Maggie Laird's ex-cop husband dies suddenly, her suburban life is turned upside down. With the bills mounting, she takes on his detective agency, with the help of neighbour 'Big Wilma'. A surprising, gritty, sometimes darkly humorous tale combining police corruption, murder, female friendship, loyalty and how an unlikely duo can beat the odds.

LONGLISTED: HEARST BIG BOOK AWARDS
"My husband is trying to kill me": a new client gets straight to the point. Maggie, still trying to rebuild her late husband's detective agency, is drawn in, but Wilma sees the case as a non-starter. What is the ugly truth that lies behind closed doors, and where's the evidence? With conflict mouning, will the agency's reputation – and Maggie and Wilma's friendship – remain intact?.

When Aberdeen housewife Debbie Milne abruptly vanishes, her husband is frantic and turns to Maggie Laird and Wilma Harcus. Maggie is reluctant to take on a 'misper' case, but Wilma leads a covert operation – trawling women's refuges and homeless squats. Soon the unlikely investigators are dragged into a deeper mystery involving trafficking, gambling and prostitution – and they're in deadly danger, with the clock ticking.

Claire MacLeary, originally from Glasgow, has lived in Fife, Aberdeen and Edinburgh. Following a career in business, she gained an MLitt with Distinction from the University of Dundee. *Payback* is her fourth novel and continues the Harcus & Laird series. *Cross Purpose* was longlisted for the McIlvanney Award 2017, and *Burnout* was longlisted for the Hearst Big Book Award 2018.